A SAM NOLAN NOVEL

WILD MEN

CHRIS RILEY

Black Rose Writing | Texas

ISBN: 978-1-68513-575-1 (Paperback); 978-1-68513-636-9 (Hardcover)
LIBRARY OF CONGRESS CONTROL NUMBER: 2024947306
PUBLISHED BY BLACK ROSE WRITING
www.blackrosewriting.com

Printed in the United States of America
Suggested Retail Price (SRP) $22.95 (Paperback); $30.95 (Hardcover)

Wild Men is printed in Gentium Book Basic

*As a planet-friendly publisher, Black Rose Writing does its best to eliminate unnecessary waste to reduce paper usage and energy costs, while never compromising the reading experience. As a result, the final word count vs. page count may not meet common expectations.

This book is dedicated to my extended family,
The Fortains.

WILD MEN

"Wisdom and peace come when you start living the life the Creator intended for you."
–Geronimo

PROLOGUE

Shiloh Parker stepped out onto his back deck and stood quietly, observing his wife, Vicki. He had just finished loading tobacco into a pipe, was about to fire it up, but then paused as he looked on at the woman. She was leaning against the deck rail, her silhouette dwarfed by the wide horizon of green forests and blue mountains beyond. Absently, Shiloh traced his thumb over the turquoise eagle embossed on his lighter as he thought about his wife.

The woman was breaking down again, losing it. Crying, sniffling, and, of course, mumbling through the sentences on the pages of notes tucked inside the folder she was holding. Occasionally, she glanced at the monumental view behind their house—the eastern slopes of the Blue Ridge Mountains—as an expression of absolute torment shuddered across her face.

Shiloh cringed. The pain he felt for his wife was almost as bad as the pain he felt for losing their daughter. Not quite, but almost.

"*... but then they were in the trees,*" Vicki continued, reading from a selected note, "*by my camp last night, stalking me, I know, hunting me, the both of them, and I heard their breathing they were that close. I could smell them, and I heard them grunting, sniffing and whispering. I heard them approaching. I heard them...*"

His wife looked up from the paper then and stared once again into the distance, her body trembling. Their house stood on a tall hill, and the deck overlooked a yawning landscape of lush wilderness, the tops of countless trees, the faraway cerulean tumble of imposing mountains, their crowns presently softened by white cottony clouds.

Somewhere—somewhere way out there—their daughter was still missing. And that fact came as an unrelenting, daily blow to Shiloh and Vicki. It was a devastating blow to anyone, in fact, who knew the young woman.

Shiloh slid his pipe and lighter into his pocket then and stepped forward, embracing his wife. His sudden closeness and sudden touch brought the woman to an uncontrollable state of tears. Like a child, she dropped her head and shrank into her husband's arms, shaking and sobbing.

"We'll find her, my dear," he said, holding back his own tears. "I promise you, we will find our daughter."

· · ·

Some hours later, his wife now in a medicated stupor on their bed, Shiloh stood alone, out on the deck. He was alternating between his tobacco pipe and a glass of Tennessee Rye while he stared out into the misty blue horizon. His mind was grasping at half-a-dozen topics, failing miserably with keeping him away from the *one* topic, the one involving his little girl.

The following week's business meetings lingered at the forefront of his thoughts, only because they were the one thing he thought about all the time, the habitual topics he mulled over day in and day out. And these thoughts were also there because Shiloh knew he'd have to do something about the meetings.

Tuesday luncheon with Frank Boyce, Vice Chairman of District 5, from the Cherokee County Board of Commissions... Old Frank won't like it, but that meeting will need to get postponed.

The construction site walkthrough scheduled for Thursday morning, nine o'clock sharp, with the partners of Eastern Band Brewery—probably not going to happen either. But Shiloh figured those IP boys won't mind that much, not after they finish sampling their latest batch of beer.

And then the Chamber Breakfast at the Biltmore, on Friday...

Shoot, it was only Sunday, and Shiloh already envisioned the end of his week, but with only one thing planned in sight.

He took a sip of whiskey, Jack Daniel's brand, Single Barrel Rye, hard and dry, which left a bold, woody flavor on his palate, and it held him for a brief second in the present moment, away from all the other thoughts haunting his mind.

Suddenly, he heard a noise behind him, and turned to look.

"Good afternoon, sir." It was Wilkins, Shiloh's personal assistant. "I have everything in order for our trip. All I need is your final confirmation."

Shiloh stared at the man. Ronnie "Long Deer" Wilkins was a spitting image of himself, minus thirty years. Standing six feet tall, with long black hair cinched back into a tight braid, and a sharp, hardened look that came with a person who survived an early life of poverty on an Indian Reservation, the blood in this man's veins was three quarters Native American. Mostly Lakota, to be precise, but with a sprinkling of Seneca and Cheyenne, and probably a few other tribes from over the years. The other quarter of his blood, which Shiloh also respected, was good old, mean-as-hell, fighting Irish.

"Shall I confirm, Mr. Parker?"

Shiloh realized he had drifted away. "Yes, do that," he said with a blink. "And tell Susanne to reschedule my meetings for this week. And maybe next week, as well."

Wilkins hesitated and then said, "We do have a number, sir. If you'd rather—"

"No, Ronnie..." Shiloh interrupted. "The conversation I mean to have can only take place face-to-face, man-to-man. Besides, it's all too easy to tell a person 'no' over the phone. Way too easy. Confirm our trip, Wilkins. And cancel my meetings for the week."

Shiloh turned back and leaned against the rail, his eyes now searching the distant wilderness. He felt Wilkins' silent departure after a few seconds, and with that, returned to the peaceful calm of being alone.

Most of the time, Shiloh couldn't stand to be alone. It seemed he was always in need of company—family, friends, even business associates—as the presence of others kept an interesting stir in the air for him. But once in a great while, he appreciated the stillness of solitude. It reminded him that there was so much more to the universe than what he could see or hear.

Solitude reminded Shiloh of a different kind of company, the company of the Great Creator perhaps, or of the many spirit animals. It was a thought that reminded him to maintain his heritage and his faith; or, at the very least, his courage. And courage—well, that was needed more than anything right now, wasn't it? Courage for him and courage for his wife. And hopefully, the Great Creator willing, courage for their daughter.

"Confirm our trip," Shiloh repeated to no one but himself, "and cancel my meetings. We're not coming back here until I get my *own* confirmation—" he drained the last of his whiskey then, and took a long drag from his pipe, blowing smoke into the air, "—from this man they call Sam Nolan."

CHAPTER 1

It was the third morning in a row that the nightmare woke Sam up. It woke him early, 3:45 AM, the small hours of the day, but there was no chance in hell he was going back to sleep. Not with the stimuli of his dream so fresh in his mind. He could still smell the forest, and taste the earth, and see the dark closeness of the night, as he crawled through a dense undergrowth of some wilderness, this time wearing full camouflage, military issue, his face painted green and brown and black, his hands gripping tightly the Army's version of a Remington Model 700 rifle, an M24 sniper weapon system—the same weapon he used while pulling missions in Afghanistan. And Sam could still feel the seething horror of worms squirming under his skin. It was a relentless feeling, as it accompanied the constant, dreadful crying he heard somewhere off in the distance.

Two nights ago, that crying had come from his long-lost spotter, Ernie Valencia. And, as it was every time he had this dream, or some version of it, when he'd finally caught up with the person crying, it would be too late. Ernie Valencia would be dead, dead as driftwood. And the death was always gruesome, with skin and hair and eyes sloughing away into piles of human rot.

Sam got out of bed and stumbled to the bathroom. He splashed water on his face three times, did some business in the toilet, and then got dressed for a run. His knees were stiff, as he'd been averaging six miles a day since the dreams had started, almost three weeks ago.

The jogging helped. Jogging kept Sam's body in a state of relaxation, and it put his mind at ease, at least long enough to get through the day, until the following night would come, and then the crying would once again seem to find him. Two nights ago, that crying had come from Ernie. But last night, and the night before, the dead body Sam had caught up with was none other than his first: little Emily Parsons.

It was only ever Ernie or Emily in his dreams, two people Sam had never been able to do anything about, which was the most frustrating part for him. He couldn't go back to the Search and Rescue days of his youth and find that four-year-old girl lost in the Gila Wilderness before her body would succumb to the harsh elements. And as for Ernie, who Sam *hoped* was dead, but didn't quite know for sure, the man's last known whereabouts was a Taliban torture cage deep inside the belly of a mountain. Sam had been there with him, tormented for months, but for what felt like a lifetime. Then, by a stroke of luck and back-channel military negotiations, which Sam still didn't completely understand, he'd been released from that mountain hell. But only him, and not Ernie.

Sam walked into the kitchen and poured himself a glass of water, drank it down in one gulp, then stretched his back and legs. When he was finished, he checked in on Lolo. She was still asleep, lying peacefully in their bed, beautiful as ever. He meant to keep it that way, as he slipped quietly outside, and then on to his morning jog.

The crisp crack of the dawn air felt good and cold, but not too cold, just right for a run. It was still dark, but that didn't bother Sam any, as with the darkness came the assuredness that most people were still asleep or just waking up, and that meant he wouldn't have to say "good-morning" to anyone. Early runs were another chance for Sam to be alone, and that was something he never took for granted, despite the comforts of living back in town now, and not up in some old Apache cave, as he'd been doing for the last few years.

When Sam got back an hour later and slightly winded, Lolo was wide awake.

"How was your run?" she asked with a smile on her face. The woman had been in a state of never-ending bliss since she and Sam had moved in together. They were living in a two-bedroom house in Silver City, an older yet comfortable rental, and situated just off Hudson and Broadway, which was conveniently near the center of town. It was an ideal location for both of their schedules. And best of all, the house had an eastern-facing dining-room window, allowing for a first peak at the morning sun. In Sam's opinion, there was no better way to start the day than a cup of coffee and a New Mexico sunrise.

"Not bad," Sam replied, as he closed the front door and came inside. Lolo was in the kitchen cooking (what, he wasn't sure, but certainly not bacon and eggs). He caught a whiff of coffee, though, and that was satisfying enough. "I took a different route this time," he said, pulling Lolo into his arms. He gave her a kiss, then helped himself to a cup of brew.

"Oh yeah," Lolo said. "And what route was that?"

Sam smiled as he took a seat at the kitchen table. "The northern route."

"So how was this northern route?" She was teasing him now, going along with Sam's playful mood. "Did you see anything interesting?"

"As a matter of fact, I did."

"And what was that?"

"There was this tumble weed... looked a little different from all the others. Not as round, though."

Lolo laughed, then sat in Sam's lap. "You've missed your calling, cowboy. But maybe it's not too late. How about we pack our bags right now and head off for New York? We'll have you doing stand-up by the end of the week."

"You would like that now, wouldn't you? Seeing me up on stage, tripping over my words like a damn fool." Sam chuckled at the thought.

Lolo got up and went back to the kitchen, her slender body moving with a feline's gracefulness. She was wearing a white tank-top and matching shorts, her black Apache hair strung up in a loose bun. She stopped at the stove, one knee bent casually, a hand on her hip, and the other stirring with a spoon something in a pan. She was standing in the perfect spot—directly in the path of the golden light seeping through the window, the morning glow bathing softly her brown shoulders and the corners of her eyes.

Sam couldn't take his eyes off the woman. Nor his mind. Not today, not ever. She reminded him of a gentle wind, soft and peaceful, stirring casually through the brambles of his thoughts, never once forceful, never once destructive.

"Just a reminder," he said, "I'm roasting chilies at the ranch today." He took a sip of coffee, then added, "How about you come with me?"

"I have that meeting this morning, but after that, absolutely." She served whatever she was making into a bowl, then brought it over and placed it in front of Sam.

"You're kidding me, aren't you? You expect me to eat oatmeal after I just went for a run?"

Lolo winked and smiled. "Your body will love you for it."

"That's debatable," Sam replied.

She shrugged. "Just imagine you're living up in that cave again, eating your dried foods, or what have you."

Grudgingly, Sam ate his breakfast as he leafed through the morning paper on the table. A minute passed, with his mind drifting between the pleasant moments there in the kitchen, the latest headlines from the local news—nothing too exciting, just enough to keep a pulse going for your standard small town gossip—and the harsh echo from last night's dream.

Quietly, Lolo sat next to him, coffee in hand. She added cream and sugar to the cup, then looked at him, staring hard with those big brown eyes as she stirred the contents in her cup with a spoon. "You had another dream last night." It wasn't a question. "I heard you mumbling in your sleep."

He looked away and out the window. "Yeah, I guess I did."

The mood slowed down between the two of them. "Sam, I really think you should see about talking with someone."

He ran his fingers through his hair and looked again at the paper, trying with all his might to dodge this sudden conversation.

"Maybe someone at the VA." Lolo pressed. "You're not the only one, babe. And there are people just like you, who you can talk to."

"They're just dreams, Lolo. They're not real. And they never will be. Just a figment of my imagination."

"Yeah, but still. All the experiences you've had. All the trauma..."

Sam rolled his fingers on the table, and seeing this, Lolo dropped the subject and spun into a different one. "So how many bushels of chilies are you cooking today?"

He was slow to respond, but then he said, "I have no idea. At least ten. Probably more."

The woman smiled then, a big heartwarming smile, one with the power to put her man back into the previous mood. "Well, whatever it is, you're in for an easy day, that's for sure."

"You've got that right," he replied, smiling as well. "I sure as hell am, aren't I?"

Sam had been working again at the family enterprise, Hidden Creek Ranch, for almost a year now, since coming down from his cave in the Gila Wilderness. True to his promise to Lolo, after the turmoil of finding his brother Bryson up in Canada, he hadn't left the woman's side for more than a full day.

"Last week was a kicker," he said, "hauling all that manure. There's more work to do on that, as well as weaning them calves. But today..." Sam chuckled lightly, "... today, I'm roasting."

"Like I said," Lolo replied, "an easy day." She took a drink of coffee, then added, "Tell you what. I'll try to get out of that meeting early. And if not, it'll only be a couple of hours."

Sam smiled lazily. His woman was the Jack of All Trades, good at just about everything she did (so she probably could get out of that meeting early), but seemingly unable to focus on any one thing. Currently, she worked at Hand on Heart, a senior citizen living center on the outskirts of Silver City. Lolo wanted to go to nursing school, and figured working at the care center would give her experience, while she picked away at a few prerequisite college courses.

Sam wondered how long the woman would keep at it. A while back, before he took off into the Gila Wilderness to live his life of solitude, Lolo had wanted to become a professional singer. She had an incredible voice and a stage presence that rivaled Reba McEntire's. But, as with all things, so it seemed, her fiery passion for singing had eventually burned out, only to be replaced by another interest.

"Well," he began, "don't you worry about it none. You can show up whenever you can. I'll be there the whole day." He took another bite of oatmeal (which, as Sam would never admit, didn't taste terrible) and then glanced at the clock mounted on a wall above the stove. It was 5:45, and he knew his mother would be up by now, and in the kitchen, fixing a hearty breakfast of meat and eggs for everyone at the ranch. If Sam hurried, he could get a seat at the table just as the food was being served.

"I better get going," he said, taking one last bite of oatmeal. He got up and kissed Lolo on the lips, then went into the other room. In fifteen minutes he was showered and dressed, and then at the door with his cowboy hat and keys. Lolo gave him a big hug and kiss before he left, and there was a sweet sadness in her eyes that about melted Sam on the spot. Damn, if he didn't love this woman.

But as he walked outside and headed toward his truck, a ghostly feeling struck him. Something about Lolo's eyes... The way she looked at him, and the buildup of morning tears at the corners. With a sudden, stark impression, that look in Lolo's eyes somehow reminded Sam of little Emily Parsons.

CHAPTER 2

"You sure you ain't burning them?" Sam's older brother, Matt, was sitting in a rocking chair he'd dragged from off the front porch of the farmhouse, drinking coffee from a clay mug, and smiling relentlessly. A 21st century cattle puncher born and raised in the Land of Enchantment, every breath and syllable that came out of his mouth—wisecrack or otherwise—exuded with the unmistakable inflection of the modern day cowboy. The boots and hat he wore added to this impression. All that was missing were a pair of chaps, which were hanging on the back wall of the barn, and a loaded six-shooter, which Sam knew was resting peacefully under the front seat of his brother's truck.

Matt was sitting twenty feet away and had been watching Sam all morning long. "Pay close attention, now," he said, adding a wink to his grin. "But don't think too hard. It ain't rocket science."

Sam glared at his brother. They were behind the ranch-house and underneath a large *ramada*, an open, loosely roofed wall-less structure, crafted mostly from lodgepole pine, and which covered a grilling station and a fifteen-foot long, custom-made picnic table. Hanging from one of the *ramada's* support beams was a boom box stereo tuned to a country station and presently playing Garth Brooks' *The Dance*. It had been roughly two hours since Sam started cooking the green chilies, which was about the same time his brother had started up on him.

"Now, if it gets too difficult for you," Matt added, "you just let me know."

"The day you take over this job is the day I die," Sam replied.

Matt laughed. He took a swig of coffee and then fired back with, "Well, I guess I better go find my apron then, seeing how you're not looking so good."

Sam was wearing an apron himself, which his mother had made out of a piece of tan canvass. Embroidered on the front, and in black thread, were the words, *Don't Mess With The Chef.* Without fail, that phrase only made things worse for Sam, as it acted as a catalyst for his older brother's bantering.

It had been a quick morning, despite the general lazy attitude of everybody at the ranch. No one was planning on working too hard today. It was a cook day after all, a day for physical rest, while preparing various foods to store for the winter. The ranch hands, Jim and Mason, were playing cards and watching the smoker down on the other side of the *ramada*, which they had been doing since long before the sun had come up. In the smoker were two large beef briskets, now smelling divine, and undoubtedly stirring the curiosity of every bear and coyote within a five-mile radius.

In the house, Sam's parents, Ruby and Tom, were getting things ready for long-term food storage—cleaning jars, organizing materials, and setting up the vacuum sealer. They had been joined by Lolo about an hour ago (as expected, she had gotten out of her work meeting early) but now the woman was over in the barn, tending to the horses. That, as Sam knew, was indeed a long-lasting passion of Lolo's, one that hadn't fizzled out, and probably never would. Once a horse lover, always a horse lover.

Around and about were Matt's family—his wife and several young children. Sam never paid much attention to the whereabouts of his nieces and nephews, other than knowing they were always there and always making bits of nonsensical noise. Although it seemed the youngsters were quieter than usual this morning, so Sam assumed they were up to no good.

He had showed up at the ranch shortly after six, and four hours were already long gone. A little grimy and sweaty, he was on his third bushel of hatch chilies, with seven more to go. Of those he had already cooked, they were rolled up in small bundles of damp cheesecloth, and set neatly in rows on the picnic table to cool. Later in the day, a host of people, including Sam, would attack the bundles and begin the laborious process of peeling away the skins and seeds, exposing the sweet and spicy fruits, which would then get canned in Mason jars.

Sam opened the lid of the grill, revealing a crowded layer of chilies. A gust of heat wafted across his face, bringing with it a strong punch of the flame-roasted smell. Using tongs, he rotated a few of the chilies and then closed the lid again. And as he did, he was met with the sight of his grinning brother, who was still sitting in the rocking chair in front of him.

"Better use some water on them flames," Matt said, "so things don't get too hot in there."

"Why don't you get off your ass already and do something?" Sam replied.

Matt chuckled in response, and at that, Sam turned around and walked off a bit. Behind him, the *ramada* opened up into a long valley of dry, yellow grass, and scattered sage. Beyond the valley and on the far horizon, he could see the dusty brown slopes of the Mogollon Mountains, and its surrounding wilderness, the mystical Gila. There wasn't a cloud in the sky. And on the wind, he thought he heard the faint sound of a white-tailed kite crying somewhere way above him. But he couldn't yet see it.

"You'll need to look much closer—closer *inside*—to see Brother Bird." It was Denali, Lolo's father and lifelong friend of the Nolan family. He lived alone in a cabin on the ranch, two miles east. Sometimes Denali walked from his cabin to the ranch-house. Other times he drove his truck. But this time, Sam wasn't sure. The old man had somehow crept up behind him, but it seemed as if he'd materialized out of thin air.

"Dammit, Nali," Sam said. "You've got to stop sneaking up on people. Especially me. I'm getting too old."

Nali nodded, then gestured to the south. "He's up there, above those trees." The old Apache was pointing to a bird of prey resting on an updraft and circling a clump of desert willows. "Once a week, he goes there. And once a week, he gets something."

"Well, damn if you aren't observant," Sam said.

"My eyes see what the land shows me. And that's all I need to see."

Sam smiled. "What are your plans for today, old friend?"

"Oh, I suppose I'll start peeling those chilies soon. And someone will need to sample that beef over there, make sure those boys aren't ruining it. There's plenty of work."

They talked for a bit about the morning, and it was a good, yet brief, conversation. Nothing had changed about the old man, and everything about that sat right with Sam. "We should go hunting, soon," Sam suddenly said. "It's been too long since our last hunt." It had been over four years since the two of them went hunting together. But in truth, Sam was thinking about when Nali used to take him and his brothers up into the mountains to hunt deer and elk the traditional way, using homemade bows.

"I could use that," Nali replied. "You're right. It has been a while."

Just then, the dogs took off. Like bullets, Bixby, Charlie, and Lady all came sprinting past Sam and Nali, on their way down the half-mile long dirt driveway leading to the ranch. The dogs weren't barking, not yet, just heading to meet what appeared to be a black suburban trudging slowly toward the house.

"Who in the heck is that?" Sam asked.

Nali didn't reply. He stared at the approaching vehicle, his silence adding more weight to Sam's curiosity.

"Let me guess," Sam said. "I need to look closer *inside* to find my answer."

Sam stood quietly and waited as the vehicle rolled in. By the time it came to a stop in the turn-about at the side of the house, Matt was up and out of his chair and whistling at the dogs, bringing them to a heel. They were barking continuously, making a ruckus, until he successfully called them to his side. Right about then was when the two long-haired Native American men stepped out of the suburban.

At this point, Sam's curiosity heightened. So did Nali's, he noticed. And, as Tom and Ruby came out of the house, and the ranch hands walked around from the *ramada* to get a look, so too, it seemed, did everyone else's.

"Good morning, folks," the older of the two strangers announced. The man walked around from the passenger side, and he was holding a small, square package. He was dressed in denim jeans, a long-sleeved flannel shirt, black leather vest, and matching boots. He wore a fat turquoise bolo around his neck, and his long gray and black hair was bound in two braids. There was an interesting glimmer in his eyes, a mixture of cunning and kindness.

Sam stared evenly at the men. Naturally, his military mind kicked in gear. He couldn't help it. And he was already assessing the individuals for potential malice—although he had no clue where such a thing would come from. He noticed the younger man looked trained, a bodyguard no doubt, perhaps former Special Forces, or practitioner of some martial arts system. Maybe even both. He wore a navy-blue suit, shined cowboy boots, and dark sunglasses. And similar to the older gentleman, he too had long hair, although it was pulled back into a single braid. Standing with hands together at his midsection, he was in a relaxed state of at ease.

"My apologies for coming out here unannounced," the older man said, as he carefully tucked the package in the crook of an elbow and stepped forward. His eyes were skipping across the faces of everyone, searching for something or someone, but Sam noticed his gaze held a second or two longer on that of Nali's. "I would not be of trouble," he continued, "only, well, it's that I come bearing a gift." He smiled and gestured to the package. "A gift and a proposition. My name is Shiloh, by the way. Shiloh Parker."

There was a pause, and then Tom Nolan stepped down from the porch and approached the man. He put his hand out, they shook, and Tom said, "Well, Mr. Parker, I'm Tom Nolan, proprietor of this here ranch. You are welcomed—but I must admit, I suspect you might have taken a wrong turn somewhere." He looked around then, studying the situation, observing the reactions of everyone, before turning back to Shiloh. "It doesn't look like any of us are expecting you."

"That is correct," Shiloh said. "But I don't think I made a wrong turn. This is Hidden Creek Ranch, is it not?"

Tom nodded.

"Well, then," Shiloh said, offering the package to Tom, "this would be for you, sir, by way of mending any pleasantries I have broken. And the person I'm looking for," he added, glancing now at the many faces around, "would be that of your son, Sam Nolan."

Everyone looked over at Sam, who, by now, had stepped closer and was standing ten feet from Shiloh.

Shiloh followed everyone's gaze, and then his own settled on Sam. "Mr. Nolan," he said, approaching Sam, his hand held out, "I have heard much about you. It is an honor to make your acquaintance."

Slowly, Sam shook the man's hand. Any concerns he had were now replaced by curiosity. It seemed apparent this man meant no harm. But as to why he was here, that was still a mystery.

"I'm not sure what you've heard, mister," Sam said, "but what can I do for you?"

"To be honest," Shiloh replied, "I did not want to interrupt anything going on out here today. I'm staying over at the Bear Mountain Lodge. I hope you and I can meet sometime this week, over coffee, or dinner perhaps. To discuss why I've come out here."

Sam felt unsure. "Out here from where?"

"I live in North Carolina, along the Cherokee Indian Reservation. I believe you're quite familiar with that area."

The comment set Sam on edge. Apparently, this man had done some digging of sorts into Sam's past. Fort Bragg, North Carolina, is home to the Army Special Operations Command, where Rangers, Green Berets, and Delta Force operatives regularly train. Sam didn't say anything in response, but he nodded his head.

"In any case," Shiloh continued, "please consider meeting with me, Mr. Nolan. Are you available sometime tomorrow, perhaps? They make a fantastic steak over at the lodge. It would be my pleasure to buy you one."

Sam considered the invitation. He was damn curious, but also apprehensive. Without knowing the man's true intentions, the only thing Sam had to go on was speculation.

"How about you first tell me why you're out here," Sam said. "What exactly is it you want from me? Then maybe I'll consider eating that steak you mentioned."

There was a pause, followed by, "Well, Sam, if you give me your word—" Shiloh glanced quickly at Tom and then at Nali, "—your word as a *Nolan* that you will at least meet with me, and hear me out, then I'll tell you right now why I've come to the Southwest."

Sam hesitated, thinking. There were no reasons he should comply with the stranger's demands. But it didn't seem it could hurt to meet with him, either. "Why not?" he said. "I'll take you up on that steak. But that's all I can guarantee."

Shiloh put his hands in his pockets and sighed. His shoulders slumped, and there was a sudden look of consternation, and of sorrow, that crossed over his face. "Sam... My daughter has gone missing. In the woods, along the Appalachian Trail. There's no reason for it, and the search has been called off. But I think I have some evidence as to what happened to her." He paused while his eyes studied Sam's face, as if searching for a reaction. "I heard about what you did up in Canada. And now, I'd like to employ you to do the same for me and my family. I'd like you to find my daughter, Sam."

Shiloh's brief explanation came as a complete surprise to Sam. Never in a million years would he have guessed this. And this surprise took the wind out of his thoughts. He was unable to process the information completely, and thus, unable to offer any type of considerable reply.

After a pause, Shiloh nodded, and then his body straightened again. "I'll see you at six, then," he said. "Tomorrow night, at the lodge. And be sure to bring your appetite."

The man turned, waved courteously at everyone, and then walked around to the passenger door of the suburban.

"Parker!" Sam said, the sudden urge to ask a question coming over him. "How long has your daughter been missing?"

Shiloh looked at Sam. "Two weeks," he said. "Two weeks today, in fact." And after a pause, the man climbed into the vehicle, and then they turned around and drove slowly away.

Off to his right, Sam heard his dad opening the box Shiloh had presented him with. There was a stir of commotion from everyone, and then Tom pulled out a black clay bowl, which he then raised into the sunshine for all to see. It was a little smaller than a bowling ball, finished in gunmetal black, and with the rim of its opening stained a deep rust color. Along the bowl's circumference were finely crafted etchings and turquoise inlays.

Tom Nolan was an avid reader, and, as such, was duly educated with the history of his environment. He knew exactly what he was holding in his hand. "I'll be damned," he said, a look of astonishment crossing his face. "This here is a Tony Da. Got to be worth ten thousand, if it was a dollar."

But that comment barely registered in Sam's mind. He was still trying to process the previous event, not to mention considering any future ones. He was only vaguely aware of the curious inspections around him, his family and friends observing Tom's gift, or looking at Sam curiously, as if begging the question, *So what are you going to do?*

And then Lolo was there, her hands wrapping around Sam's waist, bringing him in for a hug. She smelled strongly of lemongrass and hay, the combination of her body spray and working in the barn, which brought Sam at last to the present moment. He took her in his arms, exhaled, then looked around, blinking.

And that's when his eyes found that of his older brother's, who was now smiling back at him triumphantly.

"Sam," Matt said, "I do believe the chilies are burning."

CHAPTER 3

The man's demeanor had changed. Shiloh Parker, who sat across the table from Sam, looked now like an old man with one foot in the grave. There was pain in his eyes, and a tiredness in his mannerisms. Also, he seemed more personable than when he'd shown up at the ranch, less business-like. With these characteristics, Sam figured he was now observing the proverbial monkey hanging on this man's back, weighing him down with guilt and suffering.

It was the loss of his daughter, Sam presumed, and the fact that she hadn't been found. Shiloh had no way of knowing what had happened to her, or if she was even still alive, which she probably wasn't. And if that were the case, all the unanswered questions only added to the man's torment. Was his daughter's death filled with a cold darkness and agonizing pain? Just how terrible were her thoughts while scared and alone, and with the Grim Reaper standing ominously at her side? How long did her suffering last, and how terrible was her fright? Hell, some people died just from fear. Day-by-day, these questions cursed Shiloh's mind, and day-by-day they ate at his soul. Sam was sure that the unknown circumstances behind the loss of his daughter were slowly killing the man.

He had seen it before, all too many times. And to some degree, he knew what Shiloh was feeling. "Before I forget," he said, "my father would like to thank you for the gift. And," he added, setting a small leather bundle on the table, "he wants you to have this."

Shiloh took the bundle and unwrapped it, revealing a finely crafted Native American peace pipe. "Well, isn't this a beauty," he said, carefully lifting the item up and into the light.

"It's not an original," Sam offered, "but damn pretty. Made by an artist over in Santa Fe."

The pipe was crafted from blue soapstone and bleached elk antler. It was a simple design, adorned only by two raven feathers hung by a leather strap from the stem. But the pipe had a balanced weight, and it felt nice to hold.

"Just as good," Sam said, interrupting Shiloh's quiet appreciation of the gift, "are the chilies I left for you at the front desk. Two jars of New Mexico Hatch, grilled and canned by me personally. Don't go home without them."

"Very kind of you," Shiloh said, setting the pipe down on the table. "And very kind of your family. Already, things are off to a good start."

But Sam wasn't sure he felt the same. "Before you tell me anything about your daughter, Mr. Parker, I'd like to know how you got your information about me and my family. My father's not your typical rancher, and you would know that by giving him that fancy bowl."

A look of guilt crossed Shiloh's eyes. He took a drink of beer, then set the mug back down. "I'm a rich man," he began, "and what comes with that are connections. I didn't intend to pry into you and your family's history, Sam. It's just that... Well, I'm a businessman. A damn good businessman. And men like me, all we know is how to win a deal." He paused for a second, then added, "And right now, as I'm sure you can understand, I'm up against the toughest deal of my life."

For the time being, that was enough for Sam. But Shiloh continued. "Shortly after my daughter went missing, I hired a private investigator to help me in any way possible. And when they called off the search for her, that's when he gave me the newspaper article about you. That's when I got the idea to solicit some extra help."

A waiter came over to take their order, causing a momentary break in the conversation.

"I'll have the rib eye with mashed potatoes," Sam said to Shiloh, then looked away, studying his surroundings. They were sitting in the lodge's restaurant, the Café Oso Azul, a small rectangular hall with rustic furnishings and many windows. The floors were dark wood, and there were matching support poles in various spots. On the walls were paintings and photographs of local scenery, portraits undoubtedly commissioned from local artists, all dying for attention, probably even dying for a paycheck. It was a quaint and cozy restaurant, just one of a thousand similar establishments common to the Southwest.

After a minute, the waiter left, and then Shiloh continued. "So that's why I'm here, Sam. I read that article about how you went up to Canada and found your brother. And about that serial killer you dealt with—Lou something-or-other—and..." Shiloh's eyes drifted off, as if his memory had suddenly run aground. "God help us if someone like that got to my daughter..." He blinked, then looked back at Sam. "Anyway, I'm at a complete loss here. My wife, she can't function anymore. She spends most of her days now in a cloud of anti-depressants, her mind and soul frozen in a medicated coma. It's like I've lost both my daughter and my wife, Sam. I don't think I can take much more of this."

"It's tough," Sam said, "to lose someone like that. Your own child, of all people."

"It's killing me," Shiloh replied. "But I know you're the right man for the job, Mr. Nolan. Before I came out here, I had this feeling inside my gut... And I still have it. I just know you're the one who can find my daughter and bring her back to me and my wife."

Sam thought for a minute, then said, "I don't mean to be blunt, Mr. Parker, but you know there's a good chance she's no longer alive. Two weeks in the wild, and... Well, I'm assuming she was by herself."

Shiloh looked down at the wooden table and ran his hand across the grains. "I know, Sam..." He paused and looked back up. "I know what the statistics say. And yes, she was hiking alone. But even if she's de—" he couldn't finish the word. "Even if my daughter is no longer with us, my Vicki and I need to know. We need to know something, Sam. We need some closure to this nightmare, however difficult it may prove to be. Or however long it may take to end."

Sam had yet to learn the complete details behind the missing girl, as well as become sold on going out and looking for her. But already he was feeling sad for Shiloh. The few words they'd exchanged had poked at an old wound still festering deep inside Sam's heart.

The waiter came by to check on the status of their drinks, and Sam used the interruption to look around again. He was thinking about the situation, and how unconventional it all seemed: to be hired to go look for a lost girl clear on the other side of the States, and in a terrain he was currently unfamiliar with. Even with Sam's years of experience working with Search and Rescue and Special Forces, he still found it hard to consider Shiloh's proposition.

When the waiter left, Sam said, "You know, Mr. Parker, I'm just a guy with some skills, not unlike any other man. And I'm fairly sure there are at least half-a-dozen qualified individuals out there, where you're from, who can do this job just as well as I can. Probably even better."

Shiloh shook his head. "You don't understand, Sam. I've contacted every damn name in the book. I've talked to the best trackers and survivalists I could find. I even had a guy who's been working in the field for over thirty years, and who holds the record for finding the most lost persons in that area. A Cherokee man, like myself, goes by the name of Harlow Evans. He worked on the case for a while. But eventually, even he gave it up. Although..." Shiloh's words drifted off as he stared curiously at the table.

"Although, what?" Sam asked.

"There was something odd about Harlow when he gave up searching. It was like he wasn't fully convinced about his decision. As if he had something on his mind, nagging away at him. When I noticed this look on his face, I pressured the hell out of him. I asked if he'd keep looking—I begged him, actually—but Harlow had nothing else to add. And that's how he left it, I'm afraid."

"Sounds a bit curious," Sam said.

"Anyway, that's all I got. And it ain't damn near enough." Shiloh made a hopeless gesture with his hands. "I'm at the end of my rope, Sam." The old man paused. And then, ceremoniously, he retrieved a photograph from an inner pocket of his vest, which he set on the table and slid toward Sam. "There she is, by the way. The prettiest girl you've ever seen."

Sam picked the photo up and looked at it. Indeed, she was pretty—damn pretty—bearing a striking resemblance to that of Lolo.

Sam glanced back at Shiloh. "Yesterday you mentioned something about evidence... Evidence regarding your daughter."

Shiloh nodded. "That's right," he said. Then he frowned. "Something weird about that, as well. Once we started taking a good look at what we were finding, well, that's about when some of those searchers sort of lost their steam. Even Harlow, for that matter... All of them. They just started checking out."

"I don't understand," Sam said. "What kind of evidence were you finding?"

"Notes," Shiloh replied. "We found notes, written by my daughter's own hand. Several notes, in fact, scattered all across the land. They were like little bread crumbs, teasing us with bits of information."

"What kind of information? What did the notes say?"

"Well, in a nutshell, they were descriptions of her fears, and how she was being followed by two wild-looking men. After we found the notes, some people—most people, in fact—started thinking my daughter had gone crazy. Like she had lost her mind out there."

Sam thought about that for a minute. He knew that some people, after being lost in the wilderness for several days, would turn paranoid. And tragically, this paranoia would provoke them into hiding from their would-be rescuers. And it would also push them further out into the bush, and to their definite end. Sam wondered if this was a good explanation as to what happened to Shiloh's daughter.

"Well," Sam said, "it's been known to happen from time to time. When people get lost in the woods and then their fears take over... that's when minds tend to falter."

"Not my daughter," Shiloh said. He paused, took a drink of beer, then added, "She's Cherokee, Sam. Since she was a little girl, she's been walking in the woods. And she's made that trip more than once, up and down the entire Appalachian. Not for a minute do I believe she got herself lost, first of body, and then of mind. No, not for a *damn* minute. In fact, to me, what's more credible are the words she wrote on those notes."

Shiloh's statements about his daughter were hard to discredit. But Sam tried anyway. Too many times he had seen experienced hikers succumb, in one way or the other, to the hazards of being alone in the wilderness. "Well," he said, "sometimes things just happen, Mr. Parker. Even to the best of us. Sometimes the natural world has a way of taking over."

Shiloh looked Sam square in the eye. "Someday, son, you might have yourself some children, I don't know. But for a father and his daughter—well, from my perspective, at least—there's a special bond that comes with that relationship. And it's a bond that travels far beyond the natural world, my friend." He paused, then added, "Sam, you can call me crazy, but I know in my heart that my little Emily didn't lose her mind out there."

It hit Sam with the weight of an eight-pound hammer. "What did you just say?" he asked.

Shiloh hesitated, blinking.

"Did you just say your daughter's name is Emily?"

"I sure did," Shiloh replied. "Emily Parker. She's still out there and... Well, to hell with the statistics. She's alive, Sam, I just know it. In fact, I'm of the mind that those notes she wrote about wild men chasing her... I believe she was writing to me, Sam. She was telling me, telling her father, that she was in trouble. It was as if she was asking me to come help her. But I couldn't, and she knew that. So she left that trail of evidence behind, and then..."

But for Sam, Shiloh's words had slowly whittled away, and his voice had tuned out. Sam was stuck, stuck in the mud, because he couldn't get past that name he'd just heard. Emily—*Emily Parker*.

It sounded too much like Emily Parsons, and the coincidence behind this seemed more than Sam could bear. It shook his concentration and plagued him throughout the rest of the meeting. He ate a fine rib eye, and heard more about the case from Shiloh, details and whatnot, very little of which got through to Sam. And by the end of the meeting, he still couldn't give Shiloh the answer he was looking for, as there were still too many concerns lying in the way. Too many things Sam had to think about, and too many perspectives to consider.

No, Sam didn't give Shiloh what the man had come looking for. But by the end of that meeting, there was something else Sam didn't do, either. He didn't say no.

CHAPTER 4

"You're gonna go back and tell that piece of shit that them's fighting words."

"You don't understand, dude! Myron won't like that. He'll kill me if I do!"

There was a quiet chuckle, and then Jimmy James Ramsey, a towering giant of a man, pressed his knife deeper into the crux of the young hoodlum's neck. "Kill you, will he?" he said.

Jimmy-James, as he was often referred to, was a big southern boy presently wearing denim overalls and a pair of aged Doc Martens boots. He had no shirt on, and the flesh of his exposed arms and chest, bristling with hair, glistened with sweat. He stood six inches shy of seven feet, and was built carnivore-lean, with long muscular arms that could throw a football farther than anyone he knew. His hair was long and wavy, almost down to his waist, and was a mixture of black and blond, matching the shaggy beard on his face. His eyes, narrow and beady, showed both malice and dark humor as he worked his long knife under the chin of the man below him.

"Trust me, dude," the man said, "he will. Myron, he's crazy like that. He's one crazy motherfucker!"

Jimmy-James found the words ironic. And annoying. Currently, he had the man's head pressed down onto the ancient stump of a sycamore tree, used for chopping wood, among other things, and his knife, a 12-inch long Arkansas Toothpick, was slowly drawing blood from the man's neck. "First of all," he said, "you call me dude one more time and I swear to God I'll cut your damn tongue right out of your mouth. Second, if you're gonna die, then on my mama's grave, you do not want to die up here."

The man under the knife was named Roochie, a young hoodlum from the streets of Charlotte, North Carolina. He'd been tasked with the unfortunate errand of coming up into the godforsaken backwoods to deliver a message to Jimmy-James. The message was from Myron Weathers, a small-time drug dealer who used his local gang affiliations and wannabe thugs (such as Roochie) to help him distribute controlled substances throughout the city. And right now, Myron's message wasn't being taken too kindly.

Jimmy-James pulled his knife away from Roochie's neck and, in one quick jerk, lifted the man off the tree stump. He had Roochie by the collar, and he started dragging him through the dirt, handling him like a rag-doll.

Roochie, whose clothes did not fit him properly, as they were three sizes too big, held on to Jimmy's arm with one hand, and reached unsuccessfully to keep his pants from falling to his ankles with the other. It was a strangely comical affair, and lasted for approximately twenty yards, until they came to a small ramshackle building which served as an animal pen.

"Now looky here," Jimmy said as he yanked Roochie up and pinned his head onto a wooden fence rail. He grabbed him by the back of the hair and forced him to stare at the animals in the pen. Three large hogs, each weighing a hundred pounds or more, were grunting and rooting through a mixture of mud, piss, and shit. The creatures seemed anxious and hungry, and one-by-one they began to squeal and canter around.

"See that one there?" Jimmy said, pointing with his knife at one of the pigs. "Her name is Chloe. You see that little freckle she got above her eye? See that there?" Jimmy gave Roochie's head a nudge, as if to underscore his words. "Now ain't that freckle just the cutest damn thing you done seen?"

Roochie was stuck in an awkward position, his head pressed up against the fence rail just a bit higher than three feet off the ground, leaving his legs stuck between kneeling and standing. Both of his hands were on the fence for support, and his pants had slipped down past his waist, exposing his drawers. He was trembling as he looked on.

"And that one there," Jimmy continued, "the fat one... well now, I don't really take to him. He's a big old hog, as he should be, of course. But he sets to pushing the others around a bit too much. Then they get loud and start squealing a mess. A trouble maker, he is, kind of like your nigger boss. We call him Bubba, named after my second cousin, now rotting in jail, bless his soul, and they Lawd have mercy, we're gonna eat that pig come winter."

"I don't know why you're telling me this," Roochie said. "Look du—mister—I swear to God, I'm just a messenger."

Jimmy brought his face down next to Roochie's, whisper-close, then said, "And you see that last one—the little guy? See how he's all but half the size of the other two? Well, don't let that fool you, boy. He's a tough little bastard. He takes all of Bubba's shit, and every damn time he gives it right on back." Jimmy laughed, then stood tall. "His name is Baby, and he's my favorite. And I do not look forward to the day when we're gonna slaughter his little ass."

"Pigs!" Roochie cried. "I get it. You like your pigs. But what the fuck does this have to do with me?"

Jimmy-James paused for a long second as he stared at the young hoodlum. "Well now, ain't that a good question. What does this have to do with you?" Keeping Roochie's head pressed firmly against the fence rail, Jimmy turned a shoulder and said, "Come on over here, Blake."

There were three men standing around watching the show, and then one of them stepped forward. He was taller and wider than the other two. Taller and wider than anyone present for that matter, a big old southern boy with long natty hair, soiled clothes, holey pants, a walking grease stain more or less, and Mother Mary, ugly as sin. He came right up to Jimmy-James, was presently chewing on a toothpick and grinning like a salesman. A badly healed scar from an old and ill-managed harelip left a mile-wide gap below his nose, exposing a broken row of tobacco-stained teeth.

"Hold that man's head," Jimmy commanded. "Right there, just like that. Hold it good."

There was a sudden pause, as Roochie went momentarily still. "What are you gonna do?" he asked, terror swelling in his voice.

Blake spit his toothpick on the ground and then, with his two big hands, fixed Roochie's head into the rail. He straddled the hoodlum's body from behind and pushed all three hundred and forty pounds of his weight forward, pinning Roochie against the fence.

"That's good," Jimmy said. Then he added to Roochie, "Now, then. You said you want to know what them hogs have to do with you."

"Ah... yeah..." Roochie replied.

In one quick motion, slick as butter, Jimmy took his knife and sliced Roochie's ear right off.

Roochie's body jerked in sudden shock, then he let out a blaring shriek, followed by a howling scream. Blake's belly jiggled with laughter as blood squirted out of Roochie's head. The man was screaming wildly and wiggling desperately to break free, but he had no chance in hell of doing that. Big old Blake kept him in place. And after a few minutes of dreadful howling, the hoodlum gave up and settled into a motionless, groaning sob.

"Now then, you little shit," Jimmy said, "watch this." He dangled Roochie's ear in front of his face, and then the boy, still sobbing, clamped his eyes shut. "Watch, dammit!" Jimmy shouted. "Or I'll cut the other one off, so help me Lawd."

In a pitiful, weeping manner, Roochie opened one eye.

"Now watch," Jimmy said. "See which one gets it." He gave a quick whistle, then tossed Roochie's ear into the pen. Seconds later, the hogs scrambled around, butting into one another, their snouts in the mud.

Suddenly quiet, Roochie looked on, and then watched in mesmerized horror as Baby found the prize. The pig chomped the ground, lifted its head, exposing the corner of Roochie's ear sticking out of its mouth for just a quick second, then stood its ground against the other hogs and chewed away.

Roochie closed his eyes and started crying again.

"As I was saying," Jimmy continued, "you do not want to die up here. I've got three hogs there, all with appetites big as Texas, and they'll eat every damn piece of your scrawny, city-boy ass, believe you me. So then, messenger-boy, you're gonna go back and tell Myron that he done pissed me off. And you're gonna tell him that I don't like him talking trash about my product, and that he ain't got no account for changing the arrangements of our deal, no siree. And when you're done telling him that, you're gonna show him this hole in your head, and tell him this is what happens when a born fool like him thinks he can pull one over on a dumb hillbilly like me." Jimmy chuckled. "Us mountain folks, we don't take kindly to people telling us what to do, not ever. And you make sure you tell him that, too."

Roochie kept his mouth shut and nodded his head, sucking wind between sobs.

"Now take this piece of shit on out of here," Jimmy said. He stabbed his knife into the fence rail, then stood back and rolled a smoke. In that time, he watched as Blake and the other men cinched a black bag over Roochie's head, and then tossed him in the back of an old, beat-up Ford truck. They drove slowly away, the tires rolling up dust and pushing chickens across an open field.

The truck disappeared down the dirt road leading into the forest, and then a wave of mild serenity rolled in over the land. The tops of the distant trees swayed from a light breeze, and in the background came the occasional bark from one of the bloodhounds, caged in over on the other side of a single-wide mobile home. The chickens clucked, and Jimmy took a moment to think, as he stared off in the distance and smoked his cigarette down to a stub. When he was finished, he threw the roach in the dirt, stepped on it, grabbed his knife from the fence rail, sheathed it, then turned around and walked back toward an old house sitting not far from the pigpen.

The building was an aged, single story home—more of a shack really—which had been built in 1975, the year Jimmy's pa, Flint Ramsey, had come back from the Vietnam War. The house had a rustic look to it, with wooden shingles for a roof, most of which were cracked and moss-ridden. There was a slanted deck in the front and a partially torn screen door at the entrance. Two windows looked out onto the yard, the panes of which were fogged over with dust and mold.

Jimmy stepped up onto the deck, causing a labor of creaking wood. He opened the screen door and went into the house. The inside of the building was dark and gloomy, and cluttered with an assortment of slipshod furniture and various domestic ware. A score of flies were buzzing lazy circles in the front room, of which Jimmy walked past, and then into the kitchen, with intentions to make a ham sandwich.

The refrigerator was ancient and grimy-looking, and from it, Jimmy retrieved a jar of mayonnaise, mustard, and a hunk of pork covered with foil. He laid two pieces of bread onto the filthy counter, then lathered them with the condiments, using a spoon. He pulled out his knife, rinsed it briefly in the sink, then sliced two fat chunks of meat off the ham, which he then spread onto the bread. Closing the sandwich up, Jimmy took one big, messy bite, sheathed his knife again, then walked out of the house.

He stood in the yard for a minute, watching nature as he ate. The property on which he lived was a reclusive compound of sorts, containing the house and mobile home, an assortment of sheds, animal pens, storage containers, and an old, rickety barn, among other things. This was all set deep in the backcountry of North

Carolina, so the property, although in an open field, was surrounded by forests and canyons, and not much else.

The sandwich tasted good, and Jimmy glanced at it approvingly, before finishing it off. After that, he paused for a minute, thinking. Then he looked to his left, past the clearing, and toward a thicket of small oak trees. Spitting into the dirt, he turned and walked that way.

His stroll went for a hundred yards and ended ten feet from the base of a dead oak tree. Nothing else stood before him, except the entrance to the forest, the draw of a canyon up in the near distance, and a wide hatch at his feet, cleverly concealed with woodland debris.

Using both hands, Jimmy opened the hatch, revealing a four-by-four foot wide opening into the earth. There was a ladder leading down, and casually, he made his way down into the hole.

The bottom was thirty feet below. When Jimmy stepped off the ladder, he reached to his side and pulled a small chain. A dull bloom of light turned on, exposing a dimly lit tunnel, which traveled forward fifty feet, until it gave way into a mouth of shadow.

The corridor had a low ceiling, and was not built for someone Jimmy's size, so he had to crouch as he made his way forward. He walked to the end of the tunnel until he came to an opening with little light and was about the size of a small bedroom. There were two doors in this space, one to his left and the other to his right. Jimmy went to the door on his left, opened it, then stepped into another tunnel, similar to the previous one.

He walked down this earthy corridor for another thirty feet, until it opened into a much bigger room, with a ceiling supported by thick oak beams, and was tall enough for Jimmy to stand in. In this room was a collection of chairs and pillows, as well as an old twin mattress lying on a grid of box crates. The room was well-lit by a series of three naked bulbs hanging from the ceiling. The walls were earth-bare, some of which were covered by bed linens, but one of them had a series of crude shelves built into it. And on one of the shelves was a wide screen television and DVD player.

On the ground below the television was a box of DVDs containing a collection of B-rated horror flicks, comedies, old Spaghetti Westerns, war movies, and pornos. Jimmy rummaged through the collection, found one titled *Elvira's Movie Macabre*, opened the case, then slipped the DVD into the player.

Turning, he walked over to the mattress, picking up a half-empty bottle of whiskey from off a small table on his way. The television remote was covered under a pile of blankets on the bed, and Jimmy found it after a quick search and a few curses later. He reclined on the bed, pressed play, then opened the bottle of whiskey and took a drink.

He settled in and began to watch the show. In the background was a steady hum of electricity, and the distant, intermittent running of a generator, but none of these sounds took Jimmy's attention away from Elvira, and the subsequent bloodcurdling masterpiece. *Some things never get old*, he thought.

An hour into the movie, Jimmy picked up the remote and pressed pause. He was staring at the television screen, but his eyes were seeing something else, something much farther away. He dropped the remote, then took another swig of whiskey, capped the bottle, and set that down too. Then he climbed off the bed and moved toward the adjacent wall, presently covered by a yellow sheet.

Jimmy moved the sheet, and behind it was a steel door, sealed shut by a wide latch and padlock. From a chain attached to his overalls, he retrieved a key, which he then used to open the lock. He opened the door and was met with a void of darkness and a sour stench.

Jimmy James Ramsey stepped into the darkness and reached to his left, grasping a piece of string hanging from the ceiling above. Once he pulled that string, he knew a light would turn on, revealing to him what was in this room, but he paused for a minute, because hell, he knew that's where the fun was at, hiding in all them corners of suspense. Jimmy stood silently, hand on the string, calmly listening to the darkness, feeling that familiar tingle in his loins, listening for something that would make his face break out into a wide grin.

And then Jimmy heard it. The faint rustling, followed by the distinct "clink" from a metal chain.

Goddamn, some things never do get old.

CHAPTER 5

It was the next day and Sam, Matt, Tom, and Nali were sitting at the picnic table under the *ramada*, drinking beers and eating ham sandwiches. The afternoon had arrived, and they had just taken a break from doing some ranch chores. They were discussing Sam's dilemma, among other topics.

"It does seem a little unconventional, if you ask me," Tom said, "coming out here to hire you. But I know exactly what the man is feeling right now. When you're a desperate father, desperate to find your child, you'll do anything to make that happen."

"I don't suspect any ill intentions from this man," Sam said. "It is unconventional, but you're right; he's just a mighty desperate father."

Matt smiled. "Look, Sam, if you need a vacation from the work around here, you just say the word."

"Shut your trap, Matt," Tom snapped. "This is a serious deal. We don't need any of your bantering right now. Show a little respect, for Lord's sake."

Matt's smile faded as he went back to eating his sandwich.

"No," Sam said, "he's right, Tom. Not that I need a vacation," Sam gave his older brother a sneer, "but that there's too much work around here. What with the upcoming haying and irrigation chores. Pasturing the cattle. Fencing repair, and then that damn culvert we need to fix again. There's too much needing to get done. Last thing

I should be doing is running off on some wild goose chase for a few weeks."

"Well now, that's bullshit," Tom replied. "Sure, there's work—hell, there's always work. But if we get into a bind, I'll just call up Gonzales, or his boy, Cody."

Sam looked away, his mind deep in thought. There was a warm afternoon breeze stirring the prairie just beyond the *ramada*. The wind brought with it the sweet smell of grass and creosote, along with a dusty, dry earth aroma. In the southern sky, an evening rain was piling up, and it was patiently moving toward them, like a colossal stone giant rising precariously above the land.

"I don't see any use of it," Sam said, looking back at his father. "I know it won't do me any good to go out there—not when it comes to finding that girl." Sam hadn't told them what the girl's name was, or how that detail had bothered him an awful lot. He also hadn't mentioned his recurring nightmares either, except to Lolo. But knowing her, she might've said something about that to Nali. "That man already had a good tracker looking for his daughter," Sam continued, "and he came up with nothing."

"But what about that evidence?" Tom asked. "You mentioned earlier that there was some kind of evidence they'd found?"

Sam looked down at his food. "Yeah," he said. "Notes, apparently. I guess the girl thought she was being stalked by some men or something." Then he shook his head. "Her father won't admit it, but it sounds like she lost her mind out there. I've seen it happen. A person gets lost in the woods, real lost, then night comes along, with all its strange and eerie sounds. Fear kicks in... A few days of that, and it messes with a person's mind. If you're alone and not used to being in the woods—and maybe you've got no fire to warm up to, or a weapon to protect yourself with—well, that fear, it just turns to terror and runs right over you."

The other three men nodded their heads in acknowledgement.

After a minute of silence, Matt said, "But what if she *didn't* go crazy out there? What if her notes were telling the truth?"

Sam looked at his brother. "Well, I suppose that could be the case." His mind went to his recent experience up in Canada, with Lou Pine, and that man's many victims. "We all know this kind of stuff happens."

"The girl lost her mind," Nali said, "or she didn't." The old Apache was holding his beer halfway to his mouth and measuring Sam with his stare.

Sam took the man's words for all their worth. Nali was right. It didn't really matter what had happened to the girl and how she disappeared. What mattered right now was what he was going to do about it.

Sam took a bite of his sandwich and looked away. There was a sudden silence that fell upon the men, and in this stillness he noticed the sounds of the ranch, such that they were. He heard a rustling in the cottonwoods behind the house, the wind pushing through the leaves. And off to his right came a snort from one of the horses over in the barn.

"Well, did he offer you anything?" Matt asked, suddenly breaking the silence. "How much are we talking about?"

Sam nodded. "Before I left, Mr. Parker offered me an envelope with ten thousand dollars in it, all cash. That's more than I would need, of course. And certainly more than what I make around here in a month, no offense."

"Did you take the envelope?" Tom asked.

"I did," Sam replied. "Not at first, because I didn't want to. But he insisted, and then told me that if I change my mind, to keep half, just for listening, and to send the rest back to him in a money order. I'll send it all back, of course... if I don't take the job."

"That sure is a lot of money," Matt said, "to go looking through the woods for a few weeks. I say, go for it."

"It is a lot," Sam replied. "And he said there's more if I need it. Or, if I find her—a lot more. But things..." Sam paused, picking at a splinter of wood on the table, "well, things are complicated. Lolo sure as hell wouldn't like me running off for a few weeks."

Matt chuckled. "For ten thousand dollars, I think she'd get over it."

Sam didn't respond. He knew Lolo would have a hard time with him being gone. But also, a part of her would most likely understand. She was the one who had to deal with him and his nightmares. And Sam couldn't help but think that, by design, perhaps such a trip would prove to be a remedy of sorts. The fact that the lost girl's name was Emily still weighed heavily on his conscience. And this coincidence was something that would hardly get overlooked by Lolo.

Sam looked up, suddenly feeling the burn of Nali's stare.

"There is a saying," the old man said, setting his cup down and resting his palms flat on the table, as if indicating he was finished with his break and was about to stand up. "Wisdom and peace come when you start living the life the Creator intended for you."

The words were Geronimo's, the mighty Apache chief, and they were dead on. Sam could no longer deny it. Also, because Nali spoke them, he had a hunch Lolo had been talking to her father about the nightmares. Peace coming to a person who lived a life the Creator intended sure sounded like Nali's answer to not just what Sam should do about Shiloh's lost girl, but of his inner struggles as well.

"I'll let you all know what I decide," Sam said. And then he stood up from the picnic table and walked away.

•   •   •

Later that night, Sam was digging through an old duffel bag in the garage of his house. Looking through the items in the bag brought back a host of nostalgic memories. They were his military effects he'd collected over the years, each one bearing a history of his time spent as a Green Beret, and sniper. Each one with a story all its own, and each connected to the memories of particular missions.

It was bittersweet for Sam to see all these things from his past—holsters, compass with lanyard, knives, canteen, pouches and belts—to name just a small few of the items from the plethora of tactical gear crammed into the bag. He was looking for only one thing in particular, though, but apparently had to go through all his memories in order to find it.

When he ran across a field journal he used while on missions, Sam paused. Slowly, he picked the journal up and started leafing through its pages.

The book contained mission-related specifications, along with various locations, load out specs, and details such as wind speed calculations, barometric pressure values, humidity effects, distances, geographical icons, and GPS coordinates. There were also names for select missions, as well as targets, all in code. Toward the back of the journal, Sam read the pages on one mission in particular, and this drew goose bumps over his arms, as it was from his first mission with Ernie. Sam was then reminded that this particular journal wasn't his last. His last had been lost after he and Ernie got captured by the Taliban.

The memory of his lost journal brought Sam's mind back to the evidence they had found regarding Shiloh's missing daughter. Pages from *her* notebook, describing wild men in the forest, chasing her for days... or so Shiloh had claimed.

He set his field journal to the side and went back to searching through the duffel bag. Seconds later, Sam found what he was looking for. Another notebook of sorts, as it was his old address book he'd had since he was a senior in high school.

Sam pocketed the address book, then zipped up the duffel and placed it back on a shelf. Quietly, he went into the house and made his way to the office room.

Lolo was in the room and staring at their computer. She was scanning through her Facebook feed and sipping tea, and she looked cute as a college student, with her hair in a lazy bun, and her reading glasses on. Sam liked it when Lolo wore her glasses.

"You think I can borrow that damn machine for a minute?" he asked, as he started looking through his address book.

"Of course," Lolo replied. She stood, then stepped past Sam. "I'll make you some tea if you'd like."

"No thank you," he said. "But I will take a glass of water."

She kissed him on the cheek on her way out of the room, and then Sam sat down and looked at the monitor.

Lolo's Facebook account was staring right back at him, and this left an unsettling feeling in his stomach. Sam wasn't fond of computers, although he understood and appreciated the value of such technology. Mostly, he wasn't tech-minded, and had little patience for sitting down long enough to change that. But as for social media, well, that was something Sam loathed entirely. He wasn't interested in looking into other people's lives, and certainly didn't want anyone peering into his. He was happy to say he had no such social media account, regardless of Lolo's endless teasing of him. But despite her teasing, Sam also knew she was proud of his stubbornness, as he hung faithfully on to his old-fashioned ways.

The woman wouldn't let up on him needing to get a cell phone, though. It was something that genuinely bothered Lolo, that she couldn't get a hold of him whenever she pleased. To text him messages throughout the day. To *receive* messages from him. This was a battle Sam knew he would eventually lose. And thinking of his current plans, he was likely going to lose it sooner rather than later.

He found a name in his address book, then paused as he thought about all the years that had passed since he'd written that name in there. Then an idea popped into his head, and he opened a separate tab on the computer browser. He typed in the name, followed by the words "martial artist," and seconds later, was looking at a dozen different links, all of which held his interest.

"Why am I not surprised?" Sam said to himself.

He clicked on a link, and up came the website of a business. Sam found the contact page, then chuckled as he picked up the landline phone next to the computer. Briefly, he thought of what time it was, added a few hours, then chuckled again. "Knowing him, he'll answer the phone."

Sam dialed the number from the website. It rang for several seconds before a voicemail kicked in. He hung up, waited a minute, then dialed again. After three rings, someone answered.

"Yeah, what is it?"

"Hello, Madigan," Sam said. "It's Nolan... Sam Nolan."

"Say what? *Sam?* Shit, man, it's... been a while. What's happening, brother?"

Sam heard some rustling in the background and pictured Madigan sitting up in bed, turning a light on, blinking the sleep out of his eyes.

"Yes, it has," Sam replied. "It's been a long while."

"So what's up?" Madigan asked.

"Sorry to bother you," Sam said, "but I wanted to let you know that I'm gonna be out there in a few days. I'd like to meet up, if you don't mind."

"Anytime you want, man."

"Thanks," Sam said.

After a brief pause, Madigan added, "But what's this all about? You sound serious, Sam. And it is a little late for a call."

"I've got a job to do," Sam replied. "Nothing too serious, not like anything we've done, of course. Just a favor for someone out there. I thought it'd be nice to see you, though. And also, you might be able to help me out some, I don't know."

"You just say the word, and I'll do whatever I can."

"I appreciate it," Sam said. "I'll owe you one, of course."

"Well, we'll see about that. If memory serves me correctly, I'm the one who still owes you."

With that comment, Sam recalled the time he and Ernie had saved the lives of several squad members by sniping enemy combatants presently surrounding the men and moving in. Madigan was one of those squad members, and had been wounded at the time, having taken shrapnel in the back from an RPG explosion.

"It'll be good to see you, Madigan," Sam said. "I'll call when I get in town."

They said their goodbyes and then Sam hung up the phone. He turned a shoulder, and there was Lolo with a glass of water in her hand.

"Thanks," he said, taking the glass. Then he looked at her and noticed the stoic look on her face.

Sam had already discussed his plans with Lolo, and, although not happy, she was supportive of his decision. She may not have liked it, but it seemed as if she understood. The look in her eyes when he'd told her that the girl's name was Emily Parker was like the striking of a match. As Sam expected, the coincidence had not been lost on the woman.

"Like I said, I don't think I'll be more than a few weeks."

"Don't worry, Sam," Lolo replied. She paused, then added, "I've been thinking it's very kind of you to do this. I can only imagine how that girl's parents must feel."

Sam drank his water and then pulled his wallet from his pocket. He found the business card in it, picked up the phone again, and dialed the number on the card. After two rings, he got through.

"This is Parker," Shiloh answered.

"Just wanted to let you know that I'll take the job," Sam said. "I'll look you up when I get out there. Shouldn't be more than a few days."

Shiloh didn't answer at first, but Sam heard the man exhale heavily. "Thank you, Sam," he finally said. "My God... thank you."

CHAPTER 6

In less than two days, Sam had arrived at Shiloh Parker's house. He had taken a five-hour flight from El Paso to Knoxville, and then rented a Ford Explorer for the two-hour drive south-east, through the Great Smoky Mountains. It had been beautiful scenery through the dense Appalachian wilderness, with the lush trees, tangled foliage, and mountain streams. The pleasant scenery lasted for his entire trip, all the way to Cherokee, North Carolina. But the beauty didn't stop there.

Shiloh Parker's estate was on a hundred acres of gorgeous land. The entrance to his property was a freshly paved road, which ran two hundred yards, and was bordered on both sides by a neat row of pine trees and a short wall made from natural stone. Eventually, the trees gave way to a large green meadow, with a rustic-fashioned gazebo off to the right, set next to a pond, and then the main house in the near background. The house was a luxurious log home built from solid pine and smooth granite, with two massive ceiling-high windows staring out onto the front property.

To the rear of the house was a long horse stable, built in the same architecture as that of the main house, and beside it, a much larger expanse of green pasture. Beyond this field was the entrance to a forest, and yet further away, the distant peaks of the Blue Ridge Mountains. There was no denying it; Shiloh Parker had fine taste and a thick wallet.

Sam followed the driveway up to the house, and before he got out of the vehicle, he was greeted by two large Doberman Pinschers staring at him. Shiloh's assistant, Ronnie Wilkins, was there, and by the time Sam stepped out of the Explorer, Ronnie had the dogs sitting obediently on the pavement.

"Hello, Mr. Nolan," Ronnie said, extending his hand out to Sam. "Mr. and Mrs. Parker are glad you've come."

Sam shook the man's hand and then stretched his body, popping several vertebrae and both of his knees. Despite the beauty found throughout his trip, it had been a long day of traveling.

"Why don't you follow me," Ronnie said. "Mr. Parker is out back with the horses. Welcome to the estate. I trust your trip went well." He was a cool cat, with a reserved, stoic personality, commonly found in an upper class servant, such as a butler. He even looked the part—clean-shaven and wearing freshly pressed attire, a navy blazer with matching trousers cut two centimeters from the heel, a black tie to complement his long black braid, and smoothly polished shoes. Maybe he was a butler, Sam thought.

"It did," Sam replied. "It went really well. And it's pleasant to be back in the South. I spent some time here years ago." He shut the door and then followed Ronnie's lead. They walked around the side of the house, past the attached four-car garage, until they came to the stables out back.

Shiloh Parker was standing in front of the stable entrance, his hand on the bridle of a handsome-looking Leopard Appaloosa. The horse was white with brown spots and was currently saddle-less. Shiloh was running his other hand across the horse's neck and talking nicely to the creature when Sam and Ronnie came down the driveway.

"That's a fine-looking horse you've got there," Sam said, approaching Shiloh. He was pleasantly surprised to see that the man had an obvious predilection for all things equestrian. The stable was easily three times the size of the main house, and detailed with custom features, including a paved entryway and a courtyard fountain. High fashion indeed. "You never mentioned you're a rider."

Shiloh chuckled. "Well, it's not really my hobby so much as it is my wife's... And my daughter's." He reached out and shook Sam's hand. "But I do like to trot around once in a while. And I like taking care of these creatures. Something about them makes me feel... connected, I guess."

"They sure know how to teach a man the value of work," Sam replied, "if such a man is willing to learn. Not every man is, in my opinion."

"I'm glad you came," Shiloh said, looking Sam in the eye. "I'm real glad."

They walked the horse into the stable while making small talk, and Sam took a minute to absorb the finer details of the building. There were multiple rooms in the stable, along with twenty horse stalls, more than half of which were presently occupied. The building was a commercial grade equestrian facility, with grooming and wash stalls, tack rooms, several closets, tool and storage areas, and what looked like an office and small apartment on the second level. There was a viewing room in the center of the building, beyond the fountain, and it was set with fine leather couches, a large stone fireplace, as well as a standing bar. Sam had seen many stables in his life, but this one was by far the most impressive.

A young woman was in the tack room presently organizing saddle gear, but she paused with her work and came over to the men. "Do you want me to take Penny, Mr. Parker?" she asked. She was wearing muck boots and brown denim overalls, and had platinum blond hair tied back into a ponytail. "I can stall her if you want me to."

"Thanks, Maria," Shiloh said, passing the reins to the girl. "Give her an extra brushing as well. She'll like that." He turned to Sam. "Would you care to see the rest of the horses?"

"Don't mind if I do," Sam replied. "My legs can use the walking."

Shiloh took Sam on a tour through the stable, showing him his collection of horses. "I look for rescues when I can," he said, "but some of these are retired thoroughbreds. I don't play the races, though, as I don't approve of how they treat their animals."

"I've heard of such things," Sam added.

"The rest of these beauties…" Shiloh gestured to Penny, now in a grooming stall with Maria, "they're just deals that were too good to pass by. If I could, I'd have an estate ten times bigger than this, with ten times as many animals. I'm not interested in breeding. Just providing a nice home for them to retire." Shiloh paused and then looked at the ground. "It was my wife and daughter's dream to build such a ranch. We were looking at property in Virginia, in fact. But now… Well, now I don't know anymore." Shiloh looked again at Sam. "Like I said, I'm glad you came."

•　•　•

Fifteen minutes later, they were in Shiloh's office on the second story of the main house. Just as impressive as the stable, Shiloh's home was a masterful representation of wood and stone built with ornate fixtures and custom details. Adding to the striking design was the collection of fine artwork deliberately placed throughout the home. Sam saw more than one of those fancy bowls, similar to the one Shiloh had given Tom. And on a shelf here or there were pieces of traditional Native American pottery, genuine items, not the dime-store knockoffs found along tourists traps and forgotten byways.

Even Shiloh's office was hard to ignore. The walls and ceiling were paneled with walnut and mahogany, and there was a bookcase on the south wall that must have contained over a thousand volumes. The office was bigger than Sam's living room, and there were easily several thousand dollars' worth of artwork decorating the place, sculptures and paintings, a small gallery more or less. But in the center of the room, as if entirely misplaced, was a common rectangular table, the kind seen at a backyard barbeque. And on the table were a collection of topographical maps, colored pencils, notebooks, photographs, and various sheets of paper.

Shiloh was presently pouring Bourbon into two tumblers, one for him and one for Sam. His wife was standing beside them, a glass of red wine in her hand, half empty.

"We've been over this a hundred times, Sam," Shiloh said, gesturing to the table. "Looking through those maps, Emily's notes that were found, and, of course, the notes written up during our search for her. But in my heart, I just know that we've missed something." He brought the tumbler over to Sam and then took a sip of his own. "Like I said, I don't believe for a minute that my daughter got lost out there. She knew what she was doing. And even if she got herself into some kind of trouble, a broken ankle perhaps, she would've known to stay put on the trail until help came along. Hell, she would've built a goddamn bonfire without breaking a sweat." He shook his head. "I know my Emily got abducted, Sam. Just like what's in those notes of hers. She was being followed... Followed by those wild men."

"Wild men." Sam said, thinking. Shiloh had previously mentioned this, but hadn't gone into details yet. "What exactly does that mean? Were there any notes describing these characters?"

"Not much for description," Shiloh replied, "but..." He set his tumbler on the table and picked up a binder containing several loose papers. He leafed through the pages briefly, but then his wife took the binder from him.

"Emily made references to these men," Vicki said. She had all the notes on the table now, and was quickly going through them, knowing exactly where to look. Within seconds, she handed Sam four specific pages.

Sam inspected the condition of the pages before reading the words on them. They were of high-quality paper, torn roughly from perhaps a personal diary or writing journal. A little water-damaged, weathered, and wrinkled badly, but for the most part, the notes were legible.

Emily had written her thoughts in cursive, using a pen, and looking through the pages Vicki had given him, Sam read the girl's descriptions.

I think I'm being followed. I heard noises in the forest today, way off the trail, and then I caught a glimpse of a man standing beside a tree. He was a horrible-looking man, and he was staring right at me. And when I made eye-contact with him, he slowly stepped back behind the tree. I thought I saw him smile, but I couldn't tell, it was too far away. But he was definitely watching me.

Sam set the page on the table and read from another one.

I yelled at them today. I told them I knew what they were doing, that I knew they were following me. I yelled at them to go away, and then I heard them laugh. They are creeping me out! I'm so scared.

And from another page he read...

They don't even try to hide anymore. They just stare at me from the trees, and watch me, smiling. And they're getting closer. Every time I see them, they're closer.

Finally, Sam read the last page.

They made noises all day, as I ran on the trail, hoping to get away from them. I thought I lost them, but then they were in the trees by my camp last night, stalking me, I know, hunting me, both of them, and I heard their breathing they were that close. I could smell them, and I heard them grunting, sniffing and whispering, I heard them approaching. I heard them... The page had been torn at the bottom, leaving the rest of the sentence a mystery.

When Sam was finished reading, he looked up. Shiloh and his wife were staring earnestly at him, and the woman now had a page in her hand. "Let me read this one to you," she said. *"This will be my last note. I'm leaving everything behind. I'm ditching all my gear, and I'm going to run like Penny into the wild wilderness. I know I can outrun them, it's in my heritage. I am Cherokee, and this is my home. Not theirs. <u>This is my home.</u>"*

Sam thought for a minute. The notes were intriguing. He looked through all the other pages from the binder, curious to see what else was written.

"The rest are just Emily's personal ruminations," Vicki said, "and descriptions along the Appalachian before they started following her."

Interestingly, there were no dates written on the pages, so Sam couldn't determine any specific chronological order to the notes. But the pages describing the girl's incident with the strange men seemed to follow a timeline of sorts.

"I've made copies for you, Sam," Shiloh said. He went to his desk and came back with a manila folder, which he set down on the corner of the table. "Emily's pages, the search and rescue notes… Everything is in there."

"I appreciate this," Sam said, scratching his chin. "I'm curious, though. You mentioned that when you found her notes, people in the search teams started losing interest. Is that how it went?"

Shiloh shook his head. "Only the ones that described her being followed." He picked his tumbler up and took a drink. "Like I said, I believe that's when they thought my girl had lost her mind. That she had gone crazy."

"Well," Sam said, "it isn't uncommon for lost hikers, after a few days, to lose sense of their wits. It's a shame, because sometimes they run off and hide from the very people looking for them." He paused, noticing the depressed look on Vicki's face, then added, "But that's not why I'm here, Mr. Parker—to cast doubt onto this job. I've taken you by your word that your daughter was in her right mind." He gestured at the notes on the table. "And that what she wrote on them pages is the truth."

Even as he said it, Sam had a hard time convincing himself that the girl hadn't gone crazy. And her notes, the ones describing her stalkers, seemed highly implausible. Who or what would take their time to follow a young woman like that, and for what appeared to be multiple days? Why not just abduct her at the first opportunity?

Then Sam was reminded of Lou Pine.

Still, to torment a young woman on an open trail over several days, where she could easily run across other hikers to help her out... It seemed more plausible that Emily had gotten lost, and that caused her to break down mentally. Mr. Parker was convinced his daughter was too experienced with the outdoors, and could never have gotten herself into such an extreme situation. But Sam knew how these things went. Emily could have stumbled across a bear with cubs, or seen a mountain, anything that would've spooked her enough to run off. Then, after running for some time, and not paying attention to how the wilderness looked behind her, only how it looked going forward, and while in a state of panic... This was how people got themselves lost. And when a person gets lost, well, that's a game changer.

There was a sudden knock on the office door.

"Come in," Shiloh said.

Ronnie Wilkins entered, carrying a piece of paper, which he handed to Shiloh. "A message from the Board of Commissions, sir."

Shiloh read the message, then shook his head. "I told them I'll call them back when I get around to it."

Sam took out a small notebook and pen from his back pocket. He wrote the present date on the first page, and then quietly examined the various articles sitting on the table. "If you need to take a call, Mr. Parker, I can wait."

Shiloh waved a hand dismissively. "That won't be necessary, Sam. Let's continue."

"In that case, do you have a number for that Cherokee tracker you mentioned?" Sam asked. "I would like to give him a call."

Shiloh pointed to the envelope. "The first page in there is a list of all the contacts, along with their numbers and addresses. Harlow Evans is the man's name, and he lives up near Cataloochee."

Sam nodded, then scratched his chin. He was now looking at the topographical maps on the table, making sense out of the notes written on them, and in different colors. He recognized the survey lines traced on the map in red, which were the official search boundaries, by way of boots on the ground. The area within the red perimeter would have been scoured on foot, and by the various groups looking for the girl. Local Search and Rescue, state and county law enforcement, Park Rangers, as well as a host of volunteers, would have undoubtedly made up the search teams. In total, Sam estimated that the ground crews covered roughly five square miles. And beyond this perimeter was another line on the map, traced in blue. This was the area covered from the air, through the use of a helicopter, and it amounted to roughly fifty square miles.

"Exactly how many days did you search for Emily?" Sam asked.

"The official search lasted for ten days," Shiloh replied. "Five days into our search was when we found the first page from my daughter's notebook." He pointed to a spot on the map. "Right here, within this canyon."

"And how far off the trail was this note?" Sam asked. "Or was it?"

"It was," Shiloh replied. "About two hundred yards to the northwest."

"They found all her notes in that same area," Vicki said. "Within a stretch of two miles and a half-mile radius. But only on one side of the creek."

Shiloh pointed to a small, squiggly blue line on the map. "We found all her notes within this canyon," he said, "and on the south side of this creek."

"And what happened after ten days?" Sam asked. "Can you please explain to me the details of how they wrapped up the search?"

"Absolutely," Shiloh replied. "They found the notes describing the wild men on the eighth day, although they had already found several of Emily's other journal entries. But after they read about her stalkers, I could tell that they had made up their mind. In all likelihood, I think they thought these 'wild men' she was referring to might have been some of them, who were actively searching for her—just like you said could happen. Two days later, the official search was called off… I was mad as hell, Sam, and I tried to use my influence to keep things going, but the people from the park system, they were done. It seemed as if they were more than ready to put this business of my daughter's disappearance behind them. And once they pulled out, well, Harlow followed suit, along with all the others."

"Do you know where exactly Harlow searched?" Sam asked.

"As far as I know, he stayed within the same perimeter," Shiloh said. "But I'm not sure where all he went, or what he did—how he did his searching, that is. I do know he was a little unconventional. I guess that would be the right word for it. He didn't stay near anyone, and was rarely seen. He mostly stuck to himself."

"A good tracker would do that," Sam replied. "I suspect he was on the outer perimeter, away from all the noise and commotion, not to mention the disturbances on the land that come with a large search party. It would've been his best place to cut sign, lacking anything noteworthy, such as a piece of clothing."

Sam thought for a minute, then said, "Back in New Mexico, you mentioned there was something odd about this Evans feller. That there was something you thought he had on his mind, but wouldn't comment on."

"That's correct," Shiloh said. "After we found the 'wild men' notes. Best I can describe is that there was a piece of the puzzle he'd found, but couldn't place correctly, and it was eating at him. Not like he was hiding anything from me, just, well, bothered. I couldn't get anything out of the man, though. Lord knows I tried. Ultimately, he went cold, just like everybody else."

Sam was suddenly reminded of his conversation with Andre McKinnon, the Search and Rescue team leader up in Canada, who had explained his theories as to how Bryson had gone missing. "Well," Sam said, "before I get to work, I think I'll have a talk with

Mr. Evans. Faced with another tracker, maybe he'll know how to explain to me what was bothering him."

There was a momentary pause in the conversation, with Sam quietly observing the maps on the table. And with this silence came an all-too-obvious anxiousness, coming from Shiloh, and particularly his wife. Sam glanced briefly at the woman, who was holding her wineglass with two hands, as if she didn't have the strength in just one. Her body was trembling ever so slightly, and there was a hopeful, yet painful, look in her eyes.

"Do you think you can find her?" she finally said. "Do you think you can our Emily, Mr. Nolan?"

Sam hesitated, then said, "I'll certainly do the best I can, ma'am." After another pause, he added, "I know how it feels to lose someone in this manner. Someone you care about. And, frankly, I don't think there's any worse feeling a parent could go through. Such misery shouldn't be wished upon the worst of enemies." He picked up the envelope on the table, prepared himself to leave, then ended with, "I'll promise you this, Mrs. Parker: I will not give up my search as easily as those other men did."

CHAPTER 7

Early the next morning, Sam pulled into an old commercial strip mall on the southern outskirts of Asheville. It had been a little over an hour's drive from his hotel, back in Cherokee, not counting time spent to pick up coffee and donuts. The sun had just risen, and there were only a few cars in the parking lot. The strip mall consisted of tired-looking storefronts and plenty of wide-spaced parking. Sam backed his vehicle into an empty spot, sipped his coffee, and waited as he studied the building in front of him.

It was a martial arts school, and there was a rectangular sign on the roof that read "Street Fight Studio" in blocky red letters. It was the home front to Marcus Madigan's proprietary business.

Sam's former military colleague had spent decades training in martial arts of one kind or the other. The man had several black belts from multiple fighting styles (Sam couldn't remember all the different names) and over time, much like many other notable martial artists, Madigan had fashionably amalgamated his hard-earned knowledge into his own combat fighting system.

He had taught these skills while serving in the Armed Forces. Sam remembered training with his friend, first while they were stationed in Fort Bragg, and then months later, in the deserts near Kandahar. Madigan had a penchant for what he called "getting business done," and he could do so with a knife or his bare hands, using techniques designed to maim or kill opponents within seconds, and without all that sugary flare seen in martial arts flicks. There was no wasting time or energy with high kicks or flowery forms for Madigan. Five seconds in close with a SOG Bowie was all he needed. Then death would ensue and bodies would fall.

Five seconds in close.

Sam had seen the truth of that statement. And the truth was that five seconds was more than enough time for Madigan to do what he did best. The memory stood clear as an Afghan morning in Sam's mind, the day he watched through his Leupold Mark IV scope as Madigan moved stealthily out from cover and under the low light of dawn, a modern day ninja, and then he dispatched by knife two Taliban soldiers who were leaning against a water tank, chatting idly.

Madigan had moved fast, fast as electricity. His knife-wielding hand was a blur of motion, slicing, stabbing, puncturing through both men a dozen times before it was over. He had cut through wrists first, snapping tendons so Terry Taliban couldn't get any shots fired off, then into the soft spots of their bodies, the neck and solar plexus, heart and lungs. It all happened in less than five seconds. Not as quick as death from a bullet, but damn near close enough.

The poor soldiers had no time to react, Sam remembered. Their bodies shuddered violently in those moments that Madigan got his business done, their faces equipped with sudden, grim surprises, just before they fell to the desert ground like bags of sand, blood pooling out of them.

Street Fight Studio. Was there any better name for Marcus Madigan's school? Sam sure as hell couldn't think of one.

He had arrived early, and waited for another ten minutes before he spotted Madigan down the road, jogging toward the parking lot. Sam took another sip of coffee, grabbed the bag of donuts from the seat next to him, then got out of the vehicle to meet his friend.

"Sam Nolan," Madigan said, jogging up to Sam and embracing him. He was wearing a blue jumpsuit, running shoes, and looked as lean and mean as the last time Sam had seen him. "How are you doing, brother?"

"I'm good," Sam replied, "all things considered." He offered the bag of donuts to Madigan, and added, "I figured you could use some fuel for your day. Besides, you always did have a sweet tooth."

"Thanks," Madigan said, accepting the bag with a smile. "Not the best thing for my health, but there's worse." He motioned to his studio. "Come on in, Sam. You just have to see what I've built for myself over the years. How long has it been, anyway?"

"Not long enough," Sam teased.

They both chuckled and then Madigan unlocked the door, led Sam into his school, and flicked the lights on. They stepped into a spacious martial arts studio, with a floor covered mostly in foam mats. There were mirrors all across one wall, and dozens of weapons hanging on another. Sam noticed several framed pictures throughout the place, portraits of what he assumed were instructors or top students, all with serious looks on their faces. Flags, emblems, and other pictures were fitted neatly here and there, along with photos of various military personnel. But on one section of a wall there was a collection of photos highlighting Madigan's idle: the legendry, Michael D. Echanis, mercenary extraordinaire.

"This is my dream come true," Madigan said. "It's been running for several years now, and I have over two-hundred regular students, forty-three black belts, and four assistant instructors."

Sam nodded his head approvingly. "I'm not surprised, Marcus. You were always good at this stuff. What am I saying? You were great."

"You weren't so bad yourself," Madigan said. "You held your own, if I remember correctly."

"That's because I had a good instructor."

Madigan chuckled. "Those were good times, weren't they?"

Sam nodded slightly, then looked away. "Good times, indeed," he said, as he pointed to a small office in the back of the room. "I suppose that's where you get business done now."

"Some of it, at least," Madigan replied. He led Sam across the mats and into the office. They sat down, and then Madigan turned on a computer and a small desk lamp. He opened the bag of donuts, took one out, bit into it, and smiled. They chatted for a few minutes, catching up on the years that had passed, but eventually a pause interrupted their conversation, and then Madigan asked, "So what's going on, Sam? Why are you out here?"

Sam thought for a second, then told him the story, along with all the pertinent details. "It's probably a waste of time," he concluded, "but damn if I won't feel bad for not trying."

"You said that girl's been missing for two weeks?"

"More than that now," Sam replied.

Madigan shook his head. "I hate to be a pessimist, but there's no way she's still alive, my friend."

"Yeah, I'm afraid you're probably right. But those pages her daddy gave me, they were pretty compelling. Maybe there's something to it, I don't know." He explained more about Emily's notes, and in particular, the part where she described wild men stalking her through the forest. "If there's any truth to what she wrote," Sam continued, "then it's worth spending some time out there."

Madigan's face grew serious. "I heard about your escapade up in the Yukon, by the way. Finding your brother and all. You made the paper, man. And the job you pulled up there, it made its way through some of the groups like wildfire."

"Is that so?"

"Damn right it did," Madigan said. Then he smiled. "Rumors, mostly, 'cause none of us down here got the full mission briefing."

Sam shook his head. "It wasn't anything you couldn't handle. Anyway, what I did up there, that was a family affair." He paused, then added, "But perhaps that's why I feel obliged to look into this missing girl."

"Maybe so," Madigan replied, although his tone indicated he wasn't too convinced. "But if this girl is correct, with her notes about wild men in the woods, well, that's something you should consider carefully, Sam."

"How so?"

"You've seen the movie Deliverance, haven't you?"

"Now I know you're joking," Sam replied.

"I'm not. And that's the thing. I've lived out here for most of life, and I've heard some stories over the years that would make your skin crawl. Way up in them hills," he pointed to the north, "there're folks—mountain people, we call them—who still live on their own accord, with their own laws. And some of them are fucking crazy, Sam. So you just watch yourself."

"I don't expect I'll have any problems with any mountain people," Sam said.

"Even so..." Madigan paused, opened a desk drawer and withdrew a key, hidden in an old 35 mm film canister. "Come with me, Sam," he said, standing up. "I'd like to show you something."

Madigan led Sam across the mats and to a locked door in the backroom. He used the key from his desk to unlock the door, and then they went down a flight of stairs, dimly lit. There was another door at the bottom, secured by a hefty padlock, and the key for that was tied to a chain around Madigan's neck. Once he unsecured the door, he flipped a switch and led Sam into a basement that had been renovated into a small armory. There were several guns mounted on a wall, and a long work bench below that. The bench was cluttered with various tools and gadgets, rags and cleaning supplies, along with a reloading station for ammunition. Also on the bench were a laptop and tactical radios, several ammo boxes, and gunsmith tools.

"Damn, Madigan," Sam said, "looks like you're set for war. Are you still active in some way?"

"You can say that," Madigan replied. From the wall, he pulled down an M4A1 Carbine spray-painted in a woodland camouflage pattern, and handed it to Sam. "I just completed making this one," he added. "Haven't even fired it yet."

Sam handled the rifle, pulled it up and looked through the scope, a Trijicon ACOG with illuminated crosshairs. "This is a fine piece of work," he said. He looked through it again, then handed the rifle back to his friend.

"You're still missed, Sam," Madigan said. "Many of us have moved on, of course, except for a few lifers. And others... well, some of the boys aren't with us anymore, which you may or may not know about. But for many of us, there's still work to be had."

Sam thought about that for a second. "You mean Agency work?" he asked.

"Not exactly," Madigan replied. "For some, sure. Cuba and Jenner. Frenchy... Cotton, for a while. Those guys got recruited that way. And others went a little sideways, pulling security details for the Illuminati. But I'm talking about contracting, Sam. There's big business and big money for ex-soldiers like us."

"Blackwater mercenaries..." Sam said.

"Blackwater is just one company," Madigan replied. "But there're others." He hung the Carbine back on the wall, then pulled down a Heckler & Koch MP5 submachine gun. "Contracting ain't like it used to be, Sam. It's more secure now, with better pay and better rotations." He handed the machine gun to Sam and winked. "And of course, better benefits."

Sam held the gun, felt the precision of its balanced weight in his hands, how it sat so smooth and idle. It had been a long time since he'd fired this particular gun—not since his Close Quarter Combat days—but he hadn't forgotten how much he admired it. He rotated the stock and examined the safety switch. "Full auto," he said.

"Benefits," Madigan repeated with a smile.

After a minute, Sam handed the gun back to Madigan and then walked the length of the workbench. "What company are you working for, then?" he asked.

"7-Core Sentinel," Madigan replied. "Based on the outskirts of Winston-Salem. And we can always use a guy like you."

Sam paused in thought as he circled the basement, studying the various tactical gear and assorted items. Madigan had built himself a miniature base of operations, right here below his martial arts school, and the mere observation of this place sent distant memories flooding through Sam's mind. "I'm too old and worn out for this," he mumbled, as if talking to himself. He turned and looked at Madigan. "Besides, I've got a decent life going on now, with a mighty fine woman to boot."

"I figured as much," Madigan replied. Then, from a black case on the workbench, he retrieved an Iridium Extreme satellite phone, and handed it to Sam. "Do me a favor, though, and take this. It's linked to the company account. Use it anytime you need to. There's a loaded sim card in it with my number in the internal phonebook. The only number, in fact. So you can shoot me a message or call if you... run into any mountain people," he added with a wink. "That piece of work is auto-set for tracking, so keep it on you at all times, Sam. I can watch your every move. Like I said, there're all kinds of benefits with my new job."

"Thanks, Marcus," Sam said, pocketing the phone. Then an idea abruptly popped into his head. Feeling excited from what he guessed was a combination of not going on a run for a few days now, and then being surrounded by all this tactical gear, Sam said, "You think we can do some of that fancy knife work you showed me back in the day? I can use a good workout if you've got the time and energy."

"You know damn well I've got the time and energy," Madigan replied. "Let's go see just how old and worn out you really are."

•   •   •

They worked on the basics of knife fighting for thirty minutes—defensive positioning, practical striking methods, arm parries, and footwork—before they got into the more nitty-gritty techniques.

"Lesson number one," Madigan explained, "never, ever, *ever*, find yourself in a knife fight, Sam. Avoid this scenario like it's your own death, because more than likely that'll be the case."

"It's a little too late for that," Sam said. His memories swiftly brought to mind the legendary fight he'd had with Lou Pine. "But go on."

"Right, then," Madigan said. "If forced into such a situation, be quick to pull a trigger or turn and run like hell. But—and this is lesson number two—if you do find yourself in such a fight with no means of escape, just know this: you will get cut. Regardless of how experienced you are, and how inexperienced the other man is, a trip to the ER to stitch you up is the least that will happen to you."

Sam nodded his head, knowing from experience just how true his friend's words were.

Madigan reminded Sam of these important details, among others, as they practiced some rudimentary yet lethal techniques pertaining to knife fighting, including unarming a knife-wielding opponent. They tossed each other around on the mat for long minutes at a time, and Sam caught on quickly, quicker than he'd expected, as most of the techniques were the same ones Madigan had taught him back in the day—oldies but goodies. After a few hours of non-stop training, running through the same techniques repeatedly, Sam was performing them at almost full-speed.

They both broke a good sweat and then broke for an early lunch when they were finished. Madigan treated Sam to a pulled pork specialty at a local hole-in-the-wall. The smoked meat rivaled anything Sam had eaten at the ranch.

"Like I mentioned," Madigan said in between bites, "you're a wanted man, Sam. All I ask is for you to think about the possibilities of taking on a side job here or there. 7-Core won't even think twice about hiring you."

"It's a kind gesture," Sam replied, "but like I said, I've got a good life now. And I don't want to mess that up." He polished off his sandwich, then washed it down with a gulp of iced-tea, as he thought about how to frame his next sentence, the one he'd been thinking about for days now. It was, of course, the main reason he'd come to see Madigan. "I've got to ask you, though," he began, "there's something I can't help but wonder about."

"What's that?"

"It's stupid, 'cause I know someone would've told me by now, but... has anything turned up on Ernie?"

Madigan paused, then shook his head. "You're right, Sam. You would've been one of the first to know."

*　　*　　*

After a few more hours of visiting and then saying goodbye, Sam made his way back to his rental vehicle and began the hour-long drive to his hotel in Cherokee. It was a nice visit with his friend, one that brought back many memories, some pleasant, some not-so-pleasant. But eventually Sam's thoughts steered themselves toward the job he'd been paid to do.

He started thinking about the details regarding Emily's disappearance—which were minimal—as well as how he planned on searching for her. He had the groundwork of a half-baked plan set in his thoughts, but there was still more work to be done, research to apply, wrinkles to iron out. At some point, he would need to make a trip to a local sporting store and pick up some basics for heading out into the bush. And also, to accommodate for what he had in mind, he'd need to find a home improvement store as well, such as a Home Depot.

When he reached the hotel, it was early evening. The sun had edged just past the distant mountains, and the plum light of dusk was now creeping across the land. Sam pulled into the hotel parking lot, turned a corner as he headed toward the back, where his room was located, and then jerked the steering wheel hard to the right, missing by inches a black van speeding past him.

"Christ," Sam said, slamming on the brakes and looking in the rearview mirror. The van, an older model with tinted windows and a badly dented chrome fender, wheeled out onto the main road, peeled rubber at the turn, and then disappeared out of view. "Some people," he muttered. Then he slowly pulled forward into the lot, parked, got out, and went to his room...

The place had been tossed. His suitcase had been dumped on the floor and all his clothes were strewn about. The mattress of his bed was out of kilter, hanging sideways off the box spring, with the blankets and sheets thrown asunder. It hit Sam with an unexpected, disturbing blow. He had never experienced anything like this, and he instantly felt violated.

But then, as he eventually scanned through the debris of the room, picking things up, combing through his effects that had been ripped out of his suitcase and thrown about, Sam began to take a mental inventory. It seemed nothing had been taken (not that he had anything of value to take), as all his possessions appeared to be accounted for.

Curious, he took a step back and studied what was left of the crime scene, observing the signs left behind, as if he were searching for tracks in the wild.

There was something odd about all of it. Maybe this was just his imagination adding to his current feelings. But something about this crime struck Sam as being an act of desperation. It had the markings of a frustrated individual who'd been in a mad hurry, and because of this, acted at a level beyond that of any discrete grab-and-dash job common at hotels. It was as if the burglar, whoever he was, had been aggravated in his search for something in Sam's room.

Maybe it *was* Sam's imagination. This type of thing hadn't happened to him before, so he didn't have much experience on the matter to draw perspective from.

But Sam also knew that, when it came to his imagination, there was nothing there to write home about. And as for his gut-feeling, well, that had saved his bacon on more than one occasion. Considering this, if his gut was speaking correctly to him right now, then the remaining question is, what exactly was this burglar looking for?

CHAPTER 8

Somewhere along the ride out of Hillbillyville, Roochie's lights got put out, and he lost all sense and knowledge of the ensuing events. Maybe he got pistol whipped in the back of the head by one of Jimmy's relations, or perhaps fainted from loss of blood, who's to say? All that mattered was that currently he was no longer gagged, hogtied, and possibly, hopefully, no longer held to the mercy of the Inbred Mountain Clan.

Roochie wasn't one hundred percent certain of this freedom, though. He still had a black sack cinched over his head, and had no idea where he was. Also, he was feeling groggy and listless, half dead in fact. And presently, somebody was poking at his face with something, a person who could have been one of Jimmy's cousins or brothers or cousin-brother, some fat, toothless hillbilly holding another one of those machete-looking knives, which he was using to tease Roochie back to life.

"You think he's dead?"

"I don't know."

"Maybe he's got some money on him. Check and see."

"I'm not gonna check and see. You check and see."

They didn't sound like hill people, though. In fact, they sounded like kids. Roochie released a groan, then stirred a hand to his face.

"Well, he ain't dead."

"Not yet. But it looks like he's been shot. Look at all that blood."

"I know, huh?"

"Poke him again."

Things were slowly coming back to Roochie, the world that is, and he was beginning to realize he was out of the mountains. He heard sounds in the near distance, the movement of traffic, the honking of a car horn, the unnamable buzz and hum found in every city across America.

Whatever the kid was poking him with found the spot of Roochie's severed ear, and then the sting and shock was like a pail of ice cold water to his face. Roochie jerked awake and abruptly sat up. "What the fuck, man!" he said.

"Oh shit! Let's get out of here!"

He got the sack off his head just in time to see two boys turn a corner on bikes, one of them chucking a stick far and wide. Roochie looked around and collected his thoughts. He was sitting up in a dank alley surrounded by grimy cardboard boxes and loose trash. A city for certain, but which one?

He flinched as a sharp pain pulsed at his ear—or at the spot where his ear should have been. Depressed, he realized he'd woken up to a memory far worse than any nightmare he'd ever had. *That motherfucker cut my ear off... And then fed it to his pig!* He grimaced at the thought of what he must now look like. And worse, what he would have to look like for the rest of his life: some creature out of a fairy tale, a trollish monster living under a bridge, grotesquely scary looking. *Christ, I'll never get laid again.*

Roochie eyeballed a large box and thought about crawling into it to cry his life away. What else was left if he could no longer get any pussy? Why go on, if the prospects of blow jobs, sixty-nines, threesomes, and every Kama Sutra position invented had been tossed flagrantly to the wind? What else *was* left, other than...?

The Master Plan.

That's right. Roochie remembered now—the reason he'd been sent up into the hills in the first place. It was all part of the plan. And with that plan, Roochie was sure to get some revenge on that son of a bitch hillbilly. Vengeance for all his pain and suffering. Vengeance for his lost ear.

It didn't seem like much of a consolation prize, but next to suicide due to a life of abstinence, it was all Roochie had.

The hoodlum shook his head and focused, thinking about the details Myron had explained before sending him up into no-man's-land. He stood, pulled his pants up, and absently brushed debris off his legs. First order of business was to find out where the hell he was?

Roochie took a few steps, then, feeling woozy, paused and put a hand on the alley wall to brace himself. He was thirsty, craving something cold and quenching, a Coke or Mountain Dew, with lots of ice. He sifted through his pockets, found only his wallet containing several bills, and remembered those bastards had thrown his burner phone into a pond after searching him, which was something he figured they were going to do anyway. But they left his wallet, and that was good enough.

Then Roochie suddenly remembered the electronic gizmo thingy. He had forgotten about the device throughout his ordeal, and shit, that dealy taped to his armpit was the key to the entire plan. It was the key to Roochie's revenge.

He felt for it and was surprised to find it still there. Weird how he'd gotten used to the thing, how he had forgotten its presence. It'll be hell getting off, taking his armpit hair with it, but nothing like having an ear sliced off your head.

The gizmo was a small, black device, which looked like a hockey puck, only half the size. Roochie didn't really know how it worked, but as Myron had explained, it was "instrumental to the plan." Roochie figured he'd leave the thing where it was—it obviously wasn't going anywhere. And when it was time to come off, Myron or one of his crew would do a quick job of it. Or so Roochie hoped.

The stabbing pain throbbed at his missing ear again, which was now just a hole in his head. He'd have to get used to calling it that— the hole in his head. He bit his lip and wandered out of the alleyway, looking around. He saw a half a dozen cars rolling along, mild traffic. He was in some downtown section of an unknown city. It wasn't Charlotte, as Roochie knew that place the same as he knew how many joints he could roll from an eighth of weed. No, this town was much smaller, much quainter, and much less busier.

There were storefronts up and down the street, various shops selling various items. Roochie spotted a convenient store a block away and headed for it, dodging through traffic as he staggered across the street. People in cars gave him funny looks, and for the briefest of seconds, he couldn't figure out why. But only briefly. Then he remembered, and wondered how bad he really looked, with one ear missing, and his head, face, and shoulders all covered in blood.

When he entered the convenient store, an Asian girl behind the counter threw a hand to her mouth and stepped back. "Oh, dude! Are you okay?" She stared at him with a horrified look on her face.

Roochie didn't reply. He took his wallet out and laid it on the counter, then walked down a short aisle, looking for something to edge away the pain. He grabbed a box of ibuprofen off a shelf, then went to the cooler section, took out a can of Mountain Dew, popped it open and started slugging.

"Do you need me to call the police?" the girl asked.

Roochie choked, then spun around. "No!" he cried. "No, no, don't do that. Please. Do not call the police." He grabbed another can of Dew and hurried over to the counter, his hands fumbling and shaking as he pried open the box of ibuprofen. He was thinking fast. "I just had an accident, that's all. Some asshole hit me on my bike."

She didn't seem too convinced by his explanation. Her face revealed shock, terror, and suspicion all at once. Her eyes were wide and her lips were quivering. "I can call an ambulance for you. You want me to call an ambulance?"

Roochie managed the bottle of ibuprofen open, dumped half a dozen into his hand, and popped them into his mouth. He took another chug of soda, then shook his head. "Can I borrow your phone, though?" he asked.

Now the girl seemed reluctant. "Let me call you an ambulance, sir. You look bad. Real bad."

"No... I can do that myself." Roochie held out his hand. "Just let me borrow your phone, please."

"Ah... I guess you can use this one." She picked up a landline from off a bench behind the register and set it on the counter. "My grandma uses it sometimes."

Roochie didn't complain, even though he hadn't used a landline since he was ten-years old. Suspecting he'd lose his own phone along this adventure, which he did, he had memorized Myron's number. Roochie punched the buttons, and after three rings, the big boy answered.

"Who the fuck is this?" Myron said.

"It's me, Roochie." Talking somehow made the pain at the hole in his head worse. "I made it back."

"Roochie-boy! Where are you, man?"

Roochie glanced at the girl behind the counter. She was looking more curious now, less terrified. "Where am I?" he asked her.

"Uhm... Asheville."

"I'm in Asheville," he told Myron.

"Yeah, yeah, we'll be right there. Just give us a few hours. You in one piece, right?"

Roochie hesitated, thinking how best to answer that question. "More or less."

"Well sit tight, Rooch. We's on our way."

The phone clicked dead, and then Roochie handed it back to the girl. "Thanks," he said. Then he looked around, grabbed a king-sized Snickers and bag of Doritos from off an end-cap, and placed them on the counter. "How much is all this?"

She hesitated through every damn step, but eventually Roochie paid for his items, got them bagged up, and walked out of there. His appearance was still widely noticeable, drawing hideous stares from anyone who looked at him. He figured one of these gawkers would eventually dial 911, so he ducked back into the alleyway he'd woken up in, and hid behind a cardboard box. He settled in, drank his Mountain Dew and ate the candy bar, while counting in his mind exactly how many pieces he was going to cut that fucking hillbilly into.

CHAPTER 9

"Boss-man says now we whack him, so that's what we're gonna do. Whack him." Carson Ramsey pulled over onto the shoulder of the road and under a thick canopy of tree growth. He killed the lights and took his foot off the brake pedal. The black van he was driving disappeared among the evening shadows and the lingering forest. In the distance, a hundred yards away or so, he could make out the lights of a house set up on a hillside. And in that house was the reason he had driven out to the boondocks on this side of the state. "Said make it look like something random though, and I've got me an idea 'bout that."

"But why's we gotta whack him?"

"Donny... we don't need to know why, you idiot. In fact, in our business, we never need to know why. In double fact, a person don't *want* to know why. Knowing why gets a dumb fool like you, all his teeth knocked out. Knowing why sends your kind up the river and to the big house. Knowing why finds you a new home in an old ditch. *Why, why, why.* We never ask why, Donny, because we never want to know why." Even as he said it, Carson knew he'd spoken too much, too fast. And as a result, he could predict what was going to come next out of his brother's mouth.

"Okay..." Donny said, real slow like. There was a long pause, and Carson thought he heard the single rusty gear in his brother's head heavily grind away. Then Donny finally continued with, "Why again don't we want to know why?"

Sometimes Carson just didn't have the patience for the dumb boy. Sometimes—often times, in fact—Donny drove him crazy, and then the devil in Carson would slither on out, coaxed along perhaps by some late night company with Jim Beam, and then Carson would take his frustrations out on his fool of a brother. The funfest always happened deep in the night, while Donny was fast asleep, because hell, he was too dangerous to mess with any other time. But when Donny was sawing them logs, that's when Carson would creep up and punch his brother three fast times in the face, or ring his thick skull with an iron skillet, or bring a bat down hard onto his backside, one solid thump, and then Carson would dash off somewhere, unheard and unseen. Always, Donny would wake up crying and confused, with Carson nowhere to be found, and it was all just a bad, bad dream, nothing more. Carson was now thinking that tonight might transpire into one of those nights. But before then, he and his brother had business to attend to. They had a guy to whack.

"I've got me an idea, and I want you to listen up real good, Donny. So don't be thinking about your damn pee-pee, or some little girl you've seen, or whatever goes on in that brainless head of yours, because I need you to listen up."

"I'm listening, Car."

"Good. Now take this here pipe." Carson handed Donny a two-foot length of one-inch plumbing pipe, and then told him all about his idea. He explained in the slowest and shortest details possible what he wanted Donny to do with that pipe, and exactly when. And then Carson repeated his plan to his brother not twice, but three times, just to make sure it sunk into his fat head. "Like I said," he concluded, "after I say 'Good evening, sir,' that's when you do it, you hear? And just keep thinking watermelon, Donny."

"I hear you, Car. I heard you, I mean. And I know what to do now. I don't know why, and you says I shouldn't worry 'bout that, 'cause my kind don't never need to know why. But I know what to do with this here pipe, Car. And I know when to do it, so you can count on me, because... I, ah... don't know why."

Carson and Donny Ramsey were North Carolina's real-life, if not twisted version of Steinbeck's George and Lennie. They were the complete package consisting of brains and brawn, ambition and slothfulness, windfall and mishap. They came from a long line of Ramseys, a name that, over numerous generations and a healthy amount of indiscriminate barnyard copulations, had spread its tainted seed and ill-gotten druthers across the entire American south. The Ramsey name was well known among various criminal outlets, both in the mountain towns or lowland cities, and as a logical consequence, was also well known among the various law enforcement agencies. Although a Ramsey could be found just about anywhere in the southern states, the border of North Carolina and Tennessee was Carson and Donny's current stomping grounds. It was Carson who had connected "Boss-man" to the likes of his cousin, Jimmy James Ramsey. And it was Carson who had connected Jimmy-James to the likes of Myron Weathers. Like any other Ramsey with an enterprising IQ (a small and rare lot, at best), Carson had started young with establishing his connections. And over the years, he had made his way through the different counties of North Carolina, all the while racking up an impressive list of crimes. Burglary was his true passion, but he'd participated in just about anything and everything, from trespassing to murder. At thirty-two, still alive and still free, Carson was an old hat to the life of misconduct.

"Now you follow me," he said, as he stepped out of the van. "And close your door easy like. No use letting all of Carolina know we're here."

They walked quietly through the dark, along the side of the dusty road, making their way slowly toward the house up on the hill. The night was cold and dark, and somewhere in the woods came the screech from an owl. About a quarter of a mile away, off to the right, there was another house with its lights on, and it sounded like someone was out there chopping wood.

"Keep quiet, and stay in the shadows, Donny," Carson added. "And be on the lookout for dogs. Old man like this is sure to have a bloodhound or two."

Carson was correct. There were dogs, two of them, big and loud, and they got to barking just as soon as Carson and Donny started up the driveway and to the house.

"Let's hurry," Carson said, looking around. "Them dogs are chained up, but they're making one hell of a racket. Don't forget what I told you, Donny."

"I won't forget, Car."

When they got to the front of the house, Carson noticed that there was a screen door covering the main door. Moving quickly, he opened it and secured it in place, using a rocking chair from off the porch. He moved with the swift assuredness of someone who was used to impromptu situations such as this, a skill no doubt garnered from his years of casing and robbing homes. After securing the screen, Carson took his hat off, ran his fingers through his hair, then rapped his knuckles on the front door. "Get ready," he said, glancing sideways at Donny, who was standing beside him, pipe held discretely behind his back.

Seconds later, the door creaked open and the light and warmth from inside the house wavered out onto the Ramsey brothers. An old man wearing overalls and holding a book was standing there, his face alight with concern and curiosity. "Can I help you, boys?" he asked.

"Pardon me," Carson said, "but I'm looking for Harlow Evans. Would that be you?"

The old man paused, shifted his stance. "Yes. I'm Harlow. And who might you be?"

"Good evening, sir."

For all Donny's stupidity and inherent aggravations, there was a reason why Carson had kept his brother so close to his side throughout the years. Sure, Donny was dumb as dirt, and could probably serve as a case study for every mental disability in the world of psychology. But over time, Carson had learned that his little brother didn't really need a whole lot, not when it came to explaining things to him. Simplicity was the key. The golden rule of "keep it simple stupid" was the best rule when communicating with the big oaf. But more importantly, Donny was loyal as a dog, fast as a cat, and strong as a bull. So after Carson said those three simple words—Good evening, sir—it came as no surprise to him when his brother moved the way he did, bringing that pipe over their heads with such fierce accuracy, and such swift and violent power.

After the wet and crunching *thud*, Harlow Evans fell backward like a snapped timber in a windstorm, the inch wide, inch deep impression on his forehead already leaking blood.

Then Donny burst out with laughter. "Hot diggity-dog, Car! It was just like you said. A watermelon."

CHAPTER 10

Hotel Management pulled out all the stops for Sam, demonstrating southern hospitality at its finest. They refunded his initial fare and comped him another room closer to the main entrance, where the security cameras actually worked. Then they gave him a meal voucher to a steakhouse across the street—which he used that night—and explained that for this part of town, the breaking and entering that occurred to his previous room was entirely rare, and entirely random. Rare, sure. But random? Sam still had a weird feeling about that one.

The display of kindness and generosity from the management was so grand, Sam actually felt a little guilty for all the trouble. When he checked out the next morning, he assured the manager he wouldn't leave a bad review on Yelp, or Google Maps, or whatever other websites kept track of customer approvals—not that Sam knew how to leave such a review, or had the time, anyway.

And as for time—well, time was running out. Sam had been in North Carolina for two days now, and he still had places to go, and someone yet to talk to before he could get into the wilderness and start doing what he did best.

He swung by a McDonald's and ordered a coffee and Egg McMuffin to go, then sat in the parking lot and ate his breakfast while looking through the envelope Shiloh had given him. Sam had already glanced through all the notes and maps the day before, but he couldn't help wonder if perhaps he was missing something. He tried to put together what little pieces he knew, and even then, it wasn't much.

He started at the beginning. And the beginning was the day Emily struck out for the Appalachian Trail, all by her lonesome self. What a brave girl, he thought, tough and independent, not unlike her old man. On more than looks now, Emily reminded Sam of Lolo.

During his conversation with Shiloh, Sam had learned that Emily began her trip at a trailhead near Wesser, NC, off Highway 19. Her friend Jessica had dropped her off around 9:00, on a Saturday morning. They took goofy pictures of each other, holding coffee cups from Starbucks and making silly faces at the camera, all of which were texted to Emily's mother. Then Jessica got in the car and drove one way, while Emily shouldered her backpack and started walking the other.

The girl's next point of contact came from a selfie picture, taken at Fontana Dam, in the early afternoon of the following day. She had sent that picture to her mother as well, via text message, and added that she'd be in contact again, just as soon as she got to Clingmans Dome, which wasn't much more than a two-day hike. But then those two days went by without word from Emily, and after the third day, that's when Vicki's concern leveled on the verge of panic.

Shiloh got involved then, started making some calls. Records from the phone company indicated that Emily's cell phone had pinged her location from a ridge-top a few miles west of Clingmans Dome, the day after she had taken her picture at Fontana Dam. The phone had gone dead after that, so the ping was designated as Emily's "Last Known Point," and that was where the official search began.

The first page of Emily's journal was found in a canyon a few miles southwest of the LKP, and not far from Silers Bald Shelter, an informal rest stop known to hikers. The remaining pages were discovered nearby, all along south-facing canyons, and within a mile from the Appalachian Trail. There was nothing else found other than the pages from Emily's journal. No hard tracks, no personal items, no signs of a struggle or animal predation, no recent off-trail campsite or fire ring. Just those crinkled notes. And then the discouragement that comes from a trail gone cold.

But as he studied the points on the map, Sam noticed there seemed to be a possible track to the notes they'd found. Using a pencil, he connected the dots, and the result showed him that one possibility was that the girl had been traveling southwest from the main trail, assuming the first note she dropped was the one found closest to her last known point. The detail wasn't much. Just an interesting observation, and a hollow one at best.

Sam carefully organized the items in the envelope, then re-read the field journals taken from the various search and rescue teams. There was nothing substantial written in them either, just standard observations, search patterns and trail markings, points of interest, a few illustrations, but nothing concrete enough to say "Emily was here" other than the comments regarding the findings of her journal pages. Still, Sam took his time and read through every damn record, looking for oddities or patterns, anything to light a bulb in his head.

Then he took several minutes to observe the various locations on the map, indicating where the girl's notes had been found. He studied each of those points again, deciphering the lay of the land, the topography, all the geographical details that he had always found so easy to comprehend, and so easy to etch into his memory. He should have been a geographer, he was that good.

Finally, Sam considered heavily what Emily had written on those journal pages. The girl was convinced she was being stalked by "wild men."

The more Sam thought about it, the more he wondered if perhaps Emily was indeed telling the truth, and that she hadn't lost her mind out there. Maybe she had been taunted by a couple of deranged men. Sick people existed in the world. This was something Sam knew all too well. And some of these sick people could get mighty creative with their means of causing terror. Lou Pine was evidence enough of that.

Adding to this, Sam also considered what Shiloh had mentioned about his daughter, and her familiarity with being in the outdoors. On a map, the area in which Emily had disappeared seemed fairly straightforward. The Appalachian Trail cut a north by northeastern route. With a compass and some semblance of her current bearing, it seemed likely enough that Emily would have been able to find her way back to the main trail, assuming she'd gotten herself lost. And if she was hurt *and* lost, and therefore unable to find her way back to the trail, well, according to Shiloh, she would have had the sense to stay put and light a fire.

Sam took a sip of coffee and stared out the window, observing little other than what his mind was showing him. Indeed, it was a strange case, with details that kept tripping up his logic, and with explanations that kept echoing the void behind those notes the girl had left throughout the forest. The notes about the wild men chasing her.

Then, as Sam considered his thoughts, he recalled seeing something in the copied pages of Harlow Evans' field journal. Sam picked through the stack of papers on his lap, found Harlow's notes, and read through them again.

The notes were even more impressive than anything one would expect from a tracker with thirty-plus years of experience. Harlow had recorded just about every damn step he'd made through the wilderness, as he searched for the girl. He'd made copious notes and numerous details of what seemed like the entire state of North Carolina: fallen logs, with guesstimates on the ages of such deadfall; individual stones and boulder clusters, along with approximate diameters of such rocks, in inches; countless animal droppings and tracks, each one given a near-exact day of incidence; individual weather occurrences from morning to night; even wind factors on specific hillsides or ridges. There was something written down for every half-hour of every day the man had been at it. So many comprehensive details that Sam wondered if old Harlow wasn't perhaps some kind of savant.

Still, none of the information meant a lot to Sam. Nothing shed any real light on the situation. But he did find the thing that had caught his attention from earlier. Written on the bottom corner of a page were the words "Wild men?" with a question mark after them. And underneath that was the name G. Huey, which was boldly underlined.

Both details seemed entirely out of place, when stacked up against all the other stuff Harlow had written. But even so, they still didn't tell Sam anything. He had plans to call the tracker that day, though, so Sam put a dog-ear on the specific page, figuring he'd save it for Harlow. Then he tucked everything back into the envelope.

First order of business was to stock up on gear. Sam finished the last of his McMuffin, then drove to Asheville and stopped in at a sporting goods store. He purchased a small backpack, sleeping bag, and some basic camping supplies, along with a set of thermal binoculars, and a Schrade SCH survival knife. He skipped the tent and grabbed a hammock instead. Then he loaded his cart with two weeks' worth of freeze-dried food. Last but not least, he bought a sling shot for small game, just in case he needed to extend his stay a little, and live off the land.

After the sporting goods store, Sam drove to three different garden supply retailers before he found what he was looking for, which was a set of heavy wind chimes. He knew the idea he'd concocted was crazy, not to mention a long shot. But Sam also knew he needed much more to go with than what he already had.

After finishing with his shopping, Sam used the satellite phone Madigan had lent him, and dialed Harlow Evans' number. He suddenly felt like a damn fool, using a borrowed piece of expensive hardware to make a simple phone call. Everybody around him, ages five to ninety-five, was carrying the latest iPhone or Samsung, which could let them dial up and talk to their pals clear on the other side of the planet, and all in a matter of seconds. But not Sam Nolan, no siree. He might have been the only person alive who owned nothing but a landline.

Speaking of phones, oddly enough, Harlow's seemed to be off the hook. And there was no answering machine to pick up Sam's call. Figuring he'd do better face-to-face anyway, he punched Harlow's address into the Ford Explorer's GPS unit, and then began the trip up to Cataloochee. Not much more than an hour of driving, so he'd be there right around lunchtime.

*   *   *

When Sam pulled up to Harlow Evan's driveway, he noticed three sheriff cars parked along the side of the road. There were two more up near the house, along with an ambulance, and yellow crime tape strung across a chain-link fence near the driveway. More tape was dressed out by the front door, and there were easily half a dozen officers roaming about.

Sam pulled up as close to the house as he could, put the vehicle in park, then stepped out. He was greeted instantly by a junior officer.

"Can I help you, sir?" the officer said.

Sam put his hand out, and they shook briefly. "Name is Sam," he said. "I was hoping I could talk to Harlow Evans today." He looked around, eyes soaking up the details.

"You mind giving me your last name, sir?"

"Nolan. Sam Nolan."

"Thank you, Mr. Nolan. And, ah... Well, I'm afraid old Harlow is unavailable."

Sam noticed two EMTs wheeling a gurney out through the front door. And on the gurney was a black body bag, stuffed and zipped.

"I don't suppose he'll be available to talk anytime soon?" Sam asked.

The officer stared back at Sam, hesitated for a second, then pulled a small notepad out of his pocket. "You got a number I can reach you at, Mr. Nolan?"

Sam blinked and looked at the officer. "Now I know you can't tell me anything about what's going on out here, son," he said, "but that question of yours more or less spilled the beans. My guess is that no, Mr. Evans won't be available to talk anytime soon. Or ever, for that matter."

"I'm just going through the formalities, Mr. Nolan. But you're right. I can't—and won't—tell you anything. Unless, of course, you're one of Harlow's kin, which I'm almost certain you're not."

Sam gave the officer his pertinent information, which wasn't much, and then explained to him how he'd been hired by Shiloh to look for his missing daughter, and that he was hoping Harlow could answer a few questions Sam had. The officer nodded his head, obviously aware of the case of the missing girl, and it seemed he was satisfied enough with Sam's information. Then he kindly reminded Sam to stay away from the crime scene and said he'd be in touch if necessary.

Sam walked to his vehicle and got in. He put it in gear, but looked around some more, studying the situation. He noticed a few cars parked up the road, and there were several people standing near them, faces staring hard, hands on their hips or shielding their eyes from the sun. Locals, no doubt.

Sam took his foot off the brake and eased up the road until he came to a man sitting in an old pickup truck loaded with firewood. The man had one arm resting on the door and the other on the wheel, and there was a piece of straw sticking out of his mouth.

Sam made an abrupt stop. "Hey," he said. "You know anything about what happened to Harlow?"

The man eyed Sam suspiciously for several long seconds. Then, as if content with what he saw, he took the straw out of his mouth and said, "Seems old Harlow got murdered last night. A robbery of sorts. I heard the sheriff talking. And, ah… I told him I'd seen a dark vehicle out here last night, whiles I was chopping wood."

"A robbery?" Sam asked.

"That's what I heard. Don't make no sense, though. Not out here, at least. And shoot, old Harlow? What's to rob? Seems unlikely, if you ask me. Maybe this kind of stuff happens down in the city, but out here, well…"

The man paused, just long enough for Sam to finish his sentence for him. "Yeah, I know," he said. "Out here, something like that, it's just too rare, and too damn random."

CHAPTER 11

Carson and Donny were parked in reverse on the side of a Quickmart, chewing on corn dogs and sharing a big bag of Chili Cheese Fritos while idling their long day away. They were sitting in the front seat and staring out at a sprinkle of wild flowers admix a green field of alfalfa with an overgrown forest for a backdrop. The portrait was one lush tapestry of North Carolina wilderness, which neither one of them was seeing at the moment.

For Carson, his mind's eye was fixed on figuring out his next job—whatever that would be. He wasn't in any dire hurry, of course, not after getting paid for his recent undertaking (thank you kindly, Harlow Evans), but for Carson's line of work, one just couldn't make any predictions. Money never stuck around for long, jobs came and went like the seasons, and employers always got busted some time or another, then sent off to prison, or, if they were unlucky, shot dead in the face by a rookie cop. In Carson's line of work, things could dry up pretty quickly. He had to be resourceful and mindful. It paid to keep his wheels spinning and the hopper flowing. He was hoping to get another call from Boss-man, because hell, Boss-man always paid good money, always paid on time, and occasionally, even paid in advance, as he did for the case of old Harlow. But if nothing new came from the Boss-man soon, Carson figured he'd eventually mosey on down to that new housing development he'd seen over in the suburbs north of Charlotte, and start casing the area for potential targets.

As for Donny—that fool of a giant, staring out the window with huge glassy eyes, a life-sized, full-grown caricature of a toddler, alternating between shoveling Fritos into his mouth with one hand and pulling sips from a bottle of Squirt soda with the other—what was this lumbering lout thinking about right now? Well, nothing really, aside from the occasional food whim, or the soft and milky bottom of a five-year-old. Other than these rare and fleeting reflections, Donny Ramsey was thinking about nothing, nothing at all, bless his dumb soul.

It had been a long day for the brothers. A long day of remaining discreet while hiding out in the general vicinity, keeping a low profile because Johnny Law was still on a hot buzz from last night's murder up in Cataloochee. If Carson had his way, he'd be somewhere in Tennessee by now. But Boss-man had told him to stay put, just in case something interesting showed up.

And shit, as luck would have it, something interesting did show up. All of a sudden, and right then and there.

For the team of brains and brawn, ambition and slothfulness, windfall and mishap, on this long and boring day, as Carson glanced to his left at the exact moment a vehicle rolled into the Quickmart, the element of his life that materialized before his very eyes just so happened to be windfall.

The vehicle was a familiar-looking Ford Explorer, pulling in at the gas pumps. Carson kept watching, his eyes glazed over with curiosity, until they blinked upon noticing a man—a familiar-looking man—now step out of the vehicle, work the gas pump for a few minutes, and then go inside the store.

"Well, I'll be hot damned," Carson said, sporting a grin before moving into swift action. He finished his corn dog in two quick bites, passed the bag of Fritos over to Donny, lit a cigarette, and then made a call with his cell phone, all in less than ten seconds.

"Yeah?" a voice answered.

"Hey, Boss-man," Carson said. "Guess who I just saw?"

"Who?"

"Mr. Sam-I-am, that's who."

"Okay. And where did you see him at?"

"Right here, at a Quickmart, getting gas. Amazing luck, really, when you think about it. Donny and I were sitting here minding our own damn business, eating lunch and picking our noses, nothing too fancy, just watching the day drift on by, when suddenly, along comes our guy. Man, I don't think I could get any luckier. Why the hell don't I play the lottery today?"

"That is good luck. Good luck indeed."

"So then," Carson added after a pause, "what would you like us to do? You want me to kill him, too? I'm running a special this week. First whack-job gets you a second whack-job for a discount." Carson chuckled at his own joke. Then he looked over at Donny, who promptly giggled also, even though the big dummy had no idea what he was laughing at. It always went like this, Carson knew. First, he'd say something funny and then laugh, and then Donny would also laugh, but then Donny would laugh some more, and maybe Carson would play along, laugh further, then make a few silly faces and goofy noises because he was bored or felt sorry for the blockhead, and on and on that would go, until Donny would get himself into a heap of hysterical laughter, piss his pants from that, feel shameful and embarrassed, frown sadly, and then the whole circus of hilarity would come to a screeching halt. "Hell, we're parked out by the shitter," Carson continued. "Watch him come over here and take a leak. If he does that, I can send Donny in, and he'll club him like a baby seal. Then take his wallet, make it look like another robbery. How's that sound, Boss-man?"

More giggling from Donny.

"We can cross out that first job on this guy," Carson continued, smelling the paycheck at the end of this conversation, "by killing the son of a bitch here and now."

Extreme giggling from Donny.

"No, don't kill him," Boss-man said. "Not right now, at least. That would cause too much suspicion. Then some young detective would jump on the case and start connecting the dots. Just take this opportunity to finish that first job."

"Well, alright," Carson said, slightly disappointed. "I'll keep you posted."

Carson hung up, tucked his phone into his pocket, took a chug from a can of beer stashed between his legs, and then started up the van, all in less than ten seconds. "Buckle up, Donny-boy. We've got us some work to do."

Donny's massive frame was hunched over now, his head almost touching the dashboard. He was laughing deliriously, busting his gut, his mouth cranked open, a mash-up of Fritos and corn dog and Squirt soda all seeping out. He looked stoned and out of his gourd, but Carson knew better. The big fool was just in it deep right now, having one of his comical fits born from none other than the bottomless, swirling depths of his stupidity.

Carson slapped his brother's arm. "You're gonna choke, Donny. Sit up and swallow your damn food. And quit laughing."

Donny sat up and swallowed, sucked in a gulp of air, and chuckled some more. "Are we gonna whack that old man again, Car?" he said, with a *hee* and a *haw*. "Old man, Harlow. Are we gonna kill that Harlow feller again?"

Carson shook his head from the pity of it all. "Sure, Donny," he said, putting the van into gear. "Why not? Let's go kill Harlow Evans again."

He pulled in behind the Ford Explorer real smooth-like, maintaining a good distance and allowing a few cars to get in between. Carson had followed people before, mostly girlfriends in his past who had been trying to rid themselves of him, so he knew how to stay back and stay low, as well as a few other tricks. Keep the headlights off, don't signal when changing lanes or turning corners (unless a cop was present), and always drive a few miles under the mark, so as not to rouse any suspicion. Maybe this wasn't how the pros did it, but it wasn't rocket science either, and Carson was a fast learner.

He trailed Sam for a good twenty minutes until the guy pulled into a Denny's. Carson kept going. He drove three more blocks, made a right turn at an intersection, another right, and then drove back the other way and parked on the street across from the restaurant.

"Are we gonna eat lunch now?" Donny asked, staring at the big yellow Denny's sign. He had no clue what his brother was up to, and that was just fine with Carson.

"Nope," Carson said, studying the parking lot until he spotted the SUV. It was parked near the back of the restaurant, and out of view of the windows. Carson's luck was holding strong.

It appeared Sam-I-am had already gone inside, but there was currently an old couple coming out of the restaurant and taking their sweet time getting to their car. Carson bit his lip. He hated old people, and for a number of reasons of which he'd lost count. But generally, they were too slow, too cranky, too stubborn, and, most importantly, too damn nosey.

The old man held the door open for his wife before puttering over to the driver's side. He took five minutes getting his self inside, and damn near longer to start the car.

"What we gonna do?" Donny asked. He was looking back and forth between the parking lot and Carson, trying to figure out what his brother was staring at.

The old geezer took forever backing out of the lot, checking each and every mirror a dozen times before he got out onto the road. And that's when Carson made his move.

"What we gonna do?" Donny repeated.

"You ain't gonna do nothing," Carson said. He got out and walked around the other side of the van, lit a cigarette, and stood beside the passenger door.

Donny rolled the window down. "But what we gonna do?" he asked a third time.

"You're gonna stay right here, Donny," Carson replied. "Now reach in there," he added, pointing to the glove compartment, "and hand me the flashlight."

Donny fumbled with the latch, opened the compartment, then handed Carson a black Maglite. "It don't work, 'member?" he said. Then Donny blinked his eyes and looked up at the sky.

Carson yanked the flashlight out of Donny's hand and pushed it up the sleeve of his jacket. "Now you stay in the car, Donny," he said. "You understand me? Stay in the car, keep your pee-pee in your pants, and don't talk to nobody."

"Okay, Car," Donny replied. He looked confused and kept peering up at the sun, utterly baffled as to why Carson needed a flashlight right now. "I'll stay put."

"Good," Carson said. He took a pull on his cigarette, glanced around nonchalantly, then strolled across the street. When he got to Sam's SUV, Carson eased his way over to the passenger window, glanced inside, spotted what he was looking for, then dropped his cigarette on the ground and stamped it out. Then, as if noticing his shoe was untied, he squatted down to deal with that, and slid the flashlight out of his sleeve before standing back up. He looked around once more, saw that the coast was clear, and then quickly leaned his weight against the passenger window. He applied a little pressure with his arm, causing tension on the glass and some muffling for the impending sound, and then, with one solid whack, struck the window with the back-end of the flashlight.

The window shattered into a thousand pieces. And seconds later, Carson was on his way back to the van.

Donny was hopping in his seat, giggling furtively, eyes wide with wonder. "I seen you, Car," he whispered, as Carson climbed in, started the van, and took off. "You smashed that window with that flashlight, you did. That was a slick move, Car. Real slick. Slick as slick, it was."

Carson ignored his brother and pulled out his phone, dialed Boss-man.

"Yes?" Boss-man answered.

"Got her done, big guy," Carson replied.

"Good. That'll slow him down. Now get rid of it, and then call me back later today. I've got another job for you."

"That's a ten-four," Carson said. He hung up and smiled. *Well, how about that?* he thought. *Another job.* He looked at Donny then, who was staring back at him. The big dolt's face was stuck somewhere between confusion, curiosity, mischievousness, and the beginnings of another grin.

Oh, why not?

With a sudden jolt, Carson's body broke out into a barrage of childish jerks and crazy faces, farting sounds and high-pitched wails.

Donny Ramsey exploded with laughter.

CHAPTER 12

Things were getting stranger by the day. Sam was concerned, irritated, and confused. First, the break in at his hotel room, which seemed to him as if the burglar had been looking for something specific, and then acted out of rage after not finding such an item. Sure, it could have been a simple break in done by a simple drug addict, who was in a simple sweat of panic from having withdrawals, and subsequently went nuts in Sam's room after not finding something oh-so-simple, such as a wallet, piece of jewelry, loose jingle of cash, or anything to hawk down at the local pawnshop to help pay for their next fix. It could have been something simple like that. But Sam's gut feeling—that ever so nebulous voice lingering in his body, the same one that had literally saved his life on more than one occasion—told Sam otherwise.

And now this. Harlow Evans. The one and only man left in North Carolina who Sam needed to talk to, killed in his home in the backwoods town of Cataloochee, during a randomly rare burglary. The more Sam thought about the last few days, the more he considered that maybe some things about this missing girl were not so simple after all.

But then again, maybe he was just wrong about all of it.

Sam took a drive. He left Cataloochee and drove south, back toward Asheville. Hell, maybe he just needed to stop playing city detective, and then get up into those woods and start looking for that girl. Maybe he was over thinking things, connecting dots on a mental grid that had no rhyme or reason to be connected, fabricating vague clues and shaky evidence out of mere coincidence. And, if that were the case, then at this rate, it was only a matter of time before Sam went insane. Maybe, just maybe, what he really needed to do was hop on a plane and head back home, back to a world that made sense to him.

Yeah, right. Who was he kidding? Certainly not himself. There was no capacity in Sam's heart to do such a thing, despite his frustrations. He had given his word to Shiloh and Vicki, his word that he would not give up his search for their daughter so easily. And if there was anything in this damn world that *was* simple, it was the reliability of Sam Nolan's word.

Needing gas, he pulled into a Quickmart and fueled up the tank, then went inside and bought a Coke and a bag of peanuts. When he got back into the vehicle and drove off, he was still thinking. And what he was thinking was that perhaps there was someone else left to talk to, other than Harlow—who, of course, was no longer available. Sam was wondering about that name the old tracker had written in his field journal.

G. Huey.

There had to be a good reason the ever-so-meticulous Harlow Evans wrote that name on that page. Sam was suspicious, if not convinced, that the reason had to be related to Emily's disappearance. And, he was curious if the reason was also related to the other words Harlow had written, just above the person's name.

Wild men?—followed by a question mark.

Vague as they were, the details wouldn't let go of Sam. They kept nagging at him, until finally, he wondered if maybe Shiloh could shed some light on the situation. It certainly couldn't hurt to ask.

The bag of peanuts and Coke didn't quite do the job, so when Sam got into Asheville, he pulled into a Denny's, parked, and then went inside. He was seated at a booth that overlooked the Blue Ridge Mountains, a view that was most definitely worth more than what his lunch would cost him. He ordered a burger and fries, with some coffee, then promptly took out his sat phone and called Shiloh. The man answered after three rings.

"This is Shiloh."

"Mr. Parker, Sam Nolan here."

"Sam!" Shiloh said, a tinge of excitement lining his voice. "How are things going?"

"Well, they're going. I've got a few questions to ask you. And, I'm afraid, some bad news."

"Okay, then," Shiloh said. "I'm listening."

"First, the bad news."

Sam explained what had happened to Harlow, and Shiloh seemed to take the news with great difficulty. The excitement in his voice had dissipated, and it stayed that way through the rest of their conversation.

As for the name "G. Huey," Shiloh had never heard of such a person, so he had no understanding as to why Harlow had noted it in his field journal. For now, the name was still a dead end.

Sam briefed Shiloh a little more about his future plans and told him not to expect a call from him anytime soon. Then he ended the call and drank half his cup of coffee.

As he waited for his lunch to arrive, Sam kept thinking about that name. And then an idea suddenly hit him.

Marcus Madigan.

Madigan answered after only one ring, and Sam got right to business, wasting no time.

"Marcus," he began, "I was wondering if you've got anybody at that security company of yours who can track down names?"

"I can ask," Madigan replied. "Who you looking for? Other than that girl, of course."

"G. Huey," Sam said. "Someone in the area that fits that name. If you can look into that for me, and, well, if it doesn't take too long, I'd highly appreciate it. That'd be another favor I owe you."

"I'll get right on it, Sam," Madigan replied. Then he added, "You know I'm here for you, brother. Anytime, anything, anywhere, so don't go talking about favors you owe me."

"Alright then," Sam said. "But thanks, all the same." He hung up, then started in on his lunch. He took his time, pondering over all that was bothering him, and also, knowing that this might be his last good meal for a while. For the next several days, it would be nothing but camp food and water, and not much else.

When he finished the burger and fries, and after two more cups of coffee, Sam considered getting a piece of pie, because hell, why not? But then again, he was too full. So he paid his check, made a quick stop at the bathroom, then walked out of the restaurant. It was right about then that Sam's all-too-reliable gut told him something was very wrong.

And less than a minute later, he knew what that something was. It was his vehicle.

Sam stared at the smashed passenger window of his rented Ford Explorer. Tiny cubes of glittering glass littered the ground, as well as the seat inside. *Strange*, he thought, as he studied the situation. *Oh-so-very-strange.*

Strange how this just happened, and in the short span of time it took for him to eat his lunch. Strange how once again Sam had become a victim of another breaking and entering, and all in less than two days.

He looked around, observing the rest of the lot...

And strange, how no other cars got their windows smashed in. Just his.

Sam walked around the side of the vehicle, peering into the back seat, noting with an astute curiosity that all his possessions, including his brand new backpack and expensive gear, were still miraculously untouched. Strange indeed, how none of that stuff got stolen in this second—well, third, if he counted the case of old man Harlow—burglary that crossed Sam's path, since coming to the South.

So then, Sam wondered, *what in the hell* did *get taken in this smash-n-grab?*

Or maybe nothing got stolen. Nothing at all. Maybe this was just another act of random North Carolina crime, some yahoos on a drive-by, taking pot-shots with a Red Rider, and Sam's poor rental was simply parked in the wrong place, and at the wrong time.

He inspected the inside of the Explorer a little closer. And then he noticed it. Something did get taken, and Sam realized what that was. The one and only thing, apparently, and it was the manila envelope Shiloh had given him, along with all the notes pertaining to Sam's search for Emily.

Strange, my ass.

Just then, Sam's satellite phone started ringing. He answered it, and Madigan was on the other line.

"I got a name for you," Madigan said. "Address and number, as well."

"That was quick," Sam replied, still processing the crime scene he was staring at.

"Gerald Lynn Huey, with an address of 626, Macaw Lane. That's up north, northwest of Bryson City, actually. Unincorporated area, though. Off grid, and near the Tennessee border. Might be that's the person you're looking for. I've got an unlisted number as well. But, according to my sources, it hasn't been used in a long while."

"Thanks," Sam said. "The address is good enough for now." He paused, then added, "Oh, and Marcus? Looks like I'm gonna need to ask you for another favor."

CHAPTER 13

The electronic gizmo taped on Roochie's body was a LandAirSea 54 GPS tracking device. Designed primarily for vehicle theft, it came with an autonomous mobile tracking app, real-time data readouts, location history, and up to two weeks battery life. The unit was small, completely waterproof, and quite capable of being fixed on the outside hull of a boat, or in the sweaty armpit of an anxious hoodlum.

The "54", as Myron had dubbed it, led him and his crew straight down the alley and less than a foot away from the cardboard box Roochie was sleeping under. White-Collar, Myron's tech-savvy henchman, who was short and skinny, with an overgrown and unkempt afro, wearing nerdy clothes and nerdy glasses, and who looked nothing like all the other thuggish members of Myron's crew, was sitting in the front passenger seat, and straining to see over the hood of the vehicle. He had a laptop on his lap, and was indicating that they were in the approximate vicinity of the tracking unit.

"Look. He's right under there," Myron said, pointing from the driver's side window, after spotting Roochie's legs sticking out of a cardboard box. Unlike other dealers of Myron's reputation and financial status, who almost always had a personal chauffeur, Myron preferred to keep things real by driving his own vehicles.

Roochie, apparently alerted to the fact that someone was talking about him, blinked his eyes, then sat up and rested his head against the brick wall he'd been lying next to. He looked tired and dizzy, thirsty and hungry, hopeless and anxious, and cranky and scared, all at once. And his eyes showed he was in a tremendous amount of pain. The crinkled box he was under slid away from his body, and a dim light coming from a nearby street lamp shone down onto his face.

"Oh, shit!" Myron shouted. "Motherfucker's been shot! Did they shoot you, Rooch? Pounds, P-Dog," he said, glancing in the backseat, "give that boy a hand." He looked again at Roochie, who kept blinking his eyes, trying to focus. "Oh, shit," Myron repeated.

Pounds and P-Dog, two big brothers from the hood, and Myron's personal bodyguards, stepped out of the vehicle and helped Roochie to stand up.

Myron's eyes widened once he got a better look at Roochie. "*Oh, shit!*" he said again, his voice now an octave higher. "*Motherfucker's ear is gone!* What the fuck happened to you, Rooch? Don't tell me that fucking hillbilly shot your ear off?"

Roochie shook his head, then took a step toward the vehicle, which was a freshly waxed pearl Escalade, with chrome trim and 30-inch Forgiato wheels.

"Hold up," Myron said. "Get that nigga a blanket or something. And put him in the back. Don't want his blood all over my ride."

• • •

Three hours later, the whole gang was at Myron's crib in Lincoln Heights, a rough and tumble neighborhood on the north-side of Charlotte. Roochie was lying limp and helpless on a couch in the front room, absorbing all the wonderful motherly love he was getting. Licious, one of Myron's ladies, was sitting next to him, holding a damp rag in her hand, and a bowl of warm water on her lap. She was gently sponging the blood away from Roochie's head, trying to clean him up as best she could.

"I don't know, My," Licious said. "Rooch here might need to see him a doctor. We might need to take his ass to the ER."

"That is some sick shit," Freckles said, the other girl in the room, standing a good six feet from Roochie. She was leaning forward and squinting her eyes, inspecting Roochie's wound from a distance. "This boy is *fucked up*," she continued. "And I don't see what the hell a doctor's gonna do. Sew his fucking ear back on? Where is your ear, anyway? Do you even have it, Rooch? Is it in your pocket?"

Roochie shook his head, then cringed, no doubt picturing in stark detail what had happened to his ear. He would never forget, in fact, not for as long as he lived.

"Motherfuckin' cracker fed Roochie's ear to his damn pigs," Myron shouted. He was buzzing around the house, pacing back and forth between the living and dining room. Like a bi-polar nightmare, Myron was feeling both excited and angry. The excitement came from the fact that his "Master Plan" was coming together, and coming together rather quickly.

In a nutshell, Myron had been tasked with taking out Jimmy James Ramsey for no other reason than to eliminate the man's flow of homemade meth coming from out of the hills of North Carolina and onto the streets of Charlotte. At first, Myron had welcomed the Ramsey business. But then Myron's other associates, an assortment of black, Mexican, and Cuban profiteers, had caught on to their new competition, and, in turn, had also caught on to Myron's distributive connection of this new supply—the Mountain Supply, as it was called. As a quick and irrefutable result, said profiteers subsequently gave Myron an ultimatum. Get rid of Jimmy-James, or we'll get rid of you.

The problem was that Jimmy-James lived way up in the hills, didn't own a phone, and was impossible to find, which made things a little difficult for Myron, seeing how he needed to get rid of the guy.

He had learned about Jimmy from the man's cousin, Carson Ramsey. But Myron knew there was no way in hell Carson would give up Jimmy-James' hideout. If there was one thing to be said about them hillbillies, it was that not a single one of them would snitch on the other. They'd just as soon die a painful death than to be labeled as a rat.

So what then was a brother to do?

And the answer to that question became the birth of the "Master Plan."

It was all White-Collar's idea, actually. Myron didn't even know electronic gizmos such as the "54" existed, let alone how to use one of them.

"Why don't we just put a GPS tracking device on someone and send them up there in the hills to deliver a message from us?" White-Collar had explained, in his high-pitched, monotone, inflectionless voice. "That should work just fine. These tracking devices utilize a conjunction of both cellular towers and satellite signals. We should have no problem observing where it travels... presuming we affix it to someone willing, and, of course, able, to meet face-to-face with this Jimmy fellow."

"Ah, okay," Myron had said, blinking his eyes in baffled amazement to White-Collar's explanation. "Hell, why not? And we can send our white boy, Roochie. Shit, if he can't get up there, nobody can."

Thus, the Master Plan was hatched, on its way, and now, ready to be fully executed.

So why then was Myron also in a bad mood?

And the answer to that question was that, oddly enough, Myron had taken Roochie's disfigurement as some kind of personal affront. It was like a slap to the face with a glove. A declaration of war, so to speak, even though Myron had already made his own secret declaration long before.

Like an empty gas tank, Roochie seemed to be taking in all of Myron's anxious energy and using it to refuel his pride, along with his hopes of exacting revenge upon Jimmy-James. Still assuming the role of a wounded martyr, he looked up from Licious' lap and croaked out a few words. "I want vengeance, Myron."

"Oh, you'll get your vengeance, alright," Myron said. "We're gonna fuck that hillbilly's whole world up." Myron paused with his pacing, then stood in the dining room. Looming over a table were his crew: Z-Diggy, Hoodlum, Pounds, P-Dog, Cookie, Slim-pickens, and Steve. Everyone was there, except for White-Collar, who was sitting criss-cross-apple-sauce on the living room floor, plinking away at his laptop.

"Listen up, niggas," Myron announced. "I'm fixing to take this shit to the next level. We're gonna get medieval on them crackers up there. Steve, get on the horn and call Benny. Tell him to get his Cuban posse loaded for war. And tell him to bring one of them saws, or some torture shit, I don't know. Whatever the fuck they used in Scarface to cut that man's leg off."

"Why do I gotta call that motherfucker?" Steve said. Steve was mouthy, and Steve was in a bad mood, and Steve was always like this, because Steve was Steve. Everyone else in Myron's posse had a cool nickname, given to them by none other than Myron. Everyone except for Steve, that is. And Steve wasn't even his real name, which was Trayvon Lionel Grady. Shit, Steve didn't even come close.

"Oh, so you's gonna talk back to me now, eh?" Myron said. "Boy, you know I'll fuck you up."

Steve rolled his eyes, pulled out his phone, then walked into the other room.

"That's right," Myron said. "Keep on walking, bitch." After a pause, Myron looked back at his crew. "Now where the fuck was I?"

Z-Diggy looked up. "Said you wanna invite the Cubans to the party."

"Oh, yeah," Myron said. "We's gonna get fucking Rambo on them hillbillies."

While White-Collar was tinkering with his laptop on the floor, the rest of the crew was tinkering with a frightening array of weapons, all piled up on the dinning-room table. Russian made Kalashnikovs, sawed-off shotguns, 9mm Glocks and Berettas, one or two homemade jobs, an SKS assault rifle, a couple of Uzis, dozens of ammo mags, four WWII bayonets, three jungle machetes, about twenty thousand rounds of ammunition, and a handful of flares. Sprinkled around the mess were several bottles of beer, an ashtray, two bongs, and a half-empty bottle of tequila.

"I want all you motherfuckers loaded to the nine," Myron said. "White-Collar," he added, turning a shoulder, "you got that map ready yet?"

"Working on it now, boss," White-Collar said. "Just having trouble getting the printer's wi-fi reconnected. Might need to reboot. Shouldn't take more than five minutes, if not sooner."

Myron gave a slow nod, not really understanding what the hell White-Collar had just said. "Alright, then," he replied, "just do what you gotta do. But do it soon, 'cause time is of the motherfuckin' essence." He looked back at his crew. "P-Dog, Pounds, get out in the garage and bring in all them vests you got down at the surplus store. If we's fixing to get Rambo on that son of a bitch, then we's needing to get tactical, too. Motherfuckin' Ghost Recon is what I'm talking about."

A few minutes later, P-Dog and Pounds came back in from the garage, their arms loaded with a mishmash of tactical vests, which they dumped onto the floor next to the dining room table.

"Get some, niggas," Myron said. "But save that brown one for me. The one with all them fuckin' pockets on it."

Myron's crew got up and started going through the tactical vests, tweaking with a rat's nest of buckles and straps and pouches, more or less trying to figure out how to wear the damn things. After a few minutes, and looking now like a half-dressed, yet formidable enough SWAT team, they went back to their places at the table, and back to tinkering with their guns.

Steve walked into the room just then.

"What the fuck took so long?" Myron asked.

"Motherfucker put me on hold," Steve replied. "Said he was in the kitchen cooking some Cuban cuisine. Pork and beans, or some shit, I don't fucking know."

"Yeah, yeah," Myron said, "just tell me what the hell he said."

"Said he's in," Steve replied with a nod. "Said he needs some time to round up his posse, though. And that he wants to stop by the garage and pick up some power tools."

Myron smiled. "He did, did he? Fuck yeah. You all hear that? Motherfuckin' Benny's gotta make a pit stop at the *garage*. Get him some power tools, he said." Myron chuckled, then turned a shoulder and added, "Yo, Rooch. We's bringing us some power tools."

"Hey, My," Licious said from the couch, "I really don't think Rooch is doing too good. He looks so pale."

"Bitch," Myron replied, "did I ask you to tell me what you think? I don't remember asking you to tell me what you think. Did I ask this bitch to tell me what she thinks?" he said, turning to his crew. Shakes and shrugs all around. "See that, bitch? Ain't nobody here heard me ask you to tell me what you think."

"I'm just saying, My. This boy might die soon, if we don't get him looked at."

"Well, quit your saying, woman. You ain't a doctor, and this ain't fuckin' Grey's Anatomy. Roochie's fine. And I don't know what the fuck you be thinking? Motherfucker always looks pale, 'cause motherfucker's white. Besides, ain't none of his vitals got fucked up. Just had his ear cut off, that's all. And last I recall, a nigga can live without an ear."

"Yeah," Licious said, "but he's lost a lot of blood."

"Ain't that the truth," Freckles added.

"Bitches!" Myron said, storming now into the living room, pushing everyone out of his way. "Get up, Roochie," he commanded. "Get up and get your ass on over here."

With Myron's grip on his elbow, Roochie stood and staggered over to the dining room.

"Make some room for Rooch, niggas," Myron said. "Cookie, get the fuck out of that chair."

After a confusing shuffle of bodies, Roochie was now sitting at the head of the table, and surrounded by Myron and his crew. The light from the lamp above cast a spotlight onto Roochie's head, bringing into horrific focus the state of his condition. Despite Licious' attempts to clean him up, there was still dried blood everywhere, all over his head, hair, face, and clothes. And nobody present could help themselves—whether they wanted to or not—because everybody kept staring at the place where Roochie's ear used to be. Everybody kept staring at the hole in Roochie's head.

Just then, White-Collar started wiggling his boney frame through the mass of meat and blubber and testosterone. "Pardon me," he said. "Excuse me, gentlemen. Coming through. Thank you." Once he made it into the inner circle of doom, and at the edge of the table, he found Myron and said, "I'm ready, boss."

"Huh?" Myron said. "Oh, yeah. The map. The fuckin' map. Give it to us, White-Collar. Let's see what you got."

"Um..." White-Collar began, pointing meekly at the stock of an AK-47. "Could somebody please move this out of the way for me?"

"Huh?" Myron said. "Oh, yeah. P-Dog, get that shit off the table. Come on, niggas, make some room for the little brother."

Hands reached in, guns and ammo slid away, and then a wide swath of the table opened up for White-Collar.

"Thank you," White-Collar said. Then he laid out a couple of strange looking maps which he'd previously printed out, organized, and then taped together. "Now, then, let's see here... The first thing I did was pull the history data from our tracking unit... um, that would be the '54', as some of you prefer to call it." White-Collar isolated a lowly resolved map from his stack of papers and started pointing to dots and lines printed on it. "Anyway, just as I predicted, the cloud app the device came with had no trouble logging each of the data points for the entire duration that the unit was activated. We are in North Carolina, after all, and not North Korea. But the presentation of these coordinates lacked in detail. Very low pixilation, as you can clearly see."

White-Collar shuffled the maps around while everyone watched, no doubt already feeling like they were back in school.

"And that was another thing I predicted would happen," White-Collar continued. "So anyway, once I was able to pull said data, which the app displayed conveniently onto a standard grid map, as I just showed you, I recalibrated the collection points and then transcribed them onto the Google Earth platform. Uh, side-note here, fellas. Please don't ask me how I did that. I could tell you, but then I would have to kill you."

White-Collar paused, waiting for the laughter which never came, then continued.

"So anyway, after transcribing the unit's traveling coordinates onto Google Earth, I took the liberty and added a few waypoints which I thought might be of interest to some of you. And I labeled these waypoints accordingly. However, I had to use a type of shorthand method for the labeling, because, well, it's just easier that way. You'll have to refer to this handy legend I created," he lifted a piece of paper for all to see, "to decipher my waypoints.

"For example, if you see here," he pointed to a spot on the map labeled 'E.A.R.', "according to the amount of time the tracking unit remained stationed in this general area, which, as you can all see, is most likely far off any city grid, my guess is that this would be the location in which Roochie experienced the unpleasant incident pertaining to his ear. By the way, the GPS coordinates for this point are also written on the legend, should you require them. Finally, I assumed that... and, I should pause here, fellas, and mention that I never like to assume anything, because, as the saying goes, to assume something means to make an ass out of you and me..." White-Collar made a chuckle then, the kind of chuckle someone makes when sharing a joke with nobody but themselves.

A silent, collective pause hung in the air.

"The fuck that nigga just say?" someone asked.

"And so anyway," White-Collar continued, "what I assumed was that you wouldn't be driving your Escalade up there when you, ah, do what it is you plan to do, considering that right about here," he pointed now to a red squiggly line on the map, "is where the maintained, city road, turns into an unmaintained, dirt road, which, as I would also assume..." more snickering to himself, "... would not behoove the pristine condition of your vehicle, should you choose to traverse that way." White-Collar paused, looked around, saw that he was surrounded by a gaggle of blank stares and blinking eyes. "What I'm trying to say, fellas, is that you might want to procure yourselves a different form of transportation for your journey. Oh, and ah, the printer is out of ink."

After another stretch of dumbfounding silence, someone asked, "Myron, how much you paying the professor here?"

"Words out of my mouth," someone else added.

"Shut the fuck up, fools," Myron said. "And White-Collar, I know what the fuck you're trying to say. We's gonna need us some fuckin' monster trucks if we's fixing to *traverse* up in them hills. Steve," he added, smiling as he picked up the piece of paper containing the GPS coordinates to Jimmy-James' hideout, "get on the horn and call the chop-shop. Tell Machado we need a couple of his badass, four-wheel-fucking-drives."

CHAPTER 14

626 Macaw Lane was at the end of a washboard ridden, pot-hole infested, undergrowth sprawling, switch-back laden, dirt road, and all the way the hell up in the sticks. In other words, it had been a rough drive for Sam, and as he finally brought his vehicle to a stop, he let out a deep breath of air.

Sam was beat, as he'd been driving all day, or so it seemed. Driving in circles which apparently led him nowhere, if not into trouble, and all in the same northwestern corner of North Carolina.

It had taken him two hours to get from the Denny's parking lot to where he was now. Worst of all—and this thought might have been more tiring to Sam than the actual act of driving—was that he knew his day's worth of driving wasn't even close to being finished yet.

The smashed passenger window didn't help, either. The inside of the vehicle was now covered in red dust and littered with glass. Sam shook his head at the sight of it. Lord only knew how much the rental place was going to charge him to deal with the mess, assuming his insurance company didn't cover it, which they probably wouldn't.

The driveway he'd pulled into, a dirt lot more or less, was shaded entirely by an ancient oak tree standing in the front yard. Sam killed the engine and waited for the dogs to come running out. He studied the place as he waited. Behind the big oak was a small, single story rambler, freshly painted bright yellow, with white trim. He noticed a ladder leaning on the side of the house, with a paint bucket hanging from it, and a brush sticking out of that. There was an old pickup truck parked under a rickety carport, apparently the only vehicle at the residence. It was turquoise, duly faded, and with pockets of rust scattered throughout. From afar, the truck might resemble an expensive piece of Southwestern jewelry, but up close, it looked exactly as it was: three-quarters on its way to the junkyard.

Sam inhaled deeply, then let out another sigh. Curiously, no dogs had come running yet. There was no barking, no howling, no nothing. Nothing that Sam could hear anyway, other than the hushed, metallic clicks and groans of his vehicle, as it settled itself after its long haul of the day. That and the surrounding, peaceful silence of remote isolation. Sam looked around, wondering where the life of this place was at.

Maybe the man wasn't home. Maybe he and his dogs were out hunting 'coons. If that were the case, they could be gone until the following morning. It was a plausible enough scenario. People did that up here, Sam knew. But what he also knew was that he sure as hell couldn't wait that long to talk to the guy.

A cold feeling swam inside Sam's gut as he considered a second possibility for the surrounding silence. Maybe this Gerald Huey guy wasn't out hunting at all, but, in fact, maybe he was dead. Him and his dogs. They would have been killed, of course, during the process of another aberrant burglary. *Now how complete would that be?* Sam wondered sarcastically. A succinct, befitting way to round out his long day.

He looked at his watch. It was half-past three already, and he knew his day had only just begun. Sam looked up again, observing more of the property, then stepped out of the vehicle and firmly shut the door. Maybe those dogs just hadn't heard him yet. But after a few seconds of waiting, nothing came running out at him. *Well, maybe he doesn't have any dogs,* Sam thought. Entirely unlikely, way up here, but still a possibility.

Sam walked around the front of the vehicle and slowly started to approach the house.

"That's far enough, son," someone said.

And then there was that third possibility that had crossed Sam's mind, the other reason why the place was so still, and so lifeless: Maybe old Gerald was just hiding behind some tree, keeping his dogs at bay, and pointing a rifle at Sam's head.

There was a long pause as Sam waited, looking around. He finally spotted the man, and yes, he was hiding behind a tree, and of course, had himself a rifle, and, oh yeah, it was certainly pointed at Sam.

"Now," the man continued, "you sure as hell don't look like no peckerwood to me. But I ain't buying whatever it is you's selling, anyhow. So you just get back in your vehicle there and mosey along." He gave his rifle a little nudge off center, a brief point toward the road.

Sam shook his head and waited. He was just too tired to deal with this right now.

"You deaf, son?" the man said. "And blind, too? I've got this rifle aimed right between your eyes, 'case you left your glasses in the truck and cain't see."

Sam put his hands in his pockets and turned away. He studied the house.

"Go on, now," the man said, nudging his rifle again. "Go on back the way you came. 'Cause from here, there ain't no other way to go, 'cept for down. And I mean six feet down."

"Yellow?" Sam asked, looking back at the man.

There was another pause. The man glanced quickly to his house, then back at Sam. "Do I know you, son? Or are you just fooling? I don't take kindly to jokers, just so's you know."

Sam looked again at the house. "With white trim," he said, cocking his head slightly to the left. "I'm figuring this was your old lady's idea."

"Ain't got me an old lady, stranger. And here's another thing you should know. There ain't another soul up here, but me. Which means that after I put a bullet in your head and set fire to your truck, ain't nobody gonna run to the Law to tell what happened."

Sam looked around for a minute, observing the property, actively searching for signs of dogs, but not finding any. Then he looked back at the man and said, "Living up here, way in the hills... Why don't you have yourself a good dog?"

The man didn't say anything.

Sam focused his stare on the rifle the man was holding. "Winchester 88?" he asked.

"Know your guns, eh?" the man said. "Well, then you would also know, at this range, this here rifle will blow a mighty big hole in your head."

"Mister, I can't argue with you about that. Three-o-eights leave quite the trail."

"Ain't no three-o-eights in here, son. I shoot two-eighty-fours."

"Same difference," Sam said, "from this distance. But now," he added, "there's another thing that gets me wondering. Why is Gerald Lynn Huey shooting two-eighty-fours, when three-o-eights are just as effective, and easier to come by?" Sam hesitated, keeping his eyes on the man. "Maybe that's your hunting rifle then, and you need the extra range that cartridge will give you, seeing how you probably prefer shooting your deer from afar, and not sneaking up on them anymore."

There was silence, and then somewhere in the surrounding forest, a bird whistled.

"All right, just who the hell are you?" the man said. "And what do you want?"

"Mr. Huey, my name is Sam Nolan, and I'm just a simple rancher from the enchanting state of New Mexico. But I've got skills from my past, which have recently come of interest to a man by the name of Shiloh Parker. You may have heard of the guy. His daughter went missing a few weeks back, not far from here."

Gerald kept his rifle aimed at Sam. "So what does any of this have to do with me? That girl ain't around here, if that's what you're getting at?"

"Not getting at that at all, sir," Sam said. "The truth of the matter is that your name was written into the field journal of a man by the name of Harlow Evans."

"Harlow?" The rifle lowered an inch as Gerald's eyes shifted slightly to the left, off of Sam, and on to nothing.

"Harlow Evans," Sam continued, "was an experienced tracker. And he had helped look for the girl."

"Yeah," Gerald said, looking back at Sam, "I know Harlow." He paused, then added, "But what do you mean he *was* a tracker? Is Harlow dead?"

"I'm afraid so," Sam replied.

"Well, that's a shame. Harlow was a good man. Folks get up in their years, though, and... People die. Happens to us all." Slowly, Gerald lowered the rifle's aim to the ground, stepped out from behind the tree, and glanced at his feet.

"Harlow Evans was killed, sir," Sam said. "Killed in his home by a thief. But I think... Well, I guess it don't matter what I think. The point is that Harlow had a reason to write your name in his journal, and he did that when he was looking for that girl. And since I'm now the one looking for her, I was hoping I could find out what Harlow was thinking." Sam paused. "By the way, there was something else he wrote in his journal. Right next to your name, in fact."

"And what was that?" Gerald asked, looking up.

"Wild men," Sam replied.

Just as Sam had hoped, like a bullet, that word found its mark on Gerald Huey. The old man blinked, his face drew up into a thin frown, and one of eyes started to twitch.

"Wrote that down, did he?" he finally said, after a long pause. And after another, even longer pause, he looked over at his house. "You're a damn smart boy, Mr. Nolan. It *was* my old lady's idea. 'Cept I never got around to painting the thing before she died on me. One of my biggest regrets in life. Not the biggest, but one of them." He looked back at Sam. "All right then, son... How do you take your coffee?"

· · ·

Twenty minutes later, they were standing under a screened patio in the back of the house, drinking strong, black brew from ceramic mugs. In those few minutes since Sam had crossed over Gerald Huey's threshold, he'd learned that Gerald preferred to be called Jerry, and that the last of Jerry's dogs had died last winter, two winters after his wife had died, and that Jerry himself, although not diagnosed with anything, on account that he hadn't been to a doctor in well over ten years, seemed to think he was heading into that cold direction as well. In those twenty minutes of discourse, Sam had gathered enough pieces of Jerry's life to put together the corners and partial frame to a clear portrait of the man. But Sam's keen powers of observation had gathered much more than what came from their conversation.

Sure, Jerry looked like a tough mountain man, having a large head with a long gray beard, dressed in overalls and a plaid button down, wearing a smoky-tan fold up leather hat and homemade moccasins. He was as tall as Sam but twice the girth, an imposing figure, to say the least. But he was old and weathered.

There was a sad loneliness in Jerry's eyes as well, and once the man had warmed up to Sam, that same loneliness came out through his voice. For all his size and apparent strength, Jerry carried with him an obscure, yet noticeable burden, a burden born not just from the tiredness of his aged joints and worn-out muscles, or from the fatigue of his old heart, but a burden that...

Sam wasn't sure. But there was something about the old man's demeanor that spoke of a deep pain, a pain lying somewhere deep inside his soul. The kind of pain that, once it got hold of a person, it would never let go.

"I like a little rum in my coffee," Jerry said with a wink. From a pocket in his overalls, he pulled out a small silver flask. He uncapped the flask, poured a trickle into his mug, then offered some to Sam.

"Why not?" Sam said, pushing his mug forward.

Jerry added a splash, then put the cap back on and dropped the flask into his pocket.

"This is a nice view," Sam said, looking out onto a massive meadow behind the house. "On an early fall morning, wouldn't surprise me if you could sit out here and do yourself a little hunting."

Jerry smiled. "Shot me a nice buck three years ago, from right over there." He pointed to a chair sitting beside a fire barrel less than twenty feet from the back of the house. "It was the last deer I shot, in fact."

"What about bear or pigs?" Sam asked.

Jerry shrugged. "Not anymore. I haven't shot anything in a while. Well, nothing living, that is. But I shoot some *thing* every damn day. Between rifles and pistols, I'm always sending lead down range."

Sam nodded. "It's a good hobby to have," he said. "I guess I'm envious. I don't shoot that much anymore. Used to, when I was in the service. But now... I only take out a few cans once or twice a week, just to stay sharp."

Jerry looked at him. "And for fun."

Sam smiled.

Jerry turned away, then inhaled deeply. "Last time I'd seen old Harlow was nigh on five years ago. A damn good tracker, he was. Almost as good as me, in fact. Maybe better, I don't know." He paused and took a drink. "We used to hang out some, years back, a score of us, actually. Had us a shooting club, I guess. Some would call it that. 'Cept we also spent a lot of time making shine.

"Like myself—like most of us, in fact—Harlow came from a long line of southern folk. Hell, my own name... Well, I don't know how far back it goes. Before the Civil War, that's for sure. Ever hear of the Overmountain Men?"

Sam shook his head. "Doesn't ring a bell, but maybe I have. Seems I forget things the older I get."

"Made a big difference in the American Revolution, them boys did. My great, great granddaddy was one of them. He'd fought at the Battle of Kings Mountain, which, believe it or not, took place only but a few miles from here. I got lots of kin from 'round here with ties to that period. And lots of kin who'd shot a rifle for reasons more than putting food on the table. My dad's dad fought in the Great War, and then my daddy drove a Sherman over in Europe."

"How about you?" Sam asked. "You seem like you might have seen a little action in your time."

Jerry shrugged. "I was in 'Nam. But I didn't see much action over there. A few firefights here and there, but nothing to get a woody over. Saw lots of after-action, though. Lots of death. Lots of ugliness. All that damn Agent Orange bullshit. Not to mention the goddamned napalm." Jerry shook his head and looked off into the nearby trees. "War... loses its romance." He paused, then looked back at Sam. "You know who said them words, son?"

"Can't say I do," Sam said.

"'Nam," Jerry continued, "was nothing but a useless trial by fire. And maybe... Well, maybe I was a bit different from the others, 'cause I felt a heap of sorrow for them poor folks over there. Every damn one of them." He shook his head again. "'Nam whatn't no war. It was just hell, plain and simple."

They paused with their conversation, finished their coffees, then Jerry led Sam back into the house and into the kitchen. "While's you're here, and, since you're obviously fond of guns, follow me on over to my shop. Got some things to show you." He refilled both their coffees, then walked to the side of the house and into an attached garage.

"This here is where I spend most of my time anymore," Jerry said.

Sam looked around, taking in what he figured was all that was left of the old man. The interior of the garage resembled a cross between a professional gunsmith's shop and an old trading post, circa 1750. He saw an assortment of muzzle-loading rifles and recurve bows mounted on a wall, along with various other things— a cluster of rusty traps, coils of rope and strips of leather, animal hides, scores of antlers, fur hats. There were leather satchels here and there, seemingly handmade, as well as a few powder horns. In one corner of the garage sat a melting pot next to a tin pail of water, and a small table containing various tools and a couple of molds— all supplies used for casting musket balls. Next to this area, up against a wall, was a large American Security rifle safe.

The most predominant thing in the garage was a long workbench, spanning an entire wall. On it was an assortment of odds and ends, all gun related. Sam recognized tools of the gunsmithing trade, as well as a few black powder rifles, all in various stages of assembly. On one corner of the workbench was a Hornady Lock-N-Load pressing kit, with what appeared to be a bin of .284 brass shells lying next to it. On the wall above the workbench were a dozen or so framed photos of various people—friends and family, Sam figured. And mounted above all the pictures was a large oil painting of Jesus of Nazareth.

"I shot my first smokepole when I was seven years old," Jerry said. He set his coffee mug on the workbench and started leafing through a gun magazine. He opened to a page and pointed to a picture of an antique, double barrel percussion rifle. "Like that one there, 'cept the one I shot was a Moore and Company. First round knocked me plumb on my ass. But I got up and fired the other one. Been in love ever since. Got me a thirty-two caliber CVA when I was eight, going on nine, pretty as you please. They Lawd have mercy, ain't a family of boomers in these hills that still don't get nervous when I'm around."

Sam had to think for a minute, but then he remembered. "Boomer" was mountain talk for squirrel.

"Ever shoot yourself a smokepole, Sam?" Jerry asked.

"Back in the day," Sam replied. "We've got a few on the ranch, but it's been a while. My brother, though, he hunts elk with a black powder. Me... Like I said, it's been a while. But I prefer using a bow, anyhow."

"I've always loved shooting 'em," Jerry said. "Since I was a young'un. They's got a way of kicking you back every time you pull the trigger, and I like that." He laughed. "Sounds like one of them love-hate relationships, don't it?"

They talked more about guns while Jerry fiddled with a rifle part on the bench, working a small file into the groove of a piece of metal. After a few minutes, he set the part down and walked over to the large safe against the wall, opened it, took something out, and came back over to Sam.

"This here is a beauty," Jerry said, handing Sam a hefty revolver.

Sam took the gun and looked it over. It felt nice, was obviously a percussion revolver, and appeared to be an original from the eighteen hundreds.

"Ain't no 'riginal, if that's what you're thinking," Jerry said. "I put that one together several years back. It's a Colt, 1860. Same gun John S. Mosby used in the Civil War. The Gray Ghost, he was called." Jerry said that last part with a whispering tone and a wink in his eye. "He's the one said them words, by the way. About war losing its romance."

"You're right," Sam said. "It is a beauty."

"Packs a nice little punch, too. Fun gun to shoot, any damn day of the week."

They talked more about guns, and Sam wasn't surprised. He had an idea why, in fact. It was all Jerry had left in the world. And all he would make room for. He was an old man who apparently thought he had no reason left to live, and was preparing himself for that final embrace. That's why he never got anymore dogs after his last ones died. Or why he didn't hunt anymore, figuring there was no point in keeping his freezer full. And that's the reason he was now painting his house—to fulfill that one last promise he'd made to his wife, before it was too late.

But there was another reason Jerry was stalling, and Sam suspected it had to do with that burden of pain he'd detected hanging heavily on the old man's back.

Figuring all of this, Sam forgot about his intentions for the day and listened to Jerry's stories, knowing that what the man needed was time to breathe, and time to work up the courage to broach what seemed to be a mighty painful topic. Sam patiently waited him out, until, sure enough, the old man got there.

"I had but one child in my life," Jerry said, out of the blue. He pulled a picture off the wall and set it on the workbench in front of Sam. "Henry Paul Huey... That was my boy."

Sam studied the picture of the young man, who was wearing a hunter's camouflage jacket, shotgun rested over his shoulder, and holding up a wild turkey by the legs. He was smiling, and he looked just like his dad, only fifty years younger.

"He was my best friend," Jerry said, and here, his voice cracked a bit. "And that boy, he was a shooter, my Lawd. Could shoot better'n me, and a fast draw, believe it or not. Like you seen in the movies. Used to set up cans out back and then he'd pull leather, move faster than a rattlesnake. Hit every damn one, too. Guess my boy took the 'Henry' out of John *Henry* Doc Holliday." Jerry chuckled. "Never thought about that one, now did I?"

Sam just listened, knowing that this was what he'd come looking for. Somewhere along this path they were now on lay the reason as to why Harlow had written what he did into his journal.

"To tell the truth, Sam," Jerry continued, "I've been thinking a whole lot about that missing girl. Cain't help it. And the worst part is that I know how her daddy feels right now. I've been knowing it for nigh on ten years."

Sam looked at Jerry, and then Jerry looked away, staring out the open garage door and into the forest beyond his house.

"He's out there somewhere, my Henry is. He went missing while deer hunting. He was all by himself, and," Jerry looked down and shook his head, "well, I regret that. I always hunted with my boy, 'cept on that day, as I had business in town." He paused, reached for his mug, took a sip, then put it back on the bench. "Harlow helped look for Henry. We searched together, in fact, and we found us some sign up there, where's I know Henry liked to do his hunting. Harlow and I tracked that sign down a canyon. And, before it petered out, it led plumb near the hills above a place containing some of the nastiest vermin ever to walk these mountains."

"How do you mean?" Sam asked. "What vermin?"

"I mean the Ramsey boys. They's the worst things ever come to life, the whole lot of them. Ramseys are the plague 'round here... Hell, not just here, but probably the whole damn South. Boys got their heinous blood spread out far and wide. Anyway, Henry's tracks took Harlow and me down near one of them Ramsey joints, which was a dead end, mind you, but an end that left a cold feeling in my gut—a feeling that still sits with me today."

"Sounds like you suspect these Ramseys had something to do with your boy's disappearance." As Sam said the words, a collection of haunting memories rushed into his mind, memories from Afghanistan and the Yukon.

"I don't suspect nothing," Jerry said. "I know."

Sam scratched the whiskers on his chin. "Well, how do you know, then?" he asked.

"No, I ain't never found my boy, that's true, and I ain't got no workable evidence, but I still know them Ramseys had something to do with it. I know, on more than one account. The first came when one of them Ramseys got to talking one night, down in town, and not more'n a year after Henry went missing. That Ramsey boy, he was drunk and then got himself into a scuffle, nothing surprising there, but he got his ass licked in that fight, and then, just because he was sour from it, went on about how his cousin Jimmy-James had killed him a hunter not long ago, up near his place. He was bragging, said them words just to scare the man who'd whooped him. But them words, they found their way down to me. That's how things work 'round here.

"The second account came from the devil himself. I'd seen Jimmy-James one day, down in town, and he'd seen me, too. And that son of a bitch, he looked at me and he smiled, an evil little grin that told me he knew who I was, and that he knew what he'd done to me. And also, in that snicker, was the fact he knew that now I'd known what he did, but that I couldn't do shit about it. Cold as ice, that boy is. But that ain't no surprise. His old man was mean as they come."

Jerry's words got Sam thinking. He knew there were rough people up here, folks like these Ramseys, which in itself wasn't an uncommon occurrence. Any mountain region was sure to have its share of country boys causing problems for others, just the same as any city was sure to have its own source of undesirable characters. But still, it seemed to him that some dots to the puzzle he was working on were vaguely getting connected. It wasn't hard now to imagine Shiloh's daughter running across one of these Ramsey boys while hiking all alone. Could they be the source of the "Wild Men" she had written about?

A curious thought hit Sam then. "If you're saying this guy was responsible for your son's disappearance, well, then... Have you done anything about that? I don't figure you the rollover type, especially when it comes to family."

"You figured correctly. I said you was smart, didn't I?" Jerry looked down at his hands. "Truth is, ain't a day goes by that I don't think of some way to get back at that son of a bitch. But the problem is that all I've got is me. And I'm just an old man with one foot in the grave, and the other one not far behind. All my friends are dead, or cain't hardly walk no more. What's a man like me gonna do?"

"I'm not sure I'm buying this," Sam said. "You might be old, but you've got yourself a wound that has kept a hot fire burning inside of you. That alone should be enough to force you into action."

There was a pause as Jerry looked away. "I guess there's more to it," he said. "Jimmy-James ain't alone. He's got a whole army of Ramseys up there. I just don't know what I'd do without making a fool of myself. And also... up where he lives, his old man had set himself a passel of man-killing traps. Ran across one of them while's looking for Henry. Almost took my foot clean off. Like me, Flint Ramsey was in 'Nam—three tours, in fact. He was one of them tunnel rats—crazy, and fearless. Three tours over there, but he never really came back, if you know what I mean. He didn't live long, though. Agent Orange caught up to him, but not before he taught his boys a few things, including how to be mean."

Sam considered Jerry's words. Then he thought again about what Harlow had written. "What about the wild men?" Sam asked. "How's that fit into all of this? I'd seen the face you made when I first mentioned that word to you."

"That there gets into something a little deeper," Jerry said. "There's been rumors in these hills, for many years now, about wild men running around. Hell, these rumors go back further than when I was a boy." Jerry looked at Sam. "People go missing up here, Sam. All the time, they do, and no one knows why. Sure, most of the time it's because of something simple as getting lost. But there're other reasons, too. Has to be.

"Anyhow," Jerry continued, "sometime after my boy went missing, Harlow told me he'd seen a couple of wild-looking boys up there one day, while's hiking around. Said these fellers looked like they'd been living in the bush on account that they were so filthy and mangy looking. Ugly as sin, too. They'd run off when they'd seen Harlow, and after, he found a rat's nest of nice looking hiking gear where they'd been. Sure as hell didn't belong to them. But whose gear it was, ain't nobody knows."

Sam thought about this. "Did anybody ever try to root these wild men out? Track them, at least, from where Harlow had seen them?"

"Not that I know of," Jerry said. "Harlow took all that gear and turned it in to the Sherriff, but that's as much as I know. Might be they sent some boys up there to look around, but I ain't ever heard any more of it."

Sam gave it a minute, then changed the subject. "I don't suppose you have a local map around here?"

Jerry paused. "I think so," he said. "Let me go see." He got up and walked back into the house.

As the old man was gone, Sam picked up one of the magazines in front of him and started leafing through it. He was keeping his body idle while his mind worked through all the puzzling details he'd uncovered since coming out here to North Carolina. He had a strong feeling about these Ramsey fellows, and that they sure as hell might have been involved with Emily's disappearance—or someone like them, for that matter. That came as no surprise, as Sam had suspected something along this line since he'd giving serious consideration to the notes Emily had left throughout the hills. But there were other details Sam still couldn't make sense out of, no matter how hard he tried.

Harlow's murder, for example, which happened just before Sam could talk to the guy. And the break in at the hotel, followed by that of his vehicle, resulting in the theft of nothing, except for the case notes and maps Shiloh had given him. Sam was convinced that this thief—whoever he was—handled both crimes, and that's why the hotel room had gotten trashed as much as it did. The thief couldn't find what he was looking for then, because it wasn't in the room, but rather inside Sam's vehicle.

And then, of course, the most puzzling detail of them all: Why? Why was somebody trying to make things difficult for Sam? And better yet, who?

"I found a few," Jerry said, coming back into the garage. "But they's all a bit old." He handed Sam a stack of crinkled road maps.

Sam took the maps, looked through them, found one that seemed interesting, then unfolded it and laid it out on the workbench. He studied it for a second until it made sense to him. It was a multi-county map of the western half of North Carolina. It didn't contain any topography lines, was a little faded from age, but it showed enough for Sam to compare against what he remembered seeing on the maps Shiloh had given him. Not for detail, but enough for bearing.

"You think you can show me the whereabouts of that Ramsey place?" he asked.

Jerry blinked, then picked up a pair of reading glasses from off the bench. He grabbed a pencil, then studied the map. "Right about here," he said, making a little "X" on the map. He paused, then turned back to Sam, a curious look on his face. "Place is well hidden, a devil to find. But listen here, son: on a draw below three canyons, there's a high waterfall, pretty as you like. And not far below that, there's an old, rusted out 'stiller, tucked there in the woods. If'n you come across that spot, well then, you best start keeping an eye out for some of old Flint's traps."

"I appreciate the advice," Sam said.

He looked at the point Jerry made. It was hard to tell, with no contour lines or other topographical features on the map. But Sam had a few waypoints already stored in his head. And by looking at the map, finding those waypoints, and then comparing them to the mark Jerry had just made, Sam was then able to find an approximate reading between the Ramsey place and Emily's last point of contact.

And damn if that wasn't an interesting find.

CHAPTER 15

Where the hell was it?

Jimmy-James had his little house torn almost inside out. He'd started in the single-car, attached garage, where a mountain of boxes and crates and odds and ends was kept—essentially, all his ma and pa's forgotten things, which he'd put out there shortly after his mama had died, many years before. He spent two hours looking in that cave of dust and mouse turds. Granted, some of that time had been used to corner a rat, which Jimmy eventually did, then stabbed through the spine with the old Arkansas Toothpick.

After the garage, he pulled apart the living room. He looked under all the furniture, behind the curtains on the window facing the backyard, and then in the little hall closet near the kitchen. He searched every nook and cranny of that area, all to no avail. Except he did find one of his pa's lost jugs of shine, which Jimmy enjoyed during a brief break, taking several sweet swigs before getting back to his seemingly endless search.

Where in the damn hell was it?

Next, he tore through the spare bedroom, which didn't take him long, seeing how there was hardly anything in there. That room was set up to be Blake's room. But the dumb bastard hadn't stepped foot in the old shack other than to get something to eat since... Well, Jimmy couldn't remember when the last time it was. Although, as he thought more on that, along with the strange ways of his brother, a foul feeling anchored itself inside Jimmy's gut. Blake, queer fucker that he was, was always sneaking around and doing weird shit. Maybe he *had* been in the house while Jimmy wasn't around. And maybe Blake *had* taken what it was Jimmy was now looking for.

Just in case, Jimmy made a second pass through Blake's room, but at last, it wasn't in there. So when he finished searching, he paused in the hallway and thought more about his sprawling property. Then a freak memory occurred to him. Recently, he had seen Blake hanging out in the old shed behind the house. Jimmy had never given it much thought as to what the half-wit was doing back there. Something perverted, no doubt. But now Jimmy was wondering if that just might be the place to look.

He went out to the shed and searched it briefly. The inside was littered with all kinds of screwy shit, things brought in there and used by Blake.

There was an old, stained mattress on the floor, with a crumpled blanket and pillow on it, and a lantern sitting in a corner. These might have been the only "normal" things in the shed, assuming that sleeping in a barely standing building was considered normal, when there was room waiting for you in the house less than fifty feet away.

The other things were all the odd items strewn about the floor of the shed: lengths of greasy chain, several Hustler magazines, an old and rotten zucchini, a handful of soiled rubber gloves, panties and bras from the girls they'd dragged up there over the years, a can of WD-40, two pocket knives, jar of linseed oil, and a pile of dirty rags that looked like they had been used for something only Blake would have a use for. But as for what Jimmy was currently trying to find, well, it wasn't in there, either.

Where in the god-damn *hell was it?*

He found it at last—the pretty pink box. Funny, it had been in Jimmy's room all this time. The last place he'd looked, in fact. The box had been stashed in a lost corner of his closet, underneath a pile of old jackets and worn-out boots. Now it was sitting on Jimmy's bed, crinkled and smashed, a little worse for wear, but that didn't matter any.

He opened the box, stared curiously for a long second, as a look of childish awe crossed over his face. Then he lifted his mama's pearly white dress up, out, and into the dim light coming from the window.

Ooooo-eeeee, ain't she a beauty? And it sure looked like it would fit the girl.

Jimmy tried to remember the last time he'd seen his mama wear the dress. It had to be when he was a young-un, because she had filled out quite a lot once Jimmy hit his teenage years, and she stayed that way until his eighteenth birthday, after which she promptly died. So yeah, he must've been around five or six years old the last time she wore it. His mama looked real good back then, Jimmy remembered. Hell, she had always been a looker, even after she'd put on a few pounds.

Jimmy shook the dress some, made it dance in the air, sniffed it, then smiled. There was a subtle, flowery scent—his mama's smell— hiding behind the overriding musty odor. Jimmy's smile faltered. Oh, how he missed that woman.

He laid the dress down on the bed, then took a step back and stared at it, trying to picture how she would look in it. Not his mama, but the girl. Then his smile came back, knowing that she would look real nice. Fine and dandy, in fact. Although... That girl's tits weren't as big as mama's, and maybe that would play into how the dress would fit, Jimmy wasn't sure.

"One way to find out," he said with a grin. He folded the dress and put it back inside the pretty pink box, then walked out of the house.

He made his way across the yard and to the underground hatch, which was already open, on account that it was a production day. He looked into the hole, dropped the pretty pink box all the way down, then climbed down himself. When he got to the bottom, he picked up the box and then walked through the short tunnel until it opened up into the small, dimly lit room.

This was actually the first room in a labyrinth of many rooms, all interconnected by a system of tunnels which had been masterfully constructed by Jimmy's pa, as soon as the man had come home from the Vietnam war. The purpose of the underground hideout was to provide a covert place for Flint to distill his moonshine. But there was another, less obvious motive, which Flint himself hadn't even known about, as it was a seething purpose born from some black memory locked deep beneath his daily, mental collage of grisly horrors—blown limbs, fettered torsos, hanging entrails, and headless bodies—images that wantonly strolled through the halls of Flint's consciousness.

Jimmy assumed this first room was originally designed to be some type of command center to what Flint had ultimately created down there, and all in service to the fantasies of his PTSD flashback bullshit. But Jimmy didn't really know.

Now the room was a catchall for tools and other miscellanea needed for the making of meth. Mostly, the room contained empty jars and plastic containers, along with a large table filled with assorted crap.

There were two ways in and out of this room, not counting the initial entrance Jimmy had just traveled. The door to his right, which led to the rest of the underground warren, and then the door to his left, which led to where Jimmy liked to watch his movies and drink his whiskey, and do other things. Oh yeah, and to the girl, too.

Jimmy set the pretty pink box on the large table, then went through the door to his right, figuring he would check in on the boys, see how things were going.

He walked down the tunnel, turned several corners, and all the while, the noise from the generators kept getting louder and louder. He eventually came to the "Kitchen", the place where they cooked all that fine-looking ice.

The Kitchen consisted of four separate rooms, joined closely together via a short tunnel. Each of the rooms contained wide ventilation shafts that ran upwards for approximately forty feet before peeking out through the forest floor above, a hundred yards away from the main property. The openings of these ventilation shafts were cleverly concealed behind large rocks, scrabbles of brush, or fallen logs. And as an added bonus, one of the shafts served as an emergency escape route, as it was fixed with a ladder and a removable screened door at the top.

There was a hodgepodge of paraphernalia down there—everything needed for producing crystal meth—stashed into every corner of every room within the Kitchen. Such things included gas cans, propane tanks, pipes and electrical cords, rubber gloves, rubber tubing, rubber gaskets and rubber seals, thermometers and thermostats, bags of kitty litter, ice chests and hot plates, beakers and glassware, buckets of water and buckets of nothing, and a vast assortment of bins, bottles, cartons, and sacks, all containing a vast assortment of ingredients, such as alcohol, antifreeze, hydrogen peroxide, muriatic acid, sulfuric acid, battery acid, iodine crystals, lead acetate, lighter fluid, and paint thinner.

That might have been everything, but there was probably more, Jimmy didn't really know. But Jimmy didn't really care, either, and that's because Jimmy wasn't the expert on such matters.

The experts were Jimmy's three cousins—Kyle, Kenneth, and Kirby Ramsey (no stranger to the Klan, their daddy was)—who were currently down there, and doing what they did best. They were wearing gas masks and rubber gloves, and standing around a table, mixing liquids with solids, or some such thing, when Jimmy walked in. He covered his nose with his arm after catching a whiff of the strong cat piss odor. Kyle looked up after Jimmy walked in, set a beaker of clear liquid on the table, then came over.

Jimmy turned and walked back out into the adjoining tunnel, with Kyle in tow.

"What's up?" Kyle asked, taking off his mask.

"Just checking in," Jimmy said with a nod. He looked over Kyle's shoulder and studied the other brothers, curious as to how they did what they did, but not all that curious. "So when do you think you boys will be done?"

Kyle shrugged his shoulders. "You know how this shit is, man. A few hours, at least, if'n all goes well. This sure the hell ain't like making mash, Jimmy, you know that. We could blow our goddamned faces off if we fuck something up. Then where would we be?"

"Yeah, all right then," Jimmy said. But he was still feeling a little impatient. He wanted to get this next batch done and over with, then on its way, just so he could get a taste for what that son of a bitch Myron was now thinking, since Jimmy had sent his wannabe gangster back to him, and in slightly less than one piece.

"What's the damn hurry, anyway?" Kyle asked.

"Ain't no hurry," Jimmy said. "Just get it done. And then let me know when you're finished. And don't blow your fucking faces off, even if that would make you a sight better to look at."

Jimmy turned and walked away, heading back to the main entrance, stooping low so as not to scrape his head on the dirt ceiling or the occasional cross beam above. Damn if Flint wasn't a tiny fucker. How the hell the towering Jimmy had come from that man's seed was a complete mystery.

Despite his attempts to keep low, Jimmy still bumped his head on the sharp corner of a wooden beam. Holy shit, that hurt! He paused, rubbed his head briskly with his hand for a few seconds, before continuing on.

He made his way back into the first room, picked up the pretty pink box, rubbed his head again because it still hurt like a motherfucker, then went through the door to his left and down the following tunnel.

When he came into the other small room—Jimmy's favorite room—he made an abrupt stop upon witnessing the presence of his brother.

Blake was standing on the other side of the room, completely naked, and with his body pressed up against the locked steel door. The sheet that concealed the door was partially covering his blubbery rolls of flesh. He looked like he was trying to hide behind a set of curtains, but, of course, that's not what Blake was trying to do at all.

Jimmy stared for a long second, taking it all in, not believing what he was seeing, but not surprised, either.

Blake had his ugly, disfigured lips up near the door's hinge, and he was making a series of sounds—loud and labored breathing mixed with strong, sniffing inhales—while jerking himself with a piece of raw chicken.

See, now. This was the kind of shit that really pissed Jimmy off.

Jimmy sprang into action. He dropped the pretty pink box on the ground and launched himself over the bed, slamming his body into Blake's, all with the speed and power of an NFL linebacker. Blake bounced back against the adjacent wall, and then Jimmy drove not one, but several fast elbows into the fat boy's face.

Blake dropped the piece of chicken and pulled his hands up for protection, then started giggling as he tried to move away from Jimmy.

But Jimmy wasn't going to let that happen. He grabbed Blake and pushed him into the corner, then started driving knees into his gut, and more elbows into his head, until Blake's giggling faded away. Then Jimmy took him by the hair on the back of his head, turned, and slammed his brother onto the mattress.

Blake's body bounced again off the side of the mattress, and then he slid to the floor at Jimmy's feet. He opened his eyes, both of which were now bloody and puffing fast, along with his nose, and he looked up at Jimmy, then started giggling again.

"Get your goddamn fat ass out of here," Jimmy said. Then he kicked Blake in the thigh not once, but three times, just to drive his point further.

Blake curled up, then shuffled backward, still chuckling. He looked around, slowly started picking up his clothes and boots, and finally himself, as he staggered up and away from Jimmy, and toward the exit. He was still humored, but his giggling had turned into more of a soft, wheezing snicker.

Jimmy reached down, picked up the piece of chicken, then threw it at Blake. "Go on, now," he said. "Get your filthy ass out of here."

Blake paused at the tunnel entrance. He looked back at Jimmy, then said, "How come?"

"Because I say so," Jimmy replied. "That's how come."

Blake hesitated, a look of confusion making a dent in his smiling face. "You've always let me get at them before. How come I cain't get at her?"

Jimmy took a step forward. "I done told you already, you dumb ass."

"No, you didn't," Blake replied. "You just told me to stay away. You told us all to stay away. But you ain't never said why." Blake's smile was gone, replaced now by a blank stare.

Was this true? Jimmy wondered. He thought about that for a second. Goddamn, maybe it was true.

"Don't matter none," Jimmy said, after a pause. "You just stay the fuck out of here."

Slowly, Blake turned and walked out, his clothes and boots in his arms, while blood trickled down his face.

Jimmy watched his naked, fat brother meander down the tunnel, make it into the first room, then turn the corner and slip out of view.

Jimmy took in a deep breath of air. What a fucking afternoon. First, all that time he'd spent looking for his mama's dress, and tearing his house apart in the process. Then, the nagging bite of impatience found in having to wait for their latest batch of meth to cook up. And of course, that impatience was tied to Jimmy's curiosity about what Myron was thinking right now, which was the last thing he wanted to think about. Then there was that sharp bump to his head, can't forget that. And now, finally, this: Blake, the goddamn weirdo, strikes again.

Jimmy shook his head. He went over, picked up the pretty pink box, came back to the steel door, and set the box on the bed. He pulled out the long keychain attached to his overalls, then unlocked the door, opened it, picked up the box again, and went inside.

This time, Jimmy didn't hesitate. He pulled the string hanging from the light above, and the small, dingy, dank room lit up like a candle.

He looked at the girl. She was cowering in the corner, just like she always did. Jimmy wondered a little as to why that was, seeing how he hadn't laid a hand on her, not once, even after all this time. But had he laid a hand on all the others? Oh yeah, sure he did, most definitely. In his mind, that's what they were for. That's the reason why he even brought them here, anyhow. And Jimmy wasn't the only one who had laid a hand on them girls. All the Ramsey boys did, including Blake. Especially Blake.

His brother's words suddenly echoed in Jimmy's mind. *How come?*

Jimmy stared longingly at the girl, as he thought about that question.

Maybe it was because she was so damn pretty. Prettier than all the others. The prettiest, in fact, even as she looked right now, smeared head to toe in dirt, with greasy, mangy hair, a constant fear and terror swimming in her eyes. Jimmy had yet to see the girl smile, but he had an idea what her smile would look like, and he was hoping he'd see it soon.

How come?

Because she had some Indian blood in her, Jimmy could tell. And if there was one thing that came with a woman with Indian blood, it was a savage wildness found in her ways—all of her ways. And this perceived savageness was the key to Jimmy's ongoing excitement, which fueled him day in and day out, had been fueling him, ever since he and Blake started stalking this pretty little thing in the woods, just as they'd been paid to do.

How come?

Because, well—and here, Jimmy gave pause, the pain he now felt in his chest mimicking the throbbing bump on his head—because Jimmy was lonely. And he'd been lonely for quite some time. He had an odd habit of going through girlfriends just as fast as he'd gone through them other girls he'd plucked out of the woods, and that's because Jimmy was prone to boredom. For Jimmy, everyone and everything, at one point or another, seemed to grow stale and old, then spoil and turn bad, like moldy cheese. But indeed, there was something about this new girl that made Jimmy think otherwise. Something about her that made him think she had staying power.

How come?

Finally, it was because of the deepest and perhaps saddest emotion that this cute and little, yet sexy and strong Emily girl had somehow drawn out of Jimmy James Ramsey's cold and lonesome heart. This emotion he felt was pure and primal, a nostalgic pain that provoked a nurturing, caring, lustful urge inside of him, an urge to cover and protect and smoother this little thing with every ounce of love his ugly soul could muster up.

And goddamn, when was the last time Jimmy felt this way about another human being? Not since his mama had died, that's when.

And yes, that's *how come.*

"I got you something," he said, approaching the girl.

She drew her feet in, rattling the chain attached to her ankle, as she tried instinctively to make herself smaller.

"Don't need to be scared, none," Jimmy said, coming in close and setting the box at her feet. "On my mama's grave, ain't nobody gonna hurt you, sweet thing."

Emily just looked at him. There was terror in her eyes, but a sly cunningness also, or so Jimmy imagined.

He opened the box so she could see what was inside. "See now," he said, smiling. "It's just a dress. A purty white dress. And I think it would look good on you. Don't you?"

Jimmy waited, hoping she would say something. "Go on, now," he added, "try it on."

Slowly, she pulled the box closer and then examined the contents.

Jimmy's heart lurched.

Oh, sweetie, please oh please, why don't you make this boy's day now, and give me a smile.

Those were his thoughts, and those were his hopes, and they lingered on him for a while, as he waited for that girl to do something. But in the end, goddamn son of a bitch, she did not make Jimmy's day.

CHAPTER 16

Sam picked up the phone in Madigan's office, then dialed Shiloh's number. He looked around and studied the small room while he waited for the man to answer. There were several pictures on the wall, some of which were from Madigan's service days. Sam even spotted a photo with himself in it.

The picture had been taken in Kandahar, he remembered, and during a load-out in preparation for a mission. It was the same mission that had sent that RPG shrapnel into Madigan's back. In the photo, Sam was taking a drink from a canteen, and standing behind him was his spotter, Ernie Valencia, who appeared to be cleaning a spotting scope. Ernie was out of focus, slightly blurred, not unlike how he appeared in Sam's memories today. Except for when he came to Sam in the form of one of those grueling dreams.

Interesting thing about that. Sam hadn't had one nightmare since he'd left home. Hmm...

"This is Shiloh."

Sam blinked and came back to the present moment. "Good evening, Shiloh," he said, glancing briefly at his watch.

"Sam!" As always, there was a thin layer of hope lining Shiloh's voice. "How is it going? Are you, ah... Where are you?"

"I'm not in the bush just yet," Sam said, "if that's what you're wondering. But that's about to change very soon."

"Well, okay, then," Shiloh replied, and Sam heard the layer of hope quickly dissolve into disappointment.

"Look, Mr. Parker," Sam said, "I was able to track down some interesting information. And this information came from something Harlow had left behind in his journal. Anyway, I just thought you should know that maybe your daughter hadn't lost her mind out there, as you've always figured. I don't have any hard evidence on that, mind you, just a suspicion, is all. And frankly, I probably shouldn't even be telling you this. But this suspicion I have, well, it leads to a place, as well as a name."

Sam briefed Shiloh with a summarized version of the story he'd received from Jerry, making sure to include the name "Ramsey", and making sure to stress that once again, Sam had no evidence to speak of, but only an inkling of curiosity. As a side note, he mentioned the break in of his vehicle, as well as what had been taken. But Sam didn't linger on that topic. And he even turned down Shiloh's offer to make more copies of the notes and maps for him, because all Sam wanted to do right now was get the hell out of Dodge.

He finalized the conversation with a promise to give Shiloh a call just as soon as he found anything. And of course, there was a big "If" sitting next to that promise.

Sam said goodbye, hung up the phone, scratched his cheek, then looked once again at the photo of him and Ernie. He looked for a long time, a minute, maybe two, then shook his head at the sad memory of his friend. "Whatever happened to you, man?" Sam mumbled.

Madigan came in just then, a bag of food in his hand. "Are you ready, brother?" he asked.

Sam nodded his head. "Let's get going," he said, walking out of the office and into the matted area of the dojo.

Madigan handed the bag to Sam, and then they both headed for the door. "There's a carne asada burrito and three fish tacos in there," Madigan said. "Might be the poor man's version of surf 'n' turf, but that doesn't matter any. Paco's Tacos makes some of the best food you've ever tasted. And if you eat all of this, which I hope you do, you're gonna be so full, you won't need to eat for a week."

"Well," Sam said, "that might be a good thing, considering what I have in mind."

They paused at the door, as Madigan looked at Sam. "Care to tell me what that is?" he asked.

"I'll give you the skinny version," Sam said. "But let's do that on the way. It's already late, and I hate to inconvenience you any more than I already have."

Madigan shook his head. He led Sam out the door, locked the place up, and then they headed into the parking lot. "How many times do I gotta tell you, brother? I'm here for you, man, anytime, anywhere, anyhow. Shit, that's why I gave you that sat phone in the first place."

"I know, Marcus," Sam said, "but I really shouldn't need any help." He looked over at his rental vehicle, the Ford Explorer, with its smashed window and filthy interior. Sam cringed at the guilt he now felt, along with the burden of which his latest favor had saddled onto the shoulders of his friend. "But apparently I do need help," he added, looking at Madigan. "Are you sure you're okay with this?" he asked.

"You mean, am I okay with having to take that piece of junk back to the rental place for you? Or driving your sorry ass up that mountain right now, and in what will soon be the middle of the night? Or maybe for just buying you dinner?"

Sam stared at his friend, the guilt now running through his veins being as thick as tar.

Madigan laughed. "Get your ass in the truck," he said, clicking the key fob of his Chevy Suburban.

Sam didn't say anything, just gave a pitiful nod of his head, as if to agree with the implication behind Madigan's tone, that yes, indeed, Sam was being an idiot right now. He set his bag of Mexican food on the passenger seat, then transferred his hiking gear from the back of the Explorer to the back of the Suburban. Then he tossed Madigan the keys to his rental. "Like I told you, now I owe you big time," he said. "And don't you dare say otherwise."

They climbed in the Suburban and then drove off along a few side streets, through downtown Asheville, and eventually getting onto Interstate 40. It was almost 9:30 PM, and Sam's stomach was growling. He hadn't eaten since his lunch at Denny's.

"Might as well dig in," Madigan said. "We'll be on this road for a while."

Sam did just that. He dug into his dinner, eating the burrito first, and it tasted real good, just as Madigan said it would. He had probably eaten enough, but wasn't yet satisfied, so he started in on a taco.

"What was that name you mentioned to me earlier?" Madigan asked.

Sam looked up. "Ramsey," he said. "Jimmy Ramsey, in fact. Or maybe it was James. Anyway, I just have a… Well, a hunch, is all. But this hunch has put an idea into my head."

"That's right," Madigan said. "And you were going to tell me about that idea."

Sam took a bite, nodded, then told Madigan what he planned on doing. He explained how he was going to go about with his search for Emily Parker, and also what his plans were for fitting his "hunch" into the process.

Madigan seemed to take the information in stride, and then a look of stern concentration came over his face once Sam was finished talking. "Okay, then," Madigan said, "but you better not lose that sat phone. Like I told you before, there really are mountain people up there. And I would bet they don't take well to running across strangers."

Sam looked up from his taco. "Yeah, but who said I was planning on introducing myself to any of them?"

Madigan smiled at that.

They continued on I-40 for several more miles, merged onto South-19, drove that way for a while, then turned north on U. S. 441, en route to the border. It was exactly midnight when they reached their destination, the Newfound Gap parking lot, which sat smack dab in between North Carolina and Tennessee, and directly on top of the Appalachian Trail.

Sam's belly was stuffed full, but that was just fine with him. One less thing he had to worry about.

He climbed out of Madigan's vehicle, grabbed his gear from out of the back, and his friend came around to meet him. The parking lot was empty, the darkness of the night was all-enveloping, and the sky above was a black canvas of stars.

"Well, here you go," Madigan said. He turned and stared into the nearby trees, and at the mysterious darkness lying therein. Madigan gave a brief chuckle. "Seems like old times, don't it?"

Sam shouldered his backpack. "Maybe so," he replied. Then he turned, facing west, and observed the direction he was about to travel. And somewhere in that direction, among all the dark pockets of looming silence, laid not just the Appalachian Trail, but also the final question as to what had happened to Emily Parker. "But then again, maybe not," he added.

Madigan looked back at him. "I guess time will tell, won't it?"

Sam shook his friend's hand, gave a quick nod and, without so much as saying goodbye—only because operators never said goodbye before heading out—he turned around and walked into the trees. On his way, he dug out a wad of chewing tobacco from the canister in his pocket, crammed a pinch under his lip, then just about smiled.

Finally, at last, Sam Nolan was ready to get to work.

CHAPTER 17

Carson's streak of good luck went from sixty to zero in three seconds flat. He had just finished talking with Boss-man, ended the call, and then placed his phone on the dashboard of the van. Now, he was staring out into the vague darkness of a Wal-Mart parking lot and thinking about this next job he'd been given. It wasn't the end of the world, no. Not even remotely close. But it would be inconvenient at the very least, and potentially troublesome at the worst.

Initially, Carson felt like he had been asked to do a dull chore of some kind, like taking out the trash. This new job was hardly exciting. Nothing like killing somebody, or rolling over a hotel room, or even that quick yet exhilarating smash-n-grab he'd done earlier. Also, he knew this job would result in peanuts for pay. But Boss-man had said that it was *damn important*, emphasizing those last two words. So Carson wasn't about to say no. Initially, it did feel like a mundane chore. But as Carson thought more about it, he realized just how difficult this job was going to be.

"What the hell am I going to do?" he said to himself, popping open a can of Coors.

The job came in two parts. First, Carson needed to let Jimmy-James know that very soon now, Mr. Sam-I-Am was going to be up there on the mountain, slithering through the trees like a snake in the grass, and doing what he supposedly did best, which was finding lost people. Apparently, the guy was some kind of ex-G.I. Joe badass, a Navy Seal or Green Beret, who had spent a chunk of time over in the Middle East. But worse than that, according to Boss-man, Sam-I-Am now had him some suspicions about the Ramseys. How he came across these suspicions, Carson didn't have a clue. But that didn't matter right now. What mattered was that Sam was about to be up there in the hills, was apparently dangerous, and a whole lot curious. Either way, it was now Carson's job to warn Jimmy-James about this, and to let him know to keep an eye out for the guy.

In itself, this part of the job wasn't a problem, even if Jimmy didn't own a phone. All Carson had to do was dial up old man Lee Roy and give him the message, which he would then relay over to Billy Bob, who would in turn give Earl a call, and then that boy would drive on over to Jimmy's place, and just like that, the job would be done and over with.

But of course, things would not be that simple for Carson. And that was because of the second part of the job.

Boss-man told Carson to find out about the girl.

More specifically, to make damn certain that the girl—and everything about her, such as her clothing, hiking gear, identification, or anything that would ultimately have her name on it—no longer existed, just in case somebody curious came knocking. And the only way for Carson to find this out was to head on up to Jimmy's place for himself and start snooping around. Therein lay the pickle to this job.

"What the hell am I going to do?" he repeated.

First of all, the very act of getting up to Jimmy's place was one damn pain in the ass. Especially with Carson's current ride. The last time he'd gone up there, he ended up having to fix two flat tires. The road to Jimmy's compound was a notorious dirt path of potholes and rutted out washboards, not to mention overgrown with bushes and trees. The trip was always slow going, even if Carson didn't care about the paint job on his van (which he didn't), because he had to avoid blowing out another tire, or getting stuck in some ditch or pocket of loose sand. What Carson really needed was to get him a good 4x4. But there was no time for that now. Boss-man wanted this job done ASAP.

Of course, Carson could always steal a truck, just to make the trip up there a little easier.

He looked around. He was currently sitting in the driver's seat of his van, picking away at his dinner, a lukewarm bowl of Orange Chicken chow mein from Panda Express. They were parked on the outer edge of a Wal-Mart parking lot, turned in for the night. He noticed a few RVs here and there, a couple of beater cars, and an oldie but goody Ford diesel on the other end of the lot. That would do the trick, Carson thought.

But ultimately, he sighed. He knew his cousin wouldn't be too keen on him driving a smoking-hot vehicle up to his place. Knowing Jimmy, who was shrewd as a fox, it wouldn't take him long to realize that Carson's new ride was a stolen one. And if Jimmy didn't figure it out right away, Donny would eventually spill the beans, blabbering on to anyone and everyone about their "brand new truck," and then Carson would have some explaining to do. So no, stealing a ride wasn't the answer. And yes, getting up to Jimmy's place was still the first hurdle. Maybe Carson just needed to bite the bullet on this one and buy a few extra tires in the morning before he made the long drive up there.

The second, and much more challenging, hurdle, was the task of snooping around Jimmy's place without drawing any unwanted attention. Carson wasn't sure how he was going to pull this one off. And it's not like he could simply ask his cousin if the girl was now worm food, and then take Jimmy's answer as solid gold. Boss-man would want more proof than that.

Adding to the hassle, Jimmy-James was like his old man, paranoid and leery, uptight about every goddamn thing, and never the least bit easy-going. Not even when the guy was drunk or high. Hell, on the contrary to that, while under the influence, Jimmy

James Ramsey was the last person on Earth you wanted to be around. That boy made crazy look like a stroll in the park.

So yeah, having a look-see of the property was going to be a bit challenging. Risky and complicated. Carson had his work cut out for him.

He kept thinking...

Well now, he could always lie to Boss-man. Tell him that he'd looked all the hell around for the girl, searched the entire damn property, but found diddly-squat.

Carson considered this idea for a minute.

And if, let's say, later down the road, someone did find little Ms. Emily up there. Where then would that put him in the eyes of Boss-man?

Knowing Boss-man's capabilities, Carson shivered with fear at the mere thought of that scenario. Alright then, lying was out of the question.

If the girl was still alive (not an impossibility, Carson thought, knowing how perverted his cousins were), then for sure she would be somewhere down in that tunnel system Flint had dug out years ago. The same place they distilled all that white lightning back in the day, and probably where they were now cooking the meth. Carson would have to come up with a way to get down there, see for himself if, and what, remained of the girl.

Suddenly, Donny let out a long, whistling fart, momentarily breaking Carson's concentration. The big lug was sleeping in the back of the van, but he was now rustling around and smacking his chops. He always "ate" in his sleep, and sometimes afterward, would piss the bed.

Carson grabbed a half-empty, two-liter bottle of Sprite and threw it at his brother. "Wake up, Donny!" he shouted. "Get your dumb ass up."

Donny groaned, whined, then said, "Car... I gotta pee."

"You're damn right you do," Carson said. "That's why I woke you. Now get up and go outside before you piss yourself again."

Donny made slow going of it. He huffed and grunted, then got up on his knees and started rummaging in the dark, his big hands fumbling over blankets and things.

"What the hell's your damn problem?" Carson said.

"Cain't find my coat," Donny replied, crankiness in his voice. "Where's it gone, Car? Where's it at?"

"What the hell do you need your damn coat for? Just get out there and pee. Jesus Christ, Donny, it ain't even cold out."

"Ahhh," Donny whined, giving up his search. He stumbled over to the side door, opened it, then stepped outside and paused. "Put the lights on, Car," he said.

"Shit, Donny. Just go pee, goddamnit."

"But it's dark out here."

Carson looked around. It wasn't really all that dark. There were a few parking lot lamps on, dimly lit. The sky seemed pretty clear and the moon fairly large. Then Carson shook his head, knowing who he was dealing with. He turned the headlights on. "Is that better, you big baby?"

"Thanks, Car," Donny said, sliding the door shut.

Carson watched as his brother made his way over to a porta-potty a hundred feet away. Donny stopped at the door, hesitated, knocked on it, waited a second, then slowly opened it up and went inside. Observing his brother suddenly reminded Carson of the last hurdle that came with this new job.

Blake Ramsey.

A cold shiver ran down Carson's spine. He rubbed the whiskers on his chin and let out a long sigh. Blake Ramsey... their sick-minded, twisted and demented, freak of nature for a cousin.

For reasons only the Devil understood, whenever they were up there, Blake would eventually start picking on Donny. And we're not talking about your simple locker-room humor, childishly innocent, lampoon style of teasing. Blake went *after* Donny. And he wouldn't stop until Donny lost his wits (such that they were) and then the two of them got to brawling. And once the fight between those big boys started, it would take at least half a dozen grown men to get them off each other. Always, afterward, regardless of how much blood and bruising there was, Donny would be crying like a baby, and Blake would be laughing like a fool.

Carson cringed, thinking about the last time they were up there. The fight got damn near epic. It started with Blake whispering incessantly to Donny, that he wanted to see his pee-pee lubed up with Vaseline. Then Blake pulled his own pants down and started chasing Donny around the yard, making grabs at Donny's crotch, laughing and jeering. Donny tried as best he could to get away. But once Blake tackled him, got his hand down Donny's pants and his finger in his asshole, started driving home, well then, that's when it was on.

Carson almost laughed at the memory, despite all the drama that ensued from that fight, as well as the predicament he was still in. How to get over Blake Ramsey, the third and final hurdle?

Right now, somebody is sitting in a chair and saying to their self, *Just leave Donny behind. Why take him with you?*

And then Carson shuddered at the terrifying reality behind that thought. His laughter swiftly subsided, as he remembered the last time he had left Donny in the care of someone else.

Carson had been dating Annie Mae Jones at the time, a wild hellcat of a girl, who liked her crystal meth frequent and raw, the same as she preferred sex. Annie Mae wanted to spend a long weekend down in the city with Carson, Carson only, and not Carson & Donny. Seeing how he was whipped as he was, Carson made arrangements for Donny to spend that weekend with their Aunt Caroline, and boy, what a disaster that had been. Not more than twenty-four hours later, and Carson got the call. Donny was being held point blank with a scattergun after Aunt Caroline's neighbor, Charlton Ray, caught Donny in the backyard with his three little girls. Donny and the girls had been swimming in the aboveground pool, laughing and giggling, playing games like Marco Polo, Sharks and Minnows, Launch the Guppy, just having a gay old time, and not one of them was wearing a single thread of clothing. Nothing but their birthday suits on.

So no. Leaving Donny behind was never the right answer.

Carson glanced up, noticing his brother was coming out of the porta-potty. Donny stepped out and was buttoning his jeans back together. He took a few steps forward, paused, stood there for a second, then turned around and went back into the porta-potty.

"What the goddamn hell is he doing?" Carson mumbled. "Probably needs to take a shit." Carson went back to eating his chow mein. He took a few bites, and then, suddenly, like a shooting star, it hit him. He stopped eating mid-bite and looked up.

Now why didn't I think of this sooner? he thought.

Whenever Blake and Donny got into one of their scraps, Carson was as essential to getting Donny to stop the mauling as Jimmy-James was with controlling Blake. But what if Carson wasn't there at the time? What if Carson was, say, on a walk in the woods, or out hunting boomers, or running some dumb errand in town...?

Of course, Carson wouldn't be doing any of those things. But instead, he would explore the tunnels under the property.

No, it wasn't a perfect plan. Not yet, at least. But it had the blueprints of a plausible one. Carson thought he could work the wrinkles out. The key to providing him time to do his searching would be a good distraction. And what better opportunity was there for that than an epic—no, the *most* epic—brawl between Blake and Donny?

Carson finished his bite of food and chuckled to himself, now thinking about how much of a genius he was. He was going to use Blake Ramsey's own shenanigans as a means of doing his searching. *So there—fuck you, Blake.*

But then a sudden sliver of guilt crept into Carson's thoughts as he considered the potential harm his brother would receive.

Oh, well. Donny would just have to take one for the team, simple as that. He might get injured, injured badly, but he'd been hurt before. And to look on the bright side, with any luck, maybe Donny would kill that son of a bitch in the process.

Donny came out of the porta-potty just then, working his pants together again, shuffling back to the van. He got to the door and slid it open.

"All's done, Car," he said, climbing in. "Had to poo, too."

"Yep," Carson replied. "I figured as much."

Donny slid the door closed, turned, noticed his brother was looking at him, then he sat down on the mattress at the back of the van and started fumbling with a blanket. He glanced again at Carson, who was smiling. "What'cha smiling at, Car?" Donny asked.

"Not smiling at nothing," Carson replied. "You go on back to bed now, Donny. Go on back to bed, and get your rest." Carson swung back around, turned off the headlights, and resumed his dinner.

Get your rest, boy. 'Cause Lord knows you're gonna need it.

CHAPTER 18

Sam spent the first thirty minutes of the morning lying in his hammock, listening to the forest. By intent, he wasn't thinking about anything. He was just taking it all in, and quietly observing the world around him.

The birds were singing in chorus. The sky above was overcast, but only slightly. Perhaps just a thin layer of morning fog. Off to his right, he heard the skitter-scratch on bark, the sound of a squirrel running up a tree. There was no wind, and because of this, Sam could also hear all the busy things stirring on the ground below him. The rustling of bugs and tiny critters. The crackling of settling foliage. The ever-so-subtle movement of the land.

Because of the stillness of the morning, Sam could smell much of his immediate surroundings. Damp loam was the predominant odor, wet and earthy, lingering on the forest floor all around him. He caught a whiff of tree sap, and then a fleeting trace of mountain mint. There seemed to be fungi nearby as well, probably some mushrooms growing under ground cover.

In many ways, ways that Sam fully appreciated, the forests of the South were a whole lot different from the forests of the Southwest. Both were rugged and demanding of respect, but North Carolina, Tennessee, Kentucky... The woods in these parts were thicker, more condensed, than anything New Mexico had to offer.

Water was much easier to come by, but in some ways, harder to find, unless a person knew how to look. And that's because in these forests, which were chock full of standing timber and lush greenery and dense overgrowth, unlike the sparse openness found in much of the Gila Wilderness, a person could easily lose their sense of direction, and then stumble in circles for days, until they were robbed completely of energy and desire. That's when people laid down and died.

For the first thirty minutes of his day, Sam just breathed and let his senses do all the work.

He had found this spot sometime in the night, shortly after saying goodbye to Madigan. Sam had left the Newfound Gap parking lot and headed west on the Appalachian Trail, in the darkness, with only a headlamp for light, and he just walked. He walked for about an hour, then cut to his right, off the trail, and headed deep into the woods, until he found a nice spot to hang his hammock, which he promptly did. Then he'd gone straight to sleep. And he slept damn well.

After those first thirty minutes of the morning were over, Sam spent the next half hour quietly getting ready for his day. He took down his hammock and packed it into his backpack. He put away a few other things, then took out a lightweight camp burner, which he used to make a cup of coffee and a small bowl of cinnamon-raisin oatmeal.

When his breakfast was good and hot, Sam sat on a log and slowly ate his food, drank his drink, and, of course, thought about Lolo. He looked down at his bowl and smiled. Boy, would she be proud of him right now, starting his day off with such a healthy meal. Sam sighed. After only a few days out here, he was already looking forward to getting back home and seeing the woman. Not to mention his family.

He finished his breakfast, cleaned up, brushed his teeth, then got ready to break camp, little that it was. He strapped on his backpack, then headed back toward the AT, which he came across after about ten minutes of walking.

This section of the trail was wide and fairly level. It was within a long stretch of a heavily covered canopy of trees. Sam turned to his right, roughly facing westward, and began to walk, taking his time. He wasn't in much of a hurry. Well, maybe he was. But for this part of the job, a good measure of patience and time was essential, in order to get a feel for the land. To absorb the language of his surroundings, and to see just how he would fit into this wilderness.

He walked for a few miles, the terrain changing faces more than once. The heavy canopy faded away, opening up to a thin strip of granite surrounded by a grassy field freckled with shrubs. At the end of the meadow, near a tree line and off to his right, Sam noticed a group of white-tailed deer foraging on wildflowers. They flicked their tails and watched him walk by, eyes alert, ears up, but they seemed comfortable enough with his presence.

About a quarter of a mile later, the land once again densely crowded with trees, Sam spotted the fresh tracks of a black bear. He paused and studied the signs. The creature had spent a few minutes on the trail, where it had dropped some scat, then it clawed its way up a small embankment of exposed tree roots and loose gravel. It had been a small bear, Sam could tell. Not more than a few years old.

He kept going, taking his time, at medium speed, not a hurried pace, knowing that he had all day to get to where he was planning on stopping for the night. The scenery was splendid, the environment peaceful, and after a few hours of walking, Sam felt all that city tension melt away. If nothing else, he was glad to be back in the woods.

But he had a job to do, which he was doing right now, even as he strolled casually along the Appalachian Trail. Always, Sam's senses were sponging up the land, taking in the geography, studying the feel of the woods. Just the very act of observing your surroundings, and for no other reason than to "see," was a critical role in tracking a lost person. Through both instinct and experience, Sam knew this to be the case.

The hike from where he camped the previous night, to Clingmans Dome, should have taken him roughly three and a half hours to cover. But Sam did it in well over four. It was near noon by the time he reached the visitor's center of the Dome, the highest point of the Great Smoky Mountains National Park.

There were multiple cars in the parking lot, along with several people milling about—tourists and families, a couple of hikers. Sam bought a granola bar from a vending machine, dropped a few dollars in a donation jar at the information center, which he visited briefly, then found the trailhead and began the short, half-mile hike up to the observation tower.

The view from the top of the tower couldn't get any better. Now standing nearly 7,000 feet above sea level, a cool, yet slight, breeze blew past Sam. He was looking out at a sea of green, the wilds of North Carolina and Tennessee, a rolling canvas of trees, sparsely topped with small tufts of low, billowy clouds. He figured he was seeing at least twenty miles of the horizon, perhaps more.

When he was done enjoying the view, Sam made his way back down to the information center, then found a stone bench near the parking lot, where he stopped for lunch. He took out his burner and cooked a portion of dehydrated Chicken Fried Rice from Mountain House. He ate slowly, watching people as they walked around, finished his meal, then placed his trash in a nearby dumpster. Minutes later, he was back on the trail.

It was well past one o'clock, and Sam had a few more hours of walking to do before he stopped for the day. But he had plenty of time. He wasn't close to being tired and, in fact, felt like he had only just warmed up.

The land continued to change faces. Sam's walk took him through large passages of dense woods, followed by long stretches of open fields. He came across a grove of ancient spruce-fir, and then a wide meadow of grass and colorful wildflowers—the gentle whites, yellows, and blues of thimbleweed, lupine, and iris. There were parts of the trail that had been soaked from a recent rain, was still a slushy mire of mud, yet other parts that were packed hard and dry.

Sam eventually came across the Double Springs Gap shelter, a shack with a picnic table, where three hikers were presently taking a rest. Sam waved hello and kept going. He was bearing down on his destination, getting close. And when he reached the Welch Ridge Trail junction, he veered off to his right, remaining on the AT, and headed for Silers Bald, which he reached after a few minutes of walking.

There were two hikers at this shelter, apparently taking a break. Sam walked up and said hello, exchanged a bit of small talk, then moseyed along. He didn't want to bother anyone right now, and more importantly, didn't want to be bothered himself.

He was looking for a good place to camp for the night, and figured there'd be something nearby, and so close to the shelter. He strolled through the area and eventually found a well-used, improvised campsite. There was a fire ring made from large rocks, and a few fallen timbers that had been dragged over to it, obviously used as seats. It was a good spot.

Sam tied his hammock between two trees, then secured a lean-to above it, using a lightweight Trailbreak tarp, just in case he got rain in the night. He went into the forest and gathered pieces of deadfall, then made a small fire, mostly for comfort. After his camp was set up, Sam snacked on beef jerky, and then did some exploring of the area. He had a spot in mind—the Welch Ridge Trail, which he'd passed earlier. The trail split off from the AT and ran in a roughly southern direction. Slowly, Sam made his way toward his destination, through the trees and brush, until he eventually cut the trail.

The Welch Ridge Trail ran along the top of a high ridge—Welch Ridge, Sam figured—in a north/south direction, with east and westward slopes falling off it. It was the eastward slope that Sam was interested in. The canyons dropping off this side of the ridge ran perpendicular to the southern slopes of the Appalachian Trail. And it was somewhere down in that convergence of land, all that unshorn wilderness, with miles and miles of trees and untamed hollows, where Emily found her misfortune.

Of course, Sam wasn't one-hundred percent certain about this assumption. But he knew he was as damn close to that number as he could get.

He studied the view for several minutes, then slowly made his way back to his camp. He went off-trail and through the trees once again, albeit taking a slightly different path, and keeping a constant eye out for anything interesting, such as evidence from a missing girl.

Sam didn't find any evidence, of course, and he wasn't surprised. After a few minutes of walking, he was back at camp and sitting at the fire, poking a stick into the embers, and thinking about things.

He thought about a lot of things. His military days, and what might have happened to Ernie. How his brother Bryson was doing. Getting himself a cell phone. If and when he was going to ask Lolo to marry him... And, just as nerve-wracking, having to get Nali's approval on that. Sam wasn't too worried about what the old Apache would say, but it was a mild source of anxiety, nonetheless.

And briefly, Sam thought about Lou Pine... Always, he felt like he'd missed the final chapter of a horror novel, and was left to wonder how the story ended. The authorities said Lou Pine had most certainly died. They said the long fall into that river would have killed the man. They also said that if for whatever crazy reason it hadn't, then in no time, the cold and harsh elements of the Yukon would have done the old and wounded geezer in. The authorities had said a lot of things, after they couldn't find that madman's body. But none of their excuses were able to drive away the sliver of doubt Sam still carried with him.

Finally, he thought about cooking green chilies, as well as eating them, and then Sam broke away from his daydreaming and made his dinner. He cooked and then finished the remaining portion of the Chicken Fried Rice, then nibbled on a few chocolate covered banana chips for dessert. He wasn't too worried about midnight critters, but Sam hung his food bag in a tree several yards from camp, just in case. Then he made a cup of lemon tea, which he sipped for about twenty minutes as he studied the fire, before climbing into his hammock and turning in for the night. He fell right to sleep.

•   •   •

Sam woke at the crack of dawn. Quietly, he slithered out of his hammock, took it down, and then put it away. He made a quick breakfast, ate it, then eventually packed his things and got ready. He stamped out any lingering coals of the fire before breaking camp. And then he walked off into the trees.

There was a heavy fog sleeping on the land. A wet blanket of cold moisture, which obscured everything beyond twenty feet. But Sam didn't mind. He knew where he was going.

When he came across the Welch Ridge Trail, he paused. There was nothing to see of the land. No more horizon of rolling green hills, the view now replaced by a white-gray mist. The world had become eerie with fog.

Sam wasted no time. He retrieved his compass out of his pack and put it in the front pocket of his jacket. He took in a deep breath of cold air, held it for a moment, and slowly let it out. Then he walked forward, off trail, and into the misty wilderness of the Great Smoky Mountains. In less than five seconds, Sam Nolan was gone.

CHAPTER 19

The next morning, Carson bit the bullet. He walked into Wal-Mart and bought two spare tires for the van, which put him back over a hundred dollars. Not a good way to start the day.

He paid in cash because Carson Floyd Ramsey quite literally had no other options on that matter. He also bought a few snacks and things for the road and whatnot, then made Donny carry everything back to the van, while he blew off a little buyer's remorse by looking at Car And Driver magazines.

On their way out of town, they picked up breakfast at a Jack-in-the-box drive thru. Carson ordered coffee, which he rarely drank, but figured he needed to get his mind kicked into overdrive this morning. He was still thinking about his plan, had a few kinks to work out, and, somewhat on the laborious side, still needed to do a little explaining and convincing to Donny.

Not that Donny ever needed much convincing of anything. Just a bit of deception was all it took, and that big dummy would jump right off a cliff and to his death. And Carson, well, he was a master of deception. A born genius. Especially when it came to fooling his brother.

But more than coaxing, what Carson was hoping to do was give Donny fuel for his upcoming fight. Assuming Blake and Donny got into it, and Carson was about one hundred and ten percent certain they would, then the more Donny had in his head as to what he was fighting for, the more he would make a grand show of it.

In Carson's mind, he was picturing the worst brawl known to mankind. A whole heap of violence, with lots of screaming and hollering, and lots of blood and bruising. Something really dramatic. A fight with tons of flair. A fight that drew in *all* the neighbors (not that there were any up there, but if there were). A fight that would cause so much damn commotion and racket that Carson would have no problems sneaking off to do his business, and without a single soul noticing him.

So then, the question remained: What in the world would cause Donny Ramsey to fight like that? What payoff would inspire that big boy to throw all his weight into it, and for as long as it took Carson to get down into those tunnels and do a quick search for the girl?

What indeed?

Of course, Carson knew the answer.

"Hey, Donny," he said, turning onto the on-ramp and heading west on Interstate 40, out of Asheville. "What's the one thing you've always wanted to do but ain't done yet?"

Donny looked at his brother, eyes wide and curious. "I don't know," he said. "What'cha mean, Car?"

"I mean, what have you always wanted to do, but haven't done yet, even though you've always wanted to do it?" Sometimes he had to talk like a fool in order to get through to the fool.

Donny blinked. "You mean... Disney World, Car?"

Carson didn't reply. He just smiled.

"You mean Disney World!" Donny said, chuckling. "That's what you mean, don't you, Car?"

"That's exactly what I mean, Donny. Disney World!"

Donny clapped his hands, started hopping in his seat, laughing. "Does that mean we's going to Disney World, Car? Are you finally taking me to Disney World?"

"You're damn right I am, Donny!" Carson said. "We're going to Disney World. We're gonna go real soon now, in fact!"

Donny squealed with laughter.

"And when we get there," Carson continued, preparing to lay it on thick, "we're gonna stay at one of them fancy hotels and see all them fancy things, and ride *all* them fancy rides. Yes siree, Donny. We're gonna ride the rides until the park closes!"

"Oh, boy!" Donny cried. "We're gonna ride the rides, Car! All the rides, Car! I cain't wait to ride all the rides!"

"Oh, but it gets better, Donny. While's we're there, we're gonna eat all kinds of yummy food, too. I mean, ice cream and cake, donuts, pizza, hamburgers and fries... And we're gonna see all kinds of purty things, Donny. Purty things like flowers, and waterfalls, and fancy buildings, and..." he glanced over at his brother "... and *young'uns*. That's right, Donny. They's all kinds of young'uns running around Disney World, which might be the best thing about that place, you know. Young'uns running around in their skimpy little shorts, half naked. Running around barefoot. Lots of young'uns at Disney World, Donny. Thousands, in fact."

Donny's eyes grew wide with wonder. "Thousands," he repeated.

"That's right, Donny. Like I said, lots of purty things at Disney World. And we're gonna see all of it, real soon, in fact. Very soon."

Donny's mouth was open, but he was damn near speechless. "Golly gee willikers, Car, I cain't, I cain't, I cain't hardly believe it. We're going to Disney World. Let's go, Car!"

"Going to Disney World, Donny," Carson confirmed, smiling rapturously.

Then Carson paused for a good long minute, letting that wonderful fantasy blossom inside his brother's head, before he then said, "Oh... But wait..." His smiled dropped suddenly into a frown.

Donny looked at him.

"Oh, no..." Carson added, now with distress in his voice.

"What'cha mean, Car?" Donny replied. His face was stricken with alarm. "What'cha mean, oh no?"

"I just forgot about something, Donny."

"What'd you forget, Car?"

"Well, it's kind of complicated, Donny. But it's really important. Yes siree, it's mighty important. Goddamn, it's important."

"What's important?"

"See, before we can go to Disney World, I've got this job lined up that I need to do. I got something to take care of up at Jimmy-James' place."

"Okay," Donny replied in a serious tone.

"But before I can do this job," Carson continued, "there's something else that needs tending to. Something that's... kind of in our way, Donny."

"What thing, Car? Tell me. What's in our way? I'll move it, I will, so help me, Lawd." Donny's tone was now on the verge of desperation.

"Now, now," Carson said, raising a hand, "don't go getting all upset on me. It's just that, *well...*" He stretched that last word out for about a mile.

"Well, what?"

"Well, you see, Donny, what's in our way happens to be a person."

"What person?"

"And this person, now... Well, I guess I should just come out and say it."

"Say it, Car."

"I'll be frank with you, little brother..."

"Be frank, Car."

"The person in our way is cousin Blake. And that's because Blake doesn't want us to go to Disney World, Donny."

Donny's face drew up into a mean scowl. "Blake doesn't want us to go to Disney World?"

"That's right, Donny. He told me so, in fact. Right to my face, he did. This was a while back, you won't remember. But Blake, he done told me that *you*, Donny, are not good enough to go to Disney World. That you don't deserve it. And because of that, he said he wasn't gonna let me do my job, plain and simple."

Donny fumed with anger.

"Now, I know what you're thinking, Donny. But like I told you, this here situation is a bit complicated. It ain't an easy fix. There's thinking we've got to do. And we certainly can't get all jumpy about it. Can't start shooting from the hip, if you know what I mean."

"I'll kill 'em, Car, yes I will. Ain't gonna let Blake stop me from going to Disney World. I'll kill 'em. Let me kill 'em, Car. Let me kill Blake."

Carson pulled off the highway, made a couple of turns here and there through a rural neighborhood, then started driving up a few back roads, making his way up into the mountains, and to the world of deep North Carolina desolation.

"Here's the thing, Donny," he said. "In order for me to do my job so's we can get us the money to even afford to go to Disney World, I'm gonna need you to hold out from fighting Blake, until, well... until it's time."

Donny looked at him. There was hatred in his eyes, all directed at Blake, of course. "I'll kill 'em, Car," he repeated. "Ain't gonna let him stop me from going to Disney World."

"That's right," Carson said. "But you gotta wait until the right moment, Donny."

"Well, when's that?" Donny asked.

"Now, I don't really know," Carson said, speaking the God-honest truth for once. He wouldn't know when the right time to go sneaking off would be until it presented itself to him. And that depended on what Jimmy's place was like. Sometimes, the property was crawling with all kinds of kin and local boys. Other times, it was a goddamn ghost town up there. But neither one of those scenarios would necessarily give Carson the opportunity to slip away. Like casing houses, it all depended. He just had to see for himself. Carson would need to assess the situation before he made his move, and that's all there was to it.

"I'll just have to look and see, Donny," Carson continued. "But I sure as hell will let you know. And until then, you just hang tight.

You just try to put up with Blake's teasing for as long as you can until I let you know when it's time. And then, when it *is* time, well then, you let that son of a bitch have it, Donny. Let him have it real good, you hear?"

"Don't worry, Car, I will. I'm's gonna let Blake have *all* of it."

"Well, okay then. But like I said, you gotta keep your cool until I tell you it's time, Donny. Or else I won't be able to do my job. And then it won't matter what Blake says, 'cause we won't be going to Disney World anyhow."

Carson left it at that. The job was done. Donny was sitting quietly next to him, simmering in his hatred for their cousin, a stick of dynamite just waiting to go *boom!*

Carson continued with his plotting. He knew his brother would do as he was told. But what he didn't know was what Jimmy's place was gonna be like once he got there. It all depended. Yet sometimes, love it or hate it, the "unknown" was the one reason, above all the other reasons, why Carson lived the lifestyle he did. It's why he loved robbing homes and venturing through a life of crime. It seemed nothing was more exhilarating than the potential treachery that lay waiting for him in the unknown.

Carson smiled to himself, thinking about that. But then the road got rough, sudden like, and his smile switched places with a look of stern concentration, as he navigated their van up into the mountains. He dodged potholes and skirted drop-offs, weaved around muddy puddles, and over sharp rocks. But it still seemed all his effort was for nothing. Twenty minutes up the road toward Jimmy's place, and Carson got a flat tire.

Then, two hours later, he got the van stuck in a deceptively small, but deep, crater. And goddamn, they only had a mile left to go. Even with Donny's help with pushing the van, it still took them a good twenty-minutes to get out of that hole.

After all the driving, the changing of a flat tire, and then getting stuck, Carson at last got them to Jimmy-James' place, which began as a steep drive down a short canyon, and then out onto the property.

It was midday when they finally arrived, the sun blazing high and dry. They were greeted with all the normal sights: a hardscrabble yard and driveway, Jimmy's shack, the mobile home, rickety barn, roaming chickens, a few rust-buckets here and there, caged hound dogs, animal pens, scattered oak trees, woodpiles, and the wide assortment of nameless yard litter typical of any mountain home.

But Carson and Donny were also greeted with an abnormal and rather curious spectacle. It was right there in the middle of the driveway, in fact, just as they pulled up. Impossible to miss, and impossible to ignore.

That sight was none other than the villain himself. Blake Ramsey.

And not just Blake Ramsey. But a dancing Blake Ramsey, who was wearing nothing but a pair of boots and his tighty-whities, his rolls of naked, hairy fat, glistening with sweat as he jounced up and down on a piece of plywood.

Blake was clogging, clogging pretty damn well, in fact, displaying with effortless ease the traditional Appalachian folk dance. There was a boombox on the ground beside him, attached to an extension cord, and a rooster standing next to that, watching the grotesque-looking human hop about gracefully, all to the twangs of old-school, banjo-picking, Bluegrass music.

They drove by very slowly, the van passing within mere inches of their cousin, and with everyone staring at each other. Carson studied Blake curiously. Donny glared at Blake hatefully. And Blake stared back at both of them blankly, as they scooted on by, and without so much as breaking his dance routine, or even causing him to skip a beat.

"Like I said, Donny," Carson whispered, "you just wait until I tell you it's time."

CHAPTER 20

Sam wasn't really looking for the girl. Not in the way he first intended he would do, that is. The traditional methods of tracking lost people, scouring the land for evidence, hoping to cut sign somewhere—none of these tactics were in the forefront of Sam's thoughts right now.

Too much time had passed for him to find any distinct tracks, and he knew that. And if Emily were dead, he might not even be able to find her corpse, considering how many days had passed since her disappearance. In a lush wilderness like the one he was in, a dead body would get consumed by the forest and its critters in little more than a week's time. Clothes would get scattered, along with bones. Everything would get picked and pulled away in a matter of days. Of course, Sam could always get lucky and find her backpack lying on some bald patch of granite, or maybe one of her shoes, stashed in a bush or in a gulch. Something that would indicate her final route, or resting place. It was something that could still happen, to come across one of her garments, and Sam would keep an eye out for that. But again, he wasn't looking directly for Emily, or for any of her things.

Sam had been doing more thinking about the girl, along with his interesting experiences back in town. And then, of course, the story Jerry had told him about his lost boy, and of those Ramseys...

Jimmy James Ramsey. The man's full name came back to Sam after he'd thought about it for a while. Over the last day or so, a strong notion had lodged itself inside his brain. And that notion was his suspicion of the occurrence of some type of foul play regarding Emily's disappearance. But not necessarily something as simple as the abduction of a young girl hiking in the woods, all by her lonesome self. No. To Sam's way of thinking, whatever foul play that might have happened was more complicated than that.

He traveled in a general, southerly direction, but winded his way through a rough zigzag pattern, down from the mountains and into the thickly wooded lowlands. He let the forest and all its features guide his way, as it did, and would have done, for both man and beast that passed through it.

Sam kept just an easy pace, as he combed his way through the woods, taking in its features and characters, its wildness and desolate calm. Some areas he walked through, he guessed no man had traveled in years, if ever. Parts of this wilderness were untamed and rugged, densely overcrowded, and peacefully beautiful.

But in other places, Sam discovered the trademarks of man. He found an old Buck knife lying on a large stone, deeply concealed among a cluster of beech and sugar maple trees. It looked almost fifty years old. Some hunter must have accidentally left it there, after field dressing his kill. Sam put the knife in his pocket as a souvenir, then moved on.

Later, he found a really old fire ring near a creek, the area overgrown with long green grass. There were numerous rusted tin cans scattered about. An old trapper site, maybe. Or perhaps from loggers of a bygone era.

Along one swath of open granite, closely guarded by a thin grove of pine trees, he found a well-persevered arrowhead, sitting right there, gleaming in the sun. The fluted flint point was made of a whitish-gray stone, quartz of some kind, and about three inches long. Sam picked it up and studied it briefly, smiled, then set it gently back down on the ground.

His observation of the point reminded him of his large cave back home, in the Gila Wilderness, where he'd lived for a few years—and until recently, in fact. Sam could not guess how many similar arrowheads, as well as other Indian artifacts, he and his brothers had left inside that cave over the course of their lives. Dozens, at least. Maybe even over a hundred.

As he moved further down into the lower elevations, the temperature rose slightly. He crossed over creeks, got his feet a little wet, but that was okay. Sam wasn't worried about hypothermia. He avoided climbing over large mountains, just to save his energy, and also, because such routes didn't adhere to the logical order of passage. With ease, Sam simply let the forest guide his way. And it did so with amazing clarity.

By midday, Sam figured he had walked over five miles, a good stretch of distance given his pace, but with many more to go. He wasn't feeling tired, as all that running he'd been doing kept him in good shape. His pack fit well, sat close to his hips, and was fairly light. He avoided overexerting himself, kept his climbing over boulders or crawling under logs to a minimum. By noon, Sam wasn't even hungry yet, so he pushed on.

He had somewhat of a destination in his mind. A rough spot on the map in his head, and in the same general area where Jerry had marked an X on that real map. Using only a compass and his acute sense of direction, Sam did well enough to keep himself in that heading, despite the lay of the land.

At around two-thirty, he stopped in a shady glade and took a break. He set his backpack down, stretched his shoulders and back, his hamstrings, and then his calves and thighs. He drank plenty of water, even consumed one of those fancy sport gels that salesgirl had sold him at the outdoor store back in Asheville. It added a little flavor and some quick calories, nothing to complain about. But Sam was hungry now as well, so he cooked a package of Chili Mac with Beef, from Mountain House.

Not surprisingly, it tasted quite good. Backpacking food had come a long way over the years, Sam reflected. Tastier, more convenient to prepare. It was always nice to have such comforts when bushwhacking, as he was doing now, or even while meandering along some National Park trail for just a few days.

Sam only made a small portion of the meal, as he still wanted to stay light on his feet and not get bogged down with heavy digestion. When he was finished, he sat on the ground and relaxed. He leaned back against a rock and closed his eyes. And then he listened as he waited, his mind's eye focusing deeply on an area about a hundred yards out, and to the southeast of where he was sitting.

There was a reason Sam was doing this—keeping his powers of hearing, even his sixth sense of observation, that same sense that had saved his life more than once over the years—all aimed in a general direction.

And that's because for the last mile or so, before he stopped to take his break, Sam knew someone was following him.

CHAPTER 21

"Alright, then," Sam mumbled. "Don't show yourself."

He got up on his feet and shouldered his backpack, his break now over. He was tired of waiting. Whoever was following him—and Sam had a pretty good idea who that was—apparently had no intention of making himself known.

Well, that was okay. Sam figured he understood the reason.

He struck out again, leaving the pretty glade, and then back into the woods. In no time, he came across a good flowing creek with a high, flat bank running next to it. He followed the creek downstream, a good mile or so, until it opened up into wide stretches of granite containing a few small waterfalls. He kept going, following the creek, and within minutes the forest closed up again, enshrouding the flowing water with a deep and dark grove of trees.

It was here, along the banks of the river, that Sam spotted numerous well-worn game trails. Nothing curious about that. But he got a sense that something more than animals had been using these trails.

Sam looked around, tracking for real now, searching for sign. And within a few minutes, he found some.

On a trail about twenty feet up from the water, and running parallel to the creek, Sam found human tracks, albeit peculiar in one fashion.

About half of the tracks had been made from well-worn boots, almost without tread. Old boots. And the other tracks, curiously enough, had been made from bare feet. Both prints were large, likely made by adult males, and both were about the same size.

Sam did a little more searching of the area, and eventually found other tracks as well, a couple more from boots, although from a different tread, and slightly smaller. The various tracks were scattered across the forest, and they led in all different directions.

Sam paused and looked around, studying the area. People had come here, and quite often, so it seemed. Locals, hunters, Ramseys, *wild men...?*

Sam wasn't sure. But one thing he knew was that he was definitely getting closer to his objective. He was certainly approaching the right area.

Slowly, he moved on, continuing to follow the flow of the small river.

He traveled for another hundred yards. A thin tributary had broken off from the main creek, and Sam pressed on, following that. It took him along the edge of an open field, then back into the forest, where it met up with another tributary coming from the east, and then grew wider. There were all kinds of tracks here, he discovered. Both of animal and humankind.

This part of the forest seemed thinner, and Sam found several old tree stumps, indicating the logging of years past. But selective logging, he concluded, and not of a clear cut variety, which had him thinking the old harvesting had been used for local means, and not commercial.

He paused for a minute and studied the land. He was on a slight grade, ten to fifteen degrees, maybe less. But he got a sense that the mountain was about to bottom out soon.

Sam started thinking about his plan, the one he had concocted a while back. The one that included the use of those wind chimes he had in his backpack.

Also, as he looked down at the ground, he started thinking about his own tracks he was leaving behind.

Sam looked up again, focusing his stare into the trees, wondering. He felt calm though, no sense of hurry or alarm hanging over him. The forest seemed peaceful right now. There was a slight breeze, causing a mild stir in the treetops. Birds were singing in the distance, and that was always an important indicator. If there was one thing Sam knew for certain, it was that birds never sang when a predator was about, stalking its prey—man or otherwise.

Sam felt comfortable. But he knew he had arrived close enough to his destination. And he knew what time it was, too.

It was time for Sam to get to work. Real work, that is. The kind of work that would employ a few of his tracking and sniping abilities, some of his escape and evasion tactics, and many of his skills he'd learned as a youngster from Nali. The skills of the Apache.

Sam left no more tracks.

He made certain of that as he made his way back up the mountain for about a hundred yards. He kept close to some of the more crushed and packed areas of the land, where the game trails were wider and well worn. Then, in a small clearing, a perfect clearing, with a south-facing shoulder open to the wind, Sam found a good tree on the edge of the meadow, from which to hang his wind chimes.

They were medium-sized, a bit heavy, low pitched, and he hung them as high into the tree as he could, yet on the exposed side, same as the meadow, and windward. Then, getting crafty, he cracked a branch from another nearby tree, which he then angled into the limb holding his chimes. From the broken branch, Sam tied a length of fishing line discreetly to it, ran the line along the trunk of the tree, pinned it to the ground using a stick, then ran it up the hill and into the trees for a good thirty yards, until he came to a clump of brush. He backtracked then, making sure to secure the fishing line into the ground using sticks and rocks, just enough to keep the line sitting low, but not restrained.

Sam moved away then, further off into the woods. He could already hear the chimes make their distinct chorus now and then, and that was a good sign.

Trailing into the woods, he ducked under the bottom boughs of a large spruce tree, then took off his backpack. He retrieved a few things from it, then stashed it real good, covering it up with loose debris and deadfall before slipping off again, further away.

Twenty minutes later, Sam had made himself all but disappear. His body was now covered with an array of local foliage, breaking the unnatural contours of his shoulders, hips, and clothing. Every patch of his exposed skin had been painted green and brown. Sam was a walking bush, and nothing more, a master sniper who had used resources from the land to disguise anything and everything human about him. He was now part of the forest.

He moved achingly slowly back to where he had left the fishing line, which was, of course, a well-concealed place that offered him a great view.

Sam buried himself into that area, becoming one with the land, completely disappearing among twigs and leaves, brush and dry grass, undergrowth. He had the end of the fishing line with him, and every so often, when the breeze had stopped, he tugged on it, pulling ever so slightly on the branch it was attached to, in turn making move ever so gently the branch containing the wind chimes.

Sam quietly chuckled to himself. He had never learned how to play a musical instrument. But right now, he thought he was doing just fine.

CHAPTER 22

"Best place to hide something is in plain sight."

That was Flint Ramsey talking, Jimmy-James' pa.

"Goddamn 'Nam taught me that one, son. Ain't no better place than plain sight. That's how them gooks kilt a lot of our boys over thar, don't you know? Got themselves mixed in with some local business or enterprise, blend in with all them others 'cause who in their goddamn right mind would know the fucking difference, eh? Then they'd see to our young American souls, get us all comfy, smoothed over real good with drugs and little brown tits and ass, and maybe a few other things, if you know what I mean. And then, before you knew it—*kaboom!* Out went your fucking lights. Guts and gore and nothing more—'cause you've been kilt in plain sight. So let that be a lesson to you, boy. Now get on over here so's I can tan your goddamn hide."

His old man's speech and subsequent ass-whooping came after Jimmy had been caught hiding Playboy magazines he'd stolen from his pa's dresser. Over the years, low and behold, Flint's words propagated into one of Jimmy-James' hard-learned rules. If he wanted to hide something, hide it *real* good, the best place was always right there in the open, for any and all to see.

But just what was Jimmy-James hiding right now, other than Emily Parker—who, ironically, was not in plain sight?

Currently, Jimmy was hanging out in the old barn across the yard from his shack, doing some thinking. He was drinking moonshine from a Mason jar, and taking his time with consuming a plate of recently smoked venison sausage. Beside him, in plain sight, was an old 1975 International pickup truck, parked right in the middle of the barn.

The vehicle still had its original paint, a dried daisy color. There were patches of rust spotting the fenders and hood, a couple of dents here and there, one long scratch along the side. The tires seemed out of place, being relatively brand new and flared out, as the truck had a slight lift to it and a new suspension system. Under the hood was the strongest thing about the vehicle, thanks to Jimmy's mechanical talents. He had spent the last year rebuilding the engine, going over every damn bolt, gasket, and hose, with a fine wire brush. The truck ran like a hog in heat, and would tear through the mountain roads up there like nobody's business. Even if the outside of the vehicle looked like shit, the engine was a damn good piece of work, of that Jimmy had no doubt.

But in Jimmy's opinion, the engine wasn't the truck's finest feature. Not by a mile.

He strolled over to the rear of the vehicle and then dropped the tailgate. The truck bed was lined with a false bottom, a four inch flat of framed plywood. Stacked on top of that were a few bales of hay.

There was a concealed door on the exposed side of the wooden frame, near the tailgate. Jimmy stooped down and used his knife to pry it out, then reached into the gap between the plywood and the truck bed, and retrieved a length of hidden rope. He pulled the rope through the opening, and out came a long gray canvas bag.

Jimmy adjusted the bag as he set it on the tailgate. Then he zipped it open and stared wondrously at the many bundles of hundred-dollar stacks tucked inside. The little bundles totaled well over a hundred grand the last time he'd counted, which was roughly two weeks ago, under the midnight light of a full-moon, and under the weight of a fifth of bourbon. That had been a good night.

Jimmy did this now and then, the bank man's routine of coming out here in the barn to count all his cash, and in plain sight.

He had no idea what he was going to do with this money, though. That was still a damn mystery to him. But he wasn't too concerned. Just looking at all these tight little stacks of green Franklins seemed to be good enough for now.

It still boggled Jimmy's mind with how much fast money a person could make, all from producing just a small bit of that glorious white dust. His business had been running for less than three months now, and already Jimmy had more currency saved up than all the backbreaking income he'd earned in the course of his lifetime. Hanging sheetrock, framing barns, fixing fences... None of that bullshit work ever paid him much, no siree. Not this much. There was a time when Jimmy tried to grow pot, but he could never get things straight on that. He kept killing his plants with bad soil, or too much water, or never the correct amount of sunlight. Growing weed was too much damn work for Jimmy-James.

But boy, how this crank thing just sprang to life, once he'd turned the tap on it. As it turns out, it ain't so easy hiding a meth lab in *plain sight*. Flint would've known this, despite the sermon he'd given to Jimmy eons ago. It's one of the reasons he built them tunnels, after all. But that was a different time, and a different product.

Jimmy frowned suddenly. He was pretty sure his pa never had to deal with no outside middle-man fronting him seed money for his business, as Carson's connection had done. And Jimmy was absolutely *certain* his pa never had to deal with no low-life negro giving him headaches. But of course, Jimmy was also pretty sure his pa never made this kind of money, either.

He zipped the bag up and stashed it once again into the hidden compartment under the plywood frame, put the little door back in place, then closed the tailgate. He walked back over to his plate of sausage and jar of shine, took a few bites, drank a few sips, then paused to listen.

Blake was out there dancing in the yard, but Jimmy heard something else. It was a vehicle coming down the road. Then the dogs got to barking.

Jimmy took his Mason jar with him as he walked out of the barn, and into the bright light of the day, just in time to see his cousin Carson's black van roll into the yard.

He waited by the barn until his cousin pulled up. Then he walked around to the driver's side.

Carson rolled the window down. "Howdy, Jimmy," he said, smiling like a scoundrel.

Jimmy stared at his cousin, wondering why he was here. There weren't any recent payments scheduled for "Boss-man," as that son of a bitch preferred being called. Jimmy remembered the first time he'd met the guy, a while back it was, at a brewery down in Asheville, as introduced to him by Carson, of course. There was something about the dark-haired weasel Jimmy just couldn't warm up to.

"What's up?" he said.

"Come to give you a message, Jimmy."

Jimmy looked past Carson and at Donny. "Why the hell'd you bring him here?" he asked.

"Aww, Jimmy, you know I can't leave him anywhere."

Jimmy looked again at Carson. "So what's the message, then?"

"Well," Carson began, "seems there's a new sheriff in town. Not really a sheriff, that is, but maybe just as bad. Bad enough, at least." He went on then, telling Jimmy all about the military man known as Sam Nolan, and how he was now up there in the hills looking for the girl. And also, how Sam was apparently curious about the Ramseys, so don't be surprised if he comes snooping around.

Jimmy stood quietly, thinking. He was a little surprised, actually. In all his years of abducting girls off them trails, nobody had ever put out as much time and effort at finding someone as that old Indian had done. Sure, they'd throw up a fuss at first, get a hundred people out there looking in the woods, a few helicopters up in the air. But after a couple weeks of tedious searching, maybe sooner, if the weather turned on them, the whole operation of looking for a lost hiker always came to a fast close.

On a side note, that was Blake's "favorite time of year," as the idiot would say, whenever the search parties stopped looking. He always made a big production of bragging to their abductees that the search was now over, and nobody cared for them anymore, and that never in a million years would anybody ever, ever, come looking for them again. Breathing or not, that was the day those girls truly died.

Jimmy glanced briefly over at Blake, who was still dancing away. Then he looked back at Carson, curious. "How the hell did this Sam guy know about us Ramseys?" he asked.

"Beats me," Carson replied.

Jimmy paused, still thinking. "And why'd you have to come out here to tell me this? You could've just called it in."

Carson looked away. "Had me some trouble down in town," he said. "Nothing too bad. Just need to lay low for a few days, that's all."

Jimmy wasn't sure he was buying Carson's story. He looked again at Donny. The big fool was staring at something in the side door mirror, glowering like a mean old lady. "What's his damn problem?" Jimmy asked.

Carson shrugged. "I don't know. Been complaining about having a bellyache. He probably ate some bad food. You know how he is."

Jimmy looked over at the old single-wide mobile home, then said, "Well, you's can stay over in the trailer. You know the routine." He glanced again at Donny. "But keep him locked up or something. The last time... Lawd, that was a bitch of a scrap." Jimmy chuckled faintly. "And I'll have a talk with Blake, not that it'll do any good." Jimmy spat on the ground, turned, then looked up into the hills, eyes squinting. He stared for a long minute.

"Thanks, Jimmy," Carson said, sounding unsure.

Jimmy looked back at Carson. "I don't suppose you know what this soldier boy looks like?" he asked.

"Well... As a matter of fact."

"So you do?"

"I could point him out in a line," Carson replied. "Got brownish-gray hair, kind of scruffy on the face, taller than average. Not a big guy, just—"

"Yeah, yeah," Jimmy interrupted, "I don't need the fucking book on this fella'. But I'm sure glad you've seen him." He turned then, and let out a sharp whistle. "Blake! Get on over here."

After a minute, Blake arrived, a towering mound of blubber and sweat and not much else. He was breathing heavy, and he just looked at Jimmy, not saying a word, his eyes and affect being all that was needed.

"First," Jimmy began, addressing his brother, "put some goddamn clothes on. Lawd if it ain't hard on the eyes seeing you like this."

Blake didn't reply.

"Second," Jimmy continued, "run on over to Boyer's place. Get him and his brother to come on over here. They'll be around. And tell them to bring their guns. We've got some hunting to do. Don't worry; I'll tell you all about it once you get back here."

Blake nodded.

"Finally," Jimmy said, gesturing a thumb toward Carson, "you're taking him hunting with you. So make sure he's got some decent boots and a rifle."

Carson blinked. "Ah, wait a minute. What was that?"

Jimmy let slip a half-smile. "Now I know you're not gonna start complaining on me, Carson," he said. "Everybody's gotta work 'round here. Ain't no free rides, you know that. So go on now. Park your van over there under that old willow. Get yourselves settled in. There's some of them TV dinners in the freezer." He looked at Donny, smiling. "I know he likes eating them things, don't he? Ain't that right, Donny-boy? You like them TV dinners, don't you?"

Donny looked back, eyes brightening. He gave a curt nod.

"Well, alright, then, let's go," Jimmy said, turning back toward the mountain and staring up into the wooded hills above the property. "I want you boys up there within an hour. There's still plenty of daylight left." After a moment of silence, he swung back around, looking at Blake. "You hear me?"

"I hear you." Blake said. Then Blake added, "'Cept I want to go unga-bunga style. If I'm gonna hunt, I want to unga-bunga."

Jimmy shrugged. "Suit yourself. Just make sure you're up there within an hour, no more. And if you find him, if you find that soldier boy, Blake..." Jimmy paused. "Well, you can bring him back here for a little fun, if he lets you. Or just shoot him in the head and leave him to rot. Makes no difference to me."

Blake smiled, then started clogging again, right there in the dirt. "Unga-bunga," he said, turning around and dancing his way back down the driveway.

CHAPTER 23

Roochie was actually feeling better—physically, that is. The day before, he had taken a nice hot shower over at Myron's crib, which was followed by a painful, yet much needed application of anti-bacterial ointment along the grisly wound of his head. Freckles and Licious had tag-teamed that operation, their maternal genes blossoming out into full bloom, upon having to take care of the miserable-looking white boy. After his cleaning, they fed him a tasty, hot bowl of Campbell's Chicken Soup, then laid him back down on the couch and took turns softly rubbing his back, his head in their laps (earless side up).

Physically, Roochie was feeling mountains better, even with the sharp pain on the side of his head still coming and going, and at unpredictable times. But as for mentally, now, that was a different story.

Mentally, Roochie was a wreck. A few hours ago, Myron had him suited up with some kind of camouflaged military vest that must have weighed at least fifty pounds. The damn thing was stuffed with bullets and gun magazines, a giant metal flashlight, scary-looking Rambo knife, and Lord knew what else. Adding to all the weight was this crazy rifle/machine gun thing strapped to Roochie's shoulder. He'd heard one of the Cuban dudes call it a *Galil*, some Israeli job, completely foreign and completely new to Roochie. The gun was huge, weighed a ton, and Roochie still had no clear idea on how to use it. Sure, he'd been given a quick tutorial by one of the guys. But Roochie had been so frazzled at the time (was still frazzled, in fact), that most of that information went right in one ear, and straight out through, well, the hole in his head.

"I'm about ready to do this, motherfuckers," Myron said, puffing on a cigar Benny the Cuban had given him. He was in a mood, as they had been waiting around for days, or so it seemed. "Time to get this show on the road."

"Wait, are we going out right now?" Steve asked. "It'll be dark soon. I don't see no fucking nightvision shit around here."

"'Course we're not going out right now, fool," Myron replied. "Just saying, is all. Shit's about to get real, and I'm ready. So make sure your shit's ready, too."

Presently, they were all inside a giant metal warehouse within an old industrial part of Charlotte. The whole crew was there, minus the "bitches" and White-Collar, who, not surprisingly, Myron had deemed unfit for this particular occasion.

Along with the normal crew were Benny and six of his Cuban gangbangers. They all looked the same, or so Roochie thought: little wiry dudes in white tank tops, covered in tattoos and gold teeth, wearing gold chains and fat metal watches and other such fashionable bling, circa the late 90s. Except that they too were also wearing military vests and camouflage-styled pants, and handling various assault rifles and knives, which gave them the slight appearance of some Columbian anti-drug task force.

The warehouse was brimming with activity. There were tables set up near the back wall, where everyone was hanging out at. Each table was loaded with gear and ammo, water bottles, assorted bags, and, on one of them, a pair of wireless speakers currently cranking rap music.

The place smelled of grease and sweat and testosterone. Along with the music were the chaotic sounds that came from men tinkering with every type of gun imaginable.

The noise was astonishing—the racking of rifle bolts back and forth, the constant *klickty-clack-klick* of magazines being loaded with bullets. And of course, the sounds of men cracking jokes, laughing, ripping farts, and hollering.

Around the rest of the large building, both inside and out, were parked several vehicles, three of which Myron had nicknamed "The Shermans." These were older model Ford Broncos, tricked out with heavy duty suspension systems and extra wide off-road tires. They had been acquired from Machado's chop shop only hours before, and looked like they would have zero problems escorting the men up into Hillbillyville.

"Listen up, fellas," Myron announced, addressing the crowd. He reached over and turned the music down. "We's heading out at the crack of dawn, and I want all's you motherfuckers to treat this shit like we's fixing to invade fuckin' *I-rack*. Now is not the time for any of you fools to be sipping on 40s or smoking dope. We's gonna need our A-games up there, fo' sure."

Roochie blinked and looked around. He happened to have first-hand knowledge of the fact that at least half of these dudes in the building were already on their way to being drunk and/or stoned.

"Now, I know we's only fixing to kill us a couple of crackers up in the hills," Myron continued, "but you never know what the fuck you's gonna get with them hillbillies. Motherfuckers do like their guns. So we need to keep our fuckin' eyes open and our shit real." Myron kept going, pacing back and forth, preaching like General James Mattis addressing his fellow Marines. "Won't surprise me if some of you motherfuckers don't come back. I'm dead serious now. We's going in deep. Behind enemy lines is what I'm fuckin' talking about."

Everyone stared back at Myron, their faces amazingly calm (except for Steve, who was scowling as usual), their mannerisms seeming oddly ordinary and routine, somehow indicating that for them, all of this pre-battle talk *was* ordinary and routine.

Roochie wished he could say he felt the same—brave, careless, courageous, blissfully ignorant, clueless—whatever the hell these guys were feeling right now would be a whole lot better than what Roochie had going on in his head and body.

What Roochie was feeling was the shock of fear. A weak, jittery sensation in his knees and legs, and something cold and slippery uncoiling inside his stomach. He kept getting the urge to take a loose, runny shit.

Did Roochie want his revenge on that long-haired son of a bitch up there in no-man's-land? Absolutely. And was he still fuming over having one of his ears cut off, then fed to a pig? You're damn right he was. But was he ready to take his feelings to the next level by charging into the heat of battle?

Roochie wasn't so sure about that anymore.

"But here's the thing," Myron continued, "that motherfuckin' honky up there don't even know we's coming. He ain't got a fuckin' clue. Our shit is top secret. We's going up there with surprise on our side. And by the time that hillbilly figures out what the fuck is going on, motherfucker's gonna have him three bullets in his head."

A few of the guys laughed.

"And," Myron continued, "our shit needs to be quick and real, 'cause they's got themselves a kitchen up there, which I *know* we's gonna want to inspect." Myron laughed now, himself. "Knock-knock... It's OSHA. Here we come, bitches. Coming in to check your shit. And you know we's gonna take whatever we find. But like I said, our tactics gotta be real. In and out, like Seal Team Six, motherfuckers."

Something about Myron's plan just seemed a little half-baked to Roochie, which, of course, only added to his mounting anxiety. He knew little, if anything, about staging a tactical assault, and behind "enemy lines" for that matter. But Roochie had enough sense to know that what Myron seemed to have planned—not much, really, other than driving up there with guns blazing—might just be a little too forward. Roochie thought that maybe, a better idea, would be to at least do some of that sneaky recon stuff, the kind of shit he'd seen in television documentaries featuring real Navy Seals, before pulling any triggers.

"I know this place ain't no fuckin' five-star Hilton," Myron continued, gesturing to the metal warehouse, "but you motherfuckers are just gonna have to hang. Get your shit together, then find yourself someplace 'round here to crash, 'cause we's fixing to leave fuckin' *ear-ly*."

"But what about dinner?" P-Dog asked.

"Yeah," Pounds added. "I'm getting hungry."

"Stop sweating, niggas," Myron said. "I gotcha covered. Steve, you and Pounds run out and get us some pizzas. Get like forty of 'em. And make 'em Supremes, with all them fuckin' toppings. This is my treat, motherfuckers."

"Man, why do I gotta go get the pizzas?" Steve grumbled. "I ain't no errand boy."

Myron gave Steve a cold look, a look that simply shut the man up. Then he turned the music back on and puffed on his cigar.

That was it. The orders were given, and all they had left to do now was sit and wait.

Wait for death, Roochie thought.

In truth, Roochie didn't want to go back up in the hills again. And not just because he was fearing for his life, knowing that within a gun battle in the magnitude of what this was sure to be, he would become nothing but cannon fodder. But because Roochie was dreading going back to that place of his recent trauma. The place where some fat inbred used his massive belly to squeeze Roochie into the rails of a pigpen, while another, just as twisted inbred, sliced his ear off with a Rambo knife. And the same place where Roochie was forced to watch a grimy little hog consume that ear, all in one swift gulp.

Even with the hopes of possibly surviving his impending doom, as well as fulfilling his revenge, Roochie just couldn't get past the loathing notion of going back up there again. What he needed right now was something strong to loosen his nerves, or something wicked, to put a fire under his ass, regardless of Myron's stay-sober orders. Sure as shit, what Roochie needed right now was to be high as a kite.

He hauled his gear—all fifty-plus pounds of it—over to a dark corner of the building and then curled up into a ball, making himself disappear. Most of the guys were still hanging around by the tables, laughing and joking, playing with their guns, getting their shit ready, seemingly unfazed, as they listened to music and waited for the pizzas to arrive. But Roochie had no appetite for any of that. He had no appetite for anything, really. He just wished that this day, and the following day, and whatever days after that, would soon be over. And until then, he might just have to find something hot and dirty to pump into his body.

CHAPTER 24

What the hell is unga-bunga? Carson wondered, as he parked the van under the willow tree, just as Jimmy had suggested. *And do I really want to know?*

Carson shook his head, figuring that no, he didn't want to know, and that it was best to just forget about that right now. What he needed to do was take a minute to think about his situation.

He and Donny rummaged around the van for a few minutes, gathering some personal items, before heading into the single-wide mobile home. They dumped their belongings on a couch in the front room, then Carson looked around.

The place was ancient, perhaps over fifty years old, maybe the first of its kind, Carson didn't know. It was on the cusp of being dilapidated, a flaccid heap of warped walls with a sagging foundation and numerous spots on the ceiling, showing where the rain had found its way in over the years. It seemed to Carson that there had been carpet the last time he'd stayed here. But that was all gone now, and for reasons he could only guess at. Just a plywood floor was all, with black, blotchy stains here and there, and mouse turds piled in some of the corners. But the dank, wet-mold aroma lingering in the trailer was still present, same as always. And the windows were still fogged over with decades of dust and grime, giving the appearance that it was overcast outside—which, incidentally, it was.

The only bright side to the trailer was that it provided Carson and Donny with the basic essentials of a decent shelter: beds, a working bathroom, and a refrigerator supposedly stocked with a few provisions.

Carson wondered about that. His brother was most likely feeling hungry right about now.

He checked the fridge, found that it was empty, save for a couple of random bottles of old condiments. Then Carson looked in the freezer.

Just like Jimmy had said, there were TV-dinners in there. But they looked pretty damn old. They were covered with an inch of frost. Freezer burn was definitely in the ingredients for these puppies.

Carson took a dinner out and brushed it off in the sink. It was a Hungry Man, Salisbury Steak, not a bad choice. Then he pulled another and cleaned it off as well, revealing it to be the Beer-Battered Chicken. Even better.

Of course, the dinners didn't really matter to Carson. He wasn't planning on eating right now, seeing that he had no appetite. And Donny would consume just about anything without complaining.

"You ready to eat?" Carson asked.

"Okay," Donny replied, after hesitating. Donny was standing in the middle of the room, twiddling his thumbs, literally, making it painfully clear to Carson that he didn't know what to do with himself.

"Go have a seat on the couch," Carson said. He turned the oven on and took the dinners out of their respective boxes, both being for Donny (they were only Hungry Mans, after all, and not Hungry Beasts), poked holes in the plastic covers with a fork, and then put them in the oven. Then Carson closed the door, leaned back against the counter, and started thinking.

He knew something like this was going to happen. In his gut, he just knew it. It was the all-expected wrench in his plan. A mild inconvenience, sure, but a pain in the ass all the same. Carson wasn't surprised, not one bit. Because he also knew that setbacks such as these came with the territory of his lifestyle.

Let's be clear here: Carson had no qualms about following Blake and the Boyer brothers up into the woods to hunt for Sam. He even thought he might enjoy it. It would be a pleasant break from the normal humdrum, and he always liked to go hunting. The problem was that, as always, Carson was eager to get his own job done and over with. His whole life he'd been plagued with ambition. And, although this ambition had not always (if ever) directed Carson onto a sensible highway, it was still there nonetheless, plaguing him.

As such, Carson's ambition had recently put into his mind the hope that he'd be able to sneak down into them tunnels sometime today, get the information he needed for Boss-man, tend to whatever wounds Donny had received in his epic battle with Blake, and then get the hell out of there before nightfall. This was the illusion that had worked itself into Carson's thoughts that afternoon, and all thanks to his ambition. And this illusion had been completely shattered the moment Jimmy volunteered Carson for the upcoming hunting trip.

"I don't know how long I'll be out there," Carson said, more to himself, really, and less to Donny, whose mind was no doubt stuck somewhere between eating food and murdering their cousin. "So you're just gonna have to sit tight, Donny. But maybe, if we're lucky, you'll get your chance at Blake soon as we get back. That'll be a good time. He'll be tired, that's for sure."

"Okay," Donny said robotically, staring at his twirling thumbs.

"But if it don't happen today," Carson continued, "then we'll need to figure on staying the night in this shithole."

"Okay," Donny repeated.

They waited for the dinners to be done, and for Blake to get back with the Boyer brothers. While he waited, Carson explored the little trailer, looking for anything interesting, but finding nothing other than your typical run-of-the-mill artifacts of human habitation. It appeared to him that sometime long ago, an old woman had been staying here—probably Jimmy's ma, taking a break from her nutty husband and her nutty kids—as Carson found an assortment of old lady effects, such as clothing, hairbrushes, and perfume. There was musty furniture throughout the trailer, a few cardboard boxes stuffed with kid toys in one room, and a box of photo albums in another. Otherwise, the place was more or less empty.

It took about an hour for the TV-dinners to get done. And when they were, as Carson was pulling them out of the oven, that's when he heard Blake coming down the road.

Carson peeked out the little kitchen window. He saw Blake zoom by on an ATV. He watched as his cousin drove over behind the house, parked, hopped off, then went inside a small shed. A few minutes later, the Boyer brothers pulled up in a 4x4.

"Looks like it's show time," Carson said. He peeled the plastic foil off the dinners, then took them to Donny, who was still sitting on the couch. "This oughta fill you up," he added.

"Thanks, Car," Donny said, a little less gloomy now.

"I know you want to get at that boy. But like I said, you're just gonna have to wait."

"I'll wait, Car." Donny drove a fork into one of the little steaks. He blew on the slab of meat for a second, then popped the whole thing into his mouth and looked up. "Like you tol' me."

"Good," Carson said.

Just then, there was a single knock on the door, and then Jimmy walked in. He had a pair of boots in one hand and a double-barrel shotgun in the other, along with a bandolier containing extra ammo. "Got you a few things for the hunt," Jimmy said. He set the boots and bandolier on a chair, then leaned the shotgun against the wall. "Don't know if you need the boots, but there they are, just in case. Might be big, but they'll fit 'nough. Gets mighty slippery up there near the crick, where I'm sure you'll be heading. And there's snakes, too." Jimmy looked at Donny and smiled. "I knew you liked them dinners."

Donny smiled back, nodding.

"How 'bout we throw the ball 'round when you're done?" Jimmy said.

Donny kept nodding.

This was something Carson actually appreciated about his cousin. Jimmy was genuinely fond of Donny. He always seemed to find time to play with the big fool, and he talked nicely to Donny as well, at least to the extent to which Jimmy was capable of talking nicely to anyone. It was as if he viewed Donny as his prized dog, and not one of those poor mangy mutts he kept caged up behind the trailer, on account that they never learned to leave the chickens alone.

The last time they were here, Carson remembered, Jimmy and Donny had a blast tossing the football around. Donny couldn't throw a pass to save his life, and his ability to catch one was even worse, but boy did he love trying. And boy, could Jimmy throw that damn ball. That's pretty much what that game amounted to: Jimmy launching the football as far as he could, Donny running and laughing and falling down, a complete idiot, as he tried to catch it. Then Jimmy chuckling as he watched Donny schlep the ball back to him. It was a game of fetch, that's all, and they both had a great time playing it.

"Eat your food," Jimmy said, "then come on out to the barn. We'll have us some fun." He looked at Carson then. "And you can come out right now. Them boys are ready to go. And Blake, well... he'll be out soon, like it or not."

"Alright, Jimmy," Carson said, picking up the boots and looking them over.

"Also," Jimmy added, with a serious look in his eyes, "you be sure to stay by Blake or the boys. In case you've forgotten, we've got us some nasty traps 'round here. So don't be wandering off."

"Oh, I remember," Carson said, not really remembering.

"Well, alright then. Get your stuff and let's go." Jimmy looked at Donny and winked. "And I'll see you in a few minutes, big boy."

"I'll see you in a few minutes, big boy," Donny repeated dumbly.

Jimmy shook his head and laughed, then walked out.

Carson quickly switched his shoes with the boots. Then he picked up the shotgun, inspected it briefly, put the bandolier over his shoulder, and looked at his brother. Donny was staring back at him, frozen in time, catching flies with his mouth.

Carson didn't say anything. He just nodded and then walked out the front door.

*   *   *

"Hurry the fuck up!" Jimmy shouted. They were still waiting for Blake to come out and join them. The door of the shed was shut, so Carson didn't know what Blake was doing in there, other than getting ready for the hunt. But he had a suspicion his cousin was also getting ready for that thing he called "unga-bunga"—whatever the hell that was.

"Who we looking for now?" Clyde Boyer asked, in his thick and high-pitched southern twang. "Blake said somethin' 'bout a military man."

"Military man?" his brother Wayne asked. Wayne Boyer's lower lip was pushed out with a fat wad of tobacco, looking like he'd recently been punched in the jaw. He spat on the ground. "I thought we's going after another girl."

"That's right," Jimmy replied. "Just a soldier boy—no girl. But Carson here knows what the man looks like. And if you find him, you boys can do whatever the hell you want with him... before you kill him, that is."

Clyde looked at his brother and smiled, but Wayne's face remained expressionless. They were both scrawny looking men, wearing a mixture of faded Levis and old tattered flannels. Clyde had a long brown beard, and on his head was a felt fedora. His eyes were small and pig-like, not like his brother's, which were sharp and cunning, resembling those of a wily coyote.

"Whatever happened to that last girl?" Wayne asked, staring suspiciously at Jimmy. "I ain't never got a taste of her, by the way."

Carson's attention instantly peaked. He listened carefully now, curious about Jimmy's answer.

Jimmy gave Wayne a hard, threatening stare. "Don't you fucking worry about what happened to that girl. She ain't any of your goddamn business."

Wayne quickly dropped the subject. He turned away, spat on the ground again, then looked over at the shed.

"What the hell's taking him so long?" Clyde asked.

"Let's go, Blake!" Jimmy shouted. He walked over to the shed, pounded on the wall, then walked back to the men.

A minute later, the door of the shed slid open and Blake walked out.

Carson stared at his cousin, somewhat baffled by what he was seeing. For the second time today, Blake's appearance suspended Carson's belief.

"Uhhhh," Blake groaned, staring at the ground as he walked slowly toward them.

Carson noticed Blake was barefoot. Going against conventional wisdom, the man had nothing to protect his feet from sharp rocks, pointy sticks, the slippery ground, and snakes. That was only one curiosity, Carson thought, as he studied the rest of his cousin's appearance.

The only thing Blake was wearing was a single-piece poncho, made from what Carson guessed was faded deer leather, and a matching leather belt tied at the waist. The poncho went as far down as Blake's knees and was split along the sides to allow for flexible mobility. It was covered in charcoal illustrations of caveman-like stick figures and stick animals, along with a few round, screaming faces. The artwork looked like some five-year-old's interpretation of a terrible nightmare.

The rest of Blake, that which was more or less exposed—his arms, face, hair, legs, butt cheeks, genitals—were covered in a filthy black muck. Except that there were two long crimson streaks trailing down from his eyes, as if he'd been crying tears of blood.

A shiver ran through Carson. He wondered if indeed it was blood on his cousin's face.

Blake was carrying a rifle in one hand and a wooden spear in the other, the same spear Carson had seen him skewer a hog with last year. "Unga-bunga," Blake mumbled from deep in his throat, as he staggered forward.

Unbeknownst to Carson, but what he would learn soon enough was that this was the only manner in which Blake would talk to all of them for the entire time they were out hunting. He would use a dialect of his own whacky imagination, a made up language consisting of grunts and multisyllabic gibberish. It was the unga-bunga language, of course.

"Looks like rain is on the way," Jimmy said, looking into the sky. "You boys better get up there."

"Umga-doonga," Blake replied.

Jimmy ignored his brother (and so did the Boyer brothers, Carson noticed with amazement), and headed over toward the barn.

Blake turned to Carson. "Funga doh mooga?"

It was a question, Carson could tell. He heard it in Blake's tone.

"Ah…" Carson began, trying to think of a response, but then quickly giving up.

"Scoma boowallawalla," Blake said, this time to the Boyers.

Clyde and Wayne glanced at each other, blinked, then looked back at Blake.

"Unga-bunga," Blake said, turning now toward the hills behind the property. He shoved his spear into the air, and announced again, only louder, "Unga-bunga!" then started walking toward the trees.

The Boyer brothers slowly fell in line, following Blake. And then Carson followed them, shaking his head and thinking, *Really? Just what the hell have I gotten myself into?*

CHAPTER 25

The weather was turning. Rain was on the horizon, Sam could tell. Over the last hour, the wind had kicked up and dark gray clouds had rolled in above.

The wind chimes rang constantly now, without Sam's help. He just sat back in his hide and waited, hoping something would come his way.

He still felt a little foolish with this idea of his, and wondering if he was wasting his time. What were his chances of luring someone or something over to him right now? And besides, if he really put his nose to the grindstone, Sam knew he could find where those Ramseys were living, if indeed that was what he wanted to do. So why then was he sitting in the trees, waiting?

Like always, it came back to Sam's gut. His gut was telling him that this was the course of action he needed to take, regardless of how he felt about it. And also, there was that suspicion lingering in his mind, and maybe, just maybe, he was now in the position to test it.

Even so, he waited for hours. The afternoon came and went. His legs began to cramp up. The cold ground below had seeped in through his clothes and skin and then settled into his bones, causing him to shiver slightly. The wind blew stronger, and the chimes rattled and sang. He was feeling like it was going to be a long, long day.

But then Sam spotted something, which instantly focused his awareness. Two does suddenly ran into the clearing ahead of him, paused, looked back behind them, before skittering off further up the mountain. They moved right past Sam, passing within twenty yards, and they didn't seem to notice him or the wind chimes. Clearly, there was something else on their mind.

Sam knew the does had been pushed up out of the woods by something. He waited and watched.

Several minutes passed, the wind blowing in surges, frequent and strong.

Sam saw them then. He saw the men creeping slowly out of the tree line, guns in hands, their faces alert. One of them had a curious disposition about him.

They came into the clearing and stopped a good fifty yards out from Sam. There were four of them—three white-trash looking boys, and one weird-looking man, who stood taller and bigger than all the others, and who was dressed in a peculiar outfit of leather hide. All four were holding rifles of some sort, but Sam had the feeling they weren't hunting deer.

The men were talking among themselves. But it was too far to hear what they were saying. Sam considered looking through his binoculars to get a better view, but decided against it. Even though he couldn't hear their speech, the men were close enough to notice the slightest of movements made by Sam.

Within seconds, they stopped their chattering, and then the men looked in Sam's direction. They looked right at him, in fact.

A person with lesser nerves might have panicked at that moment, but Sam held strong. The men had heard, and perhaps had now seen, the wind chimes. Sam just needed to keep his cool and wait, which was something the Army had taught him how to do. And pretty damn well, at that.

The men walked closer, crossing the clearing, as they approached the tree holding the chimes. Sam dug in, making himself feel smaller, pushing his body closer to the land.

"What in the hell is that?" one of them said in a rich southern drawl.

"Them's chimes," another one replied, stepping closer. "Uncle Joe's got 'em on his porch."

The big man stepped forward, reached up, and yanked the wind chimes off the tree.

Sam could see him clearly now. He was a strange-looking fellow, with a terrible scar on his mouth from a cleft lip. He was wearing a leather poncho of some sort, which was decorated with black, primitive style drawings, some of which appeared to be howling faces. He was a filthy creature, with mud all over his body. And he had a foul, sour odor, clinging to him, the gusts of wind bringing his smell right up to Sam. There were red streaks on the man's face as well, coming down from his eyes. And his eyes were cold and gray. Altogether, he looked like a wild man!

"Well, now, what in the hell are those doing out here?" one of them said. Then he spat on the ground and looked around. He had a wad of chew in his mouth and a curious look on his face.

"Ingo moo waka seetoo," the big man said.

It was a weird language, nothing Sam had ever heard before. And he was pretty good at identifying foreign languages. That was something else the Army had taught him.

"Will you speak English for once, goddamnit!" the other man barked. "Nobody here knows what the hell you's talking about."

"Gonga moo ga," the big man replied.

"Jesus Christ, what in goddamn hell is wrong with you, Blake?" The man with the thick accent seemed flustered. He turned away and started scanning the clearing, apparently looking for something.

Then the big, wild-looking man turned and looked around as well. He looked into the trees, right where Sam was hiding, in fact. It was almost as if he and Sam had made eye contact, but Sam had faith in his camouflage. He didn't so much as blink, though. He even stopped breathing.

"I don't see nobody 'round here. Maybe some dumb hunter put those things there... Though I cain't figure out as to what for."

"Mogo wannawanna."

"Oh, for crying out loud! This is a waste of time. Jimmy's plain wrong—we ain't got nobody to hunt out here. And goddamn if it ain't about to rain. I'm going back." The man turned and walked away from the group, heading back to the tree line. Seconds later, the man with the tobacco in his mouth followed suit, and a minute after that, so did the third guy—the one who had not said a word, but who appeared to Sam as being anxious and uncomfortable.

But the big man stayed behind. He stood there for several minutes, not much more than sixty feet from Sam, looking all around, studying the landscape. He even sniffed at the wind. That surprised Sam, who was now glad he wasn't hiding upwind from the guy.

The man stood there for a long time, as if not quite convinced he was alone. But eventually, slowly, he turned and walked back into the trees, following the path the other men had taken.

Sam waited. He didn't think he'd been detected, but the way in which that man had stood for so long, and so calmly... It was as if he knew Sam was here.

A rumble of thunder rattled the distant horizon. Then, seconds later, intermittent drops of rain started to come down. But Sam continued to wait.

He waited in the cold and in the rain for at least ten minutes before he made his first move, which was an agonizingly slow stretch of his right arm. After this, he moved his other arm, and then he subtly shifted his torso and legs, letting his blood flow to distant parts of his body, and letting the subsequent tingling sensations subside, before he uncoiled further. Like a snake, Sam cautiously withdrew his body out of his cover. And then he slowly pulled back further into the trees, a moving shadow of deep green foliage against the hillside.

Sam's suspicion..? It had tested out straight as an arrow. They had come looking for him. And that's exactly what he thought would happen.

CHAPTER 26

Blake had caught up to them before they made it back to the property. He was still carrying the wind chimes, and Carson had no fucking clue why. But then again, this was Blake, master of all-things weird and unexplained.

Jimmy and Donny were standing under the covered porch of the little house, sheltered from the rain, when they all got there. There was a football lying on the ground nearby. Donny looked tired, but interested in what Jimmy was doing. He was standing next to Jimmy, watching, as the man tended something on a grill. They both looked up as Carson and the others approached.

"Well," Jimmy said, "did you find anything?" His face showed obvious disappointment.

It was coming down hard now, so Carson and the Boyer brothers found dry spots under the porch. Blake remained standing in the rain, in a small puddle of mud, in fact, staring dumbly at Jimmy while holding up the wind chimes.

"Ain't nobody on that mountain," Clyde said. "We looked all 'round. Didn't find no tracks, and no sign of that man you's mentioned."

Jimmy scowled. "What the hell you got there, Blake?"

No one said anything, as Blake just stood in place, quietly holding up the chimes.

Jimmy stepped off the porch and walked to his brother. "What in the fuck is this about?" He took the chimes from Blake and studied them. "Where'd you find these?"

"We found 'em up there in the woods, hanging in a tree," Clyde said. "Don't make no sense, I know. But, well... They's just silly chimes, is all."

Jimmy looked at Clyde. "Silly chimes," he repeated sarcastically.

"What, Jimmy?" Clyde said with a shrug. "That's what they are. Ain't no reason for 'em, I know. But what the goddamn hell? They's just porch chimes, and nothing else."

"You damn fool," Jimmy said, glancing up into the trees. He stared for a long second, silence coming down on all of them, along with the rain. "Look at these things," Jimmy said, turning back to Clyde. "These fucking things are brand new."

"Okay..." Clyde said, still missing the point.

But Carson thought he now had an idea what Jimmy was thinking.

"You goddamn idiots," Jimmy said, tossing the chimes into the mud. "That son of a bitch up there—and he is up there, you can bet your damn lives on it—he planted those fucking things so's he could get *you* to come to *him*."

There was a pause, and then Clyde said, "Well, why in the hell would he do that? Besides, we ain't seen him. He never showed hisself to us. It ain't like he was hunting us, Jimmy. We was hunting him."

Jimmy stepped closer to Clyde, anger swelling out of the pores of his face. "He did that, you damn fool, so he could trail your dumb asses right on back here."

There was another stretch of silence, and then Jimmy turned to Blake. "You should've known this," he said.

Blake smiled in reply.

"You did know, didn't you?"

Blake remained silent and smiling.

Jimmy shook his head. Then he looked back into the woods. "Goddamn idiots. I bet he's up there right now, looking down on us. You fools fell right into the man's plan."

"Well, Jimmy," Wayne said, "what the hell do you want us to do about it? You want us to go back up there? 'Cause I will."

Jimmy waited, then said, "Not right now. Not tonight. It's getting dark... Cold and rainy... And he's up there in all of that. Let's just let him sit tight. He'll be miserable as a wet coon, come morning. And that's when we'll go get him. But this time we'll bring the dogs with us."

"Well, alright then," Clyde said.

After another pause, Jimmy turned to the men and gave them a brief rundown. "Clyde, Wayne, you boys head on home. But I want you back here in the morning, first thing. And make sure you bring some of the others. I want my kin up here, when we's go looking for that man. We'll get him tomorrow, you can bet your asses on it. Then we'll have us a good old time."

Clyde looked at Wayne and nodded. "Alright then," he said, and then they both walked over to their truck, got in, and slowly drove away.

In that moment, Blake had somehow disappeared. Carson looked around, trying to see where his cousin had gone, then finally spotted him over by the shed.

Blake was naked now, his poncho lying in the mud, and he was sitting on his ATV. He started it up, then drove off as well, across the yard and then onto a small trail running into the forest, next to the road that led away from the property. In seconds, Blake disappeared once again, gone into the woods, the angry growl of his ATV fading off in the distance.

"Where's he going?" Carson asked, his mind ever-always looking for the best time to search for the girl.

Jimmy turned to Carson and gave him a funny look. "How the hell should I know?"

. . .

Sam had followed the men through the forest for a good half-mile, keeping back at least a hundred yards. He tracked their steps, even though he heard some of their chatter along the way, which made things easier for him.

He followed the men like a faint shadow, down the canyon and through the woods, up until he came across a nice-looking waterfall. It wasn't a fast-flowing stretch of water, just a trail of glistening silver that dropped thirty feet down a wall of granite, and ending in a black pool, which was surrounded by ferns and mossy stones. Not far from this pleasant place, Sam found the old and rusty moonshine distiller, half-covered with ivy and brush.

This was the place the old man Jerry had warned him about. He was now in the area where Flint Ramsey had supposedly placed some of his traps. From that point on, Sam moved with careful ease.

Slowly, he made his way further down the canyon, stepping lightly along steep ridgelines and off-trail terrain, aware of the increasing darkness enveloping him, and the cold and wet rain badgering his comfort. But Sam took his time in the growing dark and unpleasant conditions, keeping a wary eye out for booby traps, some of which were man-killers, as Jerry had explained.

None of this was new for Sam. It had been a long time, sure, but his skills of quietly navigating through a world of increasing danger were always there.

In due time, Sam found his way to where he would spend the rest of the night. It was a small granite outcrop, sitting near the bottom of the canyon. The spot was fairly exposed, bereft of woodland cover, and it offered Sam an outstanding view of what he was now guessing to be the home of the Ramseys.

It was dark now, almost completely dark. Sam carefully retrieved his ATN Binox thermal binoculars from a pouch, and then slowly glassed the property. He didn't see anybody, but he observed, and studied quite thoroughly, all the important details.

He noticed the outlines of a small house, with a recently used grill sitting out front, and on what looked to be a porch. Next to the house was a single-wide trailer, a large barn across from that, a couple of vehicles, a few random sheds and woodpiles here and there, and all of it surrounded by odds and ends, being your typical junk not uncommon to backwoods properties such as this. And none of it was more than two hundred yards away from him.

Sam pulled the binoculars away from his face and stared at the darkened land, giving himself a minute to think. Then he scanned the property once again and noticed the old van parked under a tree next to the trailer. He couldn't tell if the van was black or not, as thermal vision didn't provide him with such detail. But Sam was fairly convinced with what he was seeing—thus solidifying his suspicions, and, by now, his running theory.

He settled in. It would be a long, cold night, that's for sure. But Sam wasn't in the position to move out just yet. He needed more information. This was the place, though. He was pretty damn sure of it. And the only questions that remained were where they were hiding Emily Parker. And if she was still alive.

CHAPTER 27

Roochie was lit up.

Fuck you, Myron Weathers. To hell with you and your stupid rules of the night. No getting drunk or high, my ass. And before we're about to go on this mission of getting our dicks shot off? Those were Roochie's thoughts the night before, and they'd propelled him into his own mission of getting the highest he'd been in his life.

One of the Cubans—Jose, or maybe it was Jorge—had been the first to hook Roochie up. He got a line of crystal meth from that dude, and every grain went right up Roochie's nose.

A few minutes later, he'd smoked some dope with Cookie behind one of the "Shermans" out in the parking lot. After they'd finished their joint, they found five unopened cans of beer in the backseat of one of the Cuban's cars, along with a baggie containing four blue pills, which they assumed were Speed. Between the two of them, the pills and beers were gone in minutes.

An hour or so after that, P-Dog and Pounds each gave Roochie a pot brownie those big boys had baked, and seemed to always have on them, for snacks and whatnot.

Finally, deep in the small hours of the night, Roochie made friends with a sketchy-looking Cuban guy named Hector. That dude had the real shit. Pure ice, liquefied via his silver spoon and lucky lighter, and all of that white gold went straight up into Roochie's arm, just like Novacaine.

So what time was it now?

Christ, Roochie didn't know.

And what day was it?

He didn't have a goddamn clue.

But most of all, who in the hell was he?

He was Batman, that's who.

Or maybe he was Superman. A superhero of some kind, that's for sure. A superhero who used a big-ass gun and who carried an army vest loaded with bullets and terror. G.I. Joe, that's who he was! Sometime in the night, Roochie turned into G.I. fucking Joe.

There was a vague recollection of primal fear swimming way in the back of Roochie's head, but he wasn't sure what that was all about. Right now, he was loaded for bear, standing near an open door and watching the sun come up, and feeling like he could take on the whole damn world.

"Saddle up, niggas!" Myron turned the music on. He cranked the volume way the hell up, then re-lit the cigar he'd started the night before. "It's time to do this shit!"

It *was* time. And Roochie was *ready*. He hadn't slept a wink all night, but that was okay, because right now, it felt like four gallons of Pete's Coffee were flowing through his veins.

Slowly but surely, the place came alive with a mixture of black and Cuban dudes, groaning and hawking morning phlegm, all pulling their shit together, fumbling with their gear, rubbing their eyes and waking up. Roochie wondered what the hell was taking them so long. He'd been ready to go for hours now.

"Get your shit on, and let's get out of here," Myron said.

"But what about breakfast?" P-Dog asked.

"Yeah," Pounds added. "I'm hungry."

Myron blinked. "Fuck you, niggas! You can eat your damn breakfast once this shit is over."

Pounds and P-Dog exchanged looks as they grumbled and whined.

"Fat-ass bitches act like you's starving," Myron continued. He looked up then, addressing everyone once again. "Yo, listen up. Once we get rolling, motherfuckers best keep your damn guns down. Last thing we need is some pig to pull our assess over. We's on a top secret mission. So let's keep it that way."

"Yeah!" Roochie shouted. *Did I just say that?* he asked himself.

"That's right," Myron continued, glancing over at Roochie. "And in case I need to remind you," he added, pointing at the hole in Roochie's head, "this is the kind of shit we're dealing with. Damn hillbillies cut my nigga's ear off, and now it's time to pay the fuckin' doctor bill. Speaking of which, did you put them power tools in the trucks, Benny?"

"Fuckin' A," Benny replied. He racked the slide on his AK-47, emphasizing the general mood.

"That's what I'm talking about," Myron said, laughing. "It's time to do this, niggas. Get all's your shit ready, and let's go. We're leaving in ten minutes, and I'm setting my motherfuckin' watch."

"Word up!" Roochie shouted. But this time he knew that he said it. He was aiming his rifle at a wall and looking down its sights, picturing in his fuzzy brain the look on that hillbilly's face, after being surrounded by him and Myron, and all these other badass dudes. Just like Myron had said: it was time to pay the bill, motherfucker.

CHAPTER 28

Carson had had a rough night. He didn't get much sleep, as he'd been constantly on the lookout for Blake. The son of a bitch never came back, and there was no telling where he was. He just drove off into the woods, and in the rain, and buck-naked at that. What a weird guy.

Sure, Carson had tried to get some sleep, but he failed miserably. He'd curled up on the front couch with a blanket, figuring it was a good place for him to hear Blake's ATV, in case the asshole came back, which he didn't. But every little sound kept Carson from falling into a deep sleep. Every little midnight creak, thump, dog bark, or strong gust of wind, which actually shook the entire trailer whenever it blew by. Then there was that constant scratching at the kitchen window from a branch on the willow tree outside. Sounded like a cat trying to get in. Finally, after hours of this touch and go, sleep/no sleep nonsense, the rain ceased and then the roosters started crowing. That's when Carson simply gave up.

He was dead tired. But there was nothing he could do about that right now. What he needed was a little crank in his system to get him going. Carson was out of luck in the pharmaceutical department, but maybe there was some coffee around here somewhere.

He got up off the couch and sighed. It was cold, dammit. He shivered, put on his jacket, started looking through the tiny kitchen, then found a half-empty jar of Folgers Instant Coffee tucked away in a cupboard. He took the jar out and opened it. The coffee looked twenty years old, and it probably was. Carson sniffed the grounds, then shrugged. *It'll have to do.*

He found an old teapot, boiled some water, and in no time, had a steaming cup of instant brew under his nose. It tasted a bit stale, but smelled good enough, so it might work. Carson didn't think caffeine had an expiration date.

While he drank his Folgers, he thought about his predicament. He was thinking hard and serious about ditching this job of looking for that girl. Things had already gotten way too complicated, and within the next hour or so, Jimmy would round everyone up to go on the big hunt. For sure, Carson would be expected to join in with that fun, since he was the only one who knew what Sam looked like—not counting Donny, of course, because no one ever counted Donny. And the hunt would only extend Carson's stay up there, which was something he didn't want. What he wanted was to get his information and then get the hell out of Dodge.

The problem was that Blake was nowhere to be found, and he was part of the plan. And also, Carson wasn't quite sure where the hell Jimmy was. The last time he'd seen him was when Jimmy sauntered over to the big oak tree after eating his spare ribs, a bottle of whiskey in his hand, and then down the shaft he went, into the tunnels. A light hadn't come on in the old house all night long, so as far as Carson knew, Jimmy was still down there, underground. Which was exactly where Carson needed to be.

Yeah, maybe he *should* forget about this job. He would just have to come up with a good excuse to tell Boss-man.

Carson drank the last swallow of his coffee, started making another cup, when suddenly, from off in the distance, he heard the distinct whine of an ATV.

Fucking, finally, he thought. He stopped with what he was doing and looked out the kitchen window. The growl of the ATV got louder, and then, after a few seconds, Blake zoomed on by, the same as he'd done the day before.

Carson leaned sideways into the window, pressing his face against the glass, trying to get a better view. His cousin was still naked. But it looked like the mud he'd wiped all over himself had been cleaned off. He was white as a piece of Wonder bread. The weirdo probably spent the night sleeping on the banks of some pond or river. *Jesus Christ, he's gotta be cold.*

Carson watched as Blake got off the ATV, then went into the little shed and closed the door.

It's time! he thought.

Or was it?

Carson wasn't sure. Maybe it was. He thought it was. He hoped it was. Hell, it had to be.

Suddenly, he raced down the hall and barged into the room Donny was sleeping in.

"Wake up, Donny," Carson said, vigorously shaking his snoring brother, who was lying on the bed in an impossible tangle of blankets. "Wake the hell up!"

Donny jerked and groaned, slapped lamely at Carson's hands, then groaned some more.

"Wake up, Donny!" Carson repeated. He dropped the tone and volume of his voice and whispered into Donny's ear, "*I think it's time.*"

Donny blinked awake. He sat up and looked at Carson. "It's time?" he asked.

Carson nodded. "That's right. I think it's time, Donny."

"It's time," Donny said loftily, his gaze drifting away. He blinked again and looked back at Carson. "Time for what?" he asked.

"Dammit, Donny! What the hell time do you think I'm talking about?"

Donny stared at his brother stupidly. Then a smile crossed over his face. "Is it time to go to Disney World, Car? Is that what time it is?"

"No, you idiot," Carson said, slapping his brother across the head. "It's time to go after Blake. *Remember?* We're not going to Disney World, Donny, 'cause Blake says you ain't good enough to go. Don't you remember, now?" None of this was out of the norm, as Carson knew all-too-well. His brother's I.Q. lied somewhere near the bottom of the sea, so fugue moments such as this were almost daily occurrences. Even so, Carson was feeling a tad bit anxious, and that always made him impatient. "Come on, Donny. Get your ass out of bed, already."

Donny looked like a confused puppy. He staggered out of bed and glanced around, no doubt wondering where he was. It took a few seconds for things to come back to him, a few moments of hard-pressed thinking before he was able to put all five pieces of the puzzle back together again. And then, sure enough, Donny turned to his brother, his face making the slow but steady transgression from bewilderment to seething anger.

"*It's time,*" Donny said in a whispery voice.

"That's right," Carson said, nodding affirmatively. "Let's go, Donny. Get your clothes on. Because... It... Is... Time."

They bumbled around the trailer like Abbott and Costello, Donny gathering his clothes and putting them on while Carson paced back and forth, peeking out windows. This went on for a few minutes until Carson spotted Blake coming out of the shed.

"Oh, there he goes," Carson said. He watched as Blake walked over to the little house and onto the porch. He was wearing overalls now, and a checkered flannel. Blake opened the front door, then stepped inside. Seconds later, a light turned on in there. "He's probably getting him some breakfast." Then Carson saw the kitchen light turn on, reinforcing his suspicion.

"Is it time?" Donny asked, sidling up next to Carson. He was dressed now, more or less, and standing there with his mouth open, watching his brother. "Right now... Is it time?"

"Well," Carson said, "not exactly. Not just yet, Donny. We still need Jimmy to be out here, so's I can do what I gotta do."

Donny paused, then said, "And what do you gotta do, Car?"

Carson shrugged. "Just gotta do my job, that's all, Donny. And you don't need to worry about that."

"Okay, Car."

They waited a few more minutes. The sun was slowly rising, but it would be awhile yet before it broke the eastern ridge looming over the property. The roosters were crowing more frequently now. The dogs in the run behind the trailer were starting to yap and whine. Blake was still in the house, probably cooking eggs, or, knowing him, eating them raw, shells and all. Some of the boys would start showing up soon. But where the hell was Jimmy?

"Car," Donny said, "I think I'm getting hungry."

Carson closed his eyes and shook his head. Like clockwork, that's how Donny moved throughout his day. "You're just gonna have to wait, Donny," Carson said impatiently. "I'll let you know when it's time to eat."

Donny didn't reply, which meant he didn't quite like that answer.

Carson looked back at his brother. "And that too is Blake's fault," he said, thinking on his feet like the ever-alert criminal that he was. "If Blake had his way, Donny, he'd let you and me starve to death. And he'd laugh at us, Donny. He'd laugh at us because we can't go to Disney World, and because we was hungry, and I mean *real* hungry, Donny. Hungrier than ever before. Hungrier than ever ever. And he'd laugh, Donny. He'd laugh at us, right to our faces, he would." Carson knew he was adding more fuel to the smoldering embers inside his brother's hollow head, but that was just fine. It was perfect, in fact.

"I don't like Blake, Car," Donny hissed. His face wrapped up in a twist of fuming anger. "I don't like him a'tall, no I don't."

That's good, Carson thought, looking out the window again. *Oh, and this is even better.* He saw Jimmy then, walking back from the long yard, and then into the house. Apparently, he had spent the night down in those tunnels. Seconds later, a truck came barreling down the driveway. It pulled to a sudden stop out front, near the barn, and three men got out. Carson couldn't tell yet who they were, but that didn't matter any. *And this is damn near perfect.*

"Okay, Donny, get yourself ready."

"Oh, I'm ready, Car. I'm *very* ready."

All Carson needed now was a few minutes. He thought he remembered the tunnels and figured it would all come back to him once he got his ass down there. As kids, they used to play hide and seek in that darkened maze, after Flint had died, of course. Carson would find his way around, he was sure of it. He only needed a few minutes, and nothing more.

He thought for a second. "Alright, Donny, here's what I want you to do: You head on out there and stand by those boys, whoever they are. Just make it easy-like, like you's part of the gang, that's all. And if they ask about me, you tell 'em I'm on the shitter, okay?"

"Okay, Car."

"Where am I right now, Donny?" Carson asked.

Donny paused, eyes blinking. "You're on the shitter, Car."

"Very good, Donny. Now then, Blake will come out there soon enough, I'm sure of it. And once he does, well, that's when it'll *really* be time." Carson waited to let that sink in, then added, "That's when you can kill him, Donny."

"Oh, I'm gonna kill him, Car, yes I am. Ain't gonna let Blake keep me from Disney World, or keep us from starving to death, no I ain't. I'm ready, Car. I'm ready for it to be time."

"Alright, then," Carson said. "So go on out there now." He opened the front door, and then Donny stumbled his way outside.

Carson went back to the kitchen window and watched as his brother walked awkwardly up to the three men, all standing in front of the barn. A second later, another truck came rumbling down the driveway. It parked right behind the first one, and then two more boys got out. Goddamn, if the morning wasn't moving fast now.

Quickly, Carson left the kitchen. He put his coat on, checked to see if the flashlight in his pocket still worked, then slipped out the back door of the trailer. The coldness of the dawn hung heavily in the air, and Carson felt it on his face. He smelled the rich odor of wet grass, and the stink of dog shit coming from the run to his left.

He crouched down, snuck his way behind the trailer, behind the little shed, behind the house, behind a large walnut tree, behind a woodpile, then a rusted old tractor, and so on, and so forth. Finally, he snuck his way into the tree line, a hundred yards away from the house, and out of view of anyone. He was nowhere near the main hatch that Jimmy had just come out from, because that door was too much in the open, and for all to see. And it was probably locked, anyhow. But that was just fine with Carson. He knew exactly where the other tunnel entrance was. The secret entrance, that is.

CHAPTER 29

It had been a long and cold, wet night. Of course, the cold wasn't anything near to what Sam had experienced in Afghanistan. But still, it had been miserable in itself.

The little sleep Sam had gotten was while he was curled up into a tight ball under the thin boughs of a small pine tree, less than ten paces from the rocky outcrop overlooking the Ramsey place. A fire would be perfect right about now, but there was no way Sam would do something that foolish.

The crowing roosters had awoken him. Once awake, Sam slowly made his way over to the granite knoll, got himself down into a tight position lying flat against the rock, and started looking through his binoculars.

The property was fairly quiet. Just the roosters, a few restless dogs in what appeared to be a run or a cage, and then a couple of hogs in a pen near the barn. Sam gave it some thought. His suspicions were strong about this being the place, but he wasn't sure just yet what to do about it. The dogs—and even those hogs—would make it pretty much impossible for him to go sneaking through the property up close, stealth-like. He would have to hope and wait for something to materialize for him, then run with that. But just what would that be?

He figured if Emily was still alive, and Sam suspected she was, and if she were hidden some place other than the main house, or that trailer over yonder, then somebody would likely bring her some food soon enough. That might be Sam's only break. But if that didn't happen, what then? He just didn't know.

He waited on the icy stone slab, ignoring the freezing ache spreading throughout his body, and ignoring his desire to build a roaring fire, just to get warm and dry. *What was the plan?* he wondered. How was he going to pull this recon—and perhaps rescue—off?

Back in the day, and overseas, a good distraction was the key for tough missions such as this. Members of the team would set off some explosions on an outside perimeter, and that would draw all the tangos into that area, which would give the rest of the team a chance to move in, or set up an ambush. But nothing like that was ever a one-man gig. It was always a well-planned and well-coordinated team effort. Sam had no such luxuries now.

The hillbillies had come looking for him yesterday. That meant that they had been tipped off and suspected he was up here somewhere. They didn't find him, of course. But they found the wind chimes, and that big, weird-looking fellow took them back with him. Sam wondered if, in time, one of those guys would be smart enough to put the pieces together on that. Then they'd know for sure he was up here, and very close, watching and waiting.

Sam couldn't take any chances. He had to assume they'd be coming for him again, and probably at first light. And this time, they'd definitely bring those dogs with them. If not to track— because the dogs wouldn't know what they were looking for—then to put the fear of God into Sam. Dogs on a man's trail always induced panic. And once a man panicked, well then, it was all over.

Sam set a timer on his watch. He would have to prepare for his strong assumption that they would be coming for him this morning, and coming soon.

It was still gray and dark. The property sat at the base of a wide canyon, and the eastern ridgeline was several hundred feet above. A person down in Asheville right now might be sitting on their front porch warming up in the bright sun, but Sam figured it would be at least another fifteen minutes before the morning light pushed the shadows away from this land.

There was a sudden noise in the distance. He cocked his ear and listened. It was an approaching vehicle, probably an ATV, or a three-wheeler. It was the same sound Sam had heard the night before, albeit only faintly, as he was creeping down the draw, and to the very spot he was now at. He put the binoculars to his eyes, looking for the vehicle.

Within a few seconds, an ATV came rolling into view, driven by a naked man who looked like the same wild-looking fellow from the day before. Sam watched as the guy parked his ATV near an old shed, got off, then went inside.

That was weird, he thought. Sam really wondered what these Ramsey folks were all about.

A few minutes after the man had gone into the shed, he came back out, dressed now. Then he walked over and into the small house. Seconds later, a few lights turned on.

Maybe this was it. Maybe he was doing just as Sam had predicted: getting breakfast ready for the girl.

But then Sam spotted something else—something that surprised him. It was another figure, a tall man, staggering into view from behind some trees, off to Sam's left. He was walking toward the house, and after a few seconds, he went into it, following the first guy.

Sam was curious. He hadn't seen another manmade structure in the area from which that man had come. So where then had he been? And when did he get there? Then a blast of adrenaline rushed through Sam. Were they already hunting him, and somehow he didn't know it?

The adrenaline worked itself into Sam's brain, and then his terror—that deep, abandoned horror—started hijacking his thoughts. It was the fear of being captured again, the same as what had happened to him in Afghanistan. His haunted memories—that's what did it. They were the trigger to the gun blast now ringing inside his head, and waking all that buried, dreaded trauma. Sam closed his eyes and took a deep, deep breath, exhaling slowly.

He wasn't in Afghanistan anymore. He wasn't a prisoner to some torturous hell, lying deep within the belly of a forgotten mountain. No, Sam wasn't there anymore, so he kept his eyes closed and tried as best he could to let all that shit go, and to just keep on breathing.

He seemed to relax now. Then, after a minute, a thought occurred to him. Maybe Sam wasn't in that hell anymore. But what about Emily?

His thoughts were interrupted then by the sound of another vehicle coming from the distant woods and approaching the property. It was a truck, and it drove down a long driveway, then pulled up and parked near the barn. Three men got out, and after a few minutes, Sam spotted another guy, a big clumsy-looking fellow, walk up to them from the trailer. And a minute later, another truck came down the driveway.

It looked like they were all getting ready now. Sam checked his watch. He'd give it just a little while longer before heading further up into the hills to think, and to put some distance between them, just in case they did come looking for him again.

More minutes passed. And then another rattle of adrenaline and fear suddenly bolted through Sam. He saw a man sneaking toward him! Not directly at him, just at a slight angle to Sam's left, but sure enough, he was coming toward his position.

Sam froze. He became one with the large granite, as he focused his stare on whomever it was approaching him. Much of Sam's improvised ghillie suit, all the twigs and leafy branches, and tufts of grass that he had woven into his clothing the day before, had fallen off on his trek down the mountain, or during the night. But there was still enough to keep his silhouette broken and concealed. And it was still plenty dark. But even so...

The man crept forward, keeping behind trees and woodpiles, and whatever other structures that came available to him, as he made his way across the open field. Sam noticed the man kept looking back behind him, toward the house and the barn. He was obviously trying to stay hidden from someone, or to keep himself from being spotted.

Sam continued watching as the man got closer, real close, less than fifty feet from where Sam was lying, before slipping into the tree line. Then the man seemed to relax some. He stopped crouching, stood erect, and stared toward the barn, where the other fellows were still mingling about. Then the guy turned and walked slowly through the trees, and once again, right toward Sam!

He was too close now, maybe thirty feet. If Sam tried to make a break for it, he'd be seen for sure. Hell, if Sam so much as twitched a muscle, he might be seen. He held his breath, his body a block of cold ice as he kept his eyes on the man, thinking, and wondering what he would do, should the man spot him.

He was a scrappy-looking fellow. Kind of wiry and unkempt, your stereotypical white trash southern boy, with somewhat of a seedy disposition about him. He was, in fact, one of the four men who'd been looking for Sam the day before. The silent, nervous one.

So just what the hell was this guy nervous about?

The man suddenly stopped and then squatted down. Quietly, he started moving brush, deadfall, and other forest litter, until he exposed what looked like a round metal door of some kind. He gave it a pull, and the door creaked open, revealing a hole in the earth. The man stood up again and looked toward the barn. Then he slowly turned, crouched, and seconds later, made his way down into the hole.

Well, I'll be damned! Sam thought. *If it were a rattlesnake, it would've bitten me.*

That had to be it. A secret space below the ground.

Something vague flashed in Sam's memory then. He recalled his conversation with Jerry, the old mountain man, and what he had said about Flint Ramsey. That back in the 'Nam, the man had been a tunnel rat. Could it be that he had brought a piece of war back home with him?

Sam waited five minutes. Then, with a turtle's speed, he crawled over to the hole. He listened first, then, very slowly, peeked inside. He smelled the odors of old wet earth, and could see the rungs of an iron ladder going down. The ladder led into a darkened space, vaguely illuminated with a very dim and wavering light.

Also, Sam could now hear the distant hum of a generator, which indicated to him it wasn't just a hole he was staring down into, but maybe a system of tunnels of some sort. Or perhaps just a very large, underground chamber.

There was a chuckle from the men near the trucks. And then some of the dogs got to barking.

Well, alright then. If Sam was going to do anything, now was the time.

He rose slightly, then paused. He quickly took out his satellite phone, checked his GPS coordinates, then sent a brief text message to Madigan. He put the phone back into his pocket. And then, with caution, Sam swung his body around and onto the ladder. He held his breath, said a quick prayer, reached over and pulled the door shut, and climbed on down.

CHAPTER 30

In his eighty-plus years of living in the mountains of North Carolina, Lee Roy Gentry had seen a lot of things. Good things, bad things, weird things, boring things. Most and many kinds of things, in fact. Old Lee Roy had seen so many damn things over the years, that he was under the impression he'd seen just about all there was to see, up there in those smoky blue hills. Even so, he still enjoyed spending his time doing nothing at all, other than looking for things to see.

One of Lee Roy's favorite places to do his looking was his own property. He lived on ten beautiful acres in the deep North Carolina wilderness, the very same stomping grounds he'd called his home since his birth. His house was a cozy two-bedroom rambler slapped with cedar siding and a box gable roof covered in wooden shingles. It sat in the cool mountain shade, tucked up under a cluster of old swamp maple. There was a bubbling spring a hundred yards above the house, a small trickle that fed into a pond sitting out front, just beyond Lee Roy's sprawling garden, but not more than throwing distance from his porch—which was where Lee Roy was sitting right now. And yes, he had a damn good view.

Bass and bluegill swam in the waters of that pond. Lee Roy caught three of them fish just the other day. He'd filleted, battered, and cooked all of them in bacon fat, then sat outside in the night and ate the entire batch while being serenaded by bullfrogs and katydids. It was a pleasant meal.

The old man thought his garden was looking might pretty right about now. Field greens and turnips were on the way, onions were sprouting, and the tomatoes, Lord Almighty, they were ripe and ready. Big, fat, juicy varieties—Brandywines, Cherokee Purples, and Green Zebras—the whole lot of them tangled up like wild weeds, and spread all throughout the garden. He liked to pick the Zebras before they got too ripe, which he would slice, fry in lard, and then sprinkle some table sugar on them before they cooled.

Lee Roy always kept a few hogs out back. He slaughtered one or two a year, and before they got too big. He preferred his pork on the tender side, and his eighty-plus year diet of such meat had proven to him that the best tasting hogs were always the ones raised on corn and table scraps, and that were harvested sometime before their first birthday.

He supplemented the pork with venison, although he was too old for hunting anymore. But Lee Roy was well taken care of. At least twice a year, one of the local boys would come on by with a few steaks or roasts, and sometimes they'd bring him a whole deer, knowing that Lee Roy would return the favor by sharing his famous cold-smoked sausage, which he made with venison and pork fat, garlic, and herbs such as rosemary, sage, bay leaves, and thyme. There were other critters on his menu, of course—possums, coons, squirrels, wild turkeys, and what have you—but pork and venison seemed to make up the majority of Lee Roy's diet.

It was early morning, and presently old Lee Roy was sitting in his favorite rocking chair, just thinking, and admiring, and of course, looking. He was wearing faded jeans and an old brown corduroy coat, with worn-out boots slipped over his feet, left untied. There was an old derby bowler on his head, but it looked kind of funny, as it was two-sizes too big for Lee Roy, and sat just above his eyebrows, making his ancient face of leathered wrinkles and hollow cheeks appear almost infant-like. The hat was as old as the man, was once black, but now the same color as cigarette ash.

Lee Roy had a scatter gun loaded with bird shot resting on his lap, and that's because on mornings such as this, bright and early, and right after a hard night's rain, he knew his property would be crawling with dove and quail. He ate them too, cooked in butter and brown sugar, a little wild rice on the side.

Just then, a morning dove fluttered down from off the roof and landed on the ground not more than twenty feet from Lee Roy. *Sweet Jesus*, he thought, as he pulled his gun up and fired, blasting the little bird into a whirl of feathers and dust.

"Okay, Sadie," Lee Roy said quietly. And then the black Lab, sitting patiently on her haunches next to him, shot out and retrieved the bird. The dog brought the dove back, dropped it at Lee Roy's feet, then sat back down. Lee Roy could see that it was already shaping up to be a really nice morning.

Sometimes he thought about his old lady, Ida, on mornings such as this. She died of cancer a few years back—hell, maybe it was more than a few years, maybe it was a decade already, Lee Roy always seemed to forget. But sometimes he thought about that woman, when the morning sun was fresh and bright, as it tended to be after a good rain.

Ida liked mornings. She would come out here and refill the hummingbird feeder, sprinkle bread crumbs all around, then sit in her rocking chair and read, or maybe just look out, like Lee Roy was doing right now. She was never fond of him shooting game right outside the house, said it was lazy and uncivilized, and so back then, Lee Roy always did his hunting out on the road, which was better, anyhow.

But then Ida up and died, and Lee Roy really did get lazy, and maybe a bit primitive, and somehow he was okay with all of that.

After several minutes of silence, another dove floated down. Lee Roy chuckled to himself, pulled his gun up to his shoulder, and fired. "Okay, Sadie," he said.

There was only one road that ran in and out of Lee Roy's property, and an ill-maintained dirt road at that. It came up thirty yards off to his left, just down his short driveway. Much of his present view of the road was concealed by his garden, an assortment of bushes, and a wall of white rhododendrons—beautiful flowers, they were—but Lee Roy could still see a section of the road just fine, from where he sat.

Right now, there were quail out there on that road, he was absolutely sure of it. He heard one of them cooing a few minutes ago, and if he ever got out of his damn chair and went for a little stroll, he'd be eating quail stew this evening. But Lee Roy was getting up there in his years. Hell, he already *was* up there. And after a cold and rainy night, his old-man bones and joints felt like frozen-over nuts and bolts. It was all-too-easy for Lee Roy to just sit on the porch and let his dinner come to him.

Besides, there was no better view than what he had right now. And for a man who had seen just about everything, the best view was all that mattered.

He'd seen youngsters, of course, born and raised throughout his life. In total, he and Ida had had seven kids, all grownup now, and nowhere to be found. Two of them were dead, that he knew, and one of them got sent up to the Big House. Another one joined the Army and hasn't been seen since, and the rest, they were somewhere around these hills, he supposed. But he hadn't heard from any of them in... Well, Lee Roy couldn't remember the last time it was.

The old man had had a good and long life, though. Sure, there were troubles and woes mixed in over the years, but all in all, he couldn't complain. The woods of North Carolina had provided for him, and they treated him just right. There were parts of the world Lee Roy had never seen, and never would—big places, such as New York City or California, the Grand Canyon, or even the old countries, overseas. No, Lee Roy will never see those places, but he was okay with that too, because he had seen enough things already.

One night, a few years back, Lee Roy even saw one of them U.F.O.s. He'd been walking on the road and smoking his pipe, when all of a sudden an orange and green disk zipped in overhead, hung there for a minute or two, and then *bam!*, shot off to space. That was quite a sight.

And on another night, a long, long time ago, Lee Roy was pretty sure he'd come across one of them Bigfoot creatures. He was hunting coons up near Saddler's pond, and the dogs were off and running. He was taking his time getting to the hounds, on account that it was pretty dark, when suddenly, a towering man-like shadow crossed the trail in front of him. The smell of that thing was god-awful, and it gave a low growl before crashing off into the trees faster than a cougar, and scaring the bejesus out of Lee Roy.

There were other things the old man had seen as well, things he couldn't quite explain, or would even care to try. And many of the things he'd seen over his life were now just foggy memories that he rarely, if ever, thought about anymore. Over his eighty-some years, Lee Roy Gentry had seen quite a lot, living in the mountains of North Carolina.

But on this fine and dandy morning...

The old man suddenly heard a vehicle coming up the road. He turned his head to listen, then decided he was hearing more than one automobile.

He waited casually in his chair, rocking gently, because there was no need for him to do anything else. The vehicles came closer, and they were driving rather slowly, he could tell.

He and Sadie were both looking down the driveway, watching with curiosity as the vehicles—three in all—cruised on by, pushing dust, gravel, and several quail to the side as they passed.

It is true: old Lee Roy Gentry had seen a lot of interesting things throughout his years up there in the hills. But on this morning, he witnessed something for the first time in his life.

"Did you just see that?" he asked Sadie. "Three trucks full of spics and niggers. Goddamn, if that wasn't the strangest thing I've seen."

Wait a minute now. Wasn't this one of them things Jimmy-James had told him to keep an eye out for?

Lee Roy got up and made his way into the house, his stiff joints cracking and popping. He went into the kitchen, set his shotgun down on the counter, then picked up the phone and dialed.

A few seconds later, Billy Bob answered. "Yes'um?" he said.

"Hey, Billy," Lee Roy replied, rubbing the whiskers on his chin. "You're not gonna believe what I just saw."

CHAPTER 31

On rare occasions, the voice inside Donny's head was that of his long since dead Mema, especially when he got himself into some kind of trouble. Like the time when Donny got picked up by the police after being chased off a school grounds, because apparently, a strange grown man playing with second graders during their recess just didn't fly anymore.

Mema had lost it then, right there on the empty stage of Donny's consciousness. She went on about how he was *still* such a *bad, stupid* little boy, and that she would never forgive him for spitting into the cookie jar after eating all the cookies. (That was Carson's fault, actually. He'd set Donny up for that little stunt when they were youngsters, and *Ooooooweeeeee!* did Mema blister Donny's hide on that day.)

And then there was the time Donny got caught streaking through an old folk's home. Again, something Carson had put Donny up to, and again, something the local police had gotten involved with, and, yes, again, another time in which Donny's mind got paid a visit from Mema.

So yeah, the old hag visited Donny from time to time. But for the most part, what he heard inside his head day in and day out were the voices of Carson, and then this other feller, a stranger of sorts, who often spoke as if he were Donny, even though Donny had never met him, and had no idea what in the hell he looked like.

Both of these people were in quite the discourse right now, ignoring Donny, who seemed to be sitting on the sidelines to the conversation within his own head, and thus making it difficult for him to think.

I told you it's time, the real time, the best time, so let's make us some time, make all the time, you know it's time. That was Carson, of course.

I don't know what time it is. I just know it's time to kill Blake. Where is Blake? It is time to kill Blake. And that was the other feller, the one Donny had never met, and often wondered about.

Donny walked out of the trailer and fumbled his way down the small porch. He saw a rooster run out in front of him (it gave him a nasty look for some odd reason) and then the dog cage off to his right, which was full of dogs, all looking at him too, but in a hopeful manner, as if he had some food for them.

Donny wished he had food right now. Heck, even dog food, which he'd eaten before, once or twice, maybe more.

Stop thinking about food, you big dummy. There'll be time for food after this time is over.

He walked across the yard and then stopped when he got to the men standing by the truck. He looked up, focusing his stare on them. *They ain't Blake, Donny. He's still in the house, like I told you.*

Are you sure they's ain't Blake?

"Morning, Donny," one of the men said. Then he chuckled. "You okay? Looks like you seen a ghost."

A round of chuckles now.

Donny looked carefully at the men, trying to put their faces to names. The Boyer brothers—Wayne and Clyde, that's right, that's who he was looking at—and then the other one. Wasn't that Hardy... something-or-other?

"Where's Carson?" Hardy asked.

A bell suddenly rang inside Donny's head. "Carson'sontheshitter," he said quickly, almost too quickly, robotic-like, actually.

The three men exchanged glances.

"Well, I s'pose a man's gotta shit when a man's gotta shit," Hardy said. He looked at Donny then. "But what about you, Donny-boy? Ain't you gotta shit, too? Lawd, I bet you take some big shits, don't'cha, Donny?"

The chuckles turned into laughter.

Donny ignored them and looked toward the house, his attention trying to break free from the chaos of his mind and the discomfort of not having Carson with him right now.

I'm right here, you idiot. So you just keep your eye on the ball. And the ball is Blake. He'll be out here soon enough, and that's when you can get him, Donny. That's when you will get him.

Donny kept squeezing his hands into tight fists. *Ain't gonna let Blake eat all the food. Ain't gonna let Blake eat Disney World. Ain't gonna let Blake eat anything anymore.*

"What's his problem?" Wayne asked.

"Beats me," Clyde replied. "You okay, Donny? You seem a little tense."

"Like I said, maybe he needs to shit," Hardy said.

More laughter.

"Maybe he's all backed up," Wayne added. "You constipated, Donny?"

A truck came rolling down the driveway just then, and it pulled to a stop near the barn. Donny turned around and looked. *Is he there? Is Blake inside that truck?*

No, Donny, he's not in that truck. He's in the house, like I done told you already.

"Morning, boys," a man said, stepping out from the driver's side. Then five more fellers somehow materialized next to him. "Jimmy-James says we got us a hunting to do."

"That's right," Clyde replied. "Although I ain't so sure 'bout that. We was up there yesterday, and we ain't seen a damn thing." He spat on the ground, then looked back up. "But I'll let Jimmy tell you all 'bout it."

"Sure enough," the man said. He walked up to Donny and smacked him on the shoulder. "How you doing, big boy? Ain't seen you in a while."

Donny froze and stared long and hard at the man. He couldn't place him. But that was okay.

He ain't Blake, so he ain't mattering none. Only needs to kill me Blake.

After a second, the man chuckled, then turned away. "What'd he do, wake up on the wrong side of the bed?"

"We's thinking he needs to shit, but cain't. Personally, I believe Blake finally got to him and ruined his asshole."

Another chorus of hellacious laughter, only much louder.

"What's so funny?" It was Jimmy-James now, walking up from the house. "You boys are having too much fun already." He stopped when he got to the group, then looked around. "This all we got?"

"I let the Colbys know," Clyde said, "and I spread the word to your kin up at Higgins's Creek. Ain't no telling if they'll show, 'cause I didn't wait around to hear back."

"Well, we'll see," Jimmy said. He looked at Donny then. "Where the hell's Carson?"

"Carson'sontheshitter!" Donny rattled off.

Jimmy paused, then glanced around. "Oh he is, is he?"

Two things happened just then: one in rapid succession, and the other in *sloooowwww* motion.

A man on an ATV came racing down the mountain, the driveway, and across the yard, before pulling to a sudden stop in front of everyone.

"Hey, Jimmy-James!" the man said, in hurried fashion. "I done got a call. There's some mean-looking niggers coming down the road. Three trucks full of 'em. They'll be here in minutes."

Jimmy's eyes widened. He looked around at the men, nodded his head, then said, "Well, I'm sure glad you boys are here. Looks like our hunt will have to wait. Might be we got us some shooting to do."

And then the second thing happened, the one in slow motion.

Real leisure-like, Blake came wandering toward the group of men. He walked casually around the truck, then stopped near the entrance to the barn, staring indifferently at everyone. He was gnawing on a turkey leg and holding a tall glass of milk.

There he is! Carson's voice suddenly said.

Yes! There he is! The invisible stranger repeated.

And then, with a howling scream, Donny charged.

CHAPTER 32

Jimmy looked on with surprise as Donny screamed, ran, and crashed into Blake. That big boy hit Blake right at the waist, the perfect linebacker's tackle. The force of the collision sent Blake's turkey leg and glass of milk flying comically into the air. And with an *Oooof!* coming out of Blake, their bodies went tumbling into the barn.

God-damnit! Jimmy thought.

A couple of boys started after Donny and Blake, but then Jimmy shouted, "No, no—never mind them! Let the fools tangle if they want to. We got bigger fish to fry, boys. Grab your guns and get some cover. I'm not figuring this'll be a friendly visit we've got coming."

Everyone moved then. They grabbed their rifles from their trucks, then spread out across the property, taking cover, and positioning themselves toward the road.

Jimmy ran into the house. He went to his bedroom and grabbed the AR15 standing in the corner near his bed. Then he grabbed a few preloaded magazines (because unloaded magazines were all but worthless) from off a nightstand, and dropped them into his overall pockets. He jogged out of the house and headed toward the road leading onto his property.

In the back of Jimmy's mind, he knew something like this was going to happen. Well, he didn't really know, but he imagined it, once or twice. He could see Flint right now, wherever he was, shaking his head in angry disapproval. *This is what you get, boy, for being greedy and making that no-good city candy of yours. Should've stuck with stilling shine. And this is what you get for making dealings with a nigger, too. I always knew you were like your brother—dumb as shit.*

"To hell with it," Jimmy said to himself. He jogged to the front of the mobile home and took up a position behind a stout woodpile next to the dog run. He looked around then, noticing everyone setting up behind cover, rifles aiming forward, all waiting for what was to come.

And what exactly was coming?

Jimmy knew. Myron and his gangsters. They sure as hell weren't coming up here to talk about the football game. This was going to be nothing short of war. Briefly, Jimmy wondered how Myron had figured out where he lived. Oh well, he'll deal with that problem later... along with that soldier boy, somewhere up there on the mountain.

Earl, the one who'd brought the message to Jimmy, suddenly drove his ATV back toward the road, then into the bushes. He stopped and got off. He had a shotgun in his hand, and he hid behind a tall oak tree near the opening of the road. Everybody else looked set and ready to go.

Jimmy nodded. "Alright, then!" he shouted. "City trash come to fuck with us mountain boys... Let's show 'em what we got."

*   *   *

Let's see what these fuckin' crackers got, Myron thought.

He had to admit, though; he was a little nervous. The roads up here sucked dick, and twice he had to turn the convoy around, after accidentally driving up onto some old white folks' driveway. Damn, if those honkies didn't stare the hell out of his black ass. Looked like they ain't never seen a brother before.

Myron eventually found his way back on the trail, or so he thought. They were heading down a steep canyon, and Roochie, who was sitting in the seat right behind Myron, said that this "felt right."

But Myron was still nervous. He was worried that they no longer had surprise on their side. If these hillbillies were anything like brothers in the hood, such as when the po-lice came rolling in, motherfuckin' word would be out by now. Before the pigs finished eating their donuts, everybody in town would know they were around. And the one thing Myron didn't want to happen was for Jimmy James Ramsey to know he was coming for him.

Still, where they were seemed peaceful enough. Myron led the three-Bronco convoy down a long and steep dirt road, all shrouded with trees and bushes and shit. It felt like they were in the Amazon jungle. But he could see, down there toward the bottom of this hill, that there was a wide clearing up ahead. And the dashboard GPS was indicating that, for sure, this was the place.

"Get ready," Myron said. P-Dog was sitting in the passenger seat next to him and petting his Kalashnikov like a bitch's thigh. Pounds, Cookie, and Steve were in the back with Rooch. Brothers Grimm they were, stacked with guns and ammo, and ready for war. "I'm thinking this is the place."

Slowly, Myron pulled toward the end of the road, where the jungle broke away and the sky opened up. He could see the details of the clearing now, and hell yeah, it was your typical white trash crib, with all kinds of shit laid out front—chickens and trucks and old cars, old wooden buildings, and of course, a damn mobile home. 'Cause what kind of white trash would you be without a single-wide on your property? And then that hillbilly barn, and next to that, built just off to the side...

Myron stopped the Bronco and squinted. "Look at that, Rooch," he said. "Is that a pigpen I see? This is the place, niggas."

Just then, a shadow stepped out from behind a tree and walked right up to Myron's window.

Myron turned and looked. *Oh, shit! Motherfucker's got a gun!*

And then the shadow—who appeared to be a dirty-looking hillbilly—raised that gun and fired.

• • •

It was only a warning shot, blasting right up into the trees, probably just to scare the shit out of everyone and to let them know that these hillbillies meant business. But Roochie was in no way, shape, or form to think about such trivial details. His scattered brain, all juiced up with a cocktail of drugs and alcohol and suppressed terror, could only think of one thing at that moment: kill or be killed.

With that, Roochie stuck the business end of his big black Israeli *Galil* out his window and squeezed the trigger.

Bwwaattattaataaaaaattttaaa!!!!!!

Chaos ensued after that.

As Roochie unloaded half a magazine in a matter of seconds, everyone in the car started hollering. Roochie's gun was fitted to fire 5.56x45mm rounds, and those bullets tore through that hillbilly's body at a speed of 3,000 feet per second. Seven in all found that poor dude. They rippled through his chest and face, making small entry holes in the front, and devastating craters out the back. The man did a weird little chicken dance, jittering in place for about a second, gun falling uselessly to the ground, before he staggered backward a few feet. Then his body dropped dead, into a leaking heap of bloody meat on the side of the road.

"Oh, damn!" Myron shouted. "You just did that, Rooch! Fuckin' shit, Rooch, you just did that! Alright then, niggas, shit's real now. Let's go!"

Myron stomped on the gas and the Bronco jumped forward, off the road and onto the main property. It got fifty feet before a swarm of opposing bullets started pinging into it, like angry bees attacking a bear.

Three rounds hit the front window, and the entire glass instantly spider-webbed. Myron cranked the wheel to the left, and the vehicle swung around ninety degrees, exposing the right side of the Bronco to whoever was shooting at them. Then Myron stomped on the brakes.

"Everybody out!" he shouted.

"What the fuck?" P-Dog cried, realizing his imminent doom.

Poor P-Dog, being in the wrong place at the wrong time, and the wrong person to boot. All his weight and size made it impossible for him to crawl across the cab and then out through Myron's side of the vehicle. And P-Dog knew this. Also, big boys like him made wonderful targets. He might have known this as well, but he opened his door anyway, taking five rounds of various calibers into his chest and belly before stepping foot onto the ground. He still had enough left in him though, because that's the other thing about big dudes: it took a lot to bring them down. Despite his fatal wounds, P-Dog managed to get out of the Bronco, and then he lifted that pretty little bitch's thigh and fired.

He fired randomly, but in a general direction, fired all thirty of his shots, creating a thin plume of smoke and powder in the air, along with a whole lot of noise, before taking another bad hit to his shoulder. The gun dropped from his hand then—bye-bye, sweet thang—and then another hit, maybe not the last, but the last one that counted, went right through P-Dog's left eye, and out through the back of his head. He finally dropped too.

"This is fuckin' war!" Myron shouted, taking cover behind the Bronco's front tire.

Pounds, Cookie, and Steve were all crouching next to Myron, peeking through gaps in the Bronco, or under the vehicle, or to the side, trying to locate who was shooting at them. Trying to find a target to shoot back at.

Loud metallic pings were going off all around them, bullets careening into the Bronco from various angles.

The other two Broncos came wheeling around, turning broadside just as Myron had done, and making somewhat of a wall of metal against the general direction of where the hillbillies seemed to be firing from. Once the Broncos stopped, dudes poured out of them like rats fleeing a fire.

Roochie was lying flat on his belly—probably the smartest thing anyone could do at that moment—and he was watching all of this action unfold before him, his eyes wide as the moon. Damn, he had just killed a guy, the first living thing he'd ever killed, not counting all the bass he'd caught and eaten, or the crawdads he used to catch and torture as a kid, by driving little sticks through them, or the time he'd run over that cat...

That's right. Roochie's life was flashing before his eyes. They said that's what happened just before a person died. Was Roochie going to die today? Was he going to die right now, in fact?

Not if Roochie could help it.

He got up suddenly and made a break for it. He ran to the end of the last Bronco, passing Cubans and black dudes, who were all staying low, and all taking pot shots here and there, trying to gauge the situation while staying alive.

Roochie didn't really know what to do. But in his tweeker brain, he thought it was a bad idea to stay in the same area where people were being shot at.

He got to the back end of the last Bronco and peeked around the shoulder of some Cuban dude, who was kneeling behind the rear tire well.

It seemed there was nothing to see—just buildings and trucks and miscellaneous junk. But then Roochie spotted a man standing near the corner of the barn, firing away with a gun that looked similar to Roochie's. Wait a minute. Didn't all the guns look similar to his?

"I see one over there," Roochie said.

"Where?" said the Cuban.

"By that building," Roochie replied, pointing. Then a wallop of bullets splattered into the back of the Bronco, right next to Roochie's head. He ducked instinctively, just as the Cuban dude took Roochie's place by peeking around the vehicle.

One of the bullets found the Cuban dead in the face. He plopped down abruptly onto the ground, lifeless, half his head now looking like something Roochie had once bought at a meat market.

Oh, man, Roochie thought, realizing that could've been him. His stomach suddenly roiled. Then he turned around and vomited.

It was still chaos. But a heightened chaos now, with the cacophony of gunfire and shouting men, the smell of gun smoke and the boiling confusion swirling through Roochie's brain, along with his sudden queasiness, and the spewing of his stomach. The dead man at his feet didn't help matters any. Finally, there was Roochie's fear, that lingering dread that had been riding his shoulders ever since he'd gotten his ear sliced off, temporarily muffled for the moment, of course, thanks to all those drugs in his system. But it was still there nonetheless, a faint echo whispering his name in the background of all this chaos.

That was it. Roochie couldn't take it anymore. Panic stepped into the driver's seat of his mind and simply took over. Yelling and screaming, Roochie ran straight out into the open field.

●　　●　　●

Like the movies, it all happened pretty damn fast.

Jimmy observed the first vehicle, a 1980ish Ford Bronco, painted sky blue, chrome features, aftermarket suspension, off-road tires. Goddamn, not a bad-looking ride.

Then Earl—good old Earl—stepping out from behind the tree, walking up to that vehicle, shotgun raised high.

Right on, boy. Blast them fuckers.

Then Earl shooting into the sky, the worthless, harmless, goddamn sky...

The sky? Not the sky! Shoot the driver, you damned fool...

Too late.

The retaliating gunfire coming from the Bronco was unreal. Seemed like it should've been louder, seeing what it did to Earl's body. Jimmy watched as Earl pranced back a few steps, then went down cold.

"Let 'em have it, boys!" he shouted.

He and the others did just that. They let that Bronco have it, as it came wheeling around into the yard. It was a racket now, gunfire going off, both to the left and right of Jimmy. He fired controlled bursts, aiming for the engine block, because there was no way in hell these assholes were getting away from him now, and then a few shots into the windows.

The Bronco lurched to a sudden stop. And then some fat ass motherfucker climbed out of the passenger's side.

What a fool, Jimmy thought. *What a big, dumb fool of a nigger.*

The big boy got hit then, hit badly, even though he started shooting his own gun, and at full-auto, throwing all his bullets into the trashcan. He wasn't going to be standing much longer, but Jimmy aimed and fired, anyway. Got him right in the arm, gun dropping now. Someone else got him in the face, and it was game over for that dude.

One down. How many more to go?

Two other Broncos came spinning into the yard then, right behind the first one. There were a lot of gangsters in those vehicles, Jimmy could tell. Oh yeah, this was going to be a fucking war.

He kept up with controlled fire, conserving his ammo, shooting only at what he thought were valid targets.

In minutes, all three Broncos looked ready for the junk pile. The windows were shattered or gone, exposed tires were now all flat. This was work done by the other boys, because Jimmy only looked for something good to shoot at. Something human.

He found a target then. Some dummy poked his face around the back of a Bronco. Jimmy let loose a three-round burst, saw sparks flying against the vehicle's rear end. He let go another burst, just as a face looked back at him, and that fool, whoever he was, was now dead. Hot damn! Jimmy was almost having him some fun.

"Keep it up, boys!" he cried.

Then, amazingly, one of those gangsters did the stupidest things imaginable. He ran out from cover and into the clearing.

You got to be kidding me. This war might end sooner than Jimmy thought.

He took careful aim, leading just a tad, allowing for the movement of that running fool, who was soon to be dead. Then Jimmy pulled the trigger.

• • •

"I's killing you! See me, Blake?! I's killing you!"

Donny had Blake pinned on the ground of the barn and was straddling his waist, hands around his throat.

Bad luck for Blake. He had been body-slammed while chewing on a mouthful of turkey meat. Now, that meat was trapped halfway down his throat.

"*Stoooopppp...*" he gasped, holding onto Donny's hands, eyes bulging. "*Guunnss...*"

But Donny didn't hear him. Nor did Donny hear the gunshots now going off outside the barn. All Donny heard were the voices inside his head.

Hooooweeeee! You got him now, Donny. You got him good, boy. Now kill that son of a bitch. Kill him dead, so's we can go to Disney World.

Not gonna let Blake eat all the pumpkin pie anymore! Not gonna let Blake eat Disney World anymore! Not gonna let Blake eat assholes anymore! Sometimes, the strange feller inside Donny's head said some pretty strange things.

"Get... off... me," Blake wheezed. He had a big piece in there, stuck deep inside his gullet. A thick chunk of dense, gristly turkey meat, all jammed up into his trachea. Blake was turning blue, eyes pleading desperately, body shaking and convulsing, hips buckling. He was fading fast.

"You can't kill Disney World!" Donny hollered. "It's mine! Mine, I say! All mine!"

Blake let go of Donny's hands, then reached down, going for the gold. He managed to get hold of Donny's ballsack, and then he clenched down really hard. The pain was enough to get a jolt out of Donny, and that was all Blake needed. Like a slippery snake, he found the gap and wriggled out from underneath Donny. Then he threw a wild left, clobbering Donny across the jaw, before stepping away.

Donny staggered back. He slowly stood, his hand now holding his mouth.

Where the hell did that come from?

I don't know.

Well, just forget about it, Donny.

I don't know.

You do know! Get your ass up and get after him. It ain't over till that man is dead. So kill him, Donny. Kill him now!

Blake was half-standing, half-crouching. He was holding his throat and hacking hard, trying desperately to dislodge the piece of meat. He glanced up, catching Donny's hateful stare.

"Nooo..." Blake gasped, shaking his head and waving a hand. Then he pointed to his throat. "Cho... king..."

Ain't gonna let Blake touch me again. Ain't gonna let Blake—"

"I'm killing you for real, Blake! That's it, now. I'm killing you for real!"

Donny screamed again and rushed forward.

CHAPTER 33

It was "range day" at 7-Core Sentinel. Nobody hated range day. Everyone loved it, in fact. Especially Marcus Madigan. And for many reasons.

Here's what range day looked like for him: It started with a pre-morning jog. Just an easy-breezy three-miler, followed by a cold shower, which sucked, but was always worth it in the end, as it made the body feel nice and warm for the first few hours of the day.

After the shower, he ate a quick breakfast of scrambled eggs and sausage, coffee, glass of orange juice, and was then out the door long before the sun was up.

The drive to 7-Core's main installation took less than an hour, and that was the time Madigan used to catch up on the world outside little old Asheville. He listened to news channels and various podcasts that highlighted global events, hoping he could predict potential hotspots he might get thrown into. Always keep yourself one step ahead of the curve, that was the idea.

After the drive, Madigan would check in to 7-Core's highly secured compound, a sprawling property of over 2,000 acres, set in the wilds between Winston-Salem and Asheville. The property was just one of 7-Core's many installations throughout the world, but was used primarily as an Intel center for stateside operations and assignments, as well as for active training, just to keep contractors frosty. It included both an indoor and outdoor shooting range, as well as the eloquently named "Zombie Town," where Close Quarters Battle drills were held.

The rest of range day was made up of nothing short of eight hours of shooting guns, all kinds of guns, and shooting these guns in various ways and scenarios, such as CQB, tactical shotgun and handgun drills, rifle marksmanship, urban warfare tactics, situational awareness exercises, and advanced integrated weapons training, to name just a small part of the daily agenda. Again, nobody hated range day.

Presently, Madigan was in the indoor range with several of the guys, preparing to expend a thousand rounds with his Close Quarter Battle Receiver, a shortened, modified version of the M4Al Carbine, when he got the text message from Sam. The message contained GPS coordinates, and the following:

Deliverance country. Tangos and boobies. This must be the place. Going in.

Curious, Madigan opened Google Maps on his phone and punched in the coordinates Sam had sent him. Sure enough, the man was way up there in the hills.

Mighty interesting.

But of course, Madigan wasn't surprised. He knew what Sam Nolan was capable of. Still, he took Sam's message exactly as it was meant for him: to go on standby.

But then Madigan thought more about that and wondered what exactly Sam had gotten himself into. Picturing his good friend "squealing like a pig," he decided to send a message of his own.

Received. On alert. What's your status?

And then Madigan waited for a response. And... he waited. And then, after several minutes of not receiving anything back, which in itself wasn't a huge alarm, something inside his soldier instincts told him that being on alert just wasn't going to cut it. Not when he was this far away from the potential action. He thought quickly, put a plan together in his mind, and was then satisfied with what he had to do, and how he was going to do it.

When you move, move fast, don't think, just react, let training take over, sort it all out in the end.

In short, this was how Madigan lived his life, as it related to tactical decisions in combat, which, as any experienced operative knew, contained an ironic dichotomy. Tactical decisions and combat rarely worked together. Because combat was just another term for chaos. And although chaos was often made superfluous and grand in movies and novels, in the real life, it was a painful exercise of staying alive inside a deadly, gruesome, fast-moving, unpredictable machination containing uncontrolled gears such as Luck and Mr. Murphy, and that was pretty much it. While in combat, the better name for "decisions" was "responses". And responses were subject entirely to one's training.

Which was something Madigan had a lot of.

He initiated the "cease fire" horn near a wall. Nobody had been shooting, but he wanted everyone's attention.

"Listen up, men," Madigan said. A dozen hardened, combat-veteran faces stared back at him. "There's a situation on hand," he continued. "We've got a brother in a tight jam, and he's not far from here. I'm going out right now to help him. I need three volunteers to assist. I can't advise on anything, because I don't know anything, other than that this could be dangerous, probably will be dangerous, and is within the civilian sector. Off the books, in other words, and strictly between us. So then, do I have any volunteers?"

His last statement was taken as a joke, and Madigan knew it would be. After asking it, every hand went into the air.

$$\bullet \quad \bullet \quad \bullet$$

The tunnel system Flint had dug was broken up more or less into three parts. The main entrance section, which was accessed primarily via the door hatch at the base of the dead oak tree; the central section, where Carson had climbed down into, and which consisted of several small chambers, currently all dimly lit, and housing anything and everything needed to cook meth; and then the distant section, which split off from the central area, and headed into a darkened labyrinth that Carson had never explored as a youngster, only because it was too damn spooky down there.

Even now, as he looked toward that path leading into a darkened unknown, Carson still got the chills. What was down there, he didn't know, and he didn't want to know. But he was betting it wasn't the girl.

She would be in one of the rooms up front, near the main entrance. For convenience's sake, if nothing else. That's what Carson was figuring, at least.

He made his way back through the central chambers, zigzagging in between barrels and boxes of chemicals, and whatever else they had down there for the making of crystal meth. He glanced here and there, looking to see if there were any bags of dope lying around, as his pockets were currently quite empty, and feeling quite lonely.

Carson didn't find anything worth taking, but he didn't spend much time looking. Time was of the essence. And it was ticking by most rapidly.

She's gotta be up there in one of them rooms, he thought. *Where the hell else would she be?*

He made his way out of the last chamber and into the tunnel leading to the main entrance. The shadows had crept closer here, and the smell of dank earth was more powerful. Carson knew where he was going, and he knew it would only take a few minutes to get there. That's as long as he didn't run into any complications.

Which he did, of course. And all of a sudden.

All of a sudden, Carson felt something really cold and really sharp come out of the shadows and press into his neck. At the same time, he felt the hand of someone really strong and really determined, press his body against the cold earthen wall. And then, a fraction of a second after all of this happened, Carson heard a voice, which sounded just as strong and just as determined as the hand that gripped him, and the knife that held him, whisper into his ear.

"Tell me where the girl is, and I might not kill you."

• • •

The downside to making the day for three fellow contractors was shitting on the days of nine others. Madigan knew this would happen. It went with the territory of deciding who would and would not accompany him on this questionable mission. By way of compensation, he promised Friday-night beers and steaks at his place for everyone when this was over. And then he and his three choices quickly left the indoor range.

Not knowing what he was getting into, Madigan had played it safe by opting for a variety in his choice of teammates. With him were Chance "Chancey" Malone, former Marine Raider turned DIA operative, turned defense contractor; Burton "Boon-ass" Bunas, former Navy Seal/DEVGRU operator; and Jackson Hightower, former Army Ranger/Delta Force member. It was a quaint, colorful little squad, whose combined combat expertise would undoubtedly contribute much to whatever hell they were getting themselves into. All three men had been involved with multiple tours in country, particularly the Middle East. And all three had been shot at plenty of times.

"You know, you just made yourself a shitload of enemies back there," Jackson said.

"Yep," Madigan replied. "But they ain't babies. They'll get over it. They'll forget about it, in fact, once I serve them steak and beers."

The four-man team was presently in 7-Core's armory, quickly stocking up on gear—namely, guns and ammo.

"I figure we've got a limited amount of time for whatever we're getting into," Madigan said. "Let's keep our loads light. This might be just a sit and wait deal. Or it might be a quick reaction maneuver. I have no idea."

That was the shittiest part about it. Intel was key to a successful mission, and good intel was key to surviving such a mission. But no intel at all, other than "here you go," was akin to showing up at a gunfight without knowing who your enemy was. And, unbeknownst to Madigan, that was exactly what they were heading into.

"We're taking the chopper," Madigan said.

The other men nodded, as if they already suspected as much.

Ten minutes later, the team was good to go. Each man was decked out in black combat fatigues and olive-green tactical vests. They each had a variant of the M4-A1 Carbine sporting an assortment of accessories, such as optical sights, scopes, suppressors, and forward handgrips. Each of them also carried a sidearm, with Madigan's choice being the Browning 9mm HP, thanks to some fine training and inspiration he'd received from Britain's Special Air Service, back in the day.

The tank in the group was Boon-ass, and for this reason, he also carried with him a Kel-Tec KSG bullpup shotgun, in case something such as a door or padlock needed to get blown to smithereens.

Packed in Molle pouches on their vests were smoke grenades and flash bangs, along with extra ammo, first aid kits, flashlights, radios, and various other gear. For a quick reaction force heading into a situation they knew nothing about, they were well prepared.

"Alright, then," Madigan said, "it's go time. Everybody out to the tarmac."

•   •   •

Even in the dim light, Sam could still see the terror in the man's eyes.

"Dude, what the... I ah... I don't know what you're talking 'bout."

Sam kept his knife at the man's throat and stared at him.

"I'm serious. I don't know nothing 'bout no girl."

The knife went further into the man's skin. "You can stop lying to me now. Tell me where she's at." And then Sam pressed harder.

The man winced then. "Alright, alright... I was, ah, wondering myself. But I don't know where she's at. That's why I came down here. To look for her."

"To look for her, eh?" Sam said.

"That's right. I was just looking for her."

Sam released a little pressure on the man, then lowered the knife toward his midsection. He did a quick pat down, searching for guns or knives, finding only a flashlight, which he took. "Well then, let's go look for her," he said. "But if you make any funny moves, I'll put this piece of steel six inches into your body." It was a risky move, but Sam didn't really have any choices. "Now which way?"

The man pointed down the tunnel. "I was going that way," he said.

"Alright, then. Let's go."

They got two steps into the tunnel, and then the gunfire started.

CHAPTER 34

Roochie was being chased by a swarm of wasps. Pissed off little wasps, whizzing by his head. But those damn little things couldn't catch him, because he was on the move, oh yes, he was.

Holding his pants up with one hand and that Israeli rifle in the other, he ran straight for a big pile of heaping metal. Looked like an old rusty truck, and in his head, Roochie was running as fast as the Bionic Man. Those damn wasps, though, they were still haunting him, just zooming right on by, trying to sting his scrawny little ass.

He was almost there. Only seconds away, that was it. Seconds more, and he'd be behind a big metal shield, while everyone else was back there getting shot at. Roochie put an extra little push into his run, seeing the finish line coming up on him, and he was almost there, dammit, when suddenly—

Ouch! One of those fucking wasps finally got him. Stung him right in the thigh, it did. And it hurt like a son of a bitch!

But Roochie kept going. His run turned into a skipping-jog, but it got him where he wanted to go. And then he dropped down behind the big metal thing and looked around, breathing hard.

The wasps were really mad now. They were crashing their little bodies into the metal, making one hell of a noisy racket, as they tried to get at Roochie.

He looked at his pant-leg, watched as it stained into a dark-wine wetness, which seemed to get bigger by the second. And oh, man, did it hurt. It hurt badly. It looked bad, too. Not as bad as what had happened to that Cuban dude. But it still looked bad.

Roochie glanced over at where he'd been just seconds ago. He saw those guys hopping around like chickens, or crouching low, some of them firing their guns, that one dude on the ground, his head half gone. And a couple more guys who looked like they'd been shot up as well.

Roochie took a deep breath. Well, at least he wasn't over there anymore.

• • •

That's the same son of a bitch whose ear I cut off, Jimmy thought, as he pulled the trigger. One bullet shot out of his gun, only one, and then Jimmy's AR-15 made that distinct *click* sound, indicating that it was out of ammo.

"Dammit!"

Quickly, he detached the empty magazine, threw it on the ground, snapped a full one back into his gun, and pulled the charging handle. He looked again for that running fool. But he'd gotten down behind the old tractor, and that was some pretty good cover.

Jimmy looked around, taking inventory. All his boys still seemed to be in the fight, rifles blasting away. He didn't know where everyone was at, but he didn't see anybody lying on the ground.

He turned back to the Broncos. Those idiots weren't doing much, other than wasting their ammo, or just hiding. Jimmy stepped over to the edge of the woodpile he was behind and got down low. From here, he had a fine view of the gap between the underside of a Bronco and the ground. And just what did he see within that gap?

Legs and feets and knees. Lots of them.

They weren't kill shots. But goddamn, this was going to put the hurt on those fools. And what fun he would have in the process.

Jimmy raised his rifle, took careful aim, then fired.

• • •

"We need to flank them!"

"What the fuck are you saying?"

"I said we need to flank them."

"What the hell is that?"

"You know; get on their side, so's we can shoot them from the side. *Flank* them!"

Myron had no idea what the hell Steve was yelling. And that's because Myron had never served in the military, nor did he have the patience to play a video game such as *Rainbow Six*, *Halo*, or *Call of Duty* for six hours, in order to learn the strategic concept of flanking.

Adding to Myron's confusion was the ongoing chaotic madness they'd somehow gotten themselves into, and all in a matter of seconds. So much for coming up here with "surprise" on their side. It appeared they had rattled the hornet's nest with these damn hillbillies. And also, they were getting SHOT-UP. P-Dog was a goner, and glancing briefly down the line, Myron saw that at least one of their crew was dead, and probably more. There was a lot of hollering and firing and screaming going on. And now this motherfucker, Steve, yelling at Myron's face about something called flanking.

"Let's flank them!"

Myron shook his head. "I don't know what the fuck you're saying, fool!"

Steve gave a sour look. "Shit, Myron... You don't know shit!" Then he turned around and started yelling at one of the Cubans. They made a quick plan, and then they both came up to the front of the Bronco, where Myron was hiding behind.

"Can you at least cover us?" Steve asked Myron. "You know what that means, don't you?"

"Fuck you, nigger! I'll cover your shit... But what'cha gonna do?"

"We're gonna flank their asses," Steve replied. "Now shoot that fucking gun!"

Myron had half a mind to shoot his gun right at Steve's face. But clearly, this wasn't the time. Instead, he stood up and started spraying over the hood of the Bronco, his Russian made AKMS with folding stock popping off 7.62s like a string of firecrackers.

"Let's go," Steve said. And he and the Cuban dude ran out from cover and sprinted for what looked like the hills.

Where the fuck are they going? Myron wondered. Then a whole barrage of enemy bullets started sparking off the hood near his face, so he ducked down. *This is fucked! We're fucked!*

Myron turned and watched Steve and the other guy run as fast as they could toward the forest. They ran so fast, it reminded him of Emmitt Smith's famous 75 yard touchdown against the Redskins, back in '91.

"Where in the fuck are they going?" he wondered again, out loud.

But then—*Poof!* Just like that, both Steve and the other dude simply disappeared.

"*What?!* Where the fuck did they go?"

And what Myron didn't know was that Steve and his Cuban running mate went straight to a painful and deadly hell. Their momentum launched each of them into an uncontrolled dive down a well-concealed, fifteen-foot deep pit, filled with sharp stakes, sticking straight up—all courtesy of Flint Ramsey, now snickering in his grave.

Oh, but then the chaos got worse. Because just then, the top half of Myron's left foot blew off his leg.

• • •

The second tackle from Donny actually rattled the piece of turkey meat trapped in Blake's windpipe. But it didn't get it out. Now it was stuck at a weird angle, sort of half-in, half-out, allowing for a bit of wheezing, but still lodged down there pretty damn good.

"*Nooo...*" Blake gasped, trying once again to break free from Donny.

Donny had Blake pinned into a corner, and in a pile of rakes and ropes and other barnyard miscellanea.

That's right! Kill him again, Donny! Kill Blake again!

I's killing him again! I's killing Blake again!

"I's killing you again, Blake!"

All fighting rules were officially off the table. Donny was going at Blake like a cornered mountain lion. He scratched at Blake's eyes and bit into Blake's defending hands. He clobbered, whaled, and walloped. He gouged thumbs into soft parts, such as armpits and cheeks and ribcages and eyeballs. And Donny pulled hair, lots of hair, handfuls of hair, as he slammed Blake with elbows and shoulders and hips. With unrelenting force and speed, Donny unleashed a devastating, brutal assembly of attacks on his cousin.

"Get... off!" Blake gasped. Trapped under Donny like the piece of turkey meat in his throat, Blake was half-breathing and half-choking. He gagged and hacked, as his body tried desperately to climb up for some air. Meanwhile, Donny was beating and mauling him to a bloody pulp. And, oh yeah, can't forget, strangely, there sure was an awful lot of gunfire happening outside the barn right now, so whatever that was about.

"Get... off... me... you... son... of... a—" But then Donny destroyed the tail end of that sentence with a crushing elbow into Blake's nose.

"I's killing you for eating all the pie! I's killing you for eating Mickey Mouse! I's killing you for, for, for eating my asshole!"

Winded and fumbling for dear life, Blake found a length of rope on the ground, which he got over Donny's head, and then looped around Donny's neck, making an effective cinch. Then he started pulling outward with both hands, the rope cutting deep into Donny's neck.

And so, the epic fight between Donny and Blake Ramsey had now turned into both of them gasping for air at the same time.

• • •

"What the hell is all that shooting about?" Sam asked.

"How should I know?" Carson replied. And he didn't. He didn't know at all. But for sure, he was damn curious.

The scary-looking soldier man with the scary-looking sharp knife—here he was, Sam-I-am Nolan, in the flesh—had a queer look in his eye, as if he were thinking really hard about something.

Carson damned himself. He damned Boss-man too, because Carson knew he should've killed Sam-I-am earlier. But Boss-man had said no to that idea. Said that it wasn't a good idea. And where was Boss-man right now? Certainly not here with Carson, down in this soon-to-be grave, a sharp knife poking at his back.

"Never mind, then," Sam said, nudging Carson along. "Just find the girl."

Carson led them down the winding tunnel and toward the main entrance, where he suspected the girl might be. For one-tenth of one second, he considered turning around and fighting this guy, or maybe just running away. But he had been told that Sam was a very dangerous man. And Carson was far from an accomplished fighter, or a good runner, for that matter. Fighting or running would only end up with him being stabbed, or eventually caught—and then stabbed.

The tunnel was dimly lit. An orange glow of light wavered leisurely throughout the darkness. He looked up at the black ceiling, hearing the muffled cracks and rattles of distant gunfire, wondering just what in the hell was going on up there. Then he thought about Donny, picturing his brother in all that madness. Poor Donny. If he wasn't dead by now, he sure as hell must be in a world of terror.

"How much farther does this go?" Sam asked.

"It, ah... It goes for a bit more. There's rooms up ahead. She might be in one of them. I'm thinking she is."

"Alright, then. Keep going. And no sudden moves."

Carson kept going, heading toward the main entrance. They passed an alcove containing a wooden crate with a humming generator sitting on it, and a couple of gas cans on the side. About fifty feet later, they came to an opened door, then entered the first chamber of the tunnel system, a room with a large table and assorted bric-a-brac. The main entrance was down the tunnel off to their left. And that other little room Carson knew of—the one Donny always ran to when they played hide-n-seek down here, only because he was too afraid to go any further—was down the tunnel running straight in front of them.

"I think she might be down there," Carson said, pointing into the tunnel.

"Well then, let's go find out," Sam said. He pushed Carson ahead.

•   •   •

Roochie couldn't figure it out. How the hell could a wasp sting draw so much blood and cause so much pain? And how could a wasp sting make a fucking hole in his leg?

His pant-leg was covered in blood, all wet and sticky and cold, very cold. But it seemed the wasps had stopped coming for him. They weren't crashing their little bodies against the big metal thing anymore, so that was good.

Roochie glanced again at the Broncos. There were more men on the ground, bodies lying in weird angles, motionless. And look at Myron—he was screaming something terrible, and that was almost frightening for Roochie to see.

He turned and stared at his feet, baffled and wondering. He was still on quite the high, and the effects of that made him feel good. But also, it clouded the shit out of his thinking. Why in the hell was he up here in the mountains with all these guns shooting off? Why again had he and the crew come up here?

Oh yeah. Roochie remembered now. It was to kill that fucking hillbilly, Jimmy Ramsey. The same asshole that had cut Roochie's ear off.

He reached up and felt for his missing ear. Oddly, the spot didn't hurt anymore, as if the pain had traveled from the hole in his head to the hole in his leg. But Roochie was still pissed. The more he thought about what those inbreds had done to him, the more he wanted his revenge.

He looked down at his rifle, hoisted it up to his chin, aiming at nothing. He got up on his knees and turned, looking in the direction those hillbillies were at. And then—*oh shit!* Right there, ten feet in front of him and sneaking forward, was an ugly mountain dude. He had a big gun in his hands, was grinning widely, and Roochie saw that the man's teeth were not white, but shades of brown and yellow, that's how close he was. And the man's eyes, they were smiling too. Even as Roochie pulled the trigger and blew him away.

CHAPTER 35

The screaming was intense now. Every time Jimmy put his optic sight on a knee, or a foot, or a leg, then fired a three-round burst, one of those gangsters started screaming. But then, from off to his left, Jimmy heard one of his own boys screaming, too.

"They kilt my brother! They kilt Wayne, Jimmy! That son of a bitch shot him in the head. I'd seen it!"

It was Clyde, and it sounded like he was about to lose his shit.

Jimmy stood up quickly and looked over the woodpile. Clyde was running out in the open now, running toward the rusty tractor, and firing his gun. *No, you damn fool!* Jimmy thought, and he was about to shout those same words, but then he was too late. Clyde's body suddenly made a careening twist, bullets tearing into his chest, little clouds of dust and blood misting away from his clothes, as he then went to the ground.

"Son of a bitch!" Jimmy said, ducking back down. He moved to the other side of the woodpile, keeping low, looking for more targets. It seemed those gangsters had wizened up some. They were all hiding behind wheel wells now, or the occasional tree stump. Jimmy couldn't find a shot.

He looked over at the old tractor, wondering about that one fellow. Jimmy figured he was trying to get into a position to flank him and his boys. He had only fired one shot at the guy, and he didn't know if he'd hit him. But some of the others had been shooting at him too, and the man had definitely taken a round. Jimmy saw how he'd staggered those last few steps before getting behind the tractor. But was he dead now?

No, he wasn't.

Jimmy saw him then, hobbling from the tractor to the big old sycamore. He was wounded, wounded badly, Jimmy could tell. But he was doing the right thing. The bastard was trying to move up closer, and was moving out wider, working for a position that would bring flanking fire on to Jimmy and the others.

Quickly, Jimmy raised his gun and pulled the trigger, sending three groups of three-round bursts at the guy, all of which seemed to miss, dammit! That son of a bitch was a goddamn ghost.

• • •

"Motherfucker!!"

It was the worst pain of Myron's life. So bad, he was screaming like a little girl. Big old Myron T. Weathers, cool cat hoodlum from Charlotte, North Carolina's north side, badass motherfucker who owned fifteen blocks of crack-central, bankrolled half-a-dozen other hustles, and who, on more than one occasion, had stood on the Lord's end of a Glock nine mil, as he watched grown men pee their pants and beg for their mama's. That Myron T. Weathers, he was now crying like a little girl.

But it was the worst pain of Myron's life. And that's because the wound in his foot was now being accentuated by the fact that all around him were brothers in agony, brothers in trouble, brothers bleeding out, or brothers simply dead. Myron's crew was getting obliterated, and it was making the hole in his foot feel like he'd been shot in the heart.

"Fuck this!" he shouted. All of Myron's fear and angst suddenly turned into white-hot anger. He came to the conclusion that this was not possible anymore. That they couldn't be getting fucked in the ass like this by these damn hillbillies. Fuck this shit.

He got up and looked around, assessing the situation. The front of his foot was pouring out blood. Pounds was lying over there in the dirt, ten yards away. Looked like he was dead. Oh yeah, he was dead alright. That fat boy bought the same fate as P-Dog, both being so damn big they were impossible to miss. Looked like he'd been shot at least a dozen times.

Hoodlum and Z-Diggy were still in it, though. But they were both bleeding something fierce. Cookie was crawling on the ground, trying to get into a better shooting position, or maybe just to hide, and he'd obviously been shot in the leg. Slim-pickens looked okay, lying low behind a tire, firing steadily. But where the hell was Benny, king of the Cubans?

Myron stretched his neck and looked down the line of Broncos.

Oh, shit. Fucking Benny had never even made it out of the damn car. Dude's head was lying on the steering wheel, and there was blood all over the windshield.

Speaking of Cubans. There were only four of them left, and they looked pretty shot up. But they were still shooting back.

Myron looked to his left, past the frontend of the Bronco he was hiding behind. There was nothing over there, nothing to offer him cover. And somewhere over there was Steve and that other dude, but Myron had no idea what had happened to them.

Then he looked to his right, back down the line of Broncos. He had to do something, dammit. He couldn't just sit here and do nothing. Fuck that.

Staggering in pain, Myron quickly made his way down to the end of the Bronco. He peeked around the back of it for a brief second, looking for one of those hillbillies to shoot at, then instinctively ducked back. Then he peeked around again, spotted a dude crouching near the corner of that big barn, aiming and shooting his rifle.

Myron ducked back again, thinking *finally*, he had him a fucking target. He counted to three, lifted his AK, then swung back around. He put the iron sights on that dude, pulled the trigger, and fucking missed. Or did he? Myron pulled the trigger again, and this time he held it down, opened the damn gun all the way up on that dude, watching as dust and smoke lifted off the barn, and then off of that fucker too, as he dropped his gun and fell to the ground.

Myron ducked back behind the Bronco and crouched down, just in time. Bullets started pinging loudly into the metal behind him. "Got you, motherfucker!" he said with a laugh. "I got your fucking ass!"

But there were more of them honkies. Lots more. And how many? Myron didn't have a clue. One less now, but still, many, many more.

Myron thought he'd probably get his head blown off if he looked back there again, 'cause those damn bullets traveled so fast it was almost surreal. So he hobbled back to the front of the Bronco, then got down on his knees and peeked around that side. He couldn't see shit, so he stood up and looked over the hood, and then bullets started bouncing all around him, so he ducked back down again. Motherfuckers were on to his shit.

Staying low, Myron peeked under the front of the Bronco. And then he saw something up ahead, toward the single-wide, and about a hundred feet away from him. It was a cluster of steel oil barrels surrounded by a few wooden logs, and what looked like an old antique stove. Looked like pretty good cover to him. But there was no way in hell he could run that far without getting nailed. Not with his foot being all shot up. Although...

With an idea now in his head, Myron hustled back to the backend of the Bronco. He turned the corner, fired away with his AK until it was empty, and ducked back around. Then he popped in a fresh magazine and hobbled his way to the front of the Bronco, got down on his belly, and studied the path ahead of him.

Now, this was some scary shit.

Myron started crawling on his belly, inching forward, and under the frontend of the vehicle.

Hell yeah, this was some real scary shit.

But he kept going. Like a damn snake, flat on the ground, toward all those motherfuckers who were shooting back at him and his crew. He kept going, right out into the open. Except that, conveniently enough, the weeds and grass between Myron and that cover he was aiming for seemed a bit too high. In fact, the weeds seemed *real* high. *White folks never liked doing their fucking chores. That's what they used us niggers for. Alright, then, Jimmy-lazy-ass-motherfuckin'-Ramsey. Too good to get up off your ass and do you some yard work? Let's just see what that'll cost you.*

Staying low-rider low, Myron kept going, inching his way through the tall grass and through the tall weeds.

· · ·

The Eurocopter AS365 Dauphin, swift and silent, traveled across the early morning Carolina hills like a soaring swallow. It was painted black, unmarked, and it moved fast and low. If a person didn't know any better, watching as the thing zoomed on by, they'd think they were seeing one of those government spook choppers out of Groom Lake, or maybe from some unacknowledged special access program. Considering the jobs Madigan and his team had pulled over the years, that wasn't too far from the truth.

Their faces were striped with black and green paint. The men looked fierce and dangerous. Guns cocked and locked, eyes flinty and gleaming, stern, yet relaxed, expressions on their faces. It was just another day in the office.

"L-Z in seven minutes," the pilot said, referring to the landing zone Madigan had suggested, which was a small field downwind, and approximately a quarter of a mile from the coordinates Sam had texted him.

"Roger that," Madigan replied, speaking into his headset. He turned toward his men. "Show time in five." He received calm nods and thumbs up in return.

They didn't know what they were getting into. But they sure as hell looked ready.

•　•　•

The wasps were back again. After Roochie blasted that dude in the face, the wasps came soaring after his ass. So Roochie took off.

He waddled once again out into the open, hands holding his pants and rifle as he headed for a big tree. It was a wide tree, real wide, and Roochie was hoping if he could get behind it, he'd be all but invisible. And maybe then those wasps would forget about him.

It was a long run, and he heard at least a dozen of those little bastards scream by. Funny how they did that—fly so fast they couldn't turn their bodies around to sting him.

A few of them slammed into the tree just as Roochie made it there, flecks of bark spitting out at him. Well, what do you know? He did it again. Never mind that hole in his leg, because old Rooch was one fast and lucky son of a bitch.

Behind the big tree, Roochie suddenly chuckled. Then he laughed. Then he howled hysterically, before turning around and firing his gun. And then, fuck it—Roochie ran out into the open once more.

•　•　•

"I's... killing... you... Blake..."

Somehow, as Donny pummeled, scratched, and clawed, his world was turning blue. There was a great ring of fiery pain circling his neck, and he felt like he was being pushed underwater, forced to hold his breath.

I cain't... I cain't... breathe.

Carson had stopped talking to him. Now, it was just the voice of that strange feller, and a weakened voice at that. Everything and everybody seemed to be drifting away from Donny, off to some hazy, wild blue yonder.

He stopped the hitting and mauling. He put his hands around Blake's throat, then started choking the man, squeezing down really, really hard. His cousin's eyes were glossing over. They looked glassy and filled with milk. He'd stopped squirming, and his body was now rigid and tense.

"Youuuu.... idiot," Blake gasped.

Oddly, Blake was holding on to a length of rope, and for the life of him, Donny couldn't figure out why. *Why is he doing that, when I's a killing him?*

"Because you're stupid, that's why."

Who said that?

Donny looked up. It was the rooster. *What?* Yes, the goddamn rooster. The same one that had given him that mean look while he was leaving the trailer a few minutes ago.

The rooster was on the ground in front of him, but sauntering forward, chest puffed out, feathers ruffled, like it owned the whole damn barn. "That's right, I just said that, you son of a bitch," the rooster added, now using Mema's voice. It was staring right at Donny, its beady little eyes full of malice. "And that's because it's true, Donny Darryl Ramsey. You're the stupidest man to walk the face of the earth. You're even stupider than a chicken... which, come to think of it, you've eaten plenty of us in your sorry time, haven't you? Haven't you, you big, dumb pile of shit?"

Was this really happening? Donny blinked, hardly believing his eyes and ears.

"*You... fool...*" Blake wheezed from below him.

Then Donny clenched harder, pushing all his weight and his stupid strength into the squeeze around Blake's neck. He felt something pop in there, and Blake did a little jolt, gave a high-pitched gasp, and at the same time, the blue fog surrounding Donny turned three shades darker. And then it shrank inward, toward him, like someone was slowly closing the door to a room filled with darkness.

"No, you big dummy," said the rooster, which had grown now, was as big as Donny. "You're the one who gets to die. Not him. And once you're dead, Donny-boy, I'm gonna peck your goddamn eyeballs out. Both of them."

Oh, no, it's getting dark outside. I's afraid of the dark.

"Time to die, Donny." The rooster laughed, a great booming laugh that filled the barn and echoed throughout the rafters. "It's time for you to die."

Donny closed his eyes as a world of terror swirled before him. And then everything faded to black.

CHAPTER 36

It was a short tunnel, dank and vaguely lit, but well trodden. It led to a room which instantly gave Sam the creeps. He looked around, studying the little hole in the earth. He saw an unmade bed against the wall, blankets and sheets tousled about, along with filthy rags and a few empty bottles of whiskey. There was a television mounted on the wall to his right, and under that were crates on the ground containing what looked like DVDs. A small table was set to the side, cluttered with more movies, along with an ashtray stuffed with cigarette ash and butts, a couple of cigar nubs. The smell was mostly wet decay, but there was a sweet, oily odor lingering in the room as well.

"What is this place?" Sam asked.

"Hell if I know," Carson replied.

Sam continued to scan the room, noticing the out-of-place yellow sheet hanging in the far corner.

"Over there," he said, nudging the knife at the man's back as they walked further in. "Take that sheet down."

Carson did as he was told. He yanked the sheet away, at once revealing the locked iron door.

"I'll be damned," Sam mumbled to himself. "She's in there, ain't she?"

The man seemed a bit mesmerized, staring coldly at the door, which was secured with a fat padlock.

"Step aside," Sam said, keeping his knife poised low, out of the man's reach, but ready to stab if need be. He moved to the man's side, then gave the door a strong pound with his fist. "Emily! Emily Parker! Are you in there?"

They both listened.

"Emily Parker!" Sam shouted again, pounding on the door. "Your dad, Shiloh, sent me. Say something if you're in there!"

Then, along with the distant cracking noises coming from the gunfire above and outside, there came a soft, hopeful voice from behind the door. "Yes. Yes, I am. I'm in here!"

•   •   •

Myron couldn't believe how hard it was to crawl one hundred feet on his belly. *How the fuck do soldiers do this shit?* he wondered. And he wasn't even wearing a big old rucksack.

Having half his foot shot off sure didn't help matters any. Every few feet of crawling, the ragged tip of his foot would bonk down onto the ground, or it would catch onto an exposed root or rock, and then send a ripple of hot pain up his leg.

He didn't know how long he could keep going, messed up as he was. But Myron tried not to think about that shit. He kept his focus on getting across the weed-infested yard, then into position behind the cluster of barrels and wood and whatever.

It was a painstaking process; inch-by-inch, foot-by-foot, as the bullets whizzed by overhead, clattering into the vehicles behind him, and to his right. Those damn hillbillies hadn't caught on to Myron yet, or else they would've shot the shit out of him by now. He prayed to the Lord and to Jesus Christ, as he kept going, G.I. Joe style, all the way to the heap of cover.

He was winded as hell when he got there. And in a world of unbelievable pain. He crawled under the angle of a big log, which was lying propped up on a stack of wood and junk. He took a minute to catch his breath, his face grimacing at the stinging tenderness in his foot. Goddamn, this was one hell of a war, wasn't it?

"Motherfuckin' crackers, smoking our shit up," he mumbled quietly. "Ain't gonna let that shit happen no more, no fuckin' way."

He checked his gun, making sure nothing got messed up or had fallen out while crawling. It looked good, ready to kick some ass. Myron shimmied his body further into the concealment of the oil barrels. Then he started peeking through cracks here and there. He couldn't see shit, so he got up on his knees and peered over the barrels. Quickly, he ducked back down and smiled.

Oh yeah, these fuckers are all mine.

Getting into a squatting position, careful not to bonk his foot again, Myron prepared himself. He checked to make sure his gun hadn't slipped into the safety, figuring that kind of shit could happen, and at the worst possible moments, too. Then, as fast as he could, he stood up, aimed, and pulled the trigger.

• • •

Jimmy started taking flanking fire. From his right, someone was shooting at him. He heard screams then, new screams, screams from his own side, just as bullets started ripping into the surrounding woodpile.

He turned quickly, fired a few random shots, but couldn't tell exactly where the fire was coming from, so he ducked back around the other side of the woodpile. Big mistake. Because now he was taking fire from the gangsters behind the Broncos.

This was how soldiers died and died quickly. Jimmy panicked. He turned and ran back toward the barn, hearing bullets cut through the air. He saw one of his guys lying dead in the yard—looked like Randall—and then another one near the front of the barn. Then, as he came around the corner of the mobile home, heading toward some good cover, there he was, that wannabe gangster, right in front of Jimmy, not more than fifty feet away. The punk with the missing ear.

He was standing between the barn and the old water tank, and there was a river of blood all down his pants. But he had his gun raised, and he was aiming right for Jimmy.

Jimmy pulled his AR up and fired. At the same time, he saw a flash of yellow fire coming from the punk's gun, and then he felt something punch into his chest above his heart.

Oddly, there was no pain. Jimmy's adrenaline was running in overdrive. He saw the man drop to his knees, then Jimmy kept going.

Another man—Hardy—was lying dead against a truck, his head hanging low. Goddamn, things were unraveling pretty fast, weren't they? How could this be happening to him? And where the fuck were the rest of his kin?

He was down to his last magazine, so he ran into the house, looking for more, but not finding any. Windows started shattering then, bullets were tearing into the place. He heard dull beating sounds against the house's siding. They were coming for him, so Jimmy went out through the back door, and then headed for the old tunnels.

The pain had found him by then. His shoulder and chest burned. He was leaking blood pretty good now, and he could feel it running down his back, which meant that that man's bullet had made a mean exit wound. But Jimmy's legs were still in the game. So he pumped them hard, driving his way to the dead oak tree.

When he got to the door, and the entrance down into the tunnels, Jimmy turned around and looked. He saw a few of those gangsters running between buildings, guns firing. Looked like those fuckers were overrunning the place.

Jimmy cursed. This kind of nonsense should never happen. Not to no country boys like him.

Alright, then, you sons of bitches, he thought. *Good luck coming for me in here.* Then Jimmy climbed down into the tunnels.

. . .

Oh, man, Roochie was the fastest man alive. For the *third* time, he outran a horde of wasps. Even with a big, bad, bloody sting in his leg, he still made it.

He was behind an enormous black bucket now, some kind of tank, with the side of the barn just a few feet to his right. And not a single one of those ugly insects had found him.

He looked over at the barn and saw a dead dude on the ground. The man's eyes were open, and it seemed like he was staring at Roochie, a look of amazed wonder on his dead face. Maybe he was wondering how Roochie did it. How Roochie outran all those angry little wasps, because he sure as hell didn't.

Roochie smiled. Then he walked out from around the tank and slowly started toward the front of the barn. He had pigs to kill, he just remembered. But first, he and Myron were going to feed that mean old Jimmy Ramsey to those filthy animals. So where was that fucking hillbilly?

Wait a second. *There he is!* Right there in front of Roochie, on the run, running from wasps, his long blond hair trailing behind him.

Roochie stopped walking. A voice of icy terror suddenly started screaming inside his head, followed by a tingling jolt in his neck and face, and then at the hole where his ear once lived. He raised his *Galil* and fired. He caught a glimpse of stuff getting torn up on the mobile home behind Jimmy, right before he saw that mean man take one to the chest. And that was followed by a blossom of fire coming from Jimmy's own gun.

Oh shit, oh damn, oh man... It would seem Roochie's luck had run out. One of those wasps finally found him good. He felt its stinger bury itself deep, right into his heart. Then, weirdly, the whole world turned into some kind of indoor arena, and Roochie was a dreaming kid again, at a Guns 'N' Roses concert, sitting in the nosebleed section. All the best things in life were right there in front of him, his dreams, maybe his *only* dream. But shit, that dream was so clouded, and so very far away, that it crushed Roochie's little heart, knowing he didn't have one chance in hell at grasping it.

They were playing *Sweet Child O'Mine*, Roochie's all-time favorite. And it was the last thing he heard as he dropped to his knees, smiled pensively, then found the ground and closed his eyes.

•   •   •

Madigan was the first one out of the chopper. Seconds later, the other three were out as well, having static lined down onto the small clearing, then spreading out to form a perimeter, guns raised, covering all fields of fire.

They waited for the chopper to leave, and for the silence of the morning wilderness to come back. But it never did. Because in the forward distance, a quarter of a mile away, was gunfire. Lots of gunfire.

"That's an AK," Jackson whispered.

Madigan nodded, and so did the others. Every one of them knew the sound of that gun model, particularly when the barrels were aiming in their direction.

"There's more," Madigan said. "NATO rounds. Sounds like a war going on up there."

"Well, what are we waiting for?" Chancey said.

"Good question," Madigan replied. He gave the hand signal to move out.

He led the unit forward at a modest speed, faster than what they would have normally traveled in hostile territory, knowing that Sam was possibly up there by himself in all of that. And while moving, they maintained a two-man, staggered column formation, covering their flanks and crouching low as they leapfrogged ahead.

Madigan suddenly stopped the team. Everyone took a knee, guns raised, eyes in their sights. "A reminder," he whispered. "Rules of engagement are bunghole tight. Fire only when fired upon, or imminent threat is obtained. I don't want us killing any innocents up here."

The men gave quick nods, then Madigan moved them out again.

They swept forward, watching for booby traps and for men with guns, not exactly sure what they were getting into. After a few minutes, they approached a tree line, which opened up onto a large property with a big barn, several buildings, and lots of vehicles. It's where the war was being staged.

He stopped them again, and the men spread out, taking cover behind trees.

"Booby," Boon-ass suddenly said, pointing to a cluster of small pebbles and debris on the ground near his feet. "Looks like a trigger pad," he added. "Or a small I-E-D."

"Nice catch," Madigan whispered.

Carefully, Boon-ass cleared the debris from the pebbles, then reached in and disengaged the shotgun bullet, which was aiming straight up, ready to blow the foot off anyone unlucky enough to step on the pad.

"Man, you got some balls," Jackson said.

"I've seen a ton of these things," Boon-ass replied. He put the shell in his pocket, then smiled. "Another one for my collection."

Madigan sent a text message to Sam's sat phone, then waited. After a few minutes of no response, he started to worry. He studied the property ahead of them, determined a path, then said, "Let's go." He gave the signal, and the men crept out of the tree line, falling back into a single file column. They stayed tight, and stayed low, as Madigan took point and quickly led them across an open field, and toward the backside of the barn.

•   •   •

Sam felt a rush of optimism. He looked at the door, then pulled on the lock. It was held fast, and too thick to pry open with his knife.

He needed something to break it. A tool of some sort, which he didn't have.

Suddenly, the little wiry white trash dude was now a huge burden for Sam. He couldn't just leave him be while he looked for something he could use to break the lock. There might be a gun hidden down here, which this guy would run and get once Sam took his eyes off of him.

"I need something to break that lock," Sam said. "What's down here that I could use?"

"Mister, I don't know shit about this place."

"Don't get smart with me, boy," Sam said. He grabbed the man by the lapel, then spun him around. "Let's start looking then."

He pushed the guy forward while carefully studying the room again, looking for a tool or a heavy object of some sort. There didn't appear to be anything in here. Then Sam wondered if one of those rooms down the tunnel had something. Perhaps the chambers with all that drug making equipment. "Let's keep going," Sam said.

They walked back into the tunnel, then toward the first chamber with the table containing miscellaneous junk. There might be something in there. Sam remembered seeing a few small tools and other hardware scattered about the room.

When they cleared the tunnel, Sam heard something coming up on his right. He turned and looked.

It was a tall, long-haired hillbilly holding an AR-15, slightly crouched, and shuffling toward them. But then the hillbilly suddenly stopped.

"Oh, shit!" the wiry guy said. "Jimmy-James…"

Jimmy raised his gun at them and fired.

•　•　•

Myron killed two white boys in a single hail of bullets, and he thought he wounded another one. He unloaded a whole clip on those dudes, right into their sides. Goddamn, he was *flanking* them.

He watched as their bodies jerked and went rigid, then slid to the ground. The third guy, he ducked down behind cover, and so did Myron, once his gun ran out of ammo.

He popped the magazine and dropped it, then fished another one out of his tactical vest, slammed it in and pulled the charging handle. Back in the game, motherfuckers.

Myron glanced at his foot, then looked away. He might be a cripple after this. But damn, he just might survive this shit. That's how he was feeling, at least.

He stood up again and scanned the battlefield. He saw a man running around the trailer. Looked like Jimmy James Ramsey, but Myron wasn't a hundred percent certain.

There seemed to be less gunfire now. Everybody was dead, or wounded gravely. He glanced over at the wall of Broncos and saw movement. Then one of the Cubans stepped forward, out into the open.

"That's right!" Myron shouted, feeling a world of confidence now. "Move on in, boys. Let's mop this shit up!"

Somebody started shooting at him then, bullets ripping into the steel barrels. Myron didn't duck this time. He turned, spotted who it was—some ugly cracker behind a tree about fifty feet away—then Myron let that dude have it. The man took a full burst into his midsection, dropped his gun, then slid to the ground. "Fuck yeah! There's another one of you motherfuckers in the grave!"

Another Cuban came out from behind the Broncos, followed by Slim-pickens, their guns pointing forward, ready to shoot.

Now Myron was feeling really, really confident. He heard his own voice inside his head speaking from the past, talking about Ghost Recon *this*, Seal Team Six *that*, words meant to pump his guys up, but which were now pumping Myron up.

Like a smooth Special Forces operator (with a fucked up foot), Myron slid out from behind his cover and hobbled closer to the yard. It was time to end this thing.

CHAPTER 37

Son of a bitch, Jimmy missed. His aim was too high, and then both of those men took off.

And just who the hell were they?

It was Carson and that soldier boy. Carson had split to his left, further down into the tunnels. But that Sam fellow, he went the other way. And that way, Jimmy knew, was a dead end.

He checked his gun. It was out of bullets, dammit, and he had no more magazines. Well, that's alright. This wouldn't be the first time Jimmy opened a man's throat with his knife. But what if the soldier boy had a gun? That was a chance Jimmy would just have to take.

He dropped his AR and pulled out his AT—the old Arkansas Toothpick—then stepped forward, moving slowly and crouching low. He walked down the tunnel, came to the corner opening into the room, then paused. He didn't hear anything—no breathing, no running feet, no pulling back on the hammer of a revolver. And Jimmy didn't smell anything either, other than the tunnel system's typical aroma of mildew and wet earth.

Jimmy turned the corner and looked.

Surprise!

Somewhere in the back of his head was a blurred memory of a story his dad once told him, about how those gooks in 'Nam did all kinds of sneaky little things to catch a man off his guard. One such thing was to crouch down very low on the other side of a corner, so as to be out of a G.I.'s line of sight as he came around, knowing that that scared-as-shit American's tunnel vision would be focused on what was way *out there*, and not *down here*, below him. Those damn gooks only needed a split second's advantage to get their round off, or drive a bayonet up and forward, and Mr. G.I. was a dead G.I. Happened all the time, so Flint had said.

And now that same tactic happened to Jimmy. As he turned the corner, his eyes focusing toward the tunnel leading into the room he kept that girl in, Sam sprang up from a low crouch below and drove something cold and sharp into Jimmy's side.

"Goddamn you!" Jimmy said, backing away and slashing out with his own knife, but missing.

The soldier boy quickly stepped back, unharmed. And there was blood on his blade—Jimmy's blood.

Jimmy put a hand on his side, where he'd been stabbed. It came back wet, but he hardly felt anything. Maybe his adrenaline had cranked up again. And it wasn't a fatal wound, or so it seemed. No guts were spilling out of him. He could still breathe. "You wanna fight, eh?" he said. "Okay, then. Let's fight."

Jimmy moved closer, knife poised outward. He was a good four to five inches taller than the man, so he had the reach on him, which, as Jimmy knew, meant all the difference in a knife fight.

"Come here to look for that girl, did you?" Jimmy said with a snicker. He shuffled to the side, getting into a better position. He was looking for a good opening to thrust his knife into. "Well, I hate to disappoint you, because—" And then Jimmy found it. His opening. And he sprang forward.

•　•　•

Sam jumped out of the way, slashing outward, aiming his blade at the man's striking hand, just as Madigan had trained him. *Don't worry about the body, or the neck, or the head... But instead, go for the hands, the wrists, the tendons. Cut one of those on your enemy, and they'll drop their weapon for sure. Then you'll have all the body, neck, and head you want.*

But this guy was fast. And he was tall, too. He pulled his hand away just as Sam reached out, said a few taunts, then rushed forward.

Sam dropped and rolled to his side without thinking, instincts and training taking over as the big man's knife skimmed on by. Then Sam let the momentum of his roll bring him back up on his feet. He spun around, slashing again.

This time, his knife struck home. It cut across the man's bare arm, opening a nice red wound, right on his biceps.

"Son of a bitch," the man cursed. "You're gonna get it good now, boy."

He lunged in again, but it was a feint, and Sam took the bait. He stepped back to parry with his knife just as the man grabbed something with his free hand from the nearby table and hurled it at Sam. It was an empty bottle, a glass bottle, and it slammed right onto Sam's forehead, ringing his bell.

Sam stepped back. But the man came in again, right after the bottle throw, his knife swinging and stabbing.

Sam felt a burn across his left arm, pulled away, parried with his knife, then stepped back again, his foot finding the edge of the room.

"You're dead," the man said, lunging forward.

But this time he was too confident, and his great height bit back at him. Sam ducked low, well beneath the man's stab, and then stood and drove his own knife into the man's biceps, punching deep into the flesh, causing him to drop his knife. Then Sam followed up with an inward elbow across the man's jaw.

The big boy staggered backward, a look of shock on his face. Sam kicked away his knife, sending it underneath the table, out of reach. "Looks like you're on the losing end now, mister," Sam said. He stepped closer, and then a fresh round of gunfire went off from up above. It sounded like the battle had picked up some, and Sam noticed the man's eyes glance down the tunnel he'd come from, a look of worry rippling across his face. "Why don't you just do the right thing and let the girl go?" Sam said. "The jig is up. You'll be lucky to survive this day."

The man's worry turned into a look of hatred. "And why don't you just suck my cock, soldier boy?" Then he rushed in like a berserker, all his weight and height and speed coming recklessly at Sam, a locomotive sliding off the tracks.

He took Sam's knife in the midsection again, but his speed caught Sam off guard, and his driving momentum pushed Sam against the earthen wall. Then the man started pounding, dropping elbows and fists onto Sam's head, shoulders, ribs, stomach. Sam lost grip with his knife, or maybe it was stuck inside the guy or thrown to the side, who knew? But he brought his hands up in defense, weathering the storm as best he could.

It wasn't enough, though. And damn, the man was fast, powerful, and seemingly impossible to kill. Someone was turning out the lights then. Things grew darker for Sam as he kneeled, or ducked away, or threw his own punches and elbows against the onslaught tearing into him.

But unfortunately, Sam was unable to fend off the blows. And then the final light went out, with darkness taking over—except, of course, for the spangling strobes now circling the inside of Sam's head.

* * *

Jimmy could've killed the man, and with any luck, maybe he did. But he was out of time. Because those gangsters were up there, and he knew they were coming for him.

He left the soldier in a heap on the ground, then staggered down the tunnel. Goddamn, he was bleeding good now. In his shoulder, his arm, his gut. But Jimmy was far from being finished, a big old country boy like him. And he had yet another option to pursue, another card to play. It was lying way up there on the mountain, just waiting for him. The old cache—another lesson his dad had taught him years ago. *Keep yourself some guns and ammo and food and radio and other gear in a hidden stash. Somewhere close, but not too close, 'cause one day, you just might need it.*

Of course, Jimmy had lots of guns on his property, most of which were in the house, or maybe in the barn, but not down here. And he didn't dare go up there right now to fetch one. No. He would head for the hills to regroup and resupply. Let those thugs have their way for now, despite Jimmy's angry thoughts on the matter...

But he'd be damned if he'd let them get to his woman.

He made his way through the tunnel and into the small room. He fumbled for the key around his neck, got it off, then went to the door and opened it.

Jimmy stepped into the little chamber and pulled the light string. The dingy place lit up, and the girl recoiled from the intensity of the light, being in darkness as long as she was. Chains jingled as she pulled her legs back, curling up. There was a look of terror in her eyes. She always seemed to have that look, and it disappointed Jimmy to no end. But now wasn't the time to worry about that.

"It's time to go," he said, his tone short and tense.

"What's going on?" Emily asked. Her big eyes glanced at the ceiling.

"Nothing to worry about," Jimmy replied. He reached for another key, which was hanging from a support beam near the light. (See now, that was a nice little kicker. It was Blake's idea, actually, to leave the key to the girl's shackles just out of her reach. Not that it would've helped her escape any. But it was a pleasant tease, nonetheless.)

Quickly, Jimmy took the key, went to the girl, and unlocked the chains binding her hands and ankles. She was free now, free to run. But she wasn't going anywhere. Not without him.

She tried anyway, the little spitfire. Once the last shackle came off, Emily scrambled up and back, trying to get away from Jimmy, trying to get out. She saw he was hurt, and maybe she could use that to her advantage. And that was some damn foolish thinking on her part.

Jimmy caught her easily, his strong grip taking Emily by the back of the hair and pulling her face up to his. "You ain't running nowhere, girl. So don't you even try. Now let's go."

He kept hold of her hair and dragged her out of the chamber, into the room, and then down the tunnel. She winced as she dragged her feet in resistance. But that only made her pain worse.

"Let me go!" Emily cried.

"Shush up, girl," Jimmy replied. "And keep moving."

They went down the hall, past the small room where Sam was still lying. He looked unconscious, and hopefully he was dead, but Jimmy didn't stop to find out. He took the girl further into the tunnels, and then into the darker realm, still dragging her by the hair, her feet and legs squirming and kicking, her disheveled yet pretty face grimacing against the pain. Down into the faintly lit darkness they went, with the sounds of the gunfire from above fading with every step.

• • •

They were winning! Shit, maybe they had already won.

Myron shuffled forward, out into the open, toward the barn and the house, the main yard. The shooting had stopped for now. He walked past a couple of really dead white boys, their heads and chests ripped open. He saw two of the Cubans slink past him, about thirty yards ahead, with Slim-pickens slowly following. Over by the Broncos, there was a bit of movement. Hoodlum was standing in between two of the vehicles, his rifle half-raised. He looked messed up, lots of blood. Looked like he'd been shot in both arms and both legs.

"Anybody else?" Myron asked.

Hoodlum shook his head. "Motherfuckers killed us all. Ain't nothing back here but a bunch of dead niggers." His face twisted in agony then. "Might be I'm fixing to join 'em." He leaned against one of the Broncos, his face losing color.

Myron felt like he should say something, but oddly, he didn't want to. He was suddenly feeling exhausted, as if he'd been punched in the gut and all the wind had swept out of him.

He hobbled forward. His foot ached like a motherfucker. It looked like it stopped bleeding, and Myron didn't know how in the hell that was possible, since half of it was gone. But he kept going, despite the pain. *Job's gotta get finished. Ain't no fuckin' rest for the wicked.*

He made his way closer to the barn and the house. There were some trucks parked in between the buildings, and a black van parked under a tree, all shot up pretty good. A couple more dead white boys. Hell yeah, this was what war looked like.

Myron got to the little shack and paused. What was the plan now? The Cubans and Slim-pickens were running about, looking for more hillbillies to kill, but it didn't sound like any more of them were alive. Except for that Ramsey fool. Myron hadn't seen his body anywhere. And what about Roochie? Where the hell was Roochie?

All these unanswered questions rattling through Myron's head created a thick veil that obscured his thinking. Wasn't this called the fog of war?

But then, suddenly, he heard more gunshots, and Myron blinked and snapped out of it. He looked up and over at the barn. Curiously, the gunfire sounded different from what he'd been hearing all morning. It sounded rapid, yet controlled, and was coming from several guns. Myron heard a strangled cry, followed by a single shot, more gunfire, another cry, and then a whole heated blast of shooting, which was cut off abruptly. And then nothing but silence.

What the fuck is going on over there? Myron thought.

Something cold shivered inside Myron's guts. He adjusted his gun and took a step forward, toward the edge of the barn. He looked over at the Broncos, saw Hoodlum lying on the ground now, motionless.

What in the fuck is going on?

And then, the weirdest thing happened.

Motherfucking Ghost Recon... Seal Team Six...

Myron's very own words suddenly crawled to life, *real life*, and on the motion picture screen of this backwoods war he was trudging through. Four mean-looking, badass motherfuckers came stalking toward Myron, all decked out in black and green, their grim faces painted to match their clothes, their bodies crouched low, scary-ass looking guns aiming right at him... Goddamn, this shit was *surreal*.

And then Myron did the stupidest of all stupid things, although he didn't mean to. He just reacted, jacked up from all this death and war surrounding him.

What he did was raise his AK. Out of instincts, sure, but it was still stupid. And because Myron did this stupid thing, those recon ghosts let loose with some violent fire. Then the curtain finally came down, and the war movie he was living suddenly turned to black. Three in the body and one in the head—Myron T. Weathers got shot dead.

CHAPTER 38

The gunfire halted as they moved forward. Madigan led his team through tall grass, past a few piles of rusted junk, some old car parts, then closer toward a barn. They kept low profiles and maintained formation, Madigan on point, and the other three trailing behind, single file.

There was a rise of land just before the barn. As Madigan led them up it, he saw a dead guy lying face down on the ground. Then, from inside the barn, out came a man with a gun. A young Hispanic-looking guy holding an AK-47, and staring curiously at Madigan, as if he couldn't understand what he was seeing. And he probably didn't.

Madigan kept his sights on the man, while his other hand was swiftly motioning downward, making the universal signal for the guy to drop his gun and get his fucking ass on the ground.

But it was no use. Because the man's look of curiosity instantly switched to alarm. And then he quickly raised his gun. Bad idea.

Madigan wasted no time. He fired two shots from his M4, a double tap, hitting the dude twice in the forehead and dropping him fast.

The team didn't stop or say anything. They just kept moving.

A second later, another man appeared, and he looked the same as the last. Hispanic, tattoos, gold chain, holding a different gun though, an SK-S rifle. He didn't see Madigan and the others right away, as he was staring at the guy who had just been shot. But then he looked around, spotted the team, raised his gun, and went down hard, taking a bullet in the chest and face.

They kept moving.

Along the side of the barn now, sweeping past the guys they had neutralized, and then past two other dead men, until a black man with a shotgun stepped in front of them, aimed, and fired.

The team instantly split apart, two men jumping to the right, the other two to the left, as the spray from the shotgun blast swept harmlessly between them. Then, a quick burst from their guns later, the man with the shotgun turned to pulp.

Madigan paused.

"Everyone good?" he whispered.

"Good," they all replied.

He moved them out again. How many more of these gun-toting bad guys were there? And more importantly, was Sam still alive?

They came to the front of the barn. But before they cleared the corner, another black man appeared. He was holding an AK with a folding stock. He had a tired look in his eyes. And like the first man they had shot, he stared at Madigan with utter disbelief. And, unfortunately, just like the first guy, this man also raised his rifle. It was the last thing he did.

They didn't see any more men after that. Well, not any *living* men. The team stayed together as they scoured the property, examining the dead bodies, searching for Sam, and hoping he wasn't in with this mix.

"What the hell went on out here?" Madigan said. "Looks like a bad deal, that's for sure." He had no idea what had prompted this little war up in the boondocks. But judging by the looks of the characters involved—hillbillies and city gangsters—he thought for sure drugs must have had something to do with it.

"Secure our position," Madigan said. And then the other three spread out, took a knee, and covered their perimeter. Madigan pulled out his phone then and dialed Sam.

• • •

He woke to the sound of a girl screaming. Sam blinked his eyes, then shook his head. He was lying on the ground, pain swirling throughout his body. In seconds, he'd gotten his ass whipped by that big country boy.

Sam shook his head again, trying to come out of it. He heard the girl once more, cursing, saying something to the effect of *Let me go!*

It all came back to Sam. He slowly crawled his way into standing position while listening. She was down there, deeper in the tunnels, and with that long-haired man Sam now knew was Jimmy Ramsey.

He could hear rustling. A clear struggle was going on, as if Emily were putting up a fight.

Sam looked for his knife, but couldn't find it. He found a metal pipe, though, lying in between a heap of junk on the table. It was about a foot long and an inch thick, and was better than nothing. Forgetting about his pain, Sam grabbed the pipe and took off running.

• • •

"Let me go!" Emily cried.

"Stop your fighting, woman!" Jimmy cranked back on her hair as he shook her. "I'm getting tired of your sass."

She went still for a second, but then started kicking and squirming again.

Jimmy kept going, dragging and pushing her along. He made it into the kitchen, the chamber where they cooked the meth, and looked around. He spotted a box-cutting blade sitting on a table, which he took and put into his pocket. Then he found several lengths of rope coiled up on a barrel. He grabbed a piece and started tying it around Emily's neck.

She bit into his hand then.

"Why, you little—" Jimmy started. He smacked her hard across the face. That seemed to work. It stunned her, at least. Enough to finish tying the rope around her neck. Then he tied another length around her ankle and pulled her toward the escape route, the ladder leading up and out of the underground system.

Jimmy grabbed both of Emily's shoulders and shook her. "Now you listen to me, woman. You're going up that ladder, and that's that. And I'll be right behind you. So if you give me anymore sass, or try to run off, or you start your screaming, on my mama's grave, it'll cost you." He shoved her toward the ladder then. "Now get up there, missy!"

• • •

They were gone when he got there. But it didn't take Sam long to figure out where they went.

He ran to the ladder, the one he'd used to enter the tunnel system, and looked up. The hatch was open. A dull morning light was leaking down from above. Sam could see the wet shine of blood on several of the rungs. Then he heard a scuffle up there, a rustling of leaves, the girl being dragged or roughed up.

Sam tucked the pipe under his belt behind his back, then went swiftly up the ladder. He came out into the brightness of the morning and looked around. He spotted Jimmy and the girl up ahead, in the trees, about thirty yards away. They were struggling. The girl was clearly making things difficult for Jimmy.

Sam got the pipe out and ran toward them, clearing the distance in seconds. But also alerting Jimmy to his presence.

The tall man turned and looked. Then he swung around, pulling the girl between him and Sam. He pushed her to her knees and pulled out a blade—a box-cutter—and put it at her throat. He looked like a desperate wild man now, his long hair in disarray, his face sweaty and mean-streaked, blood trickling down his arms. He was ready to kill, and Sam knew it.

Sam stopped within five feet of Jimmy and the girl.

"I'm about tired of both of you," Jimmy said. He was staring at Sam, anger and desperation battling for control over his face. "Sick and tired."

"Just let her go, Jimmy," Sam said. "It's over."

"Nothing's over!" Jimmy pushed the blade harder against Emily's throat. She froze, and her eyes got bigger. "I'll tell you when it's over, soldier boy. It'll be over after I cut her goddamn throat, and then I kill you. And then... I'll go down there and kill the rest of those sons of bitches who shot my friends. That's when this'll all be over."

Sam shook his head. "Let her go," he repeated.

"You think you're something else, don't you?" Jimmy said. "Think you're bad enough to come up here and have your way with us mountain folks? Come up here, sneak around in our woods like you own this place. Like you was gonna come take my woman from me. Well, I got news for you, Mr. Soldier Boy. She ain't nobody's woman no more."

"Don't you do it!" Sam shouted.

Jimmy looked down then, made a move with the blade, when suddenly...

There came a loud boom.

Jimmy's head jerked to the side. He dropped the blade and released his grip on Emily, then staggered backward. His head looked partially deflated and blood was pouring out of his ears. But his eyes, they were still very much alive. And in shock, as he stared with a bewildered look at Sam. Then, one long second later, Jimmy James Ramsey fell back onto the ground and died.

Only then did Sam turn to his left.

It was the mountain man. Jerry Huey, fifty yards away, standing on the side of the hill, a black powder rifle tucked into his shoulder, slightly lowered. He was wearing old school leather, both his pants and his jacket, with fringes at the seams. He had on a coon hat as well, bushy like his beard.

In the end, Sam wasn't surprised. He knew the old man had been following him for the past couple of days.

Jerry didn't say anything. And neither did Sam. Because everything that needed to be said was already in both of their eyes.

Sam gave a brief nod. It was his way of saying thanks, and that it was good the old man finally got his vengeance for his lost son.

Jerry nodded back in reply. Then, like an old grizzly, he turned around and slowly disappeared into the woods.

• • •

A few seconds later, Sam felt a buzz in his pocket. It was the sat-phone—he had a message.

He retrieved the phone and listened to the message, which he must've missed while down in the tunnels. Sam called Madigan back.

Minutes later, they were all in the field behind the barn—Madigan and his team, Sam and Emily. Green smoke was lifting in the air, and the sound of a chopper was approaching them. Sam was reminded of old times, seeing his friend and the others all decked out in gear, ready to exfiltrate from the battlefield. With all those dead bodies lying around up there, it actually *felt* like old times.

But of course, it wasn't. It wasn't at all.

Sam looked at Emily and sighed. She was one pretty sight for sore eyes, despite her disheveled appearance. She had the vaguest of smiles on her face, a smile of Almighty relief. And she looked tired too. Very tired.

Sam's thoughts went to Shiloh and Vicki. Emily's father and mother, they just might die from the joy of seeing their daughter again. It was going to be a good day, a good day at last.

But Sam's job wasn't over. As the chopper came into view, he touched Emily's elbow and said, "I've got one question for you: Why did Ronnie Wilkins do it? Why did he have you kidnapped?"

CHAPTER 39

Sometime in the long and bitter day, and in the long and heavy darkness, Carson realized the smoke had finally settled. After everything had been silent for a good long time, he slithered out of the deepest, blackest tunnels that, as a kid, he had sworn he would never venture into. Funny how things have a way of changing once your life is on the line.

He came out through the main entrance, the big wooden hatch near the dead oak tree. The land was warm and bright and peaceful. The birds were singing, and the chickens were roaming around the yard, pecking at the ground. Everything looked and sounded pretty normal... except for all the dead dudes lying about.

Ever so quietly, Carson made his way through the property. He couldn't believe what he was seeing. But also, he wasn't that surprised. It didn't take him long to put the pieces together. He recognized Myron's corpse, along with much of that man's crew, and several other bad-looking mo-fos. It had been a raid, them coming up here to annihilate Jimmy's operation, then probably take all the drugs they could find. It's not like this scenario was unheard of among drug dealers.

Carson didn't dwell on such details, though. He was thinking about one thing and one thing only: getting the hell out of there.

But what about Donny?

Yeah, what about Donny?

Carson looked around for his brother, glancing over the bodies scattered about. Eventually, he made his way into the barn, where he found Donny lying in a heap on top of Blake. Neither of them were moving, and they both looked dead, although there were no obvious bullet holes in their bodies, like there were in all those other dudes.

As he looked at his brother, Carson suddenly felt something strange. Something he hadn't felt in... Well, ever.

Carson's feeling—*feelings*, more like it—were of remorse, sadness, and perhaps a small sense of loss.

He stepped closer, then spotted the rope around Donny's neck. It appeared Blake had strangled the life out of the poor guy.

As for Blake, he was clearly dead too, although his eyes were open, and he had a strange smirk on his face. Even in death, the son of a bitch was weird.

Instinctively, Carson put a hand on Donny's shoulder. "I'm sorry, brother. I'm sorry I let this happen to you."

After a second, Carson heard a cough come from Donny's corpse. Wait a minute. Oh shit, he wasn't dead! *Donny wasn't dead!*

"Donny!" Carson cried. Then a smile spread across his face. "Donny!" he repeated, shaking his brother.

Donny slowly lifted his battered head. "*Car....*" he squeaked.

"Donny, you're alive!" Carson replied. "You did it, Donny. You killed Blake. And you're alive, too."

"I am?" Donny said.

Carson helped Donny get the rope off of his neck, then blinked, slightly amazed with the sudden revelation that had just hit him. Apparently, among all the shooting and dying that had been going on around here, and while killing Blake and being almost killed himself, Donny had somehow fallen asleep. Or maybe he had just passed out.

But again, Carson didn't dwell on the details. He stepped back and said, "Get up then, Donny. We gotta get the hell out of here."

Their van was all shot up. And so were the other vehicles on the lot, except for Blake's quad, and Jimmy's yellow International pickup truck, which was parked right there inside the barn.

Carson checked the truck for keys and found one under the seat. Then he started the vehicle, put it in gear, and slowly rolled out of the barn, directing Donny to move some of the dead bodies out of the way.

"That's good, Donny," Carson said, as he drove the truck a little further. "Now go let them poor dogs outta that cage and then get back here."

Donny did as he was told. Then he ran back to the truck and got in. They drove slowly through the battlefield, passing several shot up dudes and several shot up vehicles, and now, several excited dogs chasing after chickens.

"Buckle up, Donny," Carson said, punching it once he cleared the last of the war-torn wreckage. "And take one last look. 'Cause we ain't ever coming back here anymore."

CHAPTER 40

"I'm telling you, Sam," Madigan said through his headset, "you won't find a job with benefits as good as this."

Sam smiled. "No, I guess I wouldn't."

The chopper landed on the front lawn of Shiloh's house, not far from the gazebo. Sam never bothered calling the man, figuring he'd give everyone a big surprise.

As soon as the chopper landed, the pilot shut the engines off. Shiloh's Doberman Pinschers came running out. They were followed by Shiloh and Ronnie, and, a few steps behind them, Emily's mother, Vicki.

Madigan opened the chopper door, and then Emily got out and ran to her father. Vicki ran up also, and they all hugged one another, crying.

Sam looked at Madigan. "Job ain't over yet, my friend. I need you to cover me."

"Roger that," Madigan replied with a grin.

They stepped out and walked toward the family. Sam was a mess. He was dirty, and there was blood on his clothes. One of his arm sleeves was half gone, and he had a bandage wrapped around his forearm, where Jimmy had cut him with his knife. He was tired as well, and it showed on his face, along with numerous swelling bruises.

Meanwhile, Madigan looked like he was just getting warmed up. He stood calmly next to Sam, gun still in hand, relaxed but ready.

"I can't believe it," Shiloh said, after giving his daughter the longest hug. He approached Sam then and gave him a hug as well. "I knew you could do it. I told you, didn't I? I knew you were the man for the job."

Sam smiled thinly. "I'm glad she made it," he said. "But make sure she sees a doctor soon. And get some decent food in her, as well."

Shiloh laughed and cried at the same time. "Oh, you know I will, my friend. You know I will." Then he glanced curiously at Madigan and the helicopter.

"Don't worry," Sam said, "he's an old friend of mine. And he owed me a favor."

Shiloh smiled, then went back to his daughter.

Sam waited a few minutes, keeping his attention on everyone as they got through the reunion. But then he stepped closer and said, "Mr. Parker... I hate to put a bad taste on this wonderful moment, but there's something that needs to be addressed."

Shiloh looked at him.

Sam gestured to Ronnie, who was quietly standing behind everyone else. "Time to fess up, boy," Sam said.

There was a silent pause as everyone glanced between Ronnie and Sam.

Ronnie chuckled nervously. "What are you talking about?"

Emily glowered at him, and he caught her look. Then his face went from feigning innocence to bubbling frustration.

"You know what I'm talking about," Sam said. "You can tell them or I will. Makes no difference to me."

"Tell us what?" Shiloh asked, his face now stricken with alarm. "What is he saying, Ronnie? What do you need to tell me?"

Ronnie moved then, fast, really fast, a knife coming out of nowhere as he grabbed Emily and pulled her into him.

"That's a bad play, son," Sam said, shaking his head. Next to him, Madigan had his rifle up and aimed, and the other three from his team came forward and started circling, guns raised as well, sights all centered on Ronnie.

Shiloh looked shocked and angered. "Ronnie!" he cried. "You let Emily go. I don't know what this is all about, but you let her go, dammit!"

Ronnie shuffled back a few steps. His eyes were huge now. He looked terrified and desperate. And for the second time today, Emily had a knife at her throat.

"I'll tell you what this is about," Sam said coolly. "For a while now, old Ronnie here has been embezzling money from you, Shiloh. And he was using that money to fund a nice little drug operation up there in the hills, courtesy of them Ramsey boys. It was going mighty well, I figure, up until Emily caught on to what he was doing. So then she confronted him about it, told him that he had to get lost, that he *better* get lost, before she came back from her hiking trip. And Ronnie wasn't gonna have any of that, so he got his Ramsey friends to take care of her. Then, after I showed up, he hired someone with a black van to follow me around, to steal all my maps and notes, to make things more or less difficult for me. It was probably the same person who killed Harlow as well."

"Is this true?" Shiloh said after a moment of silence.

It was true, as Sam had figured out. He had been slowly, yet methodically, putting the pieces of the mystery together since that day when his hotel room got ransacked. Then Emily's confirmation about Ronnie's illegitimate activities pretty much sealed the deal for his theory.

"Is this true, Ronnie...?" Shiloh repeated. "It is, isn't it?"

Ronnie looked like a coyote being cornered by wolves. His eyes were blinking fiercely, and he kept glancing around, as he held Emily close to him, knife at her throat.

Emily's eyes were closed, and she looked calm, as if she were making a silent prayer.

"I can't believe it," Shiloh said. "After all these years, and all I've done for you. Why, Ronnie?"

Ronnie didn't say anything in response.

"If you needed money," Shiloh added, "all you had to do was ask. You know that, Ronnie. All you had to do was ask."

Tears started running down Ronnie's face.

"Now take it easy, son," Sam said, raising his palms. "You've come to the end of the line. Ain't nothing left to do now but be a man."

There was a long pause, a standoff of sorts, with everyone looking at each other, the tension thick as fog.

"Ronnie *Long Deer* Wilkins..." It was Vicki then, stepping forward. "You will let my baby go right now. And then you will drop that knife and bow your head. You are in the presence of your elders, and you have shamed us. You have shamed the blood of your ancestors. You have done this, Ronnie Long Deer. You have shamed yourself."

Sam felt a chill from the strength in the woman's words.

And so did Ronnie. He released Emily, dropped the knife, then bowed his head and silently wept.

CHAPTER 41

As eager as Sam had been to get back home, he'd decided to forego the plane flight, and drive. He'd had a lot on his mind. A lot to process and, possibly, a lot to prepare for. The best way for him to do this was to be alone for a long stretch of time. Three and a half days on the road seemed to be a good amount.

It had been tough to say goodbye to Madigan. It was nice seeing his old friend again, after so many years. And Madigan was clearly reluctant to say goodbye as well. He'd reminded Sam that a good-paying position was always available at 7-Core Sentinel. Sam had to admit: a small part of him liked the idea of having a job with unique benefits.

But Sam already had employment—working on the family ranch—and in his book, that was the best job he could have asked for.

Even so, there was something sweet and fulfilling about looking for, and then finding, Shiloh's daughter, despite the dangers Sam had faced, not to mention the grim view of what might have been the worst of humanity, with what those Ramsey boys did. More than once after he'd found Emily Parker, Denali's words echoed inside Sam's head. The words about wisdom and peace coming to those who live the life they are meant to.

And speaking of peace: Sam still hadn't had anymore nightmares, since he'd taken the job from Shiloh.

Not long after Ronnie Wilkins had bowed his head and cried like a sorry child, the sheriffs came and took him away. A short time after that, the FBI had made their way up to the Ramsey property. Even though Sam knew that he and Madigan may still come under fire with a host of questions in the future, the case with all those dead dudes up there got written exactly as it was: a drug deal gone sour.

But as it turned out, there were a lot more bodies. More than the ones that had gotten shot up. In the coming weeks, Sam would learn that the remains of over fifteen young women were found on the Ramsey property. For years, those mean old boys had been abducting women from off the Appalachian Trail, and then doing God knew what to them before ending their lives.

With that in mind, Sam realized what he'd done to bring Emily back also resulted in the sparing of an untold amount of grief for the families of those other missing girls—let alone the prevention of any future abductions. It was this understanding that allowed Sam to finally take the reward money Shiloh offered him.

And how much money was that?

A lot. More than Sam had expected to earn in his lifetime. In fact, it was so much money that it had actually scared the hell out of him—the result of which prompted Sam to give a good chunk of it away.

Shortly after getting home, Sam had gone to his bank, deposited Shiloh's enormous check, then wrote two more checks of his own. One to the foundation for Missing and Murdered Indigenous Woman of America. And another to the charity for Disabled American Veterans, an organization aimed at helping veterans, as well as the families of soldiers missing in action.

And after Sam had sent those checks off, that's when he realized what had *really* happened to him in those last few weeks. And more importantly... what that would mean for Lolo.

. . .

Sam wasn't home when she found the note he'd left for her on the kitchen counter. It was a simple message, just a request for her to come meet him at the ranch as soon as possible, because he wanted to talk. He was in the barn brushing a new horse when she finally showed up.

Lolo slowly walked in, her hands in her back pockets, which meant she was nervous. Of course she was. The note Sam had left said that he wanted to talk, and Sam *never* wanted to talk.

"Hey there, cowboy," Lolo said, reluctantly approaching. She noticed the new horse and her pretty black eyebrows perked up. "Wow! Who's this fella?"

Sam smiled. "His name is Buddy." It was a fine-looking Paint, splotched the colors of black and white. "I was thinking maybe he would be a nice present for you, seeing how you had to put up with me being gone and all."

Lolo beamed as she walked up and put her hand on Buddy's neck. Then she gave Sam a big hug. After a minute, she said, "So, is this what you wanted to talk about?"

Sam hesitated. "In a way, I suppose it is. It's part of it, Lolo."

"Okay…" she said. "I'm listening."

Sam inhaled, then turned toward her. "I'm selfish, Lolo. In my heart, I'm selfish."

"What are you talking about, Sam?"

"I want you to quit your job, Lolo. And I don't want you to go to nursing school." He glanced at Buddy, then patted the horse on the neck. "You belong here, with the horses. And with me. You belong on the ranch, Lolo. Full time."

Her chest rose as her smile faded. Now the woman was really nervous, Sam could tell.

He took her hand then. "There's one more thing. I guess I'm ready to talk to someone about... well, you know. About my past."

Lolo's smile came back.

"But on one condition," Sam added.

"And what's that?"

"If you'll marry me."

There was a long pause, and now Sam was feeling dreadfully nervous, like he had made a huge mistake. "You're my wind, Lolo. You've always been. I don't know what I would do—"

"Oh, Sam!" Lolo interrupted, as she pulled him in for a hug. "Of course I'll marry you!"

And then they spent the rest of that day with Buddy, riding double along the range and under a beautiful New Mexico sunset, with Lolo's long Apache hair waving in the passing wind, waving over the beat of hooves and the flutter of clothes, and, most of all... waving in front of her permanent smile.

EPILOGUE

"NINJAAAAAAAAA!!!!!"

"There he goes again," the young woman said to her friend, who might have been her sister, because they did look alike. "What is he screaming?"

"Ahh... I think he's screaming ninja," the other woman replied with uncertainty. They exchanged awkward glances and smiles. "He was screaming the same thing earlier. On It's a Small World, if you can believe that."

"It's A Small World?" the second woman said, as if *no*, she couldn't believe it.

"Yep," her sister or friend or maybe even her lover replied.

"NIN-NIN-NINJAAAAAAA!!!"

One of them put a hand to her mouth, suppressing a giggle. The other wasn't as coy. She belted out a good laugh. "What a hoot," she said.

"I know. He's like a big kid. A really big kid."

Standing a few feet away and smiling aloofly was Carson Ramsey. Of course, it was Donny they were talking about, presently up there on the Big Thunder Mountain Railroad ride, screaming his damn head off like an overexcited toddler, being so outrageous and so loud, that everyone within a five-hundred foot radius was turning their heads to see.

And Carson didn't mind. No siree. He didn't mind one bit. And that's because he had many reasons *not* to mind.

For starters, Carson didn't have to worry about drumming up any work for a while (which was a good thing, since Boss-man got himself caught, and then sent up to the big house), because Carson's life had turned instantly for the better as soon as he found all that money in the back of Jimmy's truck.

The second reason he didn't care Donny was screaming like the fool that he was, was because, goddamnit, Carson was actually having some fun for once. Imagine that.

And the third reason was that Carson was still feeling those terribly uncomfortable, tender emotions for his brother. The same ones he'd felt when he thought Donny was dead.

Finally, Carson didn't mind bringing Donny to Disney World because this place was the motherlode.

Carson had his hands full. He was taking turns biting into a big fat corn dog, and this other tasty thing called a *churro*. And while he was enjoying his food, he was looking around, eyeballing all the strollers and wagons parked randomly about, bags and purses and backpacks hanging off of them, and with nary a person in the immediate vicinity to claim these wheeled treasure troves. Because everybody was up there on the ride, or over there on their cell phones, or back there, staring dumbly at a map. It amazed Carson how careless and trusting people could be, here at the happiest place on earth.

"Are you going to be here for a while, sir?" one of the ladies asked.

Carson blinked. It was him she was talking to. He swallowed his food. "Why, yes, ma'am," he said with a smile.

"Would you mind watching my cart, then?" she said, referring to one of those ridiculous-looking, 4-wheeler wagons with the knobby off-road tires.

"Not at all," Carson replied. "I'll watch your cart for you."

"Oh, thank you," she said. "Come on, Evelyn. Let's go get in line. That screaming guy just reminded me of how much I like this ride."

Carson could've kicked himself for not bringing Donny to Disney World sooner. This place was a gold mine, waiting to be prospected. He took another bite, two bites actually, then turned back toward Big Thunder Mountain. Just then, the train came screaming by, and he spotted his brother in the front seat, a big hairy fool with big eyes, mouth wide open, catching who knew how many flies.

Donny spotted Carson too, and his eyes lit up before the train made an abrupt turn, then disappeared into a tunnel. Even so, Carson still heard his brother's wild excitement. And he couldn't help but smile once again.

"NINJAAAAAAAAA!!!!!"

THE END

AUTHORS NOTE TO READERS

I'm often asked what inspires me to write, and the answer to that question is as nebulous to me as it probably is for those who are not writers. But every once in a while, when inspiration hits, it comes simply in the form of a title. This was the case for *Wild Men*. And once I got started with discovering how this story would unravel, I think I surprised myself with just how wild it turned out.

As with all my novels, I immersed myself into hours of research and inquiries during the writing of *Wild Men*, which I found to be most entertaining. For much of the Special Forces combat tactics, I owe a huge thanks to my longtime friend, David "TinMan" Tinsley. The knife-fighting scenes and techniques, albeit minimal in content, were all pages from my history, of which I couldn't have experienced without the help from so many friends and instructors—including Daniel Perez, Steve Jackson, Michael Higgins, and Steve George. And just like in Sam Nolan's first adventure, *Went Missing*, I owe Derek Randles high praise and gratitude for explaining the nuances of tracking and wilderness survival techniques, some of which I incorporated into *Wild Men*.

Finally, although a work of fiction, I tried to be as accurate as possible with circumstances and historical events included within the narration of this story. That being said, any errors are entirely my own fault.

ABOUT THE AUTHOR

Chris Riley lives near Sacramento, California, vowing one day to move back to the Pacific Northwest. He is the author of over 100 short stories and essays and four novels. A member of the International Thriller Writers, he is currently working on the next Sam Nolan adventure. By day, Chris teaches special education. He has earned multiple black belts, but as an admitted scatterbrain, Chris has way too many other hobbies, mastering few of them. The list includes, but is not limited to: reading, writing, swimming, video games, listening to music, teaching himself to play piano and speak Spanish, playing *Dungeons & Dragons*, painting miniatures, listening to podcasts, and spending time with his family. Find him on social media as he loves to hear from his fans.

OTHER TITLES BY CHRIS RILEY

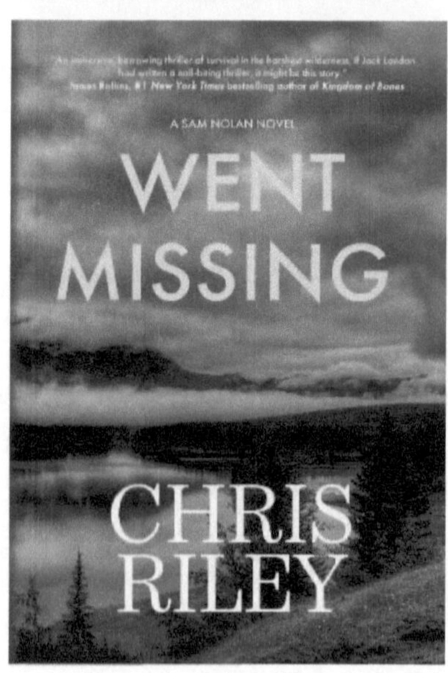

NOTE FROM CHRIS RILEY

Word-of-mouth is crucial for any author to succeed. If you enjoyed *Wild Men*, please leave a review online—anywhere you are able. Even if it's just a sentence or two. It would make all the difference and would be very much appreciated.

Thanks!
Chris Riley

We hope you enjoyed reading this title from:

www.blackrosewriting.com

Subscribe to our mailing list – *The Rosevine* – and receive **FREE** books, daily
deals, and stay current with news about upcoming
releases and our hottest authors.
Scan the QR code below to sign up.

Already a subscriber? Please accept a sincere thank you for being a fan of
Black Rose Writing authors.

View other Black Rose Writing titles at
www.blackrosewriting.com/books and use promo code
PRINT to receive a **20% discount** when purchasing.

www.ingramcontent.com/pod-product-compliance
Lightning Source LLC
Chambersburg PA
CBHW030803210726
48290CB00002B/395